Bring Down the Sun

Jamie made no attempt to hide his grin, and Kate was astounded at how his face changed. Black eyes crinkled, white teeth flashing; there was a compelling warmth that made her heart leap and beat erratically.

The stirrup shortened, he suddenly took hold of Kate's calf and fitted her shoe into the iron ring. No man had ever touched her leg before. Kate gasped as a dizzying current ran through her. Jamie said nothing, but she saw that his hand trembled as he quickly drew away and stepped back.

"Reckon that'll do, ma'am," he said and turned to go. For one flashing moment their eyes met and clung with such intensity that Kate was breathless. Astonished by her reaction, she gazed after him as he strode away. Was she losing her mind here in the vast Northwest . . . attracted to an arrogant, half-savage ma

Other Avon Books by
Elisabeth Macdonald

VOICES ON THE WIND

BRING DOWN THE SUN

Elisabeth Macdonald

AVON BOOKS ◆ NEW YORK

BRING DOWN THE SUN is an original publication of Avon Books. This work has never before appeared in book form. This work is a novel. Any similarity to actual persons or events is purely coincidental.

AVON BOOKS
A division of
The Hearst Corporation
1350 Avenue of the Americas
New York, New York 10019

Copyright © 1996 by Elisabeth Macdonald
Cover art by Jean Pierre Targete
Published by arrangement with the author
Library of Congress Catalog Card Number: 95-94907
ISBN: 0-380-77960-9

First Avon Books Printing: April 1996

AVON TRADEMARK REG. U.S. PAT. OFF. AND IN OTHER COUNTRIES, MARCA REGISTRADA, HECHO EN U.S.A.

Printed in the U.S.A.

RA 10 9 8 7 6 5 4 3 2 1

For Brian

what might have been

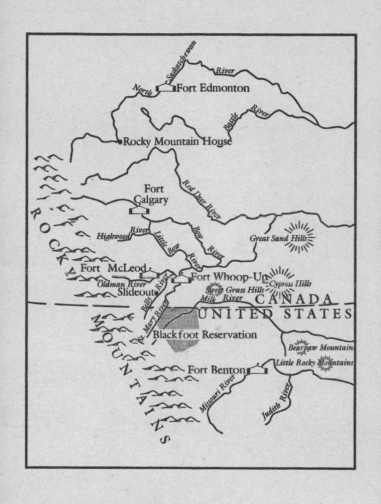

NORTHWEST TERRITORIES 1874

❧ Prologue ❧

*I*n the time beyond memory, a beautiful young maiden of the Siksika fell in love with Apisuahts, the Morning Star, as he rose above the prairies. On seeing her beauty, Morning Star loved her in return.

He took her away to the Land of the Sky and the lodge of his father, Natos, the Sun, and his mother, Kokomikeis, the Moon. They welcomed her joyfully, for they knew how lonely Morning Star had been.

The Moon gave a root digger to Morning Star's wife, saying, "This should be used only by a pure woman. You can dig all roots with it, but you must not touch the large turnip growing in the center of the meadows."

The young wife went about her work, but each time she passed the great turnip her curiosity grew. At last she yielded to temptation and dug the forbidden turnip with her root digger.

Beneath the turnip she found a hole in the sky. Looking down, she saw the camp of the Siksika with the familiar scenes of men hunting, children playing, women working. When she returned to the lodge of the Sun, she was weeping with longing for her people and the green prairies of home. As soon as Morning Star saw her tears he turned away from her in sadness, for he knew she *had disobeyed and could no longer live in the sky.*

In the Moon of Berries Ripe, the wife of Morning Star came down from the sky and went back into the lodge of her father. But her heart still lay with her husband.

At night she stayed alone on a high ridge, staring up at the Star That Never Moves, which was the hole she had made in the sky. Before daybreak, when Morning Star arose from the plains, she asked him to take her back with him.

First, he told her, she must become a medicine woman to her people; she must teach them the ceremony and the song of the sacred root digger she had brought back to earth, for that was to be an important part of the Natoas, the Sun Dance, Okan, most sacred of all Siksika rituals.

Perhaps then the Sun, knowing the love they bore each other, would once more make a place for her in the sky.

$\approx 1 \approx$

Northwest Territory
September 1874

Harsh and alien, the clanging of a bell echoed from far across the bare autumn prairie. That distant sound brought the lone horseman to a halt, his lean, hawk-nosed face frowning into the hazy distance. He was tall and straight-backed, sitting easy in a saddle covered by a cougar skin, a prized trophy among the Blackfoot. Beneath the stained and dusty, wide-brimmed felt hat, straight black hair hung to his shoulders.

Despite the familiarity of the signal, Jamie Campbell knew it was early to begin trading, only September and the furs not yet prime. The air was cold and still, almost like a snow was breeding. But there were no clouds, only the ice-blue sky arching to the empty horizon of the Canadian prairies. Tolling of the bell died away, and above him, a skein of southbound geese filled the silence with melancholy honking.

Black eyes narrowed, he pulled his buffalo coat closer and kicked the horse into motion. So the rumors he'd heard at the Blackfoot encampment were true. The American whiskey traders had returned early this year, seeking ever-greater profits from their vicious brew. For-getting the madness and the tragedy it brought, his foolish people would be trading their hard-won buffalo robes from the summer hunt . . . trading for rotgut American whiskey. His anger deepened, like a fire inside his head, as he remembered the words of his aunt, Cutting Woman, who had sent him here.

"Your brother has gone to Fort Whoop-up," the old woman had said after she welcomed him to her campfire.

The mention of his half brother brought a flood of anger and Jamie growled, "Swift Runner is a fool."

"*Wo-ka-hi*, listen," Cutting Woman countered. "Your mother is with him." She gave the pot simmering on her cook fire a forceful stir and glanced at Jamie with a significant expression. "She lives in his lodge since her husband was killed by the Cree at Belly River." She paused and waited expectantly.

Cutting Woman was the "sits-beside-him" first wife of his uncle, Crowfoot, chief of the Blackfoot confederacy. She was an important woman, and his "other" mother.

Jamie understood at once that he was expected to go to Fort Whoop-up and bring his mother, Pretty Bird, home. Despite the fact that he'd spent most of his life apart from her, the bond between them remained. After his white father deserted them, she had given her child into the care of Alec Campbell, the Hudson's Bay Company factor at Rocky Mountain House, and his Blackfoot wife. Among the many things Campbell had taught the boy was a reverence for the woman who gave him life, and responsibility for her well-being. Cutting Woman knew, as he did, that it was his duty to protect his mother from that place that was surely the hell the missionaries spoke of around the night fire at the trading post.

"Did my sister go?" he asked sharply, for he was very fond of his young half sister.

Cutting Woman shook her head and they exchanged

meaningful looks, knowing Laughing Girl was married to a jealous and protective man.

"Pretty Bird said they meant to take all their buffalo skins and their horses," she said as she dipped a wooden bowl into the pot of stewed buffalo and handed it to him.

Jamie groaned, certain the foolish and careless Swift Runner would trade the skins his mother had worked on all summer for whiskey. No doubt she'd gone hoping to trade for more needful things.

Wolfing down the food, Jamie looked at his sweated horse, as weary as he. It had been a long journey from Fort Edmonton where he'd guided the American prospectors, but they had paid well. His services as a guide were sought after in the Northwest Territory because he knew every stream, every hill, every tree and rock as no one else did. He handed the empty bowl to his watching aunt and reached for his rifle. Crowfoot would give him a fresh horse. He would ride to Fort Whoop-up and bring his mother safely home. Swift Runner could go his own way to destruction.

Even now, hours and miles later, as Jamie halted the horse on the rolling tan-colored bluffs where the prairie dropped away to riverbed at the confluence of the St. Mary and Oldman rivers, his anger at Swift Runner and the whiskey sellers had not abated.

Below him stood the infamous Fort Whoop-up, familiar from past visits during the years he'd guided and interpreted for white men in the Northwest Territory. It was the stoutest fort in all of western Canada. The walls were built of solid hewed cottonwood logs. Inside, there were storerooms, stables and living quarters for the white men. A watchtower and rampart guarded the wide gates. No Indians were allowed inside and all trading was done through a heavy wicket, the wall easily barricaded if there was trouble. The white traders could relax in safety while drunken Indians fought and often killed one another outside.

Cottonwood trees along the wide brown river were nearly bare of leaves, the yellowed grass beneath trampled by the herds of horses belonging to the crowd of Blackfoot and Bloods come to trade. The raucous sounds drifting up to him told Jamie the warriors were already far gone in drunkenness.

Repugnance clogged his throat as the horse picked its way down the autumn-bare hillside, and Jamie's anger flared again, this time toward his own hapless people. It was not just the whiskey trade that had brought the Blackfoot to this sorry and impoverished state. The traders had made the Indians completely dependent on them. Cheaper than whiskey were their offerings of flour, sugar, salt, tea and tobacco, guns and ammunition, knives and hatchets, blankets, cloth and trinkets. No longer did that once proud people make their own tools, clothing and shelter from the mighty buffalo. The buffalo robes and furs that had provided for them in the past were traded now for inferior white-man things, and traded, too, was Blackfoot pride.

"Hold up there, Jamie Campbell," a voice called, and he turned to see two horsemen riding toward him. They were leading pack horses wet to the haunches, and he knew they'd just crossed the river at the Whoop-up Trail ford.

When they were close enough to be recognized, their presence did not improve Jamie's black mood. They were wolfers, part of a group of men despised by Indians and whites alike. It was their practice to kill a buffalo, sprinkle strychnine in the carcass and collect the fur of the poisoned wolves. But it was not always wolves that died: sometimes it was valued Indian dogs, and even people. The lowest creatures on the prairies, Jamie thought with bitter irony, below even the half-breeds.

"Fixin' to whoop it up, are ye?" one of them asked with a coarse chuckle as they came abreast. "Git yerself some whiskey and a squaw?"

Jamie's look of fury silenced the man. "It's not whiskey, you scum. It's poison." He whipped his horse, wanting to get away from them before they somehow tainted him.

He watched the wolfers pound on the gates at the fort and finally be admitted. Jamie Campbell, the half-breed guide, was known there and he would be admitted, too, but what he sought was not inside the fort.

A line of Indians, men and women, stood before the stout trading wicket in the wall of the fort. Jamie rode slowly now, searching for his mother or half brother, Swift Runner. As he watched, the warriors and women traded horses, furs and the hard-won buffalo robes from the summer hunt. One robe, pushed through the wicket, bought a half gallon of the so-called whiskey, which Jamie knew was concocted inside the fort. A fiery brew of raw alcohol, flavored with chewing tobacco, pepper and bitters, with red ink for coloring, and mixed with an infinite amount of water. At that exchange, the trade price for whiskey would be fifty dollars a gallon. The rumored fifty-thousand-dollar profit Hamilton and Healy, the Americans who owned this fort, made each winter seemed easily possible. No wonder more greedy traders were moving into the area this fall.

The faces he sought were not in the line, and he rode on, past the Blackfoot and Bloods and Piegan huddled against the fort wall, seeking warmth from the white man's blanket that could never replace a buffalo robe. Some lay sprawled on the cold earth, lost in alcoholic unconsciousness. If the temperature fell during the night, they might freeze to death where they lay. In past winters, many had done just that.

Beyond the fort, toward the river, a few lodges had been pitched. Not the fine old buffalo-skin lodges, but the flimsy canvas ones sold by the traders. Jamie turned toward them. Perhaps Pretty Bird was there, watching over a drunken Swift Runner. A sense of foreboding fell over him as he rode.

Near the lodges, a fire burned fitfully. Men and women in various stages of drunken abandonment danced crazily around it. Some distance beyond, two warriors fought each other with vicious mindlessness. Another man lay beaten and bleeding nearby.

"Follows the Eagle!"

At the sound of his Blackfoot name spoken with apprehension, Jamie turned. A young warrior from Crowfoot's camp, his eyes glazed with alcohol, was trying futilely to mount his nervous and impatient horse.

"Where is my mother, Big Rib?" Jamie demanded. The man cringed away and attempted to climb on his horse as though to flee, but the animal shied and he fell to the ground. In an instant, Jamie was beside him, jerking the man upright to look into his terrified face. "My mother, Pretty Bird," he asked again, "and my worthless brother, Swift Runner—where are they?"

"Dead," Big Rib croaked, and Jamie felt the foreboding turn to ice around his heart. He shook the man violently.

"Tell me—and speak truly, or I'll kill you."

Big Rib gasped out the horrifying story, taking every opportunity to assure Jamie he had no part in the affair. "Swift Runner was very drunk and wanting to fight. But he wanted a woman, too, and he tried to take Good Young Man's woman by force. Good Young Man attacked Swift Runner. They fought, but Good Young Man had a knife and it found Swift Runner's heart.''

"My mother?" Jamie prompted, cold with fear, when Big Rib's story faltered.

"Swift Runner was bleeding. Pretty Bird ran to help him. Good Young Man was very drunk. He thought she meant to kill him and he drew the knife from Swift Runner's heart and turned it on Pretty Bird. They lie there . . ." He pointed beyond a lopsided canvas lodge to where two bodies lay sprawled on the bare autumn earth.

Dragging the reluctant Big Rib with him, Jamie went to look down on the dead faces of his mother and his half brother. His heart felt empty. Too many he loved had departed for the Sand Hills, that Blackfoot place of After-Death, where their souls wandered in eternal, invisible limbo. The memory of his young wife and the baby whose birth had brought death stabbed through him with such pain, he nearly keened aloud. That was far in the past, he told himself, angry at his momentary lapse of strength.

Now his mother lay dead before him. Pretty Bird's doeskin gown was pulled up to her waist and her thighs were dark with blood. Sourness filled Jamie's throat. The bastard had raped her.

"Good Young Man did this?" he asked, choked with fury and pain. Big Rib nodded. Even in the grief that emptied his heart, Jamie knew it was the white man's whiskey that had truly killed his mother. And it would be the cause of Good Young Man's death, too, for Blackfoot justice demanded that he follow the slayer of his mother and brother and kill him.

"Where is Good Young Man?" he demanded of Big Rib, who had been sidling away.

"That is his lodge," was the answer as Big Rib

pointed to a canvas tepee that looked ready to collapse. When Jamie strode grimly toward it, Big Rib ran for his horse and galloped away.

Jamie jerked aside the flap of the lodge. A man cursed and looked up from where he lay atop a naked Indian woman. ''Purvis!'' Jamie exclaimed, recognizing one of the worthless half-breeds who hung around the fort. ''Where is Good Young Man?''

Purvis cackled. ''Ran like hell. Knew you'd be on his trail after what him and Big Rib did to yer ma. Left his woman behind.''

The Indian woman stared up at Jamie through glazed, drunken eyes. Sickened, he knew she had sold herself for whiskey with no mourning for her husband, who now must die. Purvis turned back and thrust at her.

Grim-faced, Jamie dropped the lodge flap and looked for Big Rib. The filthy liar was gone. He had fled, knowing that when Jamie learned the truth he would have to die, just as Good Young Man must die.

With a shovel borrowed from the fort, Jamie buried his mother and half brother in the white man's way—beneath the earth. The furious grief roiling inside him was doubled by the knowledge that their departure from this life could not be accompanied by the traditional Blackfoot ceremonies. The coming of the white men with their whiskey was destroying everything he valued.

Jamie quickly covered Swift Runner's body with tamped earth. When he lifted his mother's limp, bloody body to place it in the final bed, Jamie paused to stare into her lifeless face. In spite of their long separation, he loved and honored this woman who had borne him. She had taken pride in her half-white son and his prowess as a guide and a warrior. The beaded knife sheath at his hip was a loving gift made by her clever hands.

With an aching heart, Jamie lifted his face to the faint image of the sun gleaming behind clotted clouds and chanted a Blackfoot mourning song, the sound of it lost in the drunken uproar around the fort. "Natos." He spoke to the Sun god. "Now she is a part of you. Farewell, *nikista*, my mother." When she lay in the earth, he straightened her bloody gown and smoothed her hair. Then he let his eyes be blinded by tears as he filled the grave.

"It was a poor hunt," Crowfoot said as he and Jamie smoked beside the fire in the chief's warm and spacious buffalo-skin lodge. They rested in willow backrests cushioned by furs. From the lodge poles hung Crowfoot's bison hide shield painted with his war sign, his eagle-feather headdress bag and his medicine bundle. Soft couches of buffalo robes and furs lay against the outer walls. The pleasant odor of sweet grass smoldering in the central fire blended with the tobacco from their pipe.

Crowfoot continued gloomily. "Once, the plains were black with buffalo. Now we must ride far to find meat for our people."

Weary as he had never been, Jamie passed the pipe to his uncle. Guessing that Big Rib might run to his family, Jamie had returned to the Blackfoot encampment. He'd searched every lodge for the two who had murdered his mother. No one had seen the men or knew of their whereabouts. Tomorrow he would widen his search.

"All the Blackfoot tribes have slaughtered buffalo with their fine new guns, wanting robes to buy whiskey. They even trade their horses," Jamie said bitterly. "It's the white man's whiskey that will destroy our people if we don't destroy the traders first." He had been thinking on it all the time he searched for the murderers. It must be done, and now he spoke boldly to Crowfoot.

"You are *Ni-Nah* of the Blackfoot confederacy. Chief of chiefs for the Blackfoot, the Bloods and the Piegan. You must lead the warriors against the whiskey traders. When they've been driven from the Northwest, our people will be free again, the buffalo will come back, the Blackfoot can live in the old ways." He wished all this for his mother's people, knowing that his own lonely world—half white, half Blackfoot—would never change.

Crowfoot frowned. Shifting his prized Hudson's Bay blanket from his wide shoulders, he drew deep on the long pipe. His heavy face grew thoughtful, black eyes dark with sorrow. Long braids of black hair shot with silver gleamed in the flickering firelight as he slowly shook his head.

Before Crowfoot could speak, Jamie asked, "Have you forgotten how we and the Bloods battled the Cree at Belly River only four years ago? Our warriors slaughtered them. Those same warriors still live."

A proud smile lit Crowfoot's face at the memory of that great triumph. "Smallpox had killed so many of our people, the Cree thought to find an easy victory. They underestimated the Blackfoot and the Bloods." A sigh gusted from Crowfoot and sadness deepened in his dark, lined face. "Those warriors no longer wish to find honor in fighting the enemy. Their hearts are poisoned by white man's whiskey."

The truth of his statement was like a weight on Jamie's heart. He had seen those warriors lost in drunkenness at Fort Whoop-up. "White men!" Jamie spit into the fire. "My father's people."

"Your father is dead." Crowfoot spoke the words in a flat voice.

Jamie stared at his uncle, surprised that he would know about the father who had, so many years ago, deserted Jamie and his mother. In those twenty years, neither Crowfoot nor Pretty Bird had ever spoken the man's name.

Without meeting Jamie's eyes, Crowfoot continued. "He was shot in a drunken fight among those mangy wolfers at Fort Spitzee."

"A wolfer!" So the man who had abandoned a sick woman and child in a lonely shack on the Bow River had sunk to that. Jamie felt no grief, only a faint echo of the anger he had carried all these years.

"It was he named you Jamie." Crowfoot's voice took on the low singsong of a storyteller. "Your white name, along with the name of Alec Campbell, the Hudson's Bay factor . . . your other father."

A shaft of old pain tore Jamie's heart. He had no wish to speak of the past. The kindly missionary priest, Father Scollen, had found the sick woman and child. He took them to the Hudson's Bay trading post at Rocky Mountain House, where there was warmth and food and medicine for their sickness. After a time, when she was well, Pretty Bird went to the camp of her brother, Crowfoot. Campbell and his Blackfoot wife had grown fond of the boy and begged her to leave him. Knowing the factor could give her son many things she could not, Pretty Bird had agreed.

"My true name is Follows the Eagle," Jamie reminded his uncle now. "A name I earned in my vision quest after I came to live with you."

He had come in his fourteenth year. Campbell had given him a rough kind of affection, a knowledge of the English language, the rudiments of an education and, most importantly, the knowledge of the mountains and prairies that had since served him so well. But there had been a need in him then . . . as though his Blackfoot blood called him home. Campbell's wife wept to see him go, but the dour Scotsman simply shook Jamie's hand and growled, "Watch yer back." The fact that Jamie rode out of Rocky Mountain House with two of Campbell's finest horses let the boy know the reality of Campbell's affection for him.

At Crowfoot's camp, Pretty Bird had found a new husband, a Blackfoot warrior who did not welcome her half-blood son when he had a son and daughter of his own. But Crowfoot and his wife had invited the boy to share their lodge and taught him the ways of the people. Their own children had died of smallpox, and the boy who came after was deaf and dumb.

"You have been a good son," Crowfoot said now, and Jamie's eyes stung at the rare words of approval. "Our people have need of a warrior who understands white ways."

Jamie stared into the fire, thinking of Blackfoot ways. "I have to find Big Rib and Good Young Man," he said.

"What you say is true. First we must be rid of the whiskey sellers. We hear rumors that the Canadians are sending an army to go against these traders. But where are they?" His voice grew more decisive. "The American army keeps the traders off the reservation in Montana Territory. Perhaps they would help us." The words ended on a commanding note. Jamie knew Crowfoot had given him a mission. Nothing more need be said.

The United States cavalry was stationed at Fort Shaw in Montana Territory for the purpose of keeping whiskey sellers off the American Blackfoot reservation. But the traders had to cross that reservation to reach Canada, north of what the Blackfoot called the Medicine Line. Surely he could persuade the commandant to take action. Tomorrow he must ride to Fort Shaw. Blackfoot retribution would have to wait.

2

Fort Benton, Montana Territory
1874

An earsplitting shriek burst from the steamboat's whistle as the *Josephine* crowded against the levee on the banks of the upper Missouri River. To Kate Maginnis, waiting tensely on the upper deck, the sound went on reverberating portentously, echoing back from low-hanging gray clouds until at last it was lost in the vast reaches of the prairie.

Beyond the dock lay the raw, sprawling town of Fort Benton, treeless and uninviting. A noisy, shoving crowd was converging on the steamboat landing: rough-looking men in buckskins, blanketed Indians, blue-coated American soldiers, a few prosperous types in black frock coats, but she could see no women at all.

Distant mountains chilled the cold wind tugging stray locks from her tightly coiled red-gold hair. Wide gray eyes narrowed, Kate stared out at the uninviting scene and, for a moment, was certain her courage had finally deserted her. Without her father's knowledge, and against the advice of everyone she knew, she had plunged into the western wilderness. Back in Toronto, her plan had seemed plausible when there was no real alternative.

Wryly, she thought that this was not the first time she

had gone against all logic. Certainly, her decision to become a doctor like her father, Dr. Thomas Maginnis, had been denounced as foolish by everyone, from the board of governors at the University of Toronto when they denied her entrance, to the mother of her one and only suitor.

"Take yer bags, miss?"

The rough voice startled her. Turning, she saw a man dressed in stinking buckskins, a dirty, wide-brimmed hat pulled low on his grizzled head. Half the teeth were missing in the hopeful grin he gave her. Poor creature, she thought, he probably needed whatever money she'd give him for carrying her trunks.

"Yes, please." Kate handed him the heavy case of medical instruments she had kept with her. "And I have two large trunks in the baggage hold."

"I'll see to it, ma'am." He nodded and clasped the handle of her case. Tears welled in Kate's eyes at the sight of his gnarled hands, for they reminded her of her father's twisted, arthritic hands . . . the crippled hands that had ended his medical career. She and her father had been apart for months now, with no communication possible. Soon they'd be together again, working side by side as they'd done for so many years. The thought cheered her, momentarily banishing the fears that had grown since that day last winter when her father's decision had changed their lives irrevocably.

A patient had come in that day to the little house on a shabby street outside Toronto city. A lake boatman's wife who'd been severely beaten by her brutish husband, she was one of the few who still sought the services of the crippled Dr. Maginnis.

"This cut will take stitching," Dr. Maginnis said

when the woman lay on his examining table, eyes closed and moaning softly. He pointed to the gaping wound along her cheekbone. The doctor was a stocky man with thinning gray hair and penetrating blue eyes set in a broad, kindly face.

Kate hurried to bring the tray with needles and silk thread. For eight years, ever since her mother died when she was twelve, she had been her father's assistant, just as her mother had once been. Kate kept the needles threaded and the doctor chose one, waiting as she cleansed the wound.

Holding her breath, Kate watched as he tried to bring the edges of the wound together to insert the needle. Pain filled her heart as her gaze went to his hands.

Twisted and swollen, gnarled as the branches of an ancient tree, those hands were grotesque enough to make patients fear his clumsy touch. Rheumatoid arthritis; Dr. Maginnis had made the diagnosis himself, and as his disease advanced, his practice dwindled. Those good, strong hands, which had once set broken bones so easily, brought babies forth, sewed up dreadful wounds and saved lives, now were nearly useless and in constant pain. Kate became her father's hands, guided by his knowledge until her skill equaled his. It had been a long time since those crippled hands could use a surgical needle in a way that met his exacting standards: neatly closed, no scarring.

The air in the examining room seemed charged with emotion, heavy with the doctor's need to prove his skill. At last he let out his breath in a silent, frustrated curse.

"You'll have to do the sewing," he said. Kate heard the old pain in his voice and her heart twisted at the defeat in his unhappy eyes.

Hands steady, Kate shut her ears to the woman's feeble cries of pain, something she'd learned to do over the years she'd worked beside her father. Once her mother had done these things . . . that slender, quick woman with her bright red-gold hair and warm gray eyes— Kate's image, so her father said. Mary Maginnis had been a maid in a great London house until she met a charming Irish medical student who had no money, but who convinced her a new life awaited them in Canada.

They'd settled in the growing city of Toronto on the shores of Lake Ontario and begun a practice among the city's working class. Kate had been born soon after their arrival, the only child Mary Maginnis would carry to term. In all Kate's memories, it had been a good life, growing up with adults who treated her as an equal. Until she was in school, she didn't realize how different her upbringing had been. Certainly, none of the other girls' parents encouraged them in the outlandish dream of being a doctor. A *woman* doctor? It was unthinkable.

"Do you remember when I went to Government House with Father Bruneau last month?" The question startled Kate as she and her father cleaned the small examining room after putting the battered woman in Kate's bed to sleep off a dose of laudanum.

The doctor's voice held an undertone of significance and Kate paused in her scrubbing. "I remember," she replied. Father Bruneau was a good friend who often came to play chess and argue religion with the agnostic Tom Maginnis.

Dr. Maginnis looked pleased with himself as he announced, "I've been appointed surgeon to the Northwest Mounted Police."

Stunned by the words, Kate stared at him. For months the Toronto newspapers had been filled with denunciations of Prime Minister John Macdonald and his failure to deal with the violence in the Northwest Territories. Finally, the Northwest Mounted Police force had been

organized. In the spring they would march west to drive
out the American whiskey traders whose firewater was
the root cause of turmoil and death among the Northwest
Indian tribes. Kate had read the reports as something far
removed from her life. The fact that the Northwest Territory could never be settled until the Indians were pac-
ified meant nothing to someone safe in Toronto.

Without meaning to, Kate looked at her father's
hands.

His eyes followed hers and there was a brief, painful
silence. Dr. Maginnis cleared his throat. "It's fourteen
hundred dollars a year, Kate . . . enough to pay your tuition at the Women's Medical College of Philadelphia,
along with what we'll get for sale of the house."

In the past few years, there had been many discussions
between them concerning the problem of paying her tuition to medical school. After the University of Toronto
and every medical school in Canada had refused her,
applications had gone to the United States. Desperate to
continue her education, Kate had studied for a year at
the Normal School, insisting on Latin and chemistry despite the faculty's disapproval. At last an acceptance had
come from the school from which Canada's only woman
doctor, Jenny Trout, had graduated. Philadelphia was far
away and the tuition was high. It had been settled that
Dr. Maginnis would go with Kate. He was certain he
could find a job, even if only as a lab assistant. Kate had
accepted that, but surgeon to the Northwest Mounted
Police was a sacrifice she could never allow.

"You can't do it, Papa," Kate protested at once.
"The newspapers said the Mounted Police will march
all the way from Fort Dufferin to the Northwest Territories. They'll be fighting the American whiskey sellers
and the Indians. It's too dangerous . . . and even if it
weren't . . . you can't go, Papa."

The old terror she'd thought conquered suddenly rose, smothering her with fear. The Northwest was a violent land. Kate clasped trembling hands together, struggling to conceal her reaction from her father. They did not speak of it—the violence, the ugliness, the fear—and then . . . her mother dead. With practiced deliberation, she fought back the flood of emotion.

Her father's mouth tightened stubbornly and his blue eyes hardened. "Nevertheless, my dear, I *will* go. It's my decision."

Kate's voice fell as she reluctantly spoke the hurtful words. "Did they see your hands, Papa?"

The doctor's face reddened and he looked away. His voice was so low she could scarcely hear his reply.

"I wore the new gloves Father Bruneau bought for me when he took me to the interview."

"You wore gloves all the time you were there?" She was amazed that her stringently honest father would have practiced such deception. Father Bruneau was their friend and he knew their circumstances, knew how the medical practice had shrunk until there was scarcely enough income to support the two of them. He had meant to do a kindness, but Kate wished vehemently that he had not.

Dr. Maginnis took off his bloodstained smock and tossed it in the laundry basket, ignoring her question. "It's settled," he said sternly. "You'll go to Philadelphia for your training. I'll go to the Northwest and send my salary back to you. That, with the money from the sale of this house, will pay for your tuition and your board and room."

Kate sighed, knowing from experience that this quiet reasonableness was like a stone wall. "I'm afraid for you," she objected, placing a loving hand on his shoulder. "Don't you remember the Cypress Hills massacre just last year?'' Belatedly, she recalled that only one white man had been killed compared with forty or fifty Indians. No matter. Everyone knew the frontier was dangerous. They would be a continent apart . . . and she had promised her dying mother she would always look after her father.

"You can't go, Papa," Kate rallied her arguments against this wild scheme of his. "I'll need you with me in Philadelphia."

Dr. Maginnis was scrubbing his hands in the washbasin, but looked up at her with a knowing smile. "You'll do better without me to look after and worry over."

There had been only the two of them since Mama's death, clinging to each other for comfort, and now Kate tried to swallow the ache in her throat. "But I promised Mama I'd always stay with you . . . care for you."

After all these years, her father still grieved for his wife, Kate knew, and she understood the long silence before he answered her.

"Your mother died too young, Katie. A tragedy . . ." Old sorrow twisted his features and he fell silent, staring reflectively out the window.

A tragedy . . . and a horror that haunted Kate's dreams for years after that awful day. Even now she sometimes started awake in the darkness, her throat filled with silent screams. It had been a fine spring day, with twelve-year-old Kate skipping happily beside her mother as they walked to the docks to buy fresh fish for dinner. With the purchase of a fat lake trout, Mary grasped her daughter's hand and turned homeward, past the new railroad station built close to the docks. There had been trouble between the rail workers and the lake boatmen, but nothing bad could happen on such a grand morning.

The mob of rioting men engulfed them so suddenly,

there was no time to run. They were shoved mindlessly around by struggling men who pummeled one another, then fell to the ground to wrestle and gouge. Blood spurted from battered faces. There was the ugly sound of flesh striking flesh, the cacophony of curses and shouts . . . and the terror as Kate clung to her mother, who was trying desperately to protect her daughter and fight her way free of the melee.

Two struggling men, blind in their fury, knocked Mary to the ground. "Mama!" Kate screamed, at once on her knees gathering her mother in her arms in a futile effort to protect her from the mob. The two men, locked in battle, trampled Mary's inert body with great booted feet. One man fell, his adversary on top of him. Kate stared in unbelieving horror as the man jerked a knife from his belt and cut his victim's throat in one vicious slash. Blood gushed everywhere, staining Mary's dress as she tried painfully to rise. The murderer grunted, stood up and was gone without a glance at the child who gaped at him, her mouth wide with silent screams of horror . . .

"A tragedy," the doctor said again as Kate forced herself to banish the hideous memory of murder and death. He drew a long, shuddering breath and composed his face into stern lines. "No matter what you promised, Katie, I won't allow you to sacrifice yourself for me. You will go to Philadelphia, and I . . ." He stood with his shoulders back, erect as a soldier, and continued with pride in his voice. "I will be part of the Northwest Mounted Police."

Inevitably, the day of farewell came. A warm spring wind had blown away the smoke and smells of the Toronto railroad station. On the track, the train stood huffing like a winded animal. From a distance Kate could

hear the shouts of the handlers loading the horses of the
Mounted Police. This was the day more than two hundred men, under the command of George French and
James McLeod, would travel by train through Detroit to
Fargo, Dakota Territory, then march northward to join
the troops who had spent the winter training at Fort Dufferin. This was the day her father would set out on what
he persisted in calling "his adventure," and from this
day she would be on her own. Perhaps she'd come to
the Northwest when she'd finished in Philadelphia, Papa
had said, but that seemed too distant a time to contem-
plate.

The station was crowded with families saying their
farewells. Kate glanced enviously at the family groups,
feeling more alone than she had ever felt. She stood by
herself, watching as Dr. Maginnis reported, then pushed
back through the crowd to her side.

Despite his stocky build, she thought he looked quite
dashing in his new uniform: scarlet Norfolk jacket, steel-
gray breeches tucked into shiny boots. Under his arm he
carried his white helmet and gauntlets, his hands still
encased in the black leather gloves Father Bruneau had
given him. The good priest was saying a funeral mass
this morning and had come to the house for good-byes
last night, promising Dr. Maginnis that he would see
Kate off to Philadelphia.

Her father was joined by a tall young man with fair
hair and a neat mustache who was talking animatedly.
He had a narrow, aristocratic face that was immensely
attractive and eyes of a deep blue.

"I want you to meet my friend, Inspector David Cavendish," Dr. Maginnis said as the two men stopped beside her. "He plays a mean game of chess."

The young man laughed deprecatingly, took Kate's
outstretched hand and bent to kiss it. To her dismay, she

felt herself flush as he raised his head and those warm blue eyes met hers with frank admiration. She managed to say, "I'm pleased to meet you, Inspector. My father's told me about your chess rivalry." During his training for the past two months, the doctor had spent the week at troop barracks, coming home on Sundays to regale Kate with his experiences.

"You spoke of your daughter's fine mind, Doctor," Cavendish said with amused accusation. "You didn't tell me she was also quite beautiful."

At these words, Kate was truly blushing, her face on fire. The nuances of his speech told her he was of the English upper class. It had been a conceit of her mother's, placing people by their accents, and they had made a game of it. Briefly, she wondered what he was doing in Canada, heading for the wilds of the Northwest Territory.

"This expedition will be a happier one for me because of your father," he was telling her. "Most of the men are neither educated nor intellectual." He laughed then, and turned to her father. "And none of them can play chess with such devastating precision."

"I was never a match for him," Kate admitted, liking the young man at once for his warmth and wit.

A long blast from the train's whistle interrupted. Cavendish nodded briskly. "Time to board." He held out a hand. "I'll leave you two to your farewells."

Kate held out her own hand, and once more he bent to press his lips to her fingers. She drew in a deep breath at the unexpectedly pleasant sensation.

"I hope we'll meet again, Miss Maginnis." His voice was warm.

"Yes." Dr. Maginnis spoke too eagerly, Kate thought. "Kate may be coming west to join me when things are settled out there."

Cavendish nodded, his aristocratic features serious now. "Once the Mounted Police have destroyed the whiskey forts, the Indians will be sober and the territory can finally be opened for settlement."

From the corner of her eye Kate saw that her father had turned toward the Union Jack fluttering from a flagpole above them. Across the station, the sonorous notes of "God Save the Queen" rose above the babble of voices. It was as though Dr. Maginnis was saying a final good-bye to Toronto and home.

Impulsively, Kate laid a detaining hand on David Cavendish's scarlet-clad arm. To her amazement, she heard herself say, "Inspector, will you look after my father? He's not as young as the other men, and . . ." She swallowed the pain in her throat. "I promised my mother when she lay dying that I'd always be at his side, taking care of him. Now I can't keep that promise . . ." Seeing that her father's attention had returned to them, she let her words trail off.

"It will be my pleasure, Miss Kate," Cavendish replied sincerely. To her astonishment, he kissed her hand once more before he strode away.

"A fine young man," Dr. Maginnis said and, with a sidelong glance at Kate, added thoughtfully, "There's more to life than the practice of medicine, my girl." Kate caught his meaning and frowned. Didn't he remember her heartbreak over Curtis, who had refused to understand her ambitions? When she'd refused to give them up, he'd called her cold and unwomanly, then callously broken off their attachment. Hurt to the core, she'd vowed she'd never marry.

"Why is he in Canada?" Kate asked, her eyes following the tall, lithe figure as Cavendish disappeared into the crowd. "Is he one of those remittance men wealthy families send far away to be rid of them?"

"Of course not!" the doctor protested. "He's simply an ambitious young man with a taste for adventure. As the second son of a nobleman"—so she had been right about the accent, Kate thought—"David was slated for a military career. He found Sandhurst a bore and left without finishing. Family connections got his commission in the Mounted Police." The doctor grinned. "He seems to think Canada offers more opportunity to prove himself than India or Africa."

The train whistle shrieked, interrupting him. Dr. Maginnis put his arms around her, and Kate felt tears rise. He was all she had in the world. How could she let him go into the dangerous wilderness?

"You can write me at Fort Benton in Montana Territory," he said. "It's the nearest settlement to where the Mounted Police will headquarter. We should be there by the first of September." He smiled. "I'll want to know how you're doing in medical school."

Kate nodded, struggling to hold back her tears. "I'll do fine, Papa."

"Dearest daughter." His voice was choked as he took out his handkerchief to wipe away her tears. "I have never doubted that you will do well." Once more he embraced her and kissed her forehead. "Until we're together again . . . always remember I love you."

Turning quickly, he strode off. She had one last glimpse of his red-jacketed figure as he climbed the steps into the railroad car. The noise of the locomotive drowned out the cries of farewell, and then they were gone. There was only the long train diminishing in the far distance, and a faint whistle borne backward on the spring wind.

Another piercing blast from the steamboat's whistle brought Kate back to the uncertain present. Soon she'd be with her father again, she told herself. But she couldn't help wondering whether he had managed to serve as surgeon in spite of his crippled hands. If the men had only fevers and no desperate wounds or broken bones, he'd have done well enough. If he weren't so lucky, he would need her as soon as she could join him.

Lifting the skirts of her brown stuff traveling gown, she followed the hunched little man down the stairs to the lower deck. The landing was crowded now with drays and wagons and buckboards, all being loaded with the crates and barrels issuing from the hold and the crowded decks of the steamboat. Wagons piled with buffalo robes and furs waited for the last trip of the year down the Missouri to St. Louis. Ice and low water often closed the waterway earlier than this, the captain had told Kate.

"Well, Miss Maginnis . . ." Captain Grant Marsh turned from watching over the unloading to offer Kate a tentative smile. He was a large, kindly man. When she boarded his steamboat in Bismarck, he had tried, in vain, to persuade her not to make this journey. Kate presented a stubborn face and refused to listen to his pleas. How could she have told him she'd had no choice? What else could she have done when she hadn't been able to go to medical school because there was no money for tuition?

The news had devastated Kate that day back in Toronto. Her father had gone away, certain she'd be traveling to Philadelphia within the month. That the doctor had no head for business she'd well known. Her mother had always handled the family finances. Kate hadn't known—and she was certain the doctor hadn't either—that the mortgage on the house, taken out by her mother before her death, had never been repaid. Her father's small savings could take Kate to Philadelphia, but now she had no money for tuition and books. The dream so close to coming true vanished like smoke. Even more alarming to Kate was the fact that her father had been unaware of something so important. As her mother had said, he was a man who required looking after. With that certainty in mind, she had made her decision to follow him west.

"You're in Fort Benton now, as you wished," the captain was saying with a smile. "What do you think of it?"

Kate smiled back, determined she wouldn't let him see the apprehension that was a cold lump in her chest. "It certainly isn't Toronto," she replied cheerfully. When he turned to shout an order, her forced smile faded.

Drab and dusty, the town was a haphazard collection of rough, false-fronted buildings scattered along one street leading from the steamer landing. A number of large warehouses rose above the other buildings. There seemed to be no order of any kind to the furious activity taking place. Shouting men loaded and unloaded, swore at the horses and oxen and one another. Captain Marsh had told her that west of Fort Benton lay the territorial capital, the city of Helena, which had been called Last Chance Gulch during the gold-rush days. Now she thought she might persuade her father to go there, since Fort Benton looked so unpromising. But that was to be considered later.

You made the choice, Kate told herself, and squared her shoulders. The Mounted Police had planned to be at Fort Benton in early September to pick up supplies. She could stay at the police fort, wherever it was, until Dr. Maginnis's enlistment was up. Then they would move to Fort Benton, or to Helena. Back in Toronto it had seemed a good plan. Now, facing the reality of the frontier, she couldn't rid herself of the growing certainty that she had made a terrible mistake.

"This is John Weatherby." Captain Marsh interrupted Kate's rueful thoughts. "I've asked him to give you a lift up to I. G. Baker's store." His weathered brown eyes grew doubtful. "I hope there'll be news of your father and the Mounted Police."

"The Canadian Northwest Mounted Police?" Weatherby's voice held an edge of contempt, and his thin mouth beneath a drooping gray mustache twisted ironically.

Puzzled by his attitude, Kate studied the tall figure in a black frock coat. Straightening her battered straw sailor hat, she managed a confident smile as her gray eyes met his. "My father is the surgeon with the Mounted Police. They were to be in Fort Benton by early September."

Weatherby snorted. "They've been lost for days, ma'am. Word just came that they've sent a detachment south, hoping to find Benton. Should be here today or tomorrow—if they don't get themselves lost again."

A cold frisson of fear ran down Kate's back. He shouldn't have gone, she thought painfully. I shouldn't have allowed it.

The gnarled man in buckskins appeared, dragging Kate's two trunks. All her worldly possessions reposed in those trunks, for she'd sold everything possible before she left Toronto. Unsettled by Weatherby's disconcerting remarks about the Mounted Police, she frowned as she dug in her reticule for coins to pay the eager little man. He loaded the trunks into Weatherby's waiting buckboard.

Lifting her chin, Kate bade Captain Marsh good-bye

and thanked him for his kindness. Then she allowed John Weatherby to take her elbow. Clinging stubbornly to her courage, she stepped into the strangely forbidding world of Montana Territory.

3

Only a few yards up from the river, Weatherby pulled the buckboard to a halt and, with a wave of his arm, indicated the building beside them. "I believe this is the place you're looking for, Miss Maginnis." I. G. BAKER AND CO. was lettered on a large sign above the porch of the low, sprawling store. Two fly-specked windows looked out onto the street, where a bull team consisting of a dozen yoked oxen waited for a freight wagon to be unloaded. Across the dusty street, the sound of raucous voices mixed with the tinny notes of a piano drifted out of the swinging doors of the Elite saloon and gambling hall. Next door stood a large run-down building that might once have been a hotel, but now seemed to be a garrison for American soldiers.

For a fleeting moment Kate let herself remember Toronto's blue lake, green parks and grand buildings, the comfortable little house. This town was very much like the poorest and worst part of Toronto. Kate's mouth tightened stubbornly. She was here and she would make the best of it, whatever came.

"Thank you for your help," she told Weatherby with a polite smile as he helped her down from the buckboard. She wondered if she should offer to pay him.

Something about the man repelled her, although she could not have said why.

"Here, boy!" He motioned peremptorily at a gangling youngster lounging beside the store. "Take the lady's trunks inside." And he flipped a coin to the lad. "Not everyone in Fort Benton is honest," he added by way of explanation. Lifting his wide-brimmed hat in a courtly manner, he turned to climb into the buckboard. "Enjoy your stay in our fair town, miss."

"Thank you," Kate said, again at a loss for words. She watched him drive off down the street without a backward glance. Some rough-looking men hanging around in front of the building next door stared at her. Keeping her face averted, she quickly followed the boy lugging her trunks into the store.

Several men idling beside the potbellied stove in the center of the store fell silent and turned to study her with undisguised curiosity. A mixture of odors assailed her nostrils—stale sweat, tobacco smoke, ground coffee, leather, the harsh smell of animal skins piled along one side of the long room. Behind the battered-looking counter there were shelves of canned goods, clothing, shoes, animal traps. A stout, bald man with luxuriant brown side whiskers came from behind the counter to greet her.

"Can I help you, ma'am?" he asked. Only his raised eyebrows indicated his surprise at seeing her in this place.

Kate drew the fine wool paisley shawl her mother had brought from England long ago tight around her shoulders as though it might bring her courage.

"My father is Dr. Thomas Maginnis. He's the surgeon with the Canadian Northwest Mounted Police. They were to have arrived in the Northwest Territory in September and he planned to leave a message for me here."

The idlers by the stove were snickering before Kate had finished speaking. Sotto voce, one said, "Poor damn Canucks cain't find their way across an open prairie."

Kate's glare silenced him, but didn't erase his grin. A smile flitted across Baker's broad face and disappeared under Kate's hostile eyes. "What does that mean?" she demanded.

"Just bad luck." Baker feigned a lugubrious tone. "Hired some 'breed guides didn't know their . . ." He struggled for words that could be said in front of a lady. "Didn't know the country," he finished lamely. "They ended up lost, out of supplies and horses."

Sudden fear drained through her, turning her trembling hands to ice. Her fault . . . if her father had died on the hazardous trek across southern Canada, it was her fault. He'd signed on for her . . . for the money to send her to medical school. Impractical man that he was, he'd neglected to check his title to the house that was to contribute to her tuition, or to consider that his salary would not be paid in advance. As her mother had always said, Tom needed taking care of. And Kate had sworn she would be the one to do just that.

Baker must have noted her shocked reaction to his words, for he reached out and awkwardly patted her shoulder. "It's all right, miss. The troops are safe. My driver brought word that they're camped in the Sweet Grass Hills to the north. A detachment is on the way here to pick up supplies, horses and a reliable guide."

Kate's relief was so enormous she felt faint and reached out to steady herself against the counter.

"Here!" Baker snapped. "One of you loafers give the lady a chair." When she was seated, the dizziness faded. Baker studied her for a moment, then continued. "I can tell you're a lady, Miss Maginnis. The local hotel's no place for a lady, so I'll send you to Mrs. Thompson's boardinghouse. You can stay there until the Mounted Police get here.''

A stout, forbidding-looking woman, Mrs. Thompson nevertheless welcomed Kate kindly, gave her a room of her own and offered a hot bath. Washed and shampooed, dressed in clean clothing from her trunk, Kate began to think Fort Benton more civilized than at first appearance. Tomorrow she would walk around and look it over.

"Ain't many white wimmen in this town," Mrs. Thompson told Kate over tea in the warm kitchen, where she was preparing supper for her boarders. She had just imparted the information that Mr. Thompson ran the livery stable for I. G. Baker, who was obviously the town's most important citizen. "Cain't count the saloon and dance-hall girls, of course," she added with a curious glance at Kate.

"I've come here to join my father, Dr. Maginnis." Kate smoothed the skirt of her blue bengaline gown, and sipped the hot tea. It amused her to wonder if this woman thought her a dance-hall girl, and she quickly added, "He hopes to set up a practice here."

Mrs. Thompson thawed considerably at that information. "We could use a good doctor. Only one in town spends all his time drinkin' with those saloon wimmen." She leaned forward, speaking in a confiding tone. "So few wimmen, some of the men lower themselves to marry Injuns. A disgrace, I say. Like John Healy . . . everybody knows he just married that Blood woman so her father would let him build a whiskey fort in their country.''

The whiskey forts . . . Kate sat up attentively. They were the reason for the presence of the Northwest Mounted Police. Her father's friend, Inspector Cavendish, had said the Northwest could never be settled until the danger from drunken Indians was eliminated.

". . . made over fifty thousand dollars last year trading whiskey for buffalo robes and furs." Mrs. Thompson continued her story. "When that got around, everybody wanted in on the business. I hear John Weatherby's headin' north with whiskey, too." She seemed to see nothing wrong with selling whiskey to the Indians as long as there was a profit to be made. Kate stared at her in distaste, aware now that she had reason for her quick dislike of Weatherby.

"The Indians are dying of it," she protested. "The Canadian plains are a battleground. That's why the Mounted Police have come west—to stop the whiskey trade."

Mrs. Thompson shrugged off Kate's words and stood up to take her biscuits from the oven. "Well, I say good luck to them. They'll need it."

Kate's throat tightened. The premonition of disaster had begun the day she watched her father's train fade into the distance. She'd fought against it, but it rose now, chilling her heart. The Americans wouldn't help control the Indians their whiskey made crazy. They cared only for profit and thus had created a lawless land.

Late next morning, her vigil at the front parlor window was rewarded when she saw a detachment of red-coated Mounted Police ride down the dusty length of Front Street. Grabbing her shawl, she followed them to Baker's store.

"Your father's fine," Commissioner French assured her in reponse to her frantic questions. He was a husky, intimidating man, balding, with a heavy mustache. "As fine as the rest of us," he added, glancing toward the six weary troopers clustered around the warm stove. Apparently Baker had ousted the idlers in favor of paying customers.

The appearance of the men was not reassuring. Their once brilliant scarlet coats were soiled, dusty and faded, their boots worn and patched, their bearded faces sunken and windburned. Kate remembered them parading in Toronto, sitting proudly on their horses, boots gleaming, red coats bright in the spring sunlight. Now they were scarcely recognizable, and fear for her father's well-being gripped her in spite of what the commissioner had said.

"I'll go back to the camp with you," Kate told him, forcing a positive tone. "I can help him look after the men. I've been his medical assistant for eight years now."

Commissioner French's frown deepened, his pale blue eyes hostile. "Don't talk nonsense, Miss Maginnis," he snorted and handed Baker his list of purchases: boots, gloves, stockings, blankets, corn and oats for the starving horses.

"I *will* go," Kate repeated, barely repressing a quaver of doubt in her voice.

French turned a hard-eyed gaze on her. The troopers beside the stove shifted uneasily. "This is not open to debate, miss." His voice was icy. "As long as I'm commander, there'll be no women in the camps of the Northwest Mounted Police." He gave her his back, his broad shoulders in the faded scarlet jacket like a door slammed in her face.

Dismayed, Kate stared at him. It was true; no other women had followed the Mounted Police west . . . no wives with better reason than she. But her imagination called French a liar, saw her father sick and dying, desperately in need of her care.

"We want to hire a guide," Assistant Commissioner

McLeod was saying to Baker. He was a tall man with a full, dark beard, pale eyes and a confident air. "Someone who knows the country well and is dependable. We've had enough of rascally, lying half-breeds who couldn't find their way across the street."

Baker grinned. "Reckon you'll have to make do with half-breeds." He motioned toward the young boy who earlier had carried Kate's trunks. "Go over to the Exchange, Tad. See if Jamie Campbell's there. Tell him I got a job for him." Packing the gloves French had chosen into a tow sack, he added, "Best damn guide north or south of the line. Lucky for you he got in town yesterday. He had a helluva mad on, but likely he's over it by now."

Kate had listened to this exchange, cold with uncertainty. French was ignoring her as though he'd dismissed her existence. Probably any appeal to him was useless, and she had no idea where to turn now. The bearded McLeod looked to be a kindlier man, but he was not in charge.

"Miss Maginnis," said a low voice. Kate's breath went out in a sigh of relief when she gazed into the warm eyes of Inspector David Cavendish. She hadn't recognized him behind the untrimmed full beard he now wore.

"Do you remember me? David Cavendish."

Suddenly her knees felt like water, and she sat down quickly in a vacant chair beside the glowing stove.

She had met David Cavendish only once, but now he seemed like a dear, familiar friend. Surely the only friend she had in this unwelcoming place. Without thinking, she reached out to him. At once his strong hand enclosed her small, cold one.

"You've had a hard journey, Miss Kate." The sympathy in his low voice made her eyes sting. "Your father wasn't expecting you this year, was he?"

"How is my father?" she asked tremulously, fearing the answer. "Is he all right?"

Cavendish turned so that his back was toward French, and he spoke in a low tone. "Your father is well, Miss Maginnis . . . as well as any of us."

Despite her efforts to hold them back, tears filled her eyes. "I have to go to him, Inspector. He won't survive without me."

An ironic smile touched his lips, but his eyes were still sympathetic. "He's survived so far—with a lot of help."

Some of the men overheard and chuckled as though at a private joke. Kate frowned, certain that his crippled hands had made Tom Maginnis less than competent as their surgeon. The men's attitude only made it more imperative that she be at her father's side. A man could die of his own ineptness. Somehow, despite French, she'd find a way.

A blast of cold air came through the door with a tall, rough-looking man, followed by a grinning Tad. "You wanted to see me, Ike?" the man asked in a deep voice, leaning a hip against the counter. He was at least a head taller than the scowling Commissioner French.

He might be an Indian, Kate thought, forgetting her manners and staring at the new arrival. Although his skin was a shade lighter than that of most Indians, his hair was long and black. When he removed his wide-brimmed, high-crowned hat, she saw his hair was held in place by a beaded headband. He wore a stained buckskin shirt and trousers, scuffed boots and an air of arrogance she thought should have put French on guard.

"Jamie Campbell," Ike Baker was saying. "Best damn guide in the Northwest Territories, and Montana, too. This here's Commissioner French and Assistant Commissioner McLeod of the Northwest Mounted Police. They need a guide.''

"Where to?" was the laconic reply.

"Fort Whoop-up," McLeod said, his piercing blue eyes studying the half-breed intently. "Know the way?"

The guide was silent for so long, Kate wondered if he meant to answer. He took a pickle from the crock on the counter, studied it with distaste and returned it. There was an edge of contempt in his reply. "It's on the Old North Trail. Anybody could find it."

"We need a guide." McLeod's voice was mollifying now that he saw this man was not his to command. "Pay is ninety dollars a month."

"A hundred," Campbell stated with arrogant finality.

"Done." McLeod held out a hand and Campbell took it without enthusiasm.

Nodding his approval, French also shook hands, then turned to Baker. "I need to send a telegraph to Ottawa. Is that possible?"

"I'll see if the damn thing's working today," Baker said. "Lousy buffalo keep rubbing the poles down." He disappeared into a back room.

"If you haven't heard," French said to Campbell, who was studying Kate with undisguised curiosity, much to her discomfort, "the Northwest Mounted Police have come west to close down the whiskey forts. We'll start with the worst of the lot, Fort Whoop-up. Maybe that'll get a message to the others."

Jamie Campbell straightened, his black eyes glittering. "I'll be damned," he said. "We heard you were coming, but nobody believed it. I just came from Fort Shaw, where the U.S. Army told me they couldn't do anything unless they catch the whiskey sellers moving across the American Blackfoot reservation."

"It's Canada's problem," French replied tightly. "We'll handle it."

He glanced toward the back room and lowered his voice. "I'd been informed that Baker was involved in the whiskey trade. He knows why we're here. I can't figure why he's so friendly."

"He financed Fort Whoop-up," Campbell said, an edge of bitterness in his deep voice. "But he stands to make a profit off your troops." He indicated the stack of goods French had bought. "And he probably figures the Mounted Police won't cause any more problems to the whiskey forts than the U.S. Army did."

French frowned and gave Baker a suspicious look as he accepted paper and pencil to write out his telegraph message asking for money from Ottawa.

"You need horses?" Campbell asked the watching troopers. At their affirmative reply, he promised to see what he could find and to arrange a time of departure with French. He half turned to go, then stopped to bend a curious glance at Kate.

This was her chance, she thought, and stood to face him, an appealing hand on his arm. "My father's with the Mounted Police, Mr. Campbell. I want to hire you to take me to him. It's important that I join him as soon as possible, and I'll pay you well."

Jamie stared at the young woman in disbelief. She looked tired and worried, but her full red mouth had a stubborn slant to it. Red-gold hair crowned a pale face lightly sprinkled with golden freckles. That amazing coronet of hair shone in the dim light of the store like the last gleaming of a prairie sunset. Despite the prim cut of the dark blue dress she wore, the curves of her slender figure led a man's eye. He sighed and determinedly banished the flash of sympathy he felt for her.

He knew about white women. He'd been down the

Old North Trail as far as the booming town of Denver. He'd even bedded white whores. But this was one of the "good" women—wives and sisters and mothers. All of them, it seemed to him, were too tightly bound, corseted, burdened with petticoats and long skirts and puzzling rules of conduct, never free like a Blackfoot woman. He'd always felt sorry for them, as he almost did for this girl. But she had no business here, not in Fort Benton, and certainly not at Fort Whoop-up.

"You can't go there," he told her, more harshly than he'd meant to. "There ain't a white woman in all the Northwest Territories. You'd best go back where you came from."

Jamie stalked out of the store, trying to erase the memory of a pair of troubled gray eyes as dark as the cloudy Montana sky. He couldn't be bothered with a foolish white woman. The Mounted Police would pay him top price. He'd guide them to Fort Whoop-up and help root out the whiskey-selling bastards forever. Then he had another duty. He had to kill Good Young Man and Big Rib.

❧ 4 ❧

Kate gazed out at the sere autumn landscape from beneath the heavy buffalo robe the bull-train driver had provided. Under a milky-blue sky, dried buffalo grass whispered in the cold wind that blew incessantly across endless miles of rolling prairie. In front of the massive wagon, six yokes of oxen plodded along the worn trail, their hooves raising little clouds of dust to be blown away on the wind. She glanced back at the two wagons following, their heavy canvas covers flapping in the wind, then looked again at the oddly pale horizon.

"Prairie fire." The guttural voice of the man beside her startled Kate. He pointed at the faint smudge of white on the horizon. "Too late to be lightning," he went on. "Must be the damn wolfers." Leaning out from his high seat at the front of the tall covered wagon, he expertly spit a stream of tobacco juice so that the wind carried it away.

"Will it catch up with us?" Kate asked apprehensively.

"Naw!" He shrugged massive shoulders encased in a soiled and worn Hudson's Bay capote, a short coat fashioned from a heavy Hudson's Bay blanket, and he wiped a dribble of tobacco juice from his bristly gray beard. "It'll burn out at Milk River."

The silence that had prevailed through most of the long days they'd traveled north from Fort Benton fell once more.

"Lon Green's a good man," Mrs. Thompson had said, her disapproving frown firmly in place. "If you insist on making this damn fool trip to the Northwest, best you go with him. He'll see no harm comes to you."

"If he'll take me, I'm going," Kate replied firmly, and Mrs. Thompson threw up her hands in a gesture of dismissal.

"Go, then, stubborn missy. But I lay odds you'll be travelin' with Lon on his return trip."

"Maybe," Kate answered. That word was the closest she'd come to surrendering to all the dire warnings from the Thompsons and from I. G. Baker, who'd flat out said she couldn't travel to the Northwest on any of his bull trains.

Lon Green was an independent, with his own wagons and oxen. The carefully hoarded gold coins Kate offered as her fare made his faded hazel eyes glisten. The load on this trip was destined for the old Hudson's Bay fort at Rocky Mountain House, but the trail north still led through the Sweet Grass Hills, where the Mounted Police were camped.

David Cavendish, in his efforts to discourage her, had even drawn a rough map to show her how far it was. In the few days the troopers had been billeted at the Overland Hotel, he'd spent his spare hours with her, walking around the town or sitting in the Thompson parlor. Mrs. Thompson, certain he was courting Kate, had invited him for supper.

"Wait here for your father," David had urged Kate. His handsome face was clean-shaven once more, fair mustache neatly trimmed. "He'll send for you when he has a place in Canada, or he'll come here to be with you." In his urgency to convince her, David took her hand in his, looking sternly into her eyes.

It was pleasant having her hand held, knowing that at least one person in this country was concerned about her. But as the pressure of his clasp increased, the memory of Curtis flooded back. She'd sworn she'd never again be charmed out of reality by a man's warm touch and smiling eyes. Such things were not for women like her, women with unwomanly ambitions. "Papa will understand," she said, but she could not force herself to withdraw her hand from his.

David frowned. "You don't understand, Kate. Listen to me! It's a hard country—harder than you can imagine, harder than I could have guessed the day we said goodbye in Toronto."

David quickly removed his hand from hers when Mrs. Thompson and two of the older men who boarded there came into the parlor. But for the next hour, and with meaningful glances at Kate, he regaled the company with tales of the horrors suffered by the Mounted Police in their trek across Canada.

Day after desolate day, the troops had marched through country where there was no wood or water, no grass for the animals. Great swarms of voracious mosquitoes attacked both men and animals. Half the tents were blown away in a violent windstorm. Horses grew emaciated and fell to die beside the trail. Some days they made only a few miles, with the troops struggling to move the heavy field guns over hills and through swamps. It was the first of September, with rations nearly exhausted, when they saw their first buffalo and killed five. Their bodies starved and unused to the wild meat, many troopers fell victim to dysentery. Finally it became obvious that the guides themselves were lost in unfamiliar country.

At last the struggling band of Mounted Police came up on the Milk River Ridge, where the faint blue outline of the Rocky Mountains edged the horizon. In the Sweet Grass Hills they found food for the animals, and water, and rest for exhausted troopers. From there a detachment rode to Fort Benton for supplies and a guide.

As Kate listened to his tale, her heart grew sick with guilt for the misery her father had suffered for her sake. But she would make it up to him, she vowed to herself. She would go to him, wherever the Mounted Police might be camped, and take care of him as she'd promised her mother she would. The old ache of loss caught at her as she remembered that awful day.

Mary had known she was dying. The injuries she'd suffered in the riot had ruined her health. Now fever raged through her worn body. Her desperately grieving husband knew the inevitability of her death, but he couldn't bear to face his loss. So it was young Kate her mother turned to with a tolerant smile for the weakness of men. "You will take care of your father, Katie . . . promise me. You can be his second pair of hands, just as I've been. He'll be so alone, so helpless, without me. Promise, Katie, darling." The weeping twelve-year-old girl-child had promised fervently, kissed the feverish fingers that stroked her tear-wet face and watched life fade from the proud, loving woman who had been Mary Maginnis.

Now, by bull train on a rough trail, she was on her way to keep that promise. Kate smiled to herself, wondering what David's reaction might be when she arrived. They had become friends during those brief days in Fort Benton. He was attracted to her, she knew, but she wouldn't make the mistake she had with Curtis.

He'd been a fellow student in her botany class at Normal School. Tall and fair, with dancing brown eyes and ambitions to be a teacher of science. Strolling with him about the campus, gathering leaves for their assignments, Kate had been certain he would be the loving companion she'd begun to think she'd never find. But then he introduced her to his doting mother, and Kate naively confided her own ambitions. As soon as the words left her mouth, she saw the expression of distaste on Mrs. Browne's face and lapsed into silence—too late. Soon there was a sense of Curtis's drawing away. "Unwomanly and cold," he'd called her bluntly when she confronted him. Alone, Kate wept, for her heart knew she wasn't cold. Couldn't Curtis tell that from their few stolen kisses? How could he let his mother influence him against her?

In the painful weeks following, Kate came to know that if there was ever to be a man for her, he must understand and accept her dreams. And he must know that an ambitious heart could also hold a woman's passion. David might be a man who would understand that . . . but not yet. She had resigned herself to the life of a spinster, and her heart would not be given so easily again.

David had gone away believing he'd convinced her to stay in Fort Benton. She could justify that deception with the knowledge that it had occurred before she bribed Lon Green with nearly the last of her money.

Each of the three huge wagons carried two men, the driver and his swamper. Green's companion acted as a scout, riding ahead on horseback to make sure the trail was clear and passable. Right now, he rode back toward the lead wagon at a gallop.

"Them Mounties camped just ahead—over that rise,"

the rough-looking old fellow said as he drew abreast of the wagon.

"Baker's wagons there?" Green asked and swore under his breath when the scout nodded. "Feed will be short, then." He peered up at the sun slipping down the western sky through the pale haze of distant smoke. "Pick a spot," he ordered the scout. "We'll stay close by tonight." He grinned and glanced at Kate. "This is where our lady friend leaves us."

Kate frowned. She didn't like being called "lady friend," but she swallowed her annoyance because Green and his men had been scrupulously polite in their treatment of her these past wearisome days. The memory of Mrs. Thompson's horror stories of what might happen to a lone woman on the prairies still made her shudder, even though they didn't weaken her resolve.

The wagon topped the rise to look down on a grassy coulee laced with flowing springs. Fresh horses brought from Fort Benton grazed alongside the bony remnants of the trek across Canada. Baker's oxen fed on the other side of the Mounted Police camp, where a few ragged tents lined up to face away from the wind. As soon as Green's train was spotted, a trooper mounted his horse and rode to meet it.

The eyes of the fresh-faced young policeman seemed to start from his head when he rode abreast of the lead wagon and saw Kate. "I say," he blurted out. "What you doing here?"

Lon Green gave her a protective look, then glared at the young man. "This here's Kate Maginnis," he growled. "Dr. Maginnis's daughter."

"I say," the trooper repeated, still staring at Kate as though mesmerized.

Apprehension mounting, Kate managed a smile for

the young man. "Will you please inform my father that I'm here?"

"Now!" Lon roared when the boy seemed unable to move.

"Yes, sir!" He started to rein away, then turned back and saluted. "Sub-constable Bagley, at your service, miss."

Bagley rode quickly back to the camp, stopping at what Kate surmised was the commandant's tent, since a Union Jack fluttered on a pole in front of it. Lon Green set the wagon brake and stepped down to help Kate descend from the high seat. With what she thought was unseemly hurry, he unloaded her trunks and bags, her bedroll and the "half-breed" sleeping tent she'd bought in Fort Benton, a small contraption designed for one sleeper.

Kate smoothed her hair, straightened her shawl around her shoulders and struggled to maintain a confident face as she watched Assistant Commissioner McLeod stride toward her, his expression furious.

"Young woman!" he thundered as he confronted her. "What in the name of God are you doing here after I told you, and Commissioner French told you, not to come?"

With a stubborn lift of her chin, Kate tried to still the trembling inside. "You are not my commander, sir."

McLeod's face grew dark with anger. For a moment he seemed to have lost the power of speech. Then he turned his piercing glare on Lon Green. "Don't unload her baggage here, mister. She's not staying."

Green's expression was deceptively bland. "She only paid passage this far." He spit a stream of tobacco juice dangerously near McLeod's boots. "Anyways, I'm headed fer Rocky Mountain House. Cain't take no woman in that country."

"And the Northwest Mounted Police can't have a woman in their camp," McLeod exploded, glaring at him.

"Ah, Commissioner . . ." Green drawled. "This lady ain't no trouble. On the way here she did her share, set up her own tent, helped the cook, even treated a bad cut one of my swampers got."

Obviously Green's defense didn't mollify McLeod, for he turned on Kate, looking as though he longed to shake her.

A glad cry interrupted. "Katie—darling girl!"

"Papa!"

Dr. Maginnis seized her in an embrace so fierce, all the breath went out of her. With her face pressed to his shoulder, she was blind to everything but his dear presence. Only when he held her away to look into her face did she see how thin and aged he looked. Her heart fell in fear.

"What are you doing here, my girl? I thought you were in Philadelphia."

"It turned out there wasn't enough money from the house for medical school," she told him sadly, reaching to touch his worn, sunburned face tenderly. "I had nowhere to go, Papa . . . so I came to you."

Behind her, she heard the clash of the wagon brake, the crack of Lon Green's whip, and with a huge grinding of wheels, the wagon pulled away. She'd meant to thank Green and tell him good-bye, but he obviously wanted to move on before McLeod could somehow force him to take her.

With a final wave in the direction of the departing wagon, Kate turned back to her father. The advance of his disease was obvious to her experienced eye. He should have been warm and comfortable in Toronto these past months, not struggling and starving across the unwelcoming prairies.

Dusk was falling and the wind was cold. Tom Maginnis tucked his gloved hands into the pockets of his worn woolen capote and shivered. "Come, Kate. There'll be a fire in camp."

McLeod turned from glowering after the departed Green and fixed an unhappy stare on Kate. "You'll go back to Benton on the first southbound bull train," he told her in a voice that brooked no argument.

"I'm a good doctor, sir." She faced him boldly. "I'll be a real help to my father in taking care of the troops. You won't regret it if you'll only let me stay."

His reply was simply an icy stare. "Bagley," he shouted at the young trooper, who had watched the proceedings with undisguised curiosity. "Take all this stuff to Dr. Maginnis's tent." To Kate, he spoke in the stern voice of command. "Keep your place, young woman, and behave like a lady. Don't expect my men to wait on you. You'll have to look after yourself."

"I can do all that and assist my father, too." Kate found herself shouting the words to McLeod's departing back. "You'll see," she muttered furiously. "I'll show you." And she gave her father a comforting smile as she took his arm, and they started down the slope toward the Mounted Police camp.

A blazing fire at the center of the camp sent sparks into the inky night sky. Here in the Sweet Grass Hills, the troops had found wood and water and grass. The bull trains from Fort Benton had brought warm clothes, blankets and food. They had fresh horses, and tomorrow the trek north for the long-awaited attack on Fort Whoop-up would begin. No wonder the mood tonight was festive, Jamie Campbell told himself ironically.

He sat apart from the others, away from the light of the fire, watching the young troopers make damn fools of themselves for Kate Maginnis. Most of them had shaved or at least trimmed their whiskers, brushed up their red coats, donned their new boots and come after supper to sit around the bench they'd made for her beside the fire.

The only other chair in camp, now that French and his detachment were on their way to Fort Pelly, belonged to the new commander. Jamie glanced toward McLeod's tent, where the commissioner's lantern reflected his silhouette against the tent wall. Everything was in readiness for the march tomorrow, or McLeod wouldn't have allowed the troopers this evening of freedom, but he was still in there studying maps Jamie had gone over with him earlier.

The knowledge that McLeod didn't really trust him was galling. The commander had good reason not to trust half-breed guides after his experience with those two worthless imposters who'd lit out for Fort Benton as soon as they were paid. But here in the Northwest, the word of Jamie Campbell was as good as gold. No one had questioned it until now. McLeod wouldn't even listen to his insistence that the whiskey traders would have been warned, that a full-scale attack against Fort Whoop-up would be useless.

Inevitably, Jamie's gaze rested again on the laughing girl holding court across the campfire. Her red-gold hair shone like a sunset in the firelight, her eyes bright with laughter as she answered the troopers' sallies and their questions about her trip. On one side sat her aging father, and she often touched his arm or turned to smile at him. On the other side sat the neatly shaved and obviously smitten Inspector Cavendish.

Well, Jamie had warned her not to come to the North-

west and she'd paid him no more mind than she'd paid
McLeod. Stubborn, he thought, with more guts than
most white women he'd known. Something in him was
forced to admire the indomitable spirit that had driven
her here, all the way from Toronto, to her father's side.
Jamie had already noticed Dr. Maginnis's badly crippled
hands and wondered how he'd managed all those
months as the only doctor. Kate Maginnis meant to take
care of her father. The Blackfoot honored and cared for
their elders. It seemed logical and right to Jamie. But
McLeod was right, too. A lone woman could cause trouble among all these men. Yet, watching her, Jamie
sensed a stern reserve about her that would likely keep
the troopers in their place. It was the kind of emotional
barrier he recognized from inside himself.

"Campbell."

Jamie started guiltily from his thoughts of Kate Maginnis and stood to face Commissioner McLeod.

"Can you find a gentle horse for the girl?" McLeod
nodded grudgingly toward her and the adoring troopers.
"I'll send her back to Benton on the first bull train we
come across, but until then—"

"She came north with the only driver she'd be safe
with," Jamie interrupted. "Lon Green's a steer, but he's
got a good heart."

"A steer?" McLeod stared.

"Got caught in bed with a Frenchman's wife and the
Frenchman had a knife," Jamie replied laconically, trying not to smile when McLeod swallowed hard.

"Find her a horse," McLeod growled and strode
away.

The buckskin gelding was old and slow. Jamie wondered if the horse trader had driven it in with the herd
just to be rid of it. He certainly hadn't purchased it.

When he threw one of the worn-out, badly made Canadian saddles on it, the animal stood in quiet submission.

First light streaked the eastern sky as Jamie led the buckskin across the camp where tents were being struck, supplies loaded, animals saddled in readiness for the day's march. Dr. Maginnis's tent was already down, his goods and Kate's loaded in the Red River cart that carried medical supplies. They both turned to stare in surprise at Jamie's appearance.

"I brought your horse," he said, and cursed himself for sounding stupid. Still, he thought, Kate Maginnis's glowing beauty on this cold autumn morning would strike most men dumb.

Her red-gold hair had been braided and wound in a coronet around her shapely head. She wore the same brown stuff gown she'd worn yesterday, and even its ugliness failed to dim the perfection of her figure and her slender face. Puzzled gray eyes studied him.

Dr. Maginnis paused in saddling his own horse. "I thought she'd ride with the drover on the cart," he protested mildly.

"McLeod ordered the horse," Jamie replied shortly, then excused the commander by adding, "The carts are pretty heavily loaded."

Her gray eyes narrowed, and he knew she saw through his subterfuge. At last he shrugged. "McLeod won't make it easy on you."

Kate's full pink mouth tightened stubbornly. "I can ride a horse," she declared, and reached up to stroke the buckskin's nose.

"He's gentle," Jamie assured her, his anger at McLeod rising. She touched the stirrup and he groaned inwardly, knowing it didn't matter if Blackfoot women showed their legs while riding astride, but it was unthinkable for a white woman. "Might be good if you wore a pair of your father's trousers under your skirt."

Their eyes held for a long moment until he was certain he detected a humorous twinkle in hers. "Good idea," she agreed and hurried to the cart to search through the doctor's pack.

Right there in front of him and her dumbstruck father, Kate pulled the trousers up under her skirt and buttoned them. Then she tied her woolen capote, drew on a pair of knit gloves, all the while her eyes daring the men to comment.

"I'm ready," she announced. Her father spread his arms in a gesture of defeat, and Jamie guessed the girl had won him over many times before now.

"Mount up," Jamie told her, "and I'll adjust the stirrups for you."

The patient horse stood unmoving. Kate stared at the stirrup so high on the animal's side there seemed no possibility of her foot ever reaching it. Back in Toronto, ladies slid gracefully into their sidesaddles from a mounting block. But this was not Toronto. There were no mounting blocks, no sidesaddles. Kate shrugged. She was here, and there was no going back.

Suddenly two strong hands grasped her waist and lifted her from the ground. Jamie Campbell meant to put her aboard the horse. Her left foot flailed the air, struggling to find the stirrup, while her right knee pressed painfully against the pommel. Gasping and red-faced, she at last found her seat, her legs dangling above the stirrups.

Already loosening the stirrup leathers to shorten them, Jamie Campbell did not look up at her. But beneath his wide-brimmed hat Kate was certain she saw his lips twitch in amusement. Damn him, she thought in annoyance. He could have warned her and not just thrown her onto the horse like that.

He tightened the stirrup leathers and moved to the other side. "Next time you might try mounting from the wheel of the cart," he said, and she was certain he was laughing at her.

"Thanks for the advice," Kate replied tersely, with no gratitude in her voice.

This time Campbell made no attempt to hide his grin, and Kate was astounded at how his face changed. Black eyes crinkled, white teeth flashing; there was a compelling warmth about him that made her heart leap and beat erratically. The stirrup shortened, Campbell suddenly took hold of her calf and fitted her shoe into the iron ring. No man had ever touched her leg before. Kate gasped as a dizzying current ran through her. Campbell said nothing, but she saw that his hand trembled as he quickly drew it away and stepped back.

"Reckon that'll do, ma'am," he said and turned to go. For one flashing moment their eyes met and clung with such intensity that Kate was breathless. Astonished by her reaction, she gazed after him as he strode away. Was she losing her mind here in the vast Northwest . . . attracted to an arrogant, half-savage man? Then her father asked for her help at the cart and Kate dismounted. Calling up all her well-known self-discipline, she assured herself that what had passed between her and Jamie Campbell was simply a momentary lapse brought on by strange surroundings.

The eastern sky was red and a cold morning wind had risen. By now he should be well on his way in front of the troopers, scouting out the line of march, planning for tonight's campsite. But here he was, catering to a stubborn woman just because he figured the Mountie commandant was being too hard on her.

"Thanks," she'd called after him, her voice so sharp he knew she wasn't grateful at all. Or maybe the look that passed between them had jolted her as it had him.

"Damn fool woman, anyway," Jamie muttered to himself and stalked off to where he'd left his own horse. She wouldn't be so uppity at the end of the day, when her butt and thighs were raw from riding.

Kate watched his tall, straight figure silhouetted against the glowing sky as he walked back to where his horse was picketed. He didn't want her here. McLeod didn't want her here. Only her father, who was trying hard to conceal how glad and relieved he was for her presence in spite of his guilt over the house money, wanted her here. And she'd be damned if she'd let McLeod's pettiness or the half-breed's ridicule make her give up.

The troops were forming for the march. Inspector Cavendish gave her a salute as he rode along the line. The drovers whipped the oxen drawing the squeaking Red River carts and the wagons.

"Shall I help you mount?" her father asked.

"No!" she answered curtly, stung that even he should doubt her competence. He nodded and mounted his own sorrel. As Kate took the buckskin's reins, a rider galloped up beside her and pulled to a halt.

Jamie Campbell dismounted, his dark face like a thundercloud. "Lousy Canadian government," he announced harshly, obviously not caring who heard him. "Bought the cheapest damn saddles made anywhere. They're enough to cripple a man, let alone a lady." In one swift movement, he lifted the cougar skin from his own saddle and draped it over Kate's. Before she could move or speak, he had mounted his horse and was gone.

With one hand smoothing the soft fur, Kate gazed in amazement after the galloping horse and rider until they had passed the head of the column and disappeared over a rise into the blazing morning sky.

5

*T*he cold darkness smelled of woodsmoke and horses when Kate came out of the surgery tent. She winced as she pulled the heavy wool capote she'd bought in Fort Benton tight around her. Two days on horseback was quite different from riding Toronto's streetcars for transportation. The inside of her thighs was sore, and her rear end hurt all the way up her backbone. If McLeod meant to punish her for showing up at the Mounted Police camp, he'd succeeded. But not well enough to make her consider turning back to Fort Benton . . . not until her father went with her.

With a sigh, Kate settled on a cottonwood log near their small fire, one of many winking in the darkness of the camp. Inside the surgery, Dr. Maginnis still fussed over preparations for tomorrow's attack on Fort Whoop-up. If the American whiskey sellers chose to defend their fort, there would be casualties. He and Kate must be ready to care for them.

The outline of the hills above St. Mary River was barely visible in the faint starlight. There the cannons and mortar had been placed in readiness for tomorrow's attack. A shudder went through Kate as she recalled the horrifying tales of the Indian wars and the War of 1812 she'd heard during school days in Toronto. Even then she'd thought it could scarcely have been worse than the bloody riot that had caused her mother's illness and death. Death everywhere, and the memory of the rough man's life pouring from a cut throat haunted her. Again Kate shuddered, then sat up very straight, chastising herself. She was grown now. The nightmares had faded. She had known this was a military expedition and that death was a likely part of it. "You must learn to put your emotions aside when you treat a patient"—wise words her father had repeated often. If she meant to be a doctor, she must do that. To fight death was essential to her calling.

"Good evening, Miss Maginnis."

David Cavendish's handsome figure materialized out of the gloom. Kate smiled up at him. "Won't you sit down, Inspector Cavendish?" She patted the log next to where she sat. He appeared at the surgery every evening, and Kate was certain that her father, like Mrs. Thompson back in Fort Benton, thought David was courting her. Always realistic, Kate doubted that. After all, David came from an aristocratic and noble family, although he'd never told her much about them. It didn't seem likely, she thought wryly, that he would seek marriage with a nobody—the daughter of a poverty-stricken country doctor. Nevertheless, David was intelligent, well read, charming. For now, she would simply enjoy his company and think nothing of a future with him. She certainly wouldn't allow her emotions to become involved, not after she'd learned her lesson with Curtis.

"I hope you didn't get lice from that thing." He glared with distaste at the cougar pelt lying across her saddle.

Annoyed, Kate reached to smooth the soft fur with her hand. She was certain it had spared her what would have been raw sores rather than just aching muscles. "I'm sure Mr. Campbell wouldn't have given it to me if it was infested," she said coolly.

David stirred up the fire, added a log, then sat beside her. He shook his head as though he couldn't believe her ignorance, and her annoyance grew. "Miss Maginnis, you must realize that lice are a way of life among these savages."

"Savages?" she asked, frowning as she observeed Jamie Campbell's tall figure stooping to enter Commissioner McLeod's tent across the camp. He didn't look like a savage, and her cheeks burned as she recalled how often during the days' ride her eyes had followed him as he rode far ahead of the column.

Chuckling to himself, David seemed not to hear her. "Even McLeod had a batch of lice after we made the mistake of camping on an abandoned Cree camp." He smiled at her. "Only way to get rid of them is to put all your clothes on a red anthill and let the ants clean up the lice." With a significant lift to his eyebrows, he added, "It's a primitive life out here, Kate. I agree with your father and with McLeod ... it would be best for you to return to Fort Benton. It's a wild place, but at least it's a town with other civilized women. You'd be comfortable, and out of harm's way."

"My father's readying the surgery for tomorrow," Kate remarked by way of changing the subject. She nodded toward the lighted surgery tent, where her father's shadow moved on the canvas wall.

"Yes." David's expression grew serious. "The troops will be on the move early in the morning for the attack on Fort Whoop-up. I thought I'd make sure all's well with you and the doctor."

"That's kind of you, David," she said, briefly touching his hand, suddenly aware she had used his given name. "Do you think the fighting will be bad?"

With a shrug, David nodded toward McLeod's tent, where two men's figures were silhouetted and obviously involved in an argument. "Campbell claims there'll be no fighting. Says the whiskey sellers have cleared out. McLeod doesn't trust him, and neither do I."

Kate's gaze rested on the gesticulating shadows on the wall of McLeod's tent. "We ate well tonight because of him," she replied mildly.

David didn't bother to conceal his annoyance at her defense of the half-breed. "The fact that he had a buffalo cow slaughtered and dressed out when we came into camp doesn't make him our savior. That's part of his job."

The whole camp, including the few Indians who had been trailing along with them, had feasted on roast buffalo hump and ribs. He saved us from a buffalo stampede, too, Kate thought as she watched a frowning Campbell emerge from the commander's tent.

On the second night out, everyone had slept little as a mysterious rumbling sound drifted on the air. At daybreak the camp found it was surrounded by a great herd of buffalo. Excited troopers grabbed their rifles, eager to kill one of the shaggy beasts. But Campbell rode quickly among the men, warning that even one shot could set off a stampede that would leave behind trampled goods and dead troopers. To the greenhorn Mounties, the halfbreed seemed to know everything—at least in comparison with their incompetent former guides. Still, they eyed the great beasts with covetous hunters' eyes as their column moved slowly through the vast grazing herd until at last Campbell led them out into open prairie.

"One more Mountie ready for battle." Dr. Maginnis's jovial voice interrupted them. Kate nodded agreement absently, her eyes still on Jamie Campbell as his tall figure blended into the darkness and was gone.

"I took care of Bagley's hand almost as well as you could have done, Kate." The doctor winked at her as she looked up at the young trooper staring at her in red-faced adoration.

"The hand is fine." Bagley stumbled over the words. "I can be part of the attack tomorrow."

"I'm sure you'll be a credit to the Northwest Mounted Police," Kate told him with a smile, leaving the boy speechless.

Finally, he managed to mumble, "Thank you, ma'am," gave her a smart salute and walked away reluctantly.

David had been studying the ground intently during the exchange. Now he looked up with the grin he'd barely managed to conceal. "McLeod's right, Kate. You are a hazard in camp—at least to love-struck young men like Bagley."

Dr. Maginnis chuckled. "In the past three days I've had more would-be patients show up at my surgery than I had in those three miserable months marching across Canada." He grinned at Kate.

"Not surprising," David said, his handsome face suddenly serious, his blue eyes warm with admiration. "All these months in the wilderness, and here's a lovely lady waiting to take care of them." He stood abruptly and Kate wondered if she had only imagined that warmth, for now his expression was cool and distant. "We'll attack before dawn," he said. "Best get some sleep."

"I pray we'll have no patients for our surgery tomorrow." Dr. Maginnis's face was somber.

David shrugged. "At least we'll find out just how great a liar the half-breed is."

Puzzled by his abrupt departure and lightning mood changes, Kate watched his ramrod-straight figure cross the camp to his own tent, the scarlet jacket dim in the lowering firelight. An upper-class Englishman, she thought. From her mother's stories, she pictured them all as cold and arrogant, yet David had been friendly until just now. Perhaps he was merely worried about the battle tomorrow, she told herself, and went into the surgery tent to make sure her father hadn't forgotten anything.

"McLeod thinks me a fool," Dr. Maginnis said, observing Kate roll bandages in preparation for tomorrow. He did not sound angry or disgruntled, as well he might if his statement were true. Kate paused in her work to study his face, knowing he would explain.

"Perhaps he's right. I should have insisted you return to civilization at once. The middle of a war is no place for a young woman." The rising inflection in his last words almost made a question.

"Campbell says there'll be no war, that the whiskey sellers will clear out ahead of the Canadian police." Even as she spoke, doubts rose. "Do you believe him?"

"He's a half-breed, isn't he?" The usually tolerant doctor's voice was weighted with the contempt for half bloods that was common to all Canadian whites.

"Meaning he's a liar?" Kate prompted.

Dr. Maginnis considered for a moment. "Who knows?" he finally answered and fell silent, his face a study.

Kate arranged the rolled bandages in the case and closed the lid. "We're ready for tomorrow," she said. The words caught in her throat at the sight of his unhappy face.

"I've failed you, Katie." Her father's plaintive voice broke the silence. "I'm heartsick that I was such a fool in the matter of the mortgage on our house. Have I always led you in the wrong direction?''

Knowing that he'd always done his best, Kate ached for his fearful regrets. Quickly, she stepped across the tent and leaned close to press her cheek to his. "Never, Papa—never!" she protested, angry at McLeod for his tirade at her father.

Kneeling beside his stool, she took his hands in hers and looked up into his anguished face. "You've always encouraged my dreams, even though those dreams didn't conform to what nice young ladies are supposed to want. You've been my mentor, my friend, my ally in all our battles against death. How could you blame yourself for that?''

Tears pricked her eyes as she kissed his gnarled hands. "Without a father like you," she told him earnestly, "I would have shriveled and died.''

"Oh, my dear girl," he murmured sadly, one crippled hand caressing her hair. "It fills my heart to hear those words, but still I fear for your future.''

"I told you, Papa," she chided him, hoping to lighten the mood. "We'll set up practice together in the west.''

"And when I'm gone?" he asked with a grave expression.

That possibility had never occurred to Kate. Grief struck her at the thought, but she caught back a sob and refused to accept his words. "That won't happen," she cried.

"If you were wed . . . perhaps to a man like Cavendish . . . '' he began.

"That won't happen either," she protested vehemently. The knowledge that she was destined to live her life alone was engraved on her heart, but she couldn't share it with her doting father.

"What happens will happen, Papa." It was a favorite

saying of her mother's, and they both smiled in fond remembrance. Kate stood up. "Now get some rest, Dr. Maginnis," she ordered with a smile. "Tomorrow may be a very busy day."

Trooper Bagley's bugle sounded through the icy air of predawn. Jamie was already awake, mounted on his horse and waiting beside McLeod's tent. Yesterday he'd scouted Fort Whoop-up. There had been no Indians around the fort in their usual drunken carousal. Three or four he recognized as inveterate beggars had been sitting patiently beside the closed wicket. An odd silence had hung over the usually noisy place. Jamie smiled grimly. The canny Baker had sent a messenger on a fast horse, he was certain of it. By now John Healy and his barrels of whiskey were far away.

This morning, as Jamie watched the troopers catch up their horses and prepare for the great attack on Fort Whoop-up, he didn't know whether to laugh or curse. McLeod's suspicion and distrust were galling when the integrity of Jamie Campbell was legend in the Northwest. They'd argued hotly last night, but McLeod was the commander. They would attack Fort Whoop-up.

McLeod emerged from his tent, settling his white helmet on his head. His scarlet uniform had been brushed and the buttons polished. Appearances were important to the English greenhorns, and McLeod saw himself taking the surrender of Fort Whoop-up this day.

"The Whoop-up Trail ford on the St. Mary can be tricky," Jamie said, bringing his horse alongside McLeod. "Have the men follow my lead."

The dubious look McLeod gave him aroused Jamie's ire once more. Glaring at the commander, he added harshly, "Either that or they can drown. Doesn't matter to me.'' Turning the horse, he galloped north out of the camp.

"Bloody bastards!'' McLeod drew his horse to a halt and glared toward Fort Whoop-up. The troops had just crossed the St. Mary River and circled past the trees. "The bloody gall,'' McLeod swore again, and gazed in fury at the flag fluttering in the cold breeze. "Flying an American flag on British soil! We'll see about that!'' He turned to Bagley and ordered, "Bugler, sound the charge!''

At the first notes of the bugle, the beggars Jamie had seen yesterday scattered in terror.

Slouched in his saddle, Jamie studied the glowering McLeod as the troops moved cautiously forward. He tried not to smile at McLeod's anger over the flag. It wasn't really an American flag, although it had red-and-white stripes with a field of blue stripes in the corner. Healy probably flew it in defiance, since he was one of the many Americans who believed this land should belong to the United States.

Mortars and cannon were trained on the gates. The red-coated Mounties waited their command. But an eerie silence lay over the scene. No sound came from the fort. With a puzzled frown, McLeod rode back to Jamie's side. "Come along—we'll give them a chance to surrender.''

McLeod drew his pistol as they dismounted in front of the heavy wooden gates. Drawing himself up, every inch a military man, McLeod pounded peremptorily on the gates.

Silence deepened and Jamie wondered if the place had been completely deserted. Then the gates swung slowly open and there stood the old trapper, Davey Akers, shaggy head and beard peering through the opening.

"Walk right in, General," the old man greeted them in his Yankee twang. "Been expectin' you. Come right on in."

Speechless with astonishment, McLeod turned to Jamie.

"Where's Healy?" Jamie demanded of Akers.

"Damned if I know," was the reply. "He sold out. I'm runnin' the place fer Hamilton."

"Got any whiskey?" Jamie prompted, already knowing the answer.

Akers cackled and slapped his thigh. "Campbell, you know that's agin the law."

The Mounties made short work of searching the fort, but there was no trace of whiskey or alcohol to be found. Inside, dwellings were built against the stout walls, as well as storerooms, stables, a blacksmith shop and a kitchen near the well dug in one corner. Two Blackfoot women appeared from one dwelling and began cooking in the kitchen.

"Well, you told me," McLeod said as he and Jamie met in the center of the fort after the search was concluded. Accusation was in the tone of his voice, if not in the words. He believed his guide had betrayed him to the whiskey sellers.

"So I did," Jamie replied laconically. What he would not say, what everyone in the Northwest knew, was that Jamie Campbell, Follows the Eagle of the Blackfoot tribe, did not lie.

All the remaining troops had crossed the river and set up camp around the fort. Kate had treated the one casualty, an embarrassed Mountie who had dropped a packing crate on his foot. The battle for Fort Whoop-up was over; the sun high in the hazy sky when David Cavendish rode up to the Maginnis tent. He did not look pleased as he announced, "Officers and"—he bowed toward Kate—"and ladies are invited to take dinner with the owner of Fort Whoop-up." He managed a smile and added, "Seems the old gentleman grows vegetables in the fort, so at least we'll have a change of menu."

He had wanted a battle, wanted to prove himself, Kate thought, looking into his glum face. To a soldier, it was war, but she could think of killing only as murder. Was David capable of such a thing? Deliberately, she said, "I'm glad there was no fighting and no one was hurt."

David's frown deepened. "You can thank your friend Campbell for that. McLeod's certain he betrayed us and warned the whiskey sellers to get out before we arrived."

"Then McLeod should charge him," Dr. Maginnis blustered.

"Perhaps he will." David shrugged and reined his horse around. "Akers's Indian women are cooking. Come along as soon as you can."

Jamie Campbell capable of treason and betrayal? Kate asked herself. She didn't want to believe it, even though she scarcely knew the man. Without thinking, she laid her hand on the tawny cougar skin she had draped over her saddle. The touch of it was comforting and warm. The gift had spared her pain in the past days, yet the man who had given that gift could not be trusted.

❧ 6 ❧

"It's a well-built fort," McLeod was saying. He sat at the head of the long plank table in what had obviously been the fort's mess. Akers's two Indian women scurried back and forth from the kitchen to serve their guests. Dressed in soiled and worn buckskin gowns, they kept their eyes down and never spoke a word.

Kate sat on one side of the table, between her father and Inspector Cavendish, having quickly changed into a clean gown. Opposite were the other officers Akers had invited to share a meal. The china was crazed and chipped Queensware. Most of the Mounties resorted to the knives they'd eaten with on the trail because there weren't enough forks and knives to go around. Those rare amenities had been placed for McLeod, Kate and her father.

"Old Gladstone's the best builder in the Northwest," Akers told the commander. He paused to wipe buffalo-steak juice off his unruly gray beard, then added confidently, "This here's the best location in southern Canada."

"Not much grass," McLeod replied dubiously, refilling his plate from a large bowl of boiled potatoes and

carrots. There was a bowl of cabbage cooked with onions, and one of some kind of greens, all tasting wonderful to Kate. Meat was the staple of diet on the
frontier; vegetables like these were a rarity to be
savored.

Over a mouthful of buffalo meat, Akers said, "Damn
Injuns bring their horses and stay too long . . . ruined the
grass this year. But it'll come back."

McLeod chewed his buffalo steak thoughtfully. During the silence that fell over the table, Kate stole a glance
at Jamie Campbell. He sat at the foot of the table, his
dark face like stone as he ate sparingly of this white
man's food. It surprised her that she could sense his
anger, while no one else seemed aware of it. Undoubt-
edly he knew that McLeod suspected him of betraying
the Mounties to the whiskey traders. Kate wondered
whether he was angry at being unjustly accused, or because he was guilty and had been found out.

"Despite all the fort's advantages," McLeod announced in a cold voice, his piercing gaze fixed on Akers, "twenty-five thousand dollars is an exorbitant price
for the place."

So McLeod was dickering to buy the fort for his head-
quarters. Kate glanced around the log-walled room, trying to see it as her home. It was a stoutly built fort, well
fortified against Indian attack. On the frontier, that was
the most important consideration, and no doubt the place
could be made warm and comfortable.

"Ex—what?" Akers demanded testily, frowning at
McLeod.

"He means you want too damn much money," Jamie
Campbell interpreted coolly, and added in a low voice
directed at Akers, "I doubt it's yours to sell in the first
place."

Akers glared at him, then shrugged dismissively, returning his attention to McLeod. "Twenty-five thousand, take it or leave it."

"I've been allocated ten thousand for living quarters for my troops." McLeod fixed Akers with a piercing stare. "Take *that* or leave it."

Glancing around the table, Kate saw that the other officers, including her father and Cavendish, were concentrating on their food, pointedly ignoring the negotiations between McLeod and Akers. Only Jamie Campbell watched the proceedings, his lean face impassive.

Kate drew in a shaky breath. It would have been nice to unpack, to set up a permanent surgery in this stout fort. But she had been involved in too many political discussions with Papa and Father Bruneau. If the Canadian government had given McLeod ten thousand dollars for living quarters, there would be nothing more forthcoming. That was the way things worked back in Ottawa.

Abruptly, McLeod rose from his place. "We'll continue this discussion outside," he told Akers and stalked from the room. The meal that had begun with friendly toasts and good cheer was suddenly glum and silent.

Frowning, Jamie stood and followed the two men outside. The thin, cold sunlight of early autumn lay on the bare interior of the fort. It was as though the place had been swept clean in anticipation of the Mounted Police. He wondered where the barrels of whiskey had been hidden . . . maybe beneath the sand of the river bottom, more likely loaded on fast wagons headed for another fort.

As he approached the two men standing by the smithy, he caught the sound of their angry exchange.

"Be damned with ye," Akers shouted and stalked

away, disappearing into one of the buildings. Shoulders slumped, McLeod stared after him.

In spite of the fact that the commander had doubted his integrity, Jamie felt a flash of sympathy for the man. He might be a soldier, but this was strange country, country he could never traverse without a guide. The mere knowledge that the Mounted Police were on the way had cleared out this stinking den. But there were more whiskey traders and more needed to be done. The Mounties were essential if the Blackfoot were to be saved.

"McLeod," he called, giving the man time to regain his composure. Gesturing toward the building in which Akers had disappeared, Jamie said, "I know that sly old bastard from his days with Hudson's Bay. He's a robber and a pirate."

"Nevertheless," McLeod replied stiffly, stroking his beard, composed once more, "I'd buy the damnable fort if I had the money. Winter's coming, and my men need shelter."

Not just your men, Jamie thought, his eyes on Kate Maginnis as she and her father came out of the mess. Her bright head outshone the pale autumn sun, he thought, then berated himself for a fool. Too often his gaze went to her during the day, and too often her image troubled his dreams during the darkness. With a deep, steadying breath, he looked away from her, forcing his mind back to his duties.

"There's a spot upriver," he told McLeod, "a big island where Oldman River forks, then flows back together. There's plenty of grass and sweet water—timber, too. And it's near a Blackfoot crossing. Your men and animals would fare better there than here."

McLeod studied him skeptically. "But no buildings."

Jamie shrugged. "Old Gladstone, who built this place,

is in Fort Benton. Send for him to supervise your building, and to Ike Baker for your supplies.'' He gestured
toward the red-coated officers streaming out of the mess
now, their voices a low rumble. ''You have enough men
to put up a fort before snow flies.''

''I'd like to see this place you're talking about,''
McLeod said, tight-lipped, and Jamie knew there was
still no trust between them.

''We'll head north at dawn.'' Jamie's tone was
brusque. He walked away, telling himself he was obliged
to save the greenhorn Mounties in spite of themselves,
if only because their coming had put the whiskey traders
on the run, and that would save the Blackfoot. As his
glance went again to the bright-haired woman, he knew
the reason was more than that. No matter how he might
deny it, a need grew inside him to know that Kate Maginnis was safe from harm.

He would see that done, too, Jamie told himself. As
he turned away, his glance caught the flag that had
aroused McLeod's ire. It hung limp on the tall flagpole
beside the open gates. With an ironic laugh, Jamie strode
across the fort and hauled it down. Folding it carefully,
he thought he would present it to McLeod with appropriate ceremony for the surrender of Fort Whoop-up.

The weary column of tired men, winded horses, oxen
and squeaking carts finally came to a halt. Campbell had
pushed them hard on this second day of the march west
from Fort Whoop-up. Kate's worried glance went to her
father as he sat drooping on his horse beside her. In spite
of the cold wind that had come up as the sun sank low,
the doctor's face glistened with perspiration. Gripped by
concern for him, Kate thought that surely this was a
country for young men. Impulsively she reached to
cover his gloved hand with her own.

Immediately Dr. Maginnis straightened, giving her a reassuring smile. "It's a likely place the half-breed picked for us," he said.

Even as she nodded her agreement, Kate wondered at the twists of fate that had brought them to this faraway place.

All day she and her father had ridden at the rear of the long, slow-moving train. An immense prairie sky, the ardent blue of autumn, arched over the empty miles. And ever there was the wind blowing through the cured buffalo grass. When Kate lifted her head into that wind, the clean, grassy scent of it was as familiar as though she had been born to it. Wild asters, like lost blue stars, gleamed in the sheltered places; and along the river yellow-headed blackbirds rode the swaying willows, their endless cries of "scree, scree" blending into the rustle of the wind.

This prairie world was very large, the sky even larger. The overpowering landscape should make one feel small and vulnerable, but what Kate felt was a sense of boundless freedom. Freedom from the world where women were not allowed in medical school, where girls with ambitious dreams were outsiders meant only for spinsterhood. Somehow, and with a total lack of logic, the expansiveness of this country filled her with hope for those lost dreams.

The caravan had paused on the bank of Oldman River, at a shallow ford where Jamie Campbell had led them. In all the endless miles of prairie stretching to the horizon, there was no sign of human habitation. Prairie grasses were dry and brown; the cottonwood groves along the river and clustered on the island formed by the river forks dropped golden leaves into the wind. That there was game nearby had been proved when Campbell brought two deer he had killed to the camp cooks. Now he waved an arm, signaling that they were to begin crossing to the island.

Perhaps being on an island would protect them against an Indian attack, Kate comforted herself. Although the few curious Indians who had ridden along with the Mounties at various times had seemed harmless enough. They were obviously impressed by the red coats, which, to them, signified that these men were from the Great Grandmother, the Queen, and would do no harm.

"You will lie down and rest now, Papa," Kate told her father firmly. The surgery tent was up and she'd made a cot inside.

"There's unpacking to do," Dr. Maginnis protested without conviction. His skin was pale and damp.

Kate led him to the cot and gently pushed him down, silently cursing Jamie Campbell for riding the troops so hard these past two days.

"So much to do," the doctor muttered as Kate settled his gray head on a pillow.

"I can do it, Papa," she told him firmly, then wet a cloth from their drinking-water canteen and laid it across his forehead. "You must rest or you'll be very ill."

He sighed and made a feeble gesture of protest, then fell silent. With a last worried glance at his quiet figure, Kate hurried from the tent. Later they would discuss his diagnosis—whether it was sheer fatigue or something more dangerous. Right now, there was too much to be done. The cart driver had taken the oxen away, but the saddle horses stood waiting with weary patience. They must be unsaddled and taken to pasture with the other horses. Medical supplies, clothing and gear in the cart must be unloaded.

All around her, the Mounted Policemen were busy making camp—setting up tents, building the night fires, roping off a space to corral the horses. A cold wind blew off the river, bringing the certainty that winter was near.

As she stripped saddles from the two horses, the aroma of roasting deer meat spread across the camp from the cook tent. Once she'd set up camp, Kate told herself, she'd bring some food to her father. Perhaps that would revive his strength. Then she must make everything ready to treat any of the troopers who were sick or had been hurt during the day's march.

"I'll take the horses." Jamie Campbell's deep voice startled her from her concentration on her work. Kate gasped in surprise.

For an endless moment his hand clasped over hers where she held the reins. That hand was as hard as old leather. Strength emanated from it, yet the touch was gentle, sending a shaft of warmth through Kate that left her speechless.

In the silence stretching between them, their eyes clung as though they could not look away. At last the half-breed took the reins from Kate's trembling hands, tearing his black eyes from her face. He gestured toward the tent. "The doctor?" he asked.

Drawing a deep breath, Kate forced her emotions back under control. This was madness, she told herself. Why should she feel so drawn to a man with whom she had nothing in common? Her good, logical brain seemed to cease functioning in his presence. It was as though a wanton stranger suddenly took control of a body yearning toward an alien male creature. Finally, she managed to reply, "My father is resting. He's exhausted."

Campbell stooped to look inside the tent. Turning away, he frowned into the distance. "This is Blackfoot country," he said. "A country for young men . . . not for old men like—" And he gestured toward the tent.

"Or," he added, his voice suddenly sharp with anger, "white women like you."

In one swift movement he had mounted the bay horse. Leading the other horse, he rode quickly away.

Kate stared after him, her anger rising to match his. She had been a burden to no one on this march. For one weak moment she'd allowed herself to be drawn to him. Now she wanted to shout after him that she'd done her share, treated sick men, taken care of her father. How dared the half-breed stare at her in that disturbing way, then tell her she didn't belong in this country?

Cursing softly to himself, Jamie turned the three horses in with the herd already cropping cured buffalo grass. The woman was more than the healer she claimed to be. She was a witch. How else could he explain the intensity of his reaction to her . . . the concern for her welfare that was none of his business. And the tide of longing that flooded through him in her presence. Except for the flames hidden behind those lucid gray eyes, she had given no indication that she was drawn to him in the same way.

"You damn fool, she's a white woman," he berated himself, and slapped his horse on the rump as though chastising himself.

The stirring in his loins eased now in the cold twilight. With a deep, sighing breath, Jamie headed back toward the camp. He would find Crowfoot's camp. Cutting Woman was a healer of great knowledge. Surely she had a cure for this yearning sickness that possessed him.

The cart was unpacked, the folding table that held medical supplies set up. Seeing that her father still slept, Kate hurried to gather wood to make their fire before darkness fell. As she returned with her arms full of dry cottonwood limbs, she saw McLeod and David Cavendish striding purposefully toward her.

Her heart fell at the sight of McLeod's stern face. David seemed pleased about something; a hint of the arrogance she'd found annoying gleamed in his blue eyes.

With no preliminaries, McLeod announced, "A detachment is leaving for Fort Benton tomorrow to bring supplies for building a fort. You will be traveling with them."

Stunned speechless, Kate stared into McLeod's face. She had believed the issue settled, her purpose fulfilled, that in time all her plans would work out. Now this man had the power to turn those plans upside down . . . to send her away from the father who needed her so much.

❧ 7 ❧

rowning, Kate smoothed her sleeping father's forehead and watched McLeod and David walking back through the dusk-filled camp toward McLeod's tent. David had seemed pleased with the idea of her return to, as he phrased it, "civilization." Vaguely, she wondered if it might be because he'd begun to care for her. Or was it the inspector persona speaking, always in control of his troops, proving to himself that being sent down from Sandhurst over a gambling scandal hadn't made him a less competent officer?

That was a confession he'd made to Dr. Maginnis one night back in Fargo when they'd overindulged at a local saloon. His family was appalled at the disgrace and insisted he leave England to prove himself in one of the colonies. When her father finally repeated the tale to Kate, she began to understand David's obvious need to control others, as well as his seeming constant need for reassurance that he was right.

"Winter's coming on," he had told her gravely just now. "Wild and woolly as Fort Benton is, there are civilized people there and sturdy homes." His gesture took in the tent camp. Scattered fires winked in the gathering dusk before the rows of tents. The cooks were busy preparing the night meal. Men's voices echoed among the cottonwood trees, where the surgery tent was pitched a little apart from the others.

"This is no place for a gently raised young lady like you," David had added earnestly.

Gently raised? Ironic, she'd thought. If only David had seen her scrubbing up Dr. Maginnis's bloody operating room. Would he consider that gently raised?

"I can't go until my father's well," she protested, and was quickly overruled by McLeod.

"I've checked on him," the commander said. "He's just exhausted from the long ride. By morning he'll be in charge again." He glanced over his shoulder as he strode away. "Be ready to leave at dawn."

With a smile meant to be reassuring, David patted her shoulder. "Until tomorrow, Kate," he said. "It's for the best." Then he had quickly followed his commander.

She wouldn't go, Kate told herself now. They couldn't force her to leave her father lying ill. The sounds she'd heard through the stethoscope told her Tom Maginnis suffered from more than exhaustion, unless one could say his heart was exhausted. With rest and care, he'd be fine, but only she could give them to him.

The doctor had taken a little of the broth she brought from the cook tent and was sleeping again. Wearily, Kate rose from her stool beside his cot, glancing with longing at her own cot on the opposite side of the tent. She'd lie down there so she could hear him if he needed her.

She was about to pinch out the candle when a hoarse voice outside the tent startled her.

"Dr. Maginnis . . . sir . . . I'm awful sick."

Quickly pulling back the tent flap, Kate looked into the pale, drawn face of the young trooper Bagley, who had first greeted her in the Sweet Grass Hills.

"Miss K-Kate," he stammered, "I n-need the d-doctor."

She reached out to draw him into the tent, but he turned aside, retching painfully from an empty stomach. "I'm goin' from both ends," he apologized, wiping his mouth with the back of his hand.

"It's all right," she murmured and led him to the cot that had looked so inviting a moment before. He was burning with a fever she could feel through the sleeve of his shirt, and Kate's heart clenched with fear. In the candlelight, the boy's pale face was smeared with blood from a nosebleed, and the pulse beneath her fingers was slow and thready.

"Where's the doctor?" Bagley asked.

"Dr. Maginnis is sick, too." Kate replied and tried to make her smile reassuring. "I'll have to be your doctor."

Despite his misery, Bagley managed to look embarrassed. "Never had no lady doctor," he muttered, reluctantly lying down on the cot. He quieted as she placed a cold, wet cloth over his forehead. But when she began unbuttoning his shirt, he grabbed her hand and protested weakly. "Ma'am!"

"Lie still," Kate commanded. "I'm your doctor." A cold cloth over his forehead and eyes hid from the boy the fear that flooded Kate's face. She had seen it before, back in Toronto, and she trembled for what the outcome might be for him and for the Mounties. A rose-colored rash covered his distended abdomen. Typhoid!

Working quickly, Kate brought a slop bucket for Bagley's use, hurried to the river for a bucket of fresh, cold water. Her patient managed to hold down the few sips of water she urged on him. Ingestion of liquids was important in order to avoid dehydration. Lying back on the cot, he whispered, "I hurt so bad, Miss Kate." In spite of his embarrassment, she sponged his upper body with cold water, hoping to alleviate the fever.

Bagley had fallen into a restless, laudanum-induced doze when Kate heard another voice outside the tent calling for the doctor.

"It's my mate Parks," the bewhiskered Mountie named Turner told her. "He's awful sick. Needs the doctor."

One glance at the sick man leaning heavily on his partner told Kate she had another typhoid victim. "I'm the doctor tonight," she replied and quickly snapped out her orders. The half-breed tent was set up and Dr. Maginnis moved into it, protesting weakly. Kate feared if he stayed in the tent with the typhoid victims, he'd be a victim, too. A mild dose of laudanum quieted him.

With her new patient in the doctor's cot, sponged off and lying in silent misery, Kate glanced at his companion. The man had left the tent quickly and returned looking pale and shaken. "You've got it, too," she told him, and the man groaned.

First light filled Kate's eyes as the sounds of horses and men snapped her, exhausted, out of a doze. Through the cold, clear air came the odors of breakfast being prepared in the cook tent. Kate's empty stomach rumbled. Wrapped in a blanket over her wool capote, she was resting against a packing case in front of the tent. All night she'd sponged the three feverish men, emptied their slop bucket, fed them the little laudanum she dared use to ease their pain. Her clothes were filthy, her hair awry, and she was nearly too weary to stand when David grabbed her shoulder and lifted her to her feet.

"Kate! For God's sake—what's happened here? Why aren't you ready to go to Fort Benton?"

Through a haze of fatigue, Kate stared at his anxious face. "I won't be going to Fort Benton," she replied wearily. "We have typhoid fever in camp. I've been up all night with sick men. Another man came in this morning."

"Does McLeod know this?" David demanded and Kate shook her head. She had been too busy to think about informing the commandant. "Get McLeod," David ordered a waiting trooper. "Where are your things?" he asked Kate. "We need to get started."

"I'm not going with you, David," Kate repeated, wondering if he hadn't heard her the first time or simply didn't believe she'd defy his orders. "My father's ill. These men need a doctor. I can't go."

"All the more reason to leave," David retorted. "You need to get away from this illness. You need to be in Fort Benton, where you'll be safe. This is no place—"

His tirade was interrupted by McLeod's arrival. The commandant's face grew grim as he heard Kate's story. Stooping, he went into the sick tent, spoke to the four men lying there, then stepped out into the cold morning air. He bent over the sleeping Dr. Maginnis and frowned. "He looks bad," McLeod admitted. Kate drew a relieved breath, glad her father still slept from his dose of laudanum, or he might have added his voice to David's in urging her to leave.

McLeod faced Cavendish. "Better hit the trail, Inspector. You've a long ride ahead."

"But Miss Maginnis was to go—"

"No choice," McLeod interrupted. "With typhoid in camp, we need whatever kind of doctor we can get. There'll be other detachments going to Fort Benton. She can leave when her father is well again."

Under McLeod's commanding stare, David struggled

vainly to conceal his anger and disappointment. Kate laid a placating hand on his scarlet-clad arm. "Take care of yourself, David."

Despite McLeod's frown of disapproval, David kissed her hand lingeringly. Then, without meeting her eyes, he mounted his horse, shouted a command to his men and rode swiftly out of camp. From inside the tent came Constable Parks's agonized cry, and Kate hurried to his side.

"Did you contact the Indians?" McLeod asked as he and Jamie sat down in front of the commander's tent to partake of a sparse noon meal. Supplies were running low again until the wagons came from Fort Benton, and the cooks had seized the buffalo carcass from Jamie's pack horse with gratitude. It was already on the fire for the evening meal.

"Spent two nights in the camp of Crowfoot," Jamie answered. He disliked the word "Indian," which meant nothing to his people. If he had to accept the white man's use of it, he refused to use it himself. It had been pleasant to visit in the Blackfoot leader's camp, to eat heartily of familiar food and to hear the news of the Northwest.

Concerned that no Indians had come into the Mounted Police camp, McLeod had sent Jamie to learn the reason for their absence. He had hoped to trade with them for food for his men.

"The whiskey traders spread lies among my people," Jamie said, sipping his tea and savoring the hot brew. "They said the Mounted Police meant to treat the Blackfoot the same way the Long Knife Americans are treating the Sioux. I reminded them of your red coats, which make you the Queen's men, and that the Great Grandmother in England had always treated the Blackfoot fairly." With a dismissive shrug, he added, "They'll be coming to trade soon."

McLeod looked impressed, and Jamie allowed himself a smile, remembering how little the commandant had trusted him at the beginning. "You've accomplished a lot," he said, his expansive gesture taking in the rough stockade and the stables the Mounties were erecting. The sounds of ax and saw and hammer echoed in the cold autumn air as every man bent to the task of building shelter before winter.

"The stables came first," McLeod replied. "Our horses are in bad condition."

Emaciated and sickly after the long, starving trek across Canada, the animals had gained little weight since Jamie had joined the camp. Only the horses he'd bought in Fort Benton were thriving.

"I doubt they'll make it through the winter," Jamie said flatly, certain that the commandant needed the truth.

McLeod shook his head despairingly. "We'll do what we can."

"I could take them south into Montana. There's a place on Sun River, a sheltered valley where there's always plenty of feed. By spring they'll be fit again."

He watched McLeod's face as the man considered this proposition. It was a matter of trust and they both knew it. Could McLeod give his exhausted horses into the care of the half-breed guide he hadn't trusted from the beginning? Jamie watched the commandant's face, knowing that a refusal would end their relationship. He'd been willing to help the Mounted Police, knowing they had come to save the Blackfoot from the whiskey traders, something he could not do alone. But his pride was at stake here. To his surprise, McLeod scarcely hesitated.

"How many men will you need?"

When details of the drive to Sun River had been settled, Jamie rose to begin making arrangements.

"There's typhoid fever in the camp." McLeod spoke the words reluctantly.

Typhoid! One of the many scourges the white man had brought. Crowfoot's band was following Jamie to the Mountie camp. He must warn them off before he did anything else.

"The doctor's taken ill," McLeod continued. "We have four men down, but the girl—the doctor's daughter—is taking care of them. She's doing a good job." He said the last words as though unwilling to give her credit.

"I'll warn Crowfoot not to come into camp," Jamie told him and left McLeod staring after him. Crowfoot would be warned, but first he knew he must see Kate Maginnis. Bloody hell—that damned McLeod had dumped the responsibility onto the girl he'd tried so hard to be rid of.

He strode quickly across the camp. Only when he neared the surgery tent did Jamie let himself realize he had put the bright-haired white woman before his own people.

A cold wind had come up, blowing from the north, and high clouds scudded across the sky. Jamie's experienced eye appraised the signs, and he knew that the fortunate weather the Mounted Police had enjoyed would soon end. A Northwest winter was on the way.

Kate came out of the surgery tent and stood for a moment as though disoriented, the wind tugging at her hair. An air of defeat was evident in her slumped shoulders, and when her bleak eyes met Jamie's, he drew in a sharp, painful breath.

"McLeod says there's typhoid," he began, disturbed by his overwhelming desire to comfort her, to somehow erase the pain he saw in her face.

She took a deep breath and swallowed hard. Still, her voice was hoarse when she spoke. "Constable Parks is dead." The words were a cry of protest.

Without thinking, Jamie reached out to her. Kate seized his hand and clung to it almost desperately. He thought she swallowed a sob before she managed to add, "Papa's cleaning the body." Somehow the small, strong hand lying in Jamie's communicated such sorrow, he could not bear it.

He was certain she scarcely knew Parks, so it was not a personal grief. Rather, the anger and sense of defeat surely came from her failure to save the man's life. She had lost a battle with death. With all his heart Jamie wished to give her the Blackfoot acceptance of death as a part of life . . . an inevitability.

"I'll tell McLeod," he said and reluctantly let her withdraw her hand.

Kate turned away as though to hide her face. After a moment, Jamie bent and lifted the tent flap. Three of the typhoid victims lay in a row, sleeping, moving restlessly or groaning in pain. At the back of the tent, Dr. Maginnis knelt to cover the dead man's face with a blanket. Sighing, Jamie closed the flap on the stench of the sickness and looked around for Kate. At last he spotted her over by the latrine pit, emptying a slop bucket. For one moment she let her body sag with a pervasive weariness, then straightened her shoulders and turned to rinse out the bucket.

Pride was something Jamie Campbell recognized in others, and he had seen it in this girl. He could offer her no real help with her nursing. From what he had seen of white men's medicine, it was a poor and ineffectual thing against diseases like typhoid. Across the river, in the camp of Crowfoot, there was Cutting Woman, a renowned medicine woman among the Blackfoot. She would know how to help Kate Maginnis.

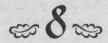

8

"**T**his is Cutting Woman," Jamie said. So
that Kate would understand the relationship, he added, "The honored wife of my
uncle, Crowfoot, chief of the Siksika Blackfoot and *Ni-
Nah* of the Blackfoot confederacy."

Crowfoot's band had gone into winter camp across
the river and had meant to visit the nearly built Fort
McLeod. But last night Jamie had warned them of the
typhoid, and until Jamie told them it was safe, they
would not enter the Mountie camp. Because Cutting
Woman was a medicine woman and a healer, he'd persuaded her to return with him this morning and give
Kate Maginnis the benefit of her Blackfoot knowledge.

"Cutting Woman is a medicine woman and a doctor,
much honored in our tribe. She came to help you with
your patients." He had already explained Kate to his
aunt.

"*Hai-yah-ho.*" Cutting Woman extended her hand.
Kate set down the bucket of fresh water she'd carried
from the river and submitted to her vigorous handshake.

Jamie's aunt was a tall, handsome woman with high
cheekbones, a prominent nose and black eyes that spar-
kled with intelligence. Speechless, Kate could only stare

at the half-breed guide and the woman he had so confidently brought to assist her.

The half-breed had presumed too much, Kate thought with a frown. She was doing all that could be done for typhoid victims and she wanted nothing to do with his savage medicine. She had lost one patient and she wouldn't risk the others with Blackfoot nostrums.

Dr. Maginnis rose from where he'd been sitting on his stool near the fire and joined them, accepting Cutting Woman's handshake. His face was pale and drawn, his movements uncertain, but he smiled at her and turned to Kate. "Perhaps she knows things we don't know. Remember, I often found the Chinese doctors in Toronto helpful."

When Jamie translated the doctor's words, Cutting Woman beamed at him approvingly. Kate observed them through a haze of weariness. Beneath the raucous noise of construction echoing under a cold gray sky, she could hear the low moans of her miserable patients. That sound filled her with anguish for the little she could do to relieve their suffering or save their lives. She had lost one patient to typhoid, and her eyes ached with unshed tears when she remembered how she'd watched Constable Parks slip away from her into death.

"Let the medicine woman help," Dr. Maginnis urged, clasping Kate's arm. "I'll help, too."

"Please, Papa." Kate placed a hand on his shoulder and urged him back toward his stool. "You must rest— *please.*" The doctor sighed and gave a defeated shrug. Slowly he moved back to his seat by the fire.

Through the open flap of the sick tent came the moans and the stench of sick men. Cutting Woman looked at Kate in grave silence, and Kate drew a ragged breath. She had never felt so helpless. Nothing she had done had brought the men any lasting relief. Why not accept the Blackfoot woman's help? she asked herself. As long as her treatment didn't become too drastic.

"Will you interpret?" she asked Jamie Campbell.

He had watched the doctor move slowly away, and now wore a troubled expression. In reply, he nodded. "My aunt speaks only a little English. It might be wise."

Kate thought there was no need for him to be sarcastic. With a sharp glance at Jamie, she followed Cutting Woman into the surgery tent, which had become the "sick tent" now. The tent was crowded by the four pallets laid out for the sick men. The cots had been removed for lack of room. Another patient had come in. Two of them slept fitfully; another lay doubled up, hugging his aching stomach. Trooper Bagley was awake and sat up with a cry of alarm when he saw Cutting Woman.

"It's all right, Bagley." Kate hurried to ease him back onto his pallet. "She's a medicine woman come to help us."

Bagley's apprehension was reflected in the faces of his companions as the two sleepers came awake. "It's all right," Kate reassured them, following Cutting Woman as she inspected each of the men, studying their faces, lifting their arms, pulling down the covers to scrutinize chests and abdomens. Finally the Blackfoot woman gave a satisfied nod and stepped outside. But she was frowning as she spoke rapidly to Jamie Campbell, who had remained outside.

"She asks what you have done for the stomach misery," Jamie translated the question as Kate came out of the tent.

"Paregoric," Kate answered. "There's little else . . ."

Jamie spoke to Cutting Woman, who raised her hands in an expression of dismay. "And for the other symptoms?" he continued.

"Laudanum . . . cold sponge baths." Kate spoke defensively now, seeing how the Blackfoot medicine woman decried her treatment. "Very little can be done for typhoid . . . just try to bring the fever down and ease the pain."

Again Cutting Woman spoke rapidly to Jamie, then turned to take a buckskin-wrapped package from the back of her waiting horse. "She wishes to try her medicine on the men," Jamie translated, "since yours hasn't worked."

In all the weary days and nights she'd attended her patients, Kate had been able to ease their misery only a little. There was no treatment for typhoid. She'd done her best and lost one man. How could this arrogant halfbreed tell her she had failed?

"Let her try, Kate," Dr. Maginnis urged once more from beside the fire, where he had been watching the proceedings intently. Kate frowned at him, then spread her hands in defeat.

"I'll explain everything she does," Jamie said, his voice stiff. Kate sensed his resentment because she hadn't welcomed Cutting Woman's help. "She'll stop if you ask her to," he added. With a sigh, Kate nodded her assent.

Chanting to herself in a low voice, Cutting Woman placed a pot of water on the embers at the edge of the fire. Then she took the buckskin roll and laid it out on the ground. Inside, neatly compartmented, lay a series of small skin bags, each painted with a different symbol. Labels—or charms? Kate wondered.

Without hesitation, Cutting Woman chose a bag and drew from it what appeared to be a white chunk of some kind of root. She interrupted her chant to speak to Jamie and he translated, "When Cutting Woman heard there was typhoid, she went to the swamps for the roots of the hellebore. It has power only in autumn, and the power fades quickly.''

Cutting Woman drew a sharp knife from the sheath at her belt and began to shave pieces of the root into the boiling pot. ''She will make a medicine from it for the men,'' Jamie continued. His aunt interrupted him with a sharp command.

''She wishes a fire in the men's tent,'' he said to Kate. Before she could protest, her father had brought the small brazier they sometimes used to heat their tent.

To the dismay of the patients who were watching the proceedings with apprehension, Jamie soon had a small fire going. Cutting Woman sprinkled sweet grass on the low flame, all the time continuing her chant. It was good the men were too sick to protest, Kate thought, or they might have run screaming from their beds.

The concoction in the pot on the fire in front of the tent smelled foul and Kate doubted the men would drink it except under duress. Did she trust Jamie Campbell and his Blackfoot aunt? They could just as easily poison her patients. Torn with indecision, Kate watched as Cutting Woman stirred the brew, continuing her soft, unintelligible chanting.

The brew in the pot thickened, but the stench did not lessen. Cutting Woman stirred, chanted, squatting beside the fire, ignoring the three patients watching through the open flaps of the tent. At last she seemed satisfied with her medicine and spoke to Jamie.

''Bring her a cup,'' he said, and Dr. Maginnis hurried to obey. Tense with doubt, Kate watched Cutting Woman measure a portion of her stinking medicine into the cup. It occurred to her then that she probably should send for McLeod.

At a command from Cutting Woman, Jamie handed

the cup to Kate and nodded toward the open flap of the sick tent.

With a quick prayer that she was doing the right thing, Kate stepped inside and knelt beside the boyish Bagley. She lifted his head so he could drink from the cup. He gagged at the odor, but with her gentle urging, managed to drink it down. Next she offered a cup to the rough-hewn Constable Turner. He spit the first mouthful out. "Bloody hell!" he groaned. "It stinks and it's bitter as gall."

Cutting Woman peered into the tent, fixed a stern gaze on Turner and spoke in an angry tone.

"Drink it, man," Jamie commanded from beside his aunt. "It'll ease your pains. Dr. Kate can't go on giving you laudanum forever."

Dr. Kate! Startled by his use of the longed-for title, Kate stared up at Jamie Campbell's serious face. Could he have guessed that she had spent most of her life pursuing the title of Doctor—all through the year at Normal School, when she was the only girl in the science classes and harassed accordingly; all the futile letters of application; even the time with Curtis when she'd half considered giving up her dream and trying to fit into the correct pattern for young women of her station, which meant being only a wife and mother.

His level gaze was on Turner, and Kate was certain Jamie Campbell didn't know he'd touched a raw place in her soul.

Gagging and sputtering, Turner finally swallowed his medicine. While Kate dosed the other men, Cutting Woman rolled up her pack of medicinals. She was tying it onto her saddle when Kate came out of the tent.

Speaking with authority, but in a kindly tone, Cutting Woman came toward Kate with both hands outstretched.

"*A-wah-heh, I-so-kin-uh-kin,*" she said, and clasped Kate's hands in hers.

"Take courage, Doctor," Jamie interpreted in reply to Kate's questioning look. Weary as she was, Kate felt the sting of tears in her eyes. Take courage . . . yes, she would need much courage; and she squeezed the woman's hands appreciatively.

"Thank you for what you've done," she told her, not yet sure she had done right by giving Blackfoot medicine to her patients. Yet Cutting Woman had an integrity of presence one could not question, and she smiled when Jamie interpreted Kate's words. Then she spoke to Jamie, obviously outlining instructions.

"You must give the medicine to your patients each day for three days. Only as much as I have shown you, or it will make them ill. After three days the fever will be gone."

With that, Cutting Woman mounted her spotted horse. Raising a hand in farewell, she waited while Jamie spoke to Kate.

"I'll ride with Sisoyaki, my aunt, to her camp. This evening I'll come by to make sure all's well."

Astounded by what had taken place here, Kate gazed after the departing figures. Again doubts surfaced. Had she been unwise to use the Blackfoot woman's medicine?

Inside the sick tent, she saw to her amazement that all the men slept—not the moaning, restless, pain-filled sleep of the past few days, but a deep, healing sleep. Kate shook her head as she turned away, knowing she had learned a valuable lesson. Across the fire from where he sat in front of the tent, her father gave her a knowing smile, and she remembered how he had always said that doctors know only a little of what there is in the world to learn.

* * *

"Cutting Woman sends you sweet grass to cleanse away the stink of sickness." Jamie held the twist of dried grass out to Kate. Their hands touched in the exchange and both drew away as though burned, each avoiding the other's eyes.

"I'll be leaving this morning," he told her after an uncomfortable silence. "I'm taking the sick horses to winter pasture at Sun River in Montana." Jamie said the words in a stiff voice while staring across the river to where early sunlight sifted through the cold mist rising off the water.

Kate wanted to ask how long he'd be away, then chided herself for the impulse. It was nothing to her. She listened attentively to his instructions for using the sweet grass to fumigate the sick tent. Another uneasy silence fell between them. After a moment, Kate swallowed her pride and said, "I can see that Cutting Woman's medicine is powerful. Do you think she'd be willing to teach me more?"

Jamie gave her a knowing look, but he didn't remind her how reluctant she'd been to use his aunt's potent brew. "Perhaps," he replied. "I'll ask her." He hesitated for a moment as though reluctant to leave. "You treated my aunt with respect," he finally said. "I thank you for that." His dark eyes were intent on her face.

"Cutting Woman commands respect," Kate told him as they walked toward his waiting horse. "If you grew up with her, how is it you speak English so well?" Perhaps she was asking a question better left unasked, but her curiosity about this contradictory man had built since that first meeting in Baker's store what seemed eons ago.

"I grew up at Rocky Mountain House," Jamie replied, reaching for the bay horse's reins. "The Hudson's Bay factor, Alec Campbell, and his half-blood wife adopted me after my father disappeared. Alec insisted I speak English with him, and he made me study with the priest during the winters, so that I learned to read and write.'' His face tightened and his voice fell. ''Sometimes I'm not sure he did me a favor. If I were all Blackfoot, it would have been easier.''

He shrugged, then continued. ''In my fourteenth summer I came to live with Crowfoot and Cutting Woman and learned their ways because it was important to me to be Blackfoot. Alec Campbell remained my friend until his death a few years ago. He even arranged for me to guide my first party to the Cypress Hills the year I turned seventeen.''

His world was so different from her own, they might have been born on different planets, Kate thought. Yet something drew her inexorably to him, something for which she had no name. In many ways he was an outsider in his world, just as she, with all her unwomanly ambitions, had been in hers.

''The fort is going up fast.'' He changed the subject abruptly, looped the reins over his horse's head and prepared to mount. ''Thanks to Old Gladstone and Baker's supply wagons, you'll be warm and dry this winter.''

Mounted in his saddle, Jamie looked down at her, his face inscrutable, a lingering sadness in his black eyes.

''*Ma-me-atsi-kimi.*'' His voice broke on the word and he reined quickly away.

Kate watched as he joined the men who held the waiting horse herd, and they moved southward under the cold-morning sun. What had he said to her? she wondered, puzzled by his tone of voice. Perhaps just a Blackfoot word for farewell. She had meant to wish him a safe journey, but he had ridden away too fast. A safe journey, she thought wryly. A safe journey for both horses and men would all depend on Jamie Campbell.

*   *   *

Work on the new fort progressed quickly. The men had voted to name it for their commander—Fort McLeod—and they raced against the onslaught of winter to finish it. Toughened by their long trek across Canada, the Mounties felled trees, wielded axes and saws and hammers as though they shared McLeod's fear that winter would catch them without shelter. The walls of the fort were a palisade of upright logs. Inside those walls were the beginnings of the men's quarters, the surgery, the mess and the permanent stables. Already the hard night frost brought difficulty. They even had to heat water to mix the icy chinking mud. Axes had to be sharpened every evening for the next day's wood chopping. There was little rest for anyone.

Wagonloads of supplies came from Fort Benton, bringing the goods Inspector Cavendish had ordered. Old Glad, as Bill Gladstone was known, the premier builder of forts in the Northwest, had arrived to supervise construction. Close behind the Mounted Police supply train came I. G. Baker's bull train, loaded with lumber and goods for the store his men started building on the riverbank opposite Fort McLeod.

Beneath a cold gray morning sky, Kate stood in front of the surgery tent. Dr. Maginnis still slept and she didn't wish to awaken him. As she watched the men hard at work on the fort, she wondered that her father could sleep with so much racket going on.

In the weeks since Jamie Campbell departed for Sun River, Kate had puzzled over their farewell, the strange word he'd spoken and the sadness in his eyes. He was a man so strong and so independent she would never have guessed he was vulnerable in any way. Yet she'd seen a flash of it, and couldn't put it from her mind.

All the typhoid patients had returned to their own

quarters. After Kate cleaned and fumigated the tent with sweet grass as Cutting Woman had instructed, life had become routine once more. She found she loved the constant movement, the knowledge of something new happening every day at the fort. An odd kind of contentment had settled over her. But now trepidation filled her heart, and she held her breath in apprehension at the sight of McLeod walking purposefully toward her, David Cavendish by his side.

"How soon can you be ready to go to Fort Benton?" McLeod asked without preamble.

Stunned, Kate stared at him, unable to speak. How could he think of sending her away after she'd proved herself during the typhoid outbreak? She turned to David for support, but when she saw his smile, she knew that was futile. He was one of those men who had no faith in the strength of females. Perhaps his upbringing had taught him to treat women like fragile, breakable china, always to be protected. He could be so charming those evenings when he came to play chess with her father, revealing bits and pieces of his life in England. When he enthusiastically described riding to the hounds, Kate swallowed her impulse to remark that it sounded like an extraordinarily useless sport.

McLeod had made David third in command, after Inspector Denny, which pleased him immensely. "I must write my family," he'd said after accepting their hearty congratulations. Studying his handsome, earnest face, Kate guessed that he desperately wanted his family's approval. She, who had always had her parents' approval, was saddened by his need, and she'd hurried to assure him he was proving himself a fine officer.

Couldn't these two men understand she had to stay? Her father had just begun to recuperate from his illness.

She was needed here, and David had heard her say she meant to stay. How could he do this?

"I have no desire to go to Fort Benton." She drew herself to her full height and faced McLeod squarely. The commandant had praised her for her work with the typhoid victims. How could he send her away?

"She's proved her worth, McLeod." A deep voice spoke the very words she'd been thinking. Jamie Campbell sat on a tall bay horse, looking down at them. He was back, and Kate's heart leaped in a way that left her momentarily breathless. There was a half smile on Jamie's lips, but his eyes grew cold when they rested on David Cavendish.

"During the typhoid you'd have been up the creek without her," Jamie continued. "You owe her for that, McLeod. Better let her stay. You'll likely need her this winter."

McLeod listened with a thoughtful expression. As he considered Campbell's words, Kate thought how far the relationship between the commissioner and his half-breed guide had developed. It seemed McLeod had come to listen to the man and trust him implicitly.

"I thought you said she wanted to go." Frowning, McLeod turned to David.

David threw Kate a look of annoyance. "I said any woman with sense would want to be out of here before winter sets in."

"Then I don't have good sense," Kate snapped. Daring to lay a hand on McLeod's arm, she went on. "I'll stay, sir, if you'll allow it. You've already seen what I can do."

"Indeed I have." He patted her hand and she knew she'd won. The humorless commander almost managed a smile. "We'll soon have quarters for you and the doctor to set up a surgery in the fort." He nodded his dismissal. "Come along, Cavendish. Baker's bull train will be leaving shortly and they're expecting you to ride along."

Looking disgruntled, David gave Kate a disapproving glance before he followed his commander.

McLeod paused and turned back toward Jamie. "Now you're here, Campbell, I'd like you to make arrangements for a reception to welcome the chiefs to Fort McLeod."

"It's time we did just that," Jamie agreed. "I'll see to it." He never called McLeod "sir," Kate realized, wondering whether anyone ever really commanded Jamie Campbell.

When McLeod was out of hearing, she looked up at Jamie. "Thank you," she said.

Their eyes held for what seemed an eternity. Kate's breath caught in her throat and her heart seemed to stop its beating. A strange, electric warmth poured over her. Then Jamie Campbell tore his glance from hers, lifting his horse's reins.

"Cutting Woman will come with the chiefs," he told her as he reined away. "She will teach you, if that is your wish."

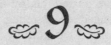

9

*S*avage splendor poured through the gates of Fort McLeod. Breathless with excitement, Kate stood in front of the fort surgery, the brilliance and color of the Indians come to confer with Commissioner McLeod dazzling her eyes. The fort had been in an uproar for days with preparations for this great gathering arranged by Jamie Campbell. Inspector Cavendish's detachment to Fort Benton had brought back extra wagons loaded with foodstuffs and presents for the chiefs.

Today it had begun. Through the wide gates of the newly completed fort they rode: Crowfoot of the Siksika Blackfoot, Red Crow of the Bloods, Bulls Head of the Piegan. Jamie Campbell rode abreast of them, and what must have been hundreds of warriors followed behind in full panoply. Feathered headdresses stirred in the cold breeze. Buckskin tunics and leggings gleamed with intricate beaded patterns: the buckskin fringing of sleeves and leggings streamed in the wind. All rode the finest of horses, which were adorned with painted robes and blankets, feathers, furs and fringed buckskins. It was a sight more splendid than anything she could have imagined.

Dr. Maginnis emerged from the log surgery that was

now their home to stand beside her. With a low whistle of admiration, he exclaimed, "Magnificent, isn't it, Katie? I wouldn't have missed this for the world.

"Campbell arranged this meeting with the chiefs," Dr. Maginnis continued thoughtfully, still staring at the impressive pageantry moving past them toward the officers' mess, where red-coated Mounties were drawn up in formation to greet their guests. "McLeod's anxious to have them understand that the Mounted Police are here only to drive out the American whiskey traders and keep the peace."

"This is an important meeting, isn't it?" Kate asked. A tremor of apprehension went through her as she realized there were enough warriors inside the fort to slaughter every Mountie in the place.

"It could make all the difference," her father replied, then added, "I don't know what McLeod and the Mounties would have come to if it weren't for Jamie Campbell." His broad face, which had begun to regain its old strength, glowed with admiration.

Kate was silent, her eyes going to the tall, erect half-breed guide. Today he rode a fine spirited horse of spotted bay and white. Dressed in his Blackfoot costume, feathers and fringed buckskin fluttering in the breeze, the intricate beading on his buckskin tunic catching the rays of cold sunlight, he made a striking figure. Something stirred inside Kate as she watched him, something so disturbing she thrust it quickly away. The man was half savage. To be drawn to him in any way was pure madness.

"There's still unpacking to be done, Papa," she said, but he did not follow her inside, remaining there to fill his eyes with the strange and magnificent panorama. To her dismay, Kate found her hands were trembling as she began to unpack the crate of rolled bandages brought from Fort Benton by I. G. Baker's teamsters. Her eyes still held the troubling image of Jamie Campbell in all his savage glory.

She would not soon forget how he'd defended her to McLeod. In a world where all men except her father seemed to be against her, she had found an unexpected ally in Jamie Campbell.

Not so with David Cavendish . . . and the thought brought a frown to her face. When she had complained to her father of David's high-handed efforts to force her return to Fort Benton, he'd laughed and given her a knowing wink. "Perhaps he wants you where you won't always have a bevy of adoring males around you. Haven't you noticed? I think he's even jealous of that poor infatuated boy, Bagley."

"Jealous!" Kate had protested in amazement. The doctor merely shrugged and turned away with a chuckle.

At the time, Kate had pondered her father's words, wondering if she could really be so blind to David's feelings. From now on she would watch herself carefully in his presence.

The officers' mess was crowded to overflowing with brilliantly costumed warriors and red-coated Mounties staring warily at one another. McLeod sat at one end of the rectangular log room, with Jamie beside him to interpret. The three chiefs were given chairs facing them and the ceremonies began.

Jamie had coached McLeod carefully in the correct protocol for dealing with the Blackfoot confederacy. Nothing must be done or said that might insult these powerful men or their followers. Hands must be shaken all around, prayers chanted, then the ceremonial smoking of the pipe. Only the head men were allowed to hold the pipe with both hands in the manner of the Bear god, so the white men must use just one hand while smoking.

With an occasional glance at Jamie for cues, McLeod followed the procedures perfectly. The chiefs appeared impressed, content with their welcome. Once the ceremonies were ended, the speeches were to begin. Jamie had warned the commander that the Indians were inclined to long-windedness, and it was important to listen with patience.

As *Ni-Nah* of the Blackfoot confederacy, Crowfoot rose first. Once again he shook hands with McLeod and his officers. Jamie leaned close to interpret for McLeod. Even those who could not hear Jamie's words seemed impressed by Crowfoot's obvious sincerity.

"We thank the gods," Crowfoot said, "and we thank the Great Grandmother for sending the Redcoats to save my people from the ravages of firewater and the cheating traders who have impoverished us." He went on at length, telling how his people had been robbed and ruined by the whiskey traders; how wives and daughters had been turned into prostitutes in exchange for whiskey; how his warriors had sold their horses for firewater and could no longer follow the buffalo so the people starved; and, most terrible of all, how his young men killed one another in their drunken fights. Crowfoot ended by fervently promising to live in peace with the Mounted Police.

Both Red Crow and Bulls Head then gave lengthy speeches endorsing all that Crowfoot had said and welcoming the red-coated Mounties to their country.

Jamie knew McLeod had grown restive during the long, rambling speeches, but the commander concealed any impatience he might have felt. Now he rose to speak.

"The Great Grandmother in England has sent the Mounted Police you call the Redcoats to enforce the law.

From now on there will be only one law. Indians and whites alike will be punished for breaking that law." He paused and added emphatically, "We did not come to take your land or to ruin your people with whiskey as the Americans have done. Whenever the chief of the whites wishes to do something in the land of the Blackfoot confederacy, it will be done only after your chiefs have given permission."

Jamie translated that speech with a passion he'd rarely felt, knowing that the coming of these honorable men had saved his people from destruction. Before he had finished, the Indians were smiling and nodding to each other, obviously well pleased by McLeod's sincere words.

They rose then to make a great ceremony of shaking hands once more. A procession began to the main mess for a feast prepared by the fort cooks. As Red Crow vigorously shook McLeod's hand, he said, "Before you came, our warriors crept along like old, sick men. Now they are not afraid to stand erect, as proud as in the old days."

Quiet had again settled over the log-walled fort. In the pale rays of the lowering sun, the Union Jack fluttered on the gleaming new flagpole of peeled cottonwood. Jamie and McLeod stood before the officers' mess, watching the departure of the last of the warriors.

"It was a success, I think," McLeod said, his eyes seeking confirmation from Jamie.

"Your words impressed them," Jamie told him, "but they won't forget your promises. If the promises aren't kept, there will be trouble."

"They will be kept." McLeod spoke with assurance and shook Jamie's hand to seal his words. He started to turn away when a warrior in full regalia rode up before them and raised a hand in greeting. Jamie recognized Eagles Tail of the Blackfoot. He spoke in a stately manner befitting the importance of the invitation to the white chief to attend a great feast at the camp across the river tomorrow. The feast would celebrate the coming of the Mounted Police to the Northwest country of the Blackfoot.

"It's an honor you can't refuse," Jamie told McLeod, and he conveyed McLeod's acceptance in the same sober manner.

Jamie had meant to take the evening meal with his uncle's family, then bring Cutting Woman to the fort to talk with Kate. You're a fool, he mentally chided himself as he caught up his horse. Why do you care whether the white woman learns Blackfoot medicine? Why do you concern yourself with her comfort and well-being? To her you're merely a half-breed savage. She's a white woman, with hair like the sun. That is a line you cannot cross.

His rueful thoughts were interrupted by a horseman galloping at full speed through the open gates of the fort. Jamie grabbed the reins and brought the careening horse to a halt. It was Purvis, the disgusting half-breed from Fort Whoop-up.

"There's been a fight at Fort Slideout," Purvis gasped, tumbling from his saddle, his rough face lined with fear. "Drunken Indians went crazy, started shooting up the place, killed one of their own, wounded two or three whites. Now they're inside the fort, helping themselves to the whiskey. It'll be a massacre."

"Where's Fort Slideout?" Hearing the noise, McLeod had come out of his office in time to hear Purvis's story.

"It's an abandoned fort south of here," Jamie replied, struggling to bring Purvis's mount under control. "The traders you ran out of Whoop-up must have moved their whiskey to Slideout.''

"We'll take a detachment immediately," the commissioner said decisively. "Campbell, you'll guide them.''

"There's men bad hurt," Purvis gasped, still out of breath and leaning heavily on the hitching rack.

"Then we'll take the doctor along," McLeod declared.

Jamie laid a detaining hand on the commissioner's arm. "You can't go. The feast in your honor at the encampment tomorrow is too important. It would be the worst of insults.''

McLeod frowned. "Can Potts interpret for me?" At Jamie's nod of assent, he growled, "Then you go to Fort Slideout.''

"Why can't I go instead of my father?" Kate demanded of Jamie as he waited for the doctor to pack his supplies. "He's not entirely well, as you can see, and I'm perfectly capable.''

"You're a woman," Jamie said, carefully not adding, "A white woman.'' Among the Blackfoot it would have made no difference—a doctor was a doctor, varying only in the degree of skill. Sometimes he found himself seesawing between the two worlds in a way that was often painful. He should not care so much what happened to the doctor's bright-haired daughter. Yet her combination of strength and vulnerability touched his heart as no other woman ever had. Not even his long-dead young wife, Meadowlark.

Abruptly he turned away, fearing his face might reveal his thoughts to those searching gray eyes.

"I'll see he's safe," he promised her, and again

cursed himself for a fool. Safety was something that could not be guaranteed on the prairies.

The doctor looked well, excited and anxious to join the detachment already forming in the compound. Inspector Cavendish would be in charge. He was a good enough man, but Jamie had never warmed to him, perhaps because of Cavendish's constant attention to Kate Maginnis—and again Jamie cursed his foolish thoughts.

"It's my job, Kate," the doctor was saying when Jamie left the surgery room. "It's what I signed on for. The fighting's all over, so the messenger said."

He leaned over to kiss her cheek as Jamie led a saddled horse up to the door. "It will be an adventure." His voice was eager, and then he was gone.

Hot with anger and frustration, Kate watched the detachment ride out of the fort, Campbell and David Cavendish leading the way. Why was her father behaving like a boy searching for adventure at his age? And why had both Campbell and McLeod insisted the doctor accompany the detachment when they both knew he'd barely recovered from the illness she was certain had been a slight heart attack? And why, oh, why, did women have no power, no control anywhere in the world? If she were a doctor . . . and her heart sank with the certainty that it could never be—because she was a woman without funds.

Kate stored away the remains of her meager meal in the hospital kitchen. Worry ate at the edges of her mind. The detachment headed for Fort Slideout had been gone four days, and still no word. She had cared for the usual cuts and bruises inevitably incurred by men still hurrying to finish the fort before winter.

The surgery was spotless as she walked through it and out the front door. An icy wind blew dust across the parade ground and set the Union Jack to snapping. The sounds of hammers and saws echoed beneath a sky roiling with gray clouds. Reaching for her shawl hanging beside the door, Kate moved purposefully toward McLeod's quarters. The commissioner had been restless since the great celebration the Indians had held to welcome him. She knew he was as anxious as she. Perhaps there had been some word.

At the sound of galloping hoofbeats, Kate stopped and glanced toward the open gates. Her heart froze as she recognized the stout pinto and its black-haired rider. Before Jamie Campbell could dismount in front of McLeod's quarters, she had run frantically to his side. Sick with fear, she seized his leg and stared up at him. "What is it?" she cried.

At the same time, McLeod hurried from his office and descended the steps hastily, his bearded face lined with worry. "Campbell?" he said just as Kate cried out again, "What is it?" without thought of the fact that she was interrupting the commander.

But McLeod did not chastise her, merely looked at Campbell and groaned softly as though steeling himself for bad news.

Jamie dismounted and took Kate's shoulders in his hands, looking down at her with a grim face. "The whiskey traders gave up without firing a shot," he said, "but the Bloods were very drunk and wanted to fight. In the melee Dr. Maginnis was knocked from his horse. His leg is shattered and I'm afraid he has a broken hip. I didn't dare move him."

"Then take me to him," Kate commanded. "I'll get my things if you'll bring me a horse." She had no need to think about her decision. She had to go.

"Wait!" McLeod's voice boomed out. "Bloody hell,

woman, you can't make that ride.'' He turned to Jamie.
"Splint the leg and bring him in.''

"The bones are sticking through the flesh,'' Jamie
replied sharply. A cry of protest broke from Kate's
throat, for she knew that now her father would be crippled.

"Let me go to him, Commissioner . . . please.'' Unthinking in her concern, Kate dared place a hand on
McLeod's arm as she implored, "I know what to do for
a compound fracture. For God's sake, let me go.''

The two men exchanged long looks. Jamie nodded.
McLeod sighed and shrugged. "Get her a horse, Campbell.'' At that moment Kate realized how totally McLeod
had come to trust his half-breed guide.

"Pack whatever you'll need,'' Jamie ordered her.
"I'll get fresh horses. It's a day's ride, but if we push
it, we'll be there by nightfall.''

Before Kate could speak, he had mounted the pinto
and ridden away toward the stables. "Thank you, sir,''
she said to McLeod and ran across the parade ground
toward the surgery. Jamie Campbell never questioned
her strength or ability because she was a woman. Perhaps the Blackfoot women were treated so, and her heart
filled with gratitude for his trust and support.

The pace Jamie set was a hard one, but Kate would
not allow herself to falter. She'd learned to ride well
enough on the trip from the Sweet Grass Hills, so that
she could keep up with him. If, as she supposed, Blackfoot women were treated as equals, that equality extended to travel by horse. Obviously Jamie had no
intention of slowing his pace for her sake.

The sun was setting as they paused on the crest of a
low hill to let the horses blow—a strangely eerie sunset,

with what seemed to be two miniature suns following the sun down the cloud-clotted sky.

"Sun dogs," Jamie explained in answer to her question. "The old ones say it's an omen . . . that it means bad weather coming."

"Then we'd better hurry," Kate replied, her voice sharp with the fear that had increased with every mile. All the way, she'd tried not to think of the awful possibilities of her father's injuries. Still, apprehension ate at her. Tension grew until it seemed to her this ride would never end. Now she whipped her horse ahead of Jamie. Almost at once he was in front of her, leading the way.

Fort Slideout was no fort, only a rough log cabin with open stables beyond. The place was half concealed by a thick stand of cottonwood and chokecherry on the bank of Oldman River, and it was ominously quiet.

Kate's heart was in her throat as she and Jamie rode down the steep bank toward where a fire marked the camp of the Mounted Police. David Cavendish turned away from the fire to peer at them. Obviously he recognized the riders, for he strode hurriedly forward, signaling them to halt.

She heard Jamie Campbell curse under his breath as David took Kate's reins and looked sadly up into her fearful eyes.

"I'm sorry, Kate . . . your father is dead."

⚜ 10 ⚜

They had wrapped him in a blanket and placed the body in a pile of snow drifted against the north side of the small cabin. David helped a stunned Kate dismount, murmuring over and over, "I'm so sorry." Solicitously taking her arm, he led her to her father's side.

Jamie followed, leading his horse and Kate's. He saw that while he had been gone, all the Indians had fled the place. Two sullen white whiskey traders, hands bound, sat on the stoop of the cabin. The Mountie detachment was stacking furs and buffalo robes to be carried back to Fort McLeod.

When she stared down at the still, silent face of her father, Kate's own pale face distorted in a mixture of pain and disbelief. Jamie's heart swelled with empathy as he remembered, a few short weeks ago, when he stood beside his dead mother, a sense of loss draining through him. With all his being he longed to reach out to Kate, to hold her and tell her that the pain would end, though the loss was forever. Instead, he stepped away when Inspector Cavendish's arm encircled her bowed shoulders and Kate covered her face against the awful sight.

Suddenly she dropped to her knees in the snow beside the body. "Papa," she whispered as though imploring him to awaken. "Oh, Papa . . ." and she lovingly stroked the cold, still face. It seemed forever that she knelt there, silent as a statue, making no sound, seeming to will her father back to life.

His need to comfort her was so intense, Jamie tightened his hands into aching fists, forcing himself to stand and watch. If only he could touch her and say the words welling in his heart. *Ma-me-atsi-kimi,* beautiful one . . . let him go. Let yourself weep or you will be sick with grief. And he thought of the Blackfoot women keening through the night for lost loved ones, giving vent to the pain of loss so that they could then get on with life.

At last, one of the troopers who had watched the heartbreaking scene in respectful silence approached Cavendish, speaking softly in his ear.

Jamie caught the words: "We've finished the grave, sir."

Cavendish nodded and laid a hand on Kate's shoulder, gently urging her away. Her eyes were blank and stunned when she looked up. "It's time, Kate," he said, adding apologetically, "We did all we could for him."

Without a word, she turned back to her father's body, leaning toward it through the packed snow to kiss the gray, dead cheek. "Good-bye, Papa," she whispered, and Jamie looked away, his eyes stinging.

Only when they laid her father's body in the grave the troopers had hacked from the cold earth did the full impact of her loss strike Kate. It hit with such force she felt her knees buckle and reached out blindly, finding David Cavendish's strong arm offering support. She leaned heavily on that arm as they stood beside the grave, and David said a short prayer, something remembered from the Book of Common Prayer back in England.

In this wild and lonely place, far from familiar scenes and faces, her father would lie forever. Aware of the sympathetic eyes watching, Kate struggled to hold back tears. Her father, her dearest friend, all she had in this world, lay in that grave. Now she was truly alone, and the world seemed unbearably empty. The knowledge that never again would anyone look on her with such pride and love, never again share her dreams, small jokes, the every day of living . . . A choked sound escaped her throat as she struggled against the overwhelming pain of grief. If she began to weep, she was certain she could never stop.

When the waiting troopers picked up their shovels to cover the grave, David led her away.

Inside the cabin, someone gave her a chair beside the stove. Another trooper brought a steaming cup of tea, muttering, "Miss Kate . . . I'm sorry."

Kate nodded and bowed her head toward the tea mug, struggling against the threatening flood of tears. Only half aware of her surroundings, she vaguely heard David and Jamie conferring about the journey back to Fort McLeod.

"The weather's about to change," Jamie said tersely. "If we hit the trail soon as it's light, we might beat the storm. But we need to move fast."

"We'll take the two prisoners." David nodded toward the two gloomily silent men sitting beside the doorway. "They have horses enough, so we can load the confiscated buffalo robes to take back to the fort."

"First light," Jamie repeated, and with an enigmatic glance at Kate, left the cabin.

*   *   *

There was one rough bunk built against the far wall and it was solicitously offered to Kate. The fire was banked, the men rolled in their blankets on the floor, and silence fell except for occasional snores and groans. Eyes aching with unshed tears, Kate stared into the darkness. In the depths of her soul she could not yet accept the reality of her father's death. It was as though when she awakened tomorrow he'd be there with his jovial "Good morning, Katie," as he had been every morning within memory. That dear man would never have deliberately left her alone in this wilderness. They had such plans for the future. Next year, when his enlistment was up, they would decide. If a town grew at Fort McLeod, as had already begun with Baker's store, a doctor would be needed there. Dr. Maginnis and his spinster daughter would set up a practice. Or they could go to Helena, even to that unlikely place, Fort Benton. But they would be together. Papa would be there forever, teaching her, encouraging her, believing in her, telling her how strong she was. How could he have known how empty of courage she felt without him? Turning her face to the wall, she let the silent tears come, washing away pain until at last she slept.

The banked fire gave off a pale glow in the darkness before dawn. Disoriented, Kate stared at the red coals until suddenly full memory hit her with such pain, she pressed a hand against her mouth to hold back a cry. Papa was dead. She was alone.

With all her strength Kate forced herself to lie still until she was certain she was under control. First light, Jamie had said. At first light they would begin the journey back to Fort McLeod, and her beloved father would be lost to her forever. This one last time, perhap the last chance of her life, she would say a final good-bye.

She had slept in her clothes and now rose silently from the bunk, stepping carefully among the sleeping Mounties as she made her way to the cabin door.

The sky was pale in these hours before first light. Frost lay on the tree limbs and the dried grass, cold as the icy air. The grave had been covered with stones, and Kate drew in a pained breath, knowing it was to protect her father's body from animal predators. Not even a flower to lay on his grave, she thought, and hot tears slid down her cold face.

"Miss Kate."

She glanced up, half angry at this intrusion on her solitary grief. Jamie Campbell's black eyes were deep with understanding in the pale light. Instinctively, she reached out to him. Holding her hand tight in his, Jamie stood beside her at the grave. After a moment, he spoke in a strange language, a sort of chant.

"A Blackfoot prayer for the dead," he told her when he had finished. Looking intently into her face, he began to translate.

"Now I go from among you, whither I cannot tell. From nowhere we come, into nowhere we go. What is life? It is the flash of a firefly in the night. It is the breath of a buffalo in the wintertime. It is as the little shadow that runs across the grass and loses itself in the sunset."

The words brought a new freshet of tears. Kate pressed her face against the rough leather sleeve of his buffalo coat and after a moment felt his hand stroking her uncovered head, a touch so comforting it might have been her father's hand.

They stood so, in perfect silence until the sounds of awakening Mounties came from the cabin.

"Kate!" It was Cavendish calling anxiously for her.

Without a word, Jamie released her and walked away.

*   *   *

The sky was a deep, sinister gray when Jamie Campbell led the column north from Forrt Slideout: Mounted Police, prisoners and packhorses loaded with the confiscated buffalo robes. Kate rode at the head of the train beside Inspector Cavendish. Three men had been left to spill the last barrel of whiskey and set fire to the cabin. It went up with a *whoosh,* flames rising eerily into the low, dark skies.

Kate looked back once at that lost, anonymous place where her father would lie forever now. Her tearless eyes ached with inner pain. She had never felt so bereft, so lost, so completely unsure of herself and her future. In those brief moments beside her father's grave with Jamie, she had felt comforted. Now the enormity of her loss came back with searing pain.

When they paused for nooning and rest, Jamie Campbell dug some buffalo chips from beneath the light snow covering the ground and got a fire going. Kate chewed listlessly on the hardtack biscuit David insisted she take and sipped a little of the hot tea that was passed. Everything around her seemed distanced and remote, as though she watched a stage play with unknown actors. She was aware that Jamie kept glancing anxiously at the low, threatening skies, and shortly he was urging the column on the way. As always he rode ahead, scouting the trail. Alone, she thought, as I'm alone now. Sometime, somewhere, she would find the opportunity to thank him for his comforting Blackfoot prayer.

Dusk descended inexorably and an icy wind whipped men and horses viciously. The change in the weather Jamie had predicted came on them with a fury. The temperature dropped. As though the heavens suddenly opened, the party was enveloped in a howling, raging blizzard. Snow swirled in every direction, for the bitter wind seemed to blow in circles.

Her weary horse lagging, her face covered by the heavy buffalo robe David had wrappped around her, Kate failed to see the column make a turn. She rode blindly ahead, wind and snow shutting out everything. At last she became aware that she could hear no voices, no other horses. Terror seized her when her worn-out horse stopped and refused to move. She had somehow strayed from the company. She was alone and lost in a Northwest blizzard.

Shouting at the top of his voice to be heard above the howling wind, Jamie gave orders. He had led the party down a steep cutbank of the river where there was some protection from wind and snow. "Unsaddle horses," he shouted. "Stow saddles and packs under a drift next to the cutbank." Then he ordered the men to take knives and shovels, any tools they had, and scoop out a cave in the sandy face of the riverbank. That done, he turned to find Kate and make sure she was led to a warm spot out of the storm.

The snow was blinding and he circled the camp again and again, finally shouting her name. "Kate! Kate Maginnis!" At the sound of his voice, Cavendish rushed toward him.

"We've lost her," he yelled to Jamie, his eyes wide with fear.

Staring into Cavendish's terrified face, Jamie cursed. He was furious with Cavendish, who should have kept her close and protected her—and furious at himself for trusting her safety to anyone else. When he'd led the men down into the riverbed, Kate must have ridden blindly ahead into the storm. "I'll find her," he told Cavendish, not bothering to conceal his anger and disgust. "Keep the men together. Try to get out of the storm. Break out those buffalo robes for every man.

Don't move from here until I come back for you.''

Before David could speak or protest, Jamie whirled his weary horse around and plunged into the blinding snow and thickening darkness.

Kate couldn't have told how long she sat there, a frozen woman on the back of a frozen horse. Wind howled about her, tore at the heavy buffalo robe she clutched to her. Darkness fell, and there was nothing in all the world but smothering, blinding snow.

I will die here, she thought. Just as my beloved father died in this wild and savage country. Her heart seemed to swell and break with longing for what had been . . . for the safe and pleasant days in Toronto. Only now did she see that ambition was a hard thing, leading one into dangerous paths. If she could call back the past year and change it all, she would.

Too late . . . too late, the wind seemed to cry. The horse refused to move. Soon she would fall from its back to lie frozen in the snow . . . to join her father in death, a hostage to the unforgiving Northwest plains.

''Kate!''

When she heard the faint voice, Kate thought she dreamed. Vaguely she realized she had fallen from her mount and lay in drifting snow beside the immobile horse.

''Kate!'' A shudder shook her as she struggled to sit up, to answer the searching voice. At last she managed to croak out the word ''Here . . . here.''

''Kate—oh, God! Katie . . . Katie.''

Someone was bending over her, lifting her up in strong, warm arms, holding her protectively against him. In the dim light she looked up into the face of Jamie Campbell and cried out in gratitude. Fiercely she pressed herself against his strength, clinging desperately as icy tears welled in her eyes. Jamie held her, his cold cheek next to hers, murmuring something comforting . . . words lost in the howling wind.

Finally, reluctantly, they moved away from each other. Jamie led her to stand between the two horses. "Don't move," he shouted, and she had to strain to hear him. "I'll make a shelter for the night. If we're lucky, the storm will blow out by morning."

Terror gripped her as he moved away, for she was fearful she would be lost and alone again. But she could hear him thrashing about in the deep, drifted snow, cursing and breathing hard. When he returned, she reached out to him with both arms.

He gave her a brief, reassuring hug, then quickly unsaddled the horses and tethered them in the shelter of some trees. Holding Kate's hand, he led her through blinding snow to where he had dug out a cave in a snowdrift against a pile of rocks.

At his urging, she crawled into the low cave, to find herself lying on the warm fur of a buffalo robe, her head pillowed on the damp cougar pelt from her own saddle. She was sobbing with relief when Jamie crawled into the cave and drew another buffalo robe over both of them.

Turning her stiff, half-frozen body onto one side, Jamie cupped his knees beneath hers and drew her back against him. He spoke apologetically. "We'll have to keep each other warm if we hope to make it through this night."

After he stripped off her sodden gloves, Jamie took her hands in his bare ones and slid them inside her capote to the last warm place on her body, beneath her breasts. Exhausted, Kate thought wryly that a real lady would have protested. She didn't care. His warmth was warming her now, his arms holding her close.

"You're safe now, Katie," he murmured, his mouth close to her ear.

"Safe . . . yes," she answered through icy lips and turned her hand to clasp his beneath her breast.

It was torture of the most exquisite kind, and Jamie stifled a groan. To lie here in the darkness, holding in his arms the one woman he desired more than anything on earth. Kate slept now, a deep, exhausted slumber. When she'd voluntarily clasped his hand, his heart had lurched in a way that made his chest ache. He had never considered that, amidst the darkness and danger, he would hold her and find himself hard with desire, wanting her. As though of their own accord, his hands moved from her waist to the swell of her hips and back to the arousing warmth of her soft breasts.

"Katie," he murmured against her hair, using the loving nickname her father had used.

She sighed, almost a sob, as though she grieved in her sleep. Jamie pressed his mouth to the bright, disheveled hair of the courageous woman who had somehow stolen all his senses. There would be no rest for him this night.

☙ 11 ❧

Gray light seeped through Kate's eyelids, gradually bringing her awake, disoriented and frightened. It was cold beyond anything she'd experienced. And there was an ache inside her, reminding her that her father was dead. Slowly, unwilling to face reality, she opened her eyes to meet Jamie Campbell's dark gaze. It came back to her in a rush—how he'd held her against him all through the bitter night, warming her with his warmth. Sometime in the darkness, stiff, cramped muscles had caused them to turn facing each other.

"*Ma-me-atsi-kimi.*" His expression was intense as he murmured the word he'd spoken to her back at Fort McLeod in what seemed lifetimes ago.

"What?" Kate asked, finding that intent gaze deeply disturbing.

"You are beautiful," he translated, and his arms tightened.

"Jamie." Kate breathed his name, reaching with cold fingers to touch his cheek.

The sound of her voice speaking his name undid all Jamie's resolve. Cupping her cheek with one hand, he brushed her lips with his. At first she stiffened with surprise; then, as his lips gently teased at hers, she returned his kiss. Kate's mouth was soft and moist, the warm taste as sweet as he had dreamed. She returned his kiss with growing fervor and Jamie felt himself harden with passion. "Katie," he whispered and pressed his mouth to the pulse at the base of her throat.

When he lifted his head to gaze into her eyes, she smiled. "You saved my life," she said.

Gratitude . . . her kiss had been given out of gratitude, not desire. Everything about him went slack, his arms falling from her shoulders. Turning away so she couldn't see his face, he said gruffly, "We'd better get started. I told Cavendish I'd come back for the detachment and guide them into the fort."

With those words, he began easing himself out of the tiny snow cave, carefully covering her with the buffalo robe. "Stay here until I saddle the horses," he ordered, his voice unnecessarily rough because of the pain in his heart.

Alone in the cave, which was iced over now from the warmth of their breath and their bodies, Kate lay beneath the buffalo robe, her thoughts in turmoil. She had kissed him back, this strange, foreign man whose wilderness expertise had saved her life. Even worse, she had longed for the kiss to go on and on, savoring the wild, strong taste of him. She'd felt his hard maleness against her leg and her whole being had responded with urgent longing. Even now her groin ached in a way she'd never felt before. She was a doctor's daughter and knew the details of sexual congress between men and women. But no one had suggested how overwhelming the touch of a man's lips could be. Certainly Curtis's furtive kisses had never aroused her like this. For the endless moment Jamie's lips had claimed hers, their two beings seemed melded, her whole body ablaze with longing.

"Kate." Jamie's voice came sharply from the mouth of the cave. Perhaps he regretted it, she thought, and knew she must put the memory of that brief moment of desire away from her forever.

Jamie had brushed caked snow from the horses and saddled them. As she eased out of the cave and stood watching, he quickly rolled up the buffalo robes and tied them behind the saddles. Kate wound her wool scarf tight around her head and pulled on damp gloves.

The sky was a pale, cold gray, indicating the storm wasn't over. The ferocious wind had abated except for occasional icy gusts. Across the endless prairies stretching before her, there was nothing to be seen but a blanket of white snow. The one man in the world who could take her home through that trackless waste stood waiting to help her mount her horse.

"Thank God!" David cried, rushing to meet her from beside the low fire the Mounties had managed to kindle in front of their sand cave.

Kate slid from the saddle into his waiting arms. At that moment she caught Jamie's eye. His mouth tightened and he quickly looked away.

"Saddle up," he shouted, as if he were in command and not David. "It'll be hard going and we've got a way to go."

He did not look at her again.

Patting her shoulder, David murmured, "I'm sorry, Kate. We should have kept better track of you. Are you all right?" She nodded silently, her eyes following the half-breed guide already mounted and riding ahead. Then David added, "Your father would never forgive me for letting you get lost like that."

At once Kate was overwhelmed by the grief she had momentarily forgotten. Her head bowed as she struggled to hold back tears, she remounted her horse and joined the column following Jamie Campbell up from the river bottom onto the snow-shrouded plains.

"I'm deeply sorry, Miss Maginnis," Commissioner McLeod said. "Your father was a good man."

The sky above Fort McLeod was cold and gray. There had been no more storm while Jamie Campbell led the detachment straight and true to the fort, but the skies held the promise of storms to come. Commissioner McLeod had greeted them with relief, and with elation for the capture of the whiskey traders and the end of one more whiskey fort.

Taking Kate's arm, he led her across the parade ground to the log surgery that was to have been her father's. It broke her heart to walk into the room and see his medical instruments ready for him to lay out in his precise way. Never again. Never again would they work side by side or dream of a future. Tightening her lips, she fought for control now as McLeod politely asked, "What are your plans?"

"I have none." An edge of bitterness crept into her voice, and she faced the commissioner squarely. "If you send me away, your troops will have no doctor at all."

Frowning, McLeod turned to stare out the open door of the surgery at the Union Jack flying above the muddy parade ground. "I'll telegraph Ottawa to send out a replacement doctor," he said, and Kate's heart fell.

"But until then," he continued in a reluctant tone, "I guess a woman doctor is better than no doctor. I've seen you work. You can handle it."

"Of course I can," Kate replied spiritedly, resenting his obvious doubts.

McLeod's frown deepened and his voice was gruff. "I can't put you on the paymaster's list, but your father's salary will go to you until our new doctor arrives. Satisfactory?"

"Quite satisfactory, sir," Kate answered, her heart lifting for the first time. However tenuous, at least she had a place.

"Several of the men are suffering from frostbite," she told him in her most professional manner. "I'm ready to treat them right away."

For a moment it seemed the humorless commander might actually smile. He bowed his head. "Good luck to you, ma'am. If you need any supplies, let me know."

With a heady sense of triumph, Kate watched him tramp across the muddy parade ground toward his quarters. She'd prove to him she was a good doctor. And she'd prove to David Cavendish, who kept insisting she must return to Fort Benton at once, that she was capable of making it on her own. As for Jamie Campbell . . .

The thought of him brought a rush of feeling Kate tried to deny. Even though she'd promised herself to forget the night they'd spent in each other's arms, the memory of his kiss returned to haunt her dreams. You mustn't think of it, Kate scolded herself.

She focused on the task of arranging the surgery. Would there be enough arnica to treat all the frostbite? Suddenly the absence of her father, her co-worker, seized her with such a profound sense of grief that she cried aloud. Covering her mouth, she tried to stifle the sobs that came unbidden. She had built her life around her father and his ambitions for her. Always, he had made her feel strong and confident. Alone now, she had the awful realization that without him she was not nearly as strong and independent as she had believed.

A knock at the door reminded her that she had no

time to grieve. She'd told David to send the men who needed treatment to the surgery right away. They were at the door and she was their doctor.

Oldman River was iced over and Kate rode at a slow pace, knowing her horse's footing was precarious. Now that winter lay on the prairies, supplies were slow in coming from Fort Benton. The arnica bottles were empty and there were new frostbite victims every day. It had occurred to her that perhaps Baker's store had what she needed, so she'd asked Bagley to bring up her horse for the short journey across the river to the new town of McLeod.

The I. G. Baker store in McLeod was a smaller copy of the one in Fort Benton, with a porch across the front and a similar sign above. She tied her horse at the hitching rack, lifted her skirts to avoid the mud of the street and went up the steps. Pausing, she looked around at the beginnings of a town. Wooden sidewalks had been laid from one business to another. Next door, hastily constructed of rough lumber, a billiard hall was being patronized by several off-duty Mounties. Beyond it, a small log cabin housed a barbershop and a shoemaker. On the other side of Baker's store, farther back from the river, a corral and some rough stables made up a livery. A far cry from the elegance of downtown Toronto, Kate thought, and wondered again how she had come so far.

Inside the store, she went at once to the welcome warmth of the round iron stove. Behind a makeshift counter stood Mr. Conrad, one of Baker's partners sent to expand the company's business to the Fort McLeod area. The log-walled store was small and crowded. A plank resting on two barrels served as the counter. Walls were lined with rough lumber shelves stuffed with all kinds of goods. Traps hung against the walls, and the smell of buffalo hides stacked in the adjacent lean-to storeroom pervaded the place. A plank partition at the back of the store walled off Conrad's living quarters.

"Miss Maginnis," he said, smiling and coming toward her with his hand outstretched, for they had met briefly at the store in Fort Benton. "How are you, ma'am?" She took his hand and he sobered. "I'm sorry about your father. Terrible thing. He was a fine man."

"Thank you," she murmured, fighting back the tears any mention of her father brought. "I've come to see what you have in stock that I might need," she said, pleased with how steady her voice came out.

"Glad to help," he replied heartily. "I hear you've been acting doctor at the fort. The men speak highly of you."

"I'm pleased to hear that," she answered. If she would have been more pleased to have her father at her side, it was good to know she had replaced him to some extent.

"Anything you want." He waved an inviting hand. "Help yourself." He went back behind the counter to wait on two customers—trappers by the scroungy look of them and the traps they were buying. Over in the corner, a morose-looking Mountie was trying on boots, his own ragged ones lying beside him on the floor.

Kate took the two bottles of arnica he had, a box of boric acid and one of Epsom salt. Nothing else seemed of any medicinal value. The purse in the pocket of her heavy capote felt very slim, and she hesitated when he gave her the total.

As though he sensed her hesitation, Conrad said, "Shall I charge it, miss? Most of the men are charging what they need. I'm told Commissioner McLeod is to leave this week for Helena, where he'll pick up the payroll for his men."

"That's good news." Kate brightened. "Yes, charge it. I'll pay as soon as the commissioner returns." Seemingly unconcerned, Conrad nodded and gave her the bill to sign. How easy to go into debt, Kate thought, but perhaps McLeod would reimburse her.

The trappers departed. The unhappy Mountie continued his search for a pair of boots that fit. Stout and bewhiskered, Conrad was a convivial man and now seemed to want to prolong his conversation with Kate.

"This place will grow in the next year," he informed her, taking in the whole town with an all-encompassing wave of his hand. "Settlers will be moving in now that the Mounted Police have settled the Indian problem."

"The whiskey problem," Kate corrected him mildly, then remembered that Conrad was an American who very likely had bankrolled some of the whiskey traders.

"Oh, yes." Conrad dismissed her comment, immersed in his own rhetoric. "We'll have to expand the store come spring, maybe add a pharmacy." He smiled and nodded at her. "Your father thought that a good idea, especially if he settled on a practice here."

Kate hadn't been aware of her father's conversation with Conrad, but she merely smiled and agreed that a pharmacy would be a fine addition to the town. It seemed to her the meager population of McLeod couldn't possibly support such an enterprise, but it was nothing to do with her.

When the Mountie greeted Kate politely and offered to pay Conrad for the boots he was wearing, she was finally able to break away from the loquacious storekeeper. Thanking Conrad politely, she went out to her waiting horse.

Thin sunlight filtered through high clouds as she rode back across the river. The fort seemed almost deserted on this bitter day except for two men chopping firewood in one corner near the palisaded log walls. To her surprise, there was a horse in front of the surgery and her heart lurched as she recognized the big stout bay only one man ever rode.

Jamie Campbell sat on a campstool, leafing idly through one of Dr. Maginnis's illustrated medical books. Light from the doorway fell on his bowed head, black hair gleaming, for his hat lay on the floor. Broad shoulders were hunched beneath a heavy buffalo-skin coat and one long brown finger followed the lines of words as he read softly to himself.

"Jamie."

He started at the sound of her voice and rose from the stool. "Dr. Kate," he said, and in spite of herself, Kate smiled on hearing the title only he had ever used. For an intensely awkward moment they stared at each other, Kate trying not to remember his arms around her, his mouth on hers.

Tearing his eyes from hers, Jamie leaned over to pick up a buckskin bag that lay beside his wide-brimmed hat. "Cutting Woman sends you these sumac leaves. Steep them in water overnight, then let those who have frostbite soak the affected limbs in it."

Gratitude filled Kate's heart. He hadn't forgotten his promise that his aunt would teach her more Blackfoot medicine.

"She couldn't come herself," he explained. "Her only son has been very ill with a lung infection."

"Will he be all right?" Kate asked, wondering whether she could offer to help.

"He's recovering already, but because he's all she has, my aunt watches over him." In his dark eyes Kate saw both affection and approval for Cutting Woman.

"She sent exactly the right thing," Kate told him. She set the two small bottles of arnica on the table and smiled at him. "One of the men has a frostbitten nose."

Jamie laughed. A tremor went through her at the deep, joyful sound, for it occurred to her that she had never heard him laugh before. "Then perhaps a poultice would help more than a soaking." He chuckled, handing her the buckskin bag.

"Please thank your aunt for me," she said, moving past him to the small iron stove that served the surgery. She saw that he had replenished the fire and she quickly put the kettle on. "I'll make some tea," she told him and sat on the campstool on the other side of the table, where her medical instruments lay covered by a clean towel.

Another awkward moment passed as they looked at each other and quickly away. Kate cleared her throat and began bravely. "I hope to spend some time with Cutting Woman, to learn what she can teach me."

"Very wise," Jamie replied, closing the book almost reluctantly and placing it on the corner of the table. "Perhaps when spring comes, you can visit the Blackfoot camp and gather herbs with her."

"When spring comes . . ." Kate repeated, wondering where on this earth she would be when spring came again.

"The prairies are beautiful that time of year," Jamie hastened to tell her as she rose to take the boiling kettle from the stove and set the tea to steep. "There's fresh green grass everywhere, and flowers—so many flowers, so many colors, you wouldn't believe it."

Their fingers touched as she handed him a steaming mug of tea. Kate saw him flinch at that contact and knew he'd felt the same electric surge that shook her. She studied her mug of tea, not daring to meet his eyes. Regaining control, she asked in a surprisingly steady voice, "Are you going to Helena with McLeod for the payroll?"

"Of course," he replied with a surprised expression. "Who else could get him there and back?"

"It's a long way." She watched him blow gently on the tea, then sip it gingerly. "And it's the dead of winter."

Jamie grinned. "It's the dead of winter half the year in the Northwest. We can hardly hibernate like the bears."

"It might be nice." She smiled at him and he chuckled. "When you come back—" She broke off, shocked by the direction of her thoughts—what she wanted when he came back.

"I'll go to Crowfoot's camp," he said almost brusquely, and rose to set his tea mug on the table. "Winter camp is a good time." He settled his battered hat on his head, avoiding her eyes. "There are ceremonies to be taught to the young ones, stories to be told and memorized around the lodge fire. My people are a proud and happy breed . . . at least they were until the coming of the whites. I hope that now the whiskey traders are gone, they can be again."

Jamie went out the door so abruptly that Kate was left with a reply stuck in her throat. She stood in the doorway to watch him ride across the parade ground, tall and proud in the saddle. All her being longed to call after him, to tell him how much she wanted to see the prairie in the spring, and to see it with him.

He was gone. You're a fool, Kate, she chastised herself, turning back to the surgery, which seemed suddenly unbearably empty. He had said he'd return to his people, and she was certain he always would. If he'd aroused something in her no other man ever had, something she'd thought herself incapable of feeling, it was futile to dream on it, for their two worlds could never meet.

⪻ 12 ⪼

Christmas was something Kate tried to not think about. It would be the first without her father, alone and far from her childhood home. As the time came on, she was besieged by memories of Christmases past. Back in Toronto, far away from the Northwest wilderness, they had made it a happy time. Father Bruneau always came after mass, bringing Tom Maginnis his annual bottle of Irish whiskey; neighbors and friends stopped by, most with gifts of food for the doctor's scanty larder. Amid jokes and stories, laughter and song, the whiskey disappeared and the food was consumed. "Good night" and "Merry Christmas" echoed in the snowy darkness as the guests departed, having brought friendship and comfort to the widowed doctor and his daughter.

This year there would be no friends to cheer her, and Kate remembered too well the desolate Christmas after her mother's death, when the friends who came could share only their tears.

Would this Christmas be another to break the heart? Kate wondered as she was about to close the door on the young Mountie whose black eye and bloody nose she'd treated with cold compresses. He'd refused to state how the injury had been acquired, and she thought that, in any case, discipline was not her business.

It seemed to her the men brought her small injuries they wouldn't have bothered her father with, but she couldn't fault them for that. She suspected they had a sort of conspiracy going to occupy her time and keep her company. Most of them lingered after treatment, plying her with questions or talking of home. Another man was already on his way across the parade ground, saluting her last patient as they passed. Kate smiled when she recognized Inspector David Cavendish.

McLeod came by occasionally to inquire if she was being supplied with firewood and water as well as food from the kitchens, but David came every day.

"Good afternoon, Kate," he said, stiffly formal as always.

"Good afternoon, David." She stepped aside to let him in the door.

Pulling off his fur hat and heavy gloves, David moved a stool in front of the only window of the surgery. Kate smiled to herself, knowing he sat there so that everyone in the fort would know there was nothing untoward in his visit.

"Tea, David?" Kate asked as she set the kettle to boil, as though this wasn't an almost daily ritual.

"Thank you, yes." He loosened the heavy buffalo-skin coat he wore, one of those McLeod had ordered made from confiscated skins when winter uniforms failed to arrive from Ottawa. The well-worn red coats were saved for dress occasions now, and the Mounties dressed like any other frontiersmen in skins and furs.

"I hear another whiskey fort was raided," she said, placing the precious sweet biscuits from Baker's store on a china saucer that had been her mother's.

"Some place called Fort Kipp," David answered.

"Unfortunately, we lost a man on the trail. O'Reilly went looking for a lost horse, got lost himself and froze to death."

"I heard," Kate replied, thinking again how hard and unforgiving this country was.

"Denny and Campbell brought in three prisoners," David continued. "McLeod was glad to get the money for their fines, since the payroll still hasn't arrived from Ottawa."

"What a crime they went all the way to Helena and the money wasn't sent there." Kate forced a casual tone. "Is Campbell off on another raid?" She kept her face turned away from David, fussing with pouring the tea. Since the day he'd delivered the sumac leaves, she had seen Jamie only at a distance. It seemed to her they had shared some important moments . . . the comforting beside her father's grave, and the night in the snow cave, which must have affected her more than him. After the friendly sharing of his last visit, she had found herself waiting in vain for him to come by again. Why did her eyes seek that wild man? And why did his face haunt her dreams? The memory of the night in his arms seemed fraught with new meaning each time she rehearsed it in her mind. She dared not let David see her expression when Jamie's name was between them.

"Gone to the Blackfoot village, I suppose," David replied easily. "That's where he belongs. For all I know, he may even have a wife there."

Pain lanced through Kate, so that she slopped tea onto the table. It was something she hadn't considered—that the man for whom she carried this secret, forbidden yearning might belong to another woman.

"I've brought news to cheer you," David announced, taking the tea mug from hands she forced to steadiness. "McLeod and the officers extend their invitation for you to join them at Christmas dinner." He smiled at her over the mug. "We're trying to make an occasion of it. Some of the younger men are very homesick at the thought of the holiday."

"How kind of you to include me." Kate sat down and sipped her tea, deliberately putting Jamie Campbell from her mind. "I was afraid Christmas would be a hard time for me." Touched that the men had cared to make her part of their celebration, she bowed her head. The memory of her father's absence was too strong and she could not hold back the tears slipping down her cheeks.

David took her hand in his and gently stroked it. "I know," he murmured sympathetically. "All of us want to help you through this bad time, Kate. The men revere and respect you for your goodness and courage. You're a woman in a million." He lifted her hand to his lips for a brief touch.

As though his words had embarrassed him, he quickly downed his tea and stood up. "Until tomorrow, then. I'll come to escort you to the officers' mess at noon."

"Thank you, David." She stood, too, watching in amusement as he tied the ungainly coat around him and jammed the fur hat on his fair hair. He looked quite unlike the dapper officer she remembered from the Toronto train station.

Looking out the window as he strode across to his quarters, Kate felt herself warm with affection for him. His concern for her reputation was touching, and they were never alone for more than a few minutes. Although he thought her decision to stay in Fort McLeod unwise, he'd accepted the commissioner's judgment and tried to make things easier for her when he could. Her father had been fond of David and spoke highly of him, even hinted at a match with Kate. It occurred to her that if David should actually ask her to marry him, she would be wise to agree. She would be, as they said in Toronto, "marrying up." Yet she was certain his world in England on a vast estate, in a great manor house, was as different from hers as the Blackfoot village where Jamie Campbell now dwelled.

And she knew very well she could marry no man until she had banished Jamie Campbell's image from her dreams.

Father Scollen, the missionary priest, said grace over tables the men had decorated with evergreens and bright red berries.

A cheery fire burned in the large stone fireplace at the end of the rectangular room. One wall was the palisaded logs of the fort itself; the others were laid in the traditional longitudinal manner and chinked with mud. No linen covered the plank tables. Tin plates and mugs served for china. The mood was determinedly festive. Loud male voices punctuated by bursts of laughter echoed across the room.

Earlier, the priest had celebrated a Christmas mass, welcoming Catholics and Protestants alike. Last night, at Kate's request, the good father had said a requiem mass for the soul of that unregenerate agnostic, Thomas Maginnis, who had been raised a Catholic in faraway Ireland. As she knelt there, listening to the rhythmic rumble of the priest's voice echoing the mass said for her mother long ago, she had felt a sense of closure. It was as though this ceremony sent her father to rest in a peaceful and proper way, quite unlike that hurried, primitive burial in the wilderness. In quite another way, the words Jamie Campbell had spoken at the graveside that cold, sad morning had comforted her as nothing else could.

A scraping of chairs and a mumble of voices followed

the priest's "Amen," ending the grace. When everyone was seated, Kate on McLeod's left, Father Scollen on his right, the commissioner rose to make a toast with wine that had been a gift from Mr. Conrad and the I. G. Baker Company. Conrad himself sat across from Kate. A crate of wineglasses, mostly unbroken, had accompanied the wine.

"The Northwest Mounted Police have cleaned out the whiskey traders," McLeod announced grandly, "and we've driven the Americans from the Northwest. God save the Queen, and God save Canada!"

"Hear! Hear!" the men responded in lusty affirmation. Even the American, Conrad, applauded.

Kate wondered if only she remembered the awful price paid: her father dead, the young trooper frozen on the trail, the constable dead of typhoid. It was a hard life. No payroll had come through for the Mounted Police. Uniforms and clothes were nearly worn out. Most of the men were sorely in debt to Baker's store for necessities they had purchased on credit. To McLeod's chagrin, when he returned from Helena without a payroll, fifteen disaffected Mounties had simply fled with horses and gear, heading for the supposed riches of the mines in Montana Territory.

Serving of a grand feast began: roast buffalo hump, wild duck, broiled trout, vegetables from the garden at Fort Whoop-up. The cooks had outdone themselves, and everyone fell to with a will.

The commissioner's plate was filled, but he sat staring at it as though lost in melancholy. Not only the young men were homesick, Kate thought with a smile. "My wife will be coming out next spring," he'd told Kate as he greeted her at the door. "Next Christmas will be quite different from this one."

"For all of us," Kate had answered with false brightness, too aware of the uncertainty of her own future.

David Cavendish sat across from Kate, next to Father Scollen. His worn and faded scarlet coat had been brushed and pressed. Despite the shabby coat, he looked dapper, his fair mustache neatly trimmed, his hair newly cut. How handsome he was, all blond, narrow-faced Englishman, Kate thought as David laughed at a sally from one of their tablemates. His eyes met hers across the table, and the admiration she saw there warmed her heart. What would it be like to kiss him? Kate wondered. How would she respond? Would David's kiss fill her with aching longing as Jamie Campbell's had done, an ache that still haunted her in the darkness of night?

"Merry Christmas, Kate." David leaned toward her, his blue eyes warm. Standing, he lifted a glass to her. "To our lovely surgeon," he said. "May the future hold only happiness for her."

"Hear! Hear!" resounded around the table, and the men burst into applause.

Flushing, Kate rose and lifted her glass to them. "To the finest men under the Queen's flag," she said. Delighted shouts of "Hear! Hear!" answered. Glasses were lifted, and her eyes misted at the affection in the faces turned to her.

A plum pudding the cook had concocted from wild plums was brought in then, aflame with brandy, and there were shouts of approval from the men.

Kate watched the red-coated officers around the table enjoy this brief respite from hard work and deadly responsibility. With David's words they had wished her a happy future. But what that future held, she could not fathom. She only knew it would not be what she had planned with such certainty back in Toronto.

*　　*　　*

"So," Crowfoot said, his heavy-lidded eyes cold with disapproval.

Jamie closed the flap of the buffalo-skin lodge and let down the inside covering meant to keep out the winter winds. It was late and all the occupants of the lodge lay sleeping on the fur couches around the perimeter—all except Crowfoot. The fire in the center of the lodge burned low. Its flickering light reflected off the prominent nose and high cheekbones of the chief. Wrapped in a Hudson's Bay blanket, Crowfoot sat cross-legged on his own couch, puffing moodily on a pipe decorated with beading and eagle feathers.

The pipe was a ceremonial one, so Jamie knew his uncle had sought answers from the gods for whatever was disturbing him. The scent of sweet grass pervaded the lodge.

"So," Crowfoot said again in a hard voice, his black eyes riveting Jamie. "You seek relief with the whore when there are young women who would be wife to you. Is that not a fool's choice?"

Jamie sucked in a breath. He had seated himself on his own couch to the right of Crowfoot and started to pull off his damp winter moccasins. Only a man of Crowfoot's authority would dare speak to another warrior in such a manner.

He hadn't bothered to conceal his visit to the lodge of the outcast woman who lived by accommodating the needs of single men. It had been an unsatisfactory joining, quickly ended. A fool's choice, perhaps, but there were times when a man seemed to burst with his seed, especially if there was an unattainable woman at the heart of his desire.

"The woman is clean," he replied without looking at his uncle as he leaned over to place his moccasins near the low fire.

Crowfoot passed the pipe to Jamie, who took it in his right hand. As he drew in the harsh smoke, he met his uncle's serious eyes and knew this was to be an important counseling.

"Five years now," the old man began in the voice he used to tell tales of the gods, "five snows have come and gone since Meadowlark's shadow fled to the Sand Hills, along with the child who never breathed. It is long enough, my son, to grieve."

Jamie bowed his head. How could he say to this revered man that he no longer grieved, that he could scarcely conjure up the face of the girl he had loved in his youth, or that his heart longed for a woman forbidden to him?

"You need a wife, Follows the Eagle." Crowfoot's words were a command. "A man should have a wife to keep his lodge, care for his horses, bear his sons."

Unable to think of a reply that would not offend the chief, Jamie silently handed the ceremonial pipe back. Crowfoot puffed, blowing smoke to the four winds, then carefully extinguished the pipe.

With a satisfied smile, he looked into Jamie's eyes. "I have spoken with Cutting Woman. She agrees you should have a wife and she will choose a maiden suited to you, one with all the skills a Blackfoot wife should have."

"And what if I don't agree with her choice?" Jamie asked, resenting such high-handed planning of his life.

Crowfoot gave a dismissive shrug as he turned to arrange his bed for the night. "Then she will find another."

By the time Jamie had banked the fire, Crowfoot was already snoring in his blankets. Sleepless, Jamie lay on his own couch and stared up at the shaft of moonlight slanting through the smoke hole of the lodge. Her hair was brighter than moonlight, bright as the core of the sun, and the image of her face filled his mind. "Katie," he whispered, remembering the taste of her lips, knowing Crowfoot's counsel had been in vain. He could wed no other woman while this futile longing for Kate Maginnis possessed him.

He must forget her. To go away would be best. When spring came, he would return to a duty neglected these many months in favor of the Redcoats: he must kill Big Rib and Good Young Man, or he was no warrior of the Blackfoot.

❧ 13 ❧

"**S**o the whiskey traders have moved into the Cypress Hills?" McLeod frowned across his desk at Jamie. "Does that mean they'll be stirring up the Sioux?"

Jamie shrugged. "Likely. The Cypress Hills are a rendezvous for several tribes, and the Sioux are looking for allies in their fight against the American Long Knives."

A wandering Piegan hunter had come north on the heels of the Black Wind, the warm chinook that blew across the plains this time of year, melting the snow, scattering the game, only to be followed by a renewal of winter. He'd stayed a few days in the village of Crowfoot, telling tales of the drunkenness and murder the whiskey traders had brought to the Cypress Hills.

"The traders can't operate in this area any longer," Jamie told McLeod, "so they've moved east to sell their rotgut."

"We'll put a stop to that," McLeod growled. He pulled a roster from his desk drawer and studied it, frowning. "Inspector Walsh and B Troop," he announced decisively. "That's seventy-five men. Can you get them to the Cypress Hills and put up a fort before spring sends those whiskey-selling bastards south to the States?''

With a wry smile, Jamie rose and picked up his hat. ''You know I can,'' he said coolly.

McLeod managed a rare grin. ''Damn right I know you can, Campbell. Find Walsh and bring him here. I want you on the trail as soon as possible.''

Jamie stood on the stoop in front of McLeod's quarters and looked across the parade ground, now deep in mud from the chinook thaw. The sky was a clear blue and the breeze had a nip to it, auguring the return of winter. The surgery door was closed, but someone moved beyond the window. For a moment Jamie couldn't catch his breath. All these weeks he'd longed to see her. If only he had a glimpse to carry away with him to the Cypress Hills. Even as the thought went through his mind, he knew it was madness. She was not for him and it was best he would be far away. Far away, too, from Cutting Woman's daily litany of the charms and accomplishments of this eligible girl or that one as she sought to make a suitable match for him. If the bright-haired woman hadn't ensnared his heart and mind, perhaps he would have chosen one of them and lived the life of a Blackfoot warrior. But try as he had this winter, it was only Kate who filled his dreams.

The surgery door opened and Inspector Cavendish paused on the stoop, turning to kiss Kate's outstretched hand. A suitable match . . . and Jamie's heart fell at the thought. He'd heard Cavendish was of noble blood and he knew that meant wealth and comfort. Kate deserved wealth and comfort with one of her own—not a half-blood misfit who could give her nothing.

At that moment Jamie swore by Natos, the Sun god, that he would not go near her again. He would put her out of his heart. Turning abruptly to avoid Cavendish, he hurried to the quarters of Inspector Walsh.

Now that bull teams made regular trips up the Old North Trail from Fort Benton, supplies and news were easier to come by. T. C. Power had built a store to compete with Baker, and a hotel of sorts with a cafe attached had gone up opposite the billiard parlor. The attractions of the town provided the Mounties with some relief from the excruciating boredom of their first Northwest winter. From remarks Kate had overheard, she surmised that the hotel provided diversion of another sort—Indian women, including one whose husband had cut off her nose as punishment for her adultery.

Bagley had come to tell her the payroll had arrived and she was to go to McLeod's office. At last she and the Mounties could pay their bills at Baker's store and buy some new clothing to replace those garments rapidly falling into rags. She would pay her bill this very day and see if Conrad had any new stock.

The fort was extraordinarily quiet as Kate picked her way through the half-frozen mud toward McLeod's quarters. With B Troop off to the Cypress Hills, the place seemed half empty. Jamie Campbell had gone to guide them, and she told herself she was glad for his absence. A glimpse of him riding up to McLeod's quarters was always enough to leave her disturbed and restless.

B Troop, under the command of Inspector Walsh, was to build a fort and root out the whiskey traders as the Mounties had done here in Whoop-up country. This time Jamie Campbell would surely be away long enough to fade from her mind and heart. Perhaps he wouldn't return at all.

As she mounted the steps to McLeod's quarters, she saw Gladstone, the builder, measuring the abandoned B Troop barracks. Puzzled, she stepped into the warmth of McLeod's office, Spartanly furnished with a campaign desk, two chairs and an iron stove with a roaring fire in it.

"Miss Maginnis." He indicated the chair opposite him and at once began counting out money. "This is your father's pay, which will now go to you." He shoved the bills across the desk. Kate picked them up and folded them carefully, then waited, sensing that the commissioner had more on his mind than payroll.

The silence grew heavy as McLeod avoided her eyes, fiddling with the papers before him. At last he drew a deep breath and said bluntly, "If you're careful, that should be enough money to get you back to Toronto. I'll arrange your transportation from here to Fort Benton."

Stunned in spite of the fact that she had been expecting something of the sort, Kate could only stare at him. He had tried to send her away from the first day. This time he would likely succeed. Her mind cast wildly about for some solution. There was nothing for her in Toronto without her father, no family, few friends. Nor did Fort Benton seem as likely a place as it would have been with Dr. Maginnis beside her. With a sinking heart, she knew that no matter how she might resist, in the end it would have to be Toronto . . . a place that now seemed as alien to her as the Northwest Territories had seemed just last fall.

"But, sir—" she began, and he interrupted harshly.

"A new doctor has been recruited, Samuelson by name. He'll be coming out as soon as the boats are moving up the Missouri. He'll escort my wife, and the wives of Inspector Winder and Inspector Shurtliff. Gladstone will remodel B Troop quarters for married officers and their wives.''

McLeod paused. His face reddened and he still avoided Kate's resentful eyes. "I've said from the beginning," he continued defensively, "this is no place for a single woman. You'll be better off with your relatives in Toronto."

"I have no relatives," Kate snapped, unable to keep the bitterness from her voice. "No place to go—except perhaps to the hotel in town." Her voice broke with anger.

McLeod squirmed with embarrassment. "No need for crude remarks, young lady. I'm simply doing my duty." His voice hardened on the last words and his pale blue eyes were cold. "I'm sure by the time spring comes, you'll have made arrangements for your future."

"Thanks for your concern, Commissioner." Kate stood up, giving him an angry stare. Stuffing the bills she was holding into the pocket of her skirt, she lifted her chin defiantly and walked out into the icy wind that blew winter back to the plains.

Thanks to the skill of men who had already built one fort, Fort Walsh went up in six weeks on the western slopes of the Cypress Hills. On their arrival, B Troop had no sooner put up their tents than they were confronted by a band of hostile Sioux. While Jamie struggled to convince the Indians that these men were not the hated Long Knives of the United States Army, a band of friendly Cree rode up. The Sioux scattered.

In the weeks since, seven whiskey traders had been arrested and put out of business. News that the Redcoats were honest in their intentions spread quickly, so that Jamie was able to arrange a council: the chiefs of the

Bloods and Piegan, Cree, Assiniboin and Sioux to meet with Inspector Walsh.

Spring began to creep across the prairies. Ice had broken up on the rivers. Rivulets ran from under every snowbank. Grass was greening on the south slopes. Soon the flowers he had promised Kate would appear. He would not see them with her this or any other year. If McLeod had sent her away before he returned, it would be best. She would make a life in her world; perhaps he would take Crowfoot's advice, marry and live as a Blackfoot. Deliberately, Jamie put such thoughts away, and turned to the business of the council meeting.

All the tribes seemed to be trying to outdo one another in the brilliance of their finery: eagle-feather war bonnets, painted buffalo-skin shields, lances heavy with feathers and scalp hair, horses draped with furs. All the warriors' faces and bare chests were bright with paint.

The chiefs gathered around a fire, for the weather was chill. Mounted warriors waited restively behind them. The Blackfoot seldom roamed this far east, but their relatives, the Bloods and Piegan, were there, along with the dour northern Sioux, the careless Cree and the Assiniboin.

At last the serious ritual of smoking together ended. The Redcoat chief, Inspector Walsh, rose to speak. He was a stocky man with a bristling mustache and a fierce temper. Jamie stood beside him to interpret with signs and by the languages of the attentive chiefs.

"We have been sent by the Great Grandmother to bring law and order, to keep peace among the tribes. Whiskey selling is against the law and we have driven out the whiskey traders. But the Indians must obey the law, too. There must be no cheating or stealing or warfare among you. The Redcoats will always deal honorably with those who keep the law.''

One after another, the chief of each tribe responded at length, welcoming the Redcoats and promising to cooperate. Pipes were passed again and smoked to seal the words of friendship.

Walsh turned to Jamie. "I think we've reached them—that they understand." Despite the positive words, he frowned and there was a question in his eyes.

"I hope so," Jamie replied carefully. "It would be a good thing if the Sioux went back south of the Medicine Line. They try to lead the others into their own war."

"We'll see to it that the peace is kept," Walsh stated in his forceful way. Jamie watched him move among the crowding Indians, shaking hands.

Walsh was a white man. He could never understand a people whose life and honor had once depended on waging war and stealing horses. Perhaps Walsh had made a beginning. Jamie feared it was a small one, but driving out the whiskey traders was most important of all. This past winter it had kept him from all other duties, including Blackfoot revenge.

Amid the confusion he was confronted by an old friend. Red Crow, chief of the Bloods, had often been a visitor in the camps of Crowfoot. Riding up to Jamie, he extended a hand. "Come to my fire tonight, my friend," the older man said, shaking hands vigorously. "We will talk."

Stern and dignified, Red Crow sat in front of his lodge, holding the ceremonial pipe in both hands. He blew smoke to the earth, the sky and the four winds, then passed the pipe to Jamie. As he carefully repeated the chief's actions, Jamie wondered why he had been invited here. It was well known that Red Crow disliked half bloods. He had been a famous warrior in his youth, and such an intemperate drinker at the whiskey forts that he had killed his own brother in a drunken rage. He'd once been a violent and arrogant man, and the deaths and the devastating poverty that were the result of the whiskey-trading years had left their mark on him. Fortunately, he had grown into a wise and benevolent chief of the Bloods.

"Crowfoot is your *nis-ah,* your uncle," Red Crow began when the pipe had gone round the circle of chosen warriors gathered before the fire in Red Crow's spacious lodge.

Jamie nodded, certain now that Red Crow had asked him here because he wanted something. "My honored uncle, and my second father," he agreed.

"And you are Blackfoot?"

"My heart is Blackfoot," Jamie replied, placing a hand on his chest gravely.

"The Blackfoot and the Bloods are brothers," Red Crow intoned. Again Jamie nodded, studying the low flames of the center fire that cast their shadows on the walls of Red Crow's lodge. He waited for the chief to at last come to the point of what he wished to ask.

After many more compliments and pledges of friendship, Red Crow said, "My brother, Running Bear, gave his daughter in marriage to a Blackfoot. He is a bad man. He beats this fine girl and threatens her father. We wish you to take him away, to the camps of the Blackfoot or . . ." There was a significant pause. "Or to the Sand Hills."

Anger leaped in Jamie. With an effort, he kept a bland expression on his face. It was not his place to punish this man. Red Crow was chief. Running Bear was surely a coward, or he would have protected his daughter. Yet Jamie could not afford to antagonize Red Crow, not at this stage in the Mounted Police negotiations.

"Who is this man?" he asked, playing for time.

"Big Rib." Red Crow spit out the name.

Big Rib! The sound of that name was like a knife in Jamie's gut. Big Rib . . . murderer of his mother and his brother, the man he had sworn to kill in order to achieve Blackfoot justice.

Closing his eyes, Jamie leaned his head back, longing to cry out his anger and shame that he had lost his warrior's vision. In the months since the coming of the Mounted Police, he had let go from his heart and mind the Blackfoot vengeance he was bound by blood ties to take against his mother's murderers. That vengeance was required by all that being a warrior meant. Had he so lost himself in the white world, in his hunger for the bright-haired woman, that the medicine vision he had fasted and prayed for had gone from him?

It must be done. Fighting for control, Jamie asked in a voice trembling with rage, "Where is he? The murderer of my mother must die."

"*Kyi . . . Kyi . . .*" Red Crow cried out. "*I-nit-si-wah,* kill him, kill him now!"

The moon was down, the night black and cold, when Jamie's horse gave out. Big Rib had gone from his lodge and from the camp, warned somehow long before Red Crow had revealed his name. Jamie had told Walsh he must go, and he'd followed the trail through the darkness of the prairie night, trusting his instincts as always. But the trail was cold. Big Rib might have seen him at the council and taken flight then. He was headed west, and Jamie would follow. This time he swore nothing would make him forget that he was a warrior with a vision from the Sun god, a Blackfoot warrior with a tradition of honor to uphold.

He would mete out justice to Big Rib and Good Young Man. Seething with emotion, Jamie swore by Natos, his Sun god, that he would dedicate himself to that end. When the summer Medicine Lodge was built, he would give of himself to Natos in the *Okan,* the Sun Dance, the Blackfoot's most powerful medicine.

❦ 14 ❧

After yet another confrontation with McLeod, Kate was certain she couldn't find the courage to defy him again. At any rate, she had already lost the battle. With a sigh, she wiped the sweat from her upper lip and glanced out the window. Dust kicked up by the hot summer wind blew across the parade ground. Leaves of the cottonwood trees stirred listlessly, the sky above them a deep, cloudless blue. Except for the two sentries, the fort seemed deserted. Everyone off duty would certainly be staying out of the day's heat.

In the center of the surgery floor stood the trunks she could no longer delay packing. By not packing them yesterday, she'd incurred McLeod's wrath, but she'd managed to avoid going with him to Fort Benton. He had gone with Inspectors Shurtliff and Winder, all planning to collect their wives, who would be arriving on the riverboat, escorted by the new doctor. With traveling time and a rest in Fort Benton, they would be away for more than two weeks.

"I told you we'd be leaving today," McLeod had shouted when Kate said she hadn't packed anything and wasn't ready to go. "We can't wait on you." His face had been purple with rage above his dark beard as he stamped out of the surgery.

Trembling from the encounter, Kate told herself the commissioner had more reason than she to be short-tempered. She understood his anger. All spring he'd waited impatiently for word of his wife's coming, only to be frustrated by one delay after another. He was certainly not going to let Kate's defiant behavior keep him from the long-awaited reunion with his wife.

Remembering that painful scene now, Kate slumped in her chair, eyes closed tightly as she tried to fight off the sense of despair that threatened to leave her helpless. Perhaps it had been foolhardy to defy McLeod this last time, knowing she could win nothing. The new doctor was on the way. She had to vacate the surgery—to go . . . somewhere. Where? The word echoed over and over in her mind. The raw, wild town of Fort Benton held no allure for her, nor the suggested destination of Helena. She was Canadian, born and bred. She would always be Canadian.

There was a knock at the door, and Kate looked up to see that David Cavendish was still bent on the mission McLeod had given him—to reason with stubborn Miss Maginnis and convince her to return to Toronto. She sighed resignedly.

"Kate," he said, shaking his head as if at a recalcitrant child, "this is foolishness. You know you can't stay here."

It flashed through her mind that she could if he would marry her. A hundred times he'd indicated his fondness for her, although he'd never committed himself in words. In the unpanicked, objective part of her mind, Kate knew that young men of David's class were expected to marry wealthy heiresses. She would be a fool to hope for that reprieve—and worse, she didn't love him.

"McLeod meant to pay your passage to Toronto, Kate. Both he and I want to see you safely back among your own people."

"I have no people there—or anywhere." Self-pity overwhelmed her and tears stung her eyes. "No home anywhere."

"You have friends—many friends, your father told me," he protested, taking her hand and stroking it soothingly.

So I would go and be a burden to the poor people who are my friends . . . at least until I could find employment. And employment as what? A nursemaid, companion to an aging invalid? The thoughts raced through her mind even while she knew her objections carried no weight. She would have to go.

"My father's here," she managed to mumble, hating herself for the self-pity, her mind still casting frantically about for a different solution.

"Your father is dead, my dear." David's voice was low and sympathetic. "You must go back to civilization and make the kind of life he'd have wished for you." Straightening, he smiled into her eyes. "I'll be taking the next detachment to Fort Benton and I'll see you safely on your way home then." Clasping her hand, he raised it to his lips and kissed the palm lingeringly. The caress was so unusual, Kate stared at him in shocked surprise as he continued. "I'll be in Toronto next spring on my way home to England, and I plan to spend some time there."

What had he really meant? Kate wondered when he had left her with the firm admonition to begin her packing. In speaking of Toronto, had he meant to court her there? That a lasting and legal relationship might be possible between them? Any woman, certainly one as alone as she, should be overjoyed at the possibility. But Kate felt only an overweening sadness, and her hand went involuntarily to stroke the softness of the cougar skin thrown over the back of her chair.

She hadn't seen Jamie all through the glorious spring he had promised her. Every time she walked among the lush, flowered meadows along the river, she thought of him and wondered how he fared in the Cypress Hills. Then Bagley mentioned he'd seen the half-breed when he reported to McLeod before joining the Blackfoot encampment. Wiser than I, Kate thought, he meant to sever the tenuous, and forbidden, connection between them.

In the depths of winter Stone Calf, Cutting Woman's only living child, had fallen ill, a sickness of the lungs white men called pneumonia. Medicine men came and danced, offering their best remedies. Cutting Woman called on all her skills, but nothing seemed to work. At last she prayed to Natos, the Sun god, vowing she would build the summer Medicine Lodge, the most sacred of all Blackfoot ceremonies, if only her son survived his illness.

The role of Medicine Woman was a sacred one, available only to an honored and virtuous wife. It was a sacrifice, too, for the woman and her husband must purchase costly medicine bundles. The Medicine Woman was responsible for the success of the entire ceremony. If anything went awry, it would bring disaster on all her people.

Now it was the season of the ripening of the sarvis berries. Stone Calf was well and happy. The great summer encampment of the Siksika people had come together on the plains to build the sacred Medicine Lodge, to offer prayers and songs to the Sun god and to perform the ultimate sacrifice of warriors, the *Okan,* the Sun Dance.

Jamie came from Crowfoot's lodge at the center of the camp and paused for a moment to survey the huge encampment stretching far across the prairie. Towering clouds marched across a deep blue sky, blown by the incessant prairie wind. They were rainless clouds and wouldn't interfere with the ceremony to come.

This was the third day of the four-day march toward the site chosen for the Medicine Lodge. Each day's march was a great dress parade with all the people clad in their finest clothes, riding their best horses, the warriors displaying their weapons and their painted buffalo-skin shields. Jamie would take part in the final ceremony, the Sun Dance, as he had vowed to the Sun god that night in the Cypress Hills.

Tonight word had come to him that his beloved half sister, Laughing Girl, was in labor with her first child. From the time he had come as a boy to live with Crowfoot's band, she had been a favorite of his. A group of children running at their games bumped into him and he smiled, recalling games with his small half sister, the toys he'd made for her.

Before a fine, painted lodge a courting couple stood embracing, wrapped in a blanket that indicated the girl's acceptance of her suitor. Jamie quickly looked away. He had been only eighteen when he courted Meadowlark and won her. It seemed a lifetime since he'd proudly brought his gift of horses to her father's lodge and been accepted. Their happiness had been short-lived. She died in childbirth. He had been wandering ever since.

The summer encampment was a time for such courting, for renewing of friendships, for feasting and trading, for games and races and councils. It was a happy time as well as one of deep religious significance to the people.

After his futile pursuit of Big Rib, he'd briefly reported to McLeod before joining the summer encampment. The commissioner had asked that he act as guide to Fort Benton, where McLeod imtended to meet his wife. He'd added, as if it were of little importance, "Miss Maginnis will be going with us on her way back to Toronto."

Jamie's heart had fallen at the words. Back to Toronto . . . a world away. It's best, he'd chastised himself, best for her and best that you forget her.

Soon she would be gone. He wouldn't see her again, and now he must turn all his thoughts to his Blackfoot duties. His vow to the Sun god would be renewed in the Sun Dance. Once again his medicine would be powerful and he would take revenge on the murderers of his mother as prescribed by Blackfoot tradition.

When Jamie explained his commitment to the Blackfoot summer encampment, the commissioner agreed that Jerry Potts could act as guide on this particular trip. A part of Jamie was relieved, knowing how harrowing the trip would have been for him . . . taking her away forever. But several days later, he'd laughed aloud with unexpected relief when he stopped by Baker's store and Conrad told him Kate had refused to accompany the commissioner to Fort Benton. She was still in the Northwest. He would see her again.

As he strolled through the bustling Blackfoot summer camp, Jamie could hear the distant shouts of men involved in racing their horses. Buffalo Runner sat before his lodge, smoking a medicine pipe. Knowing the man performed a ritual to the gods on behalf of his young wife, Jamie waited until he had finished.

"*Hai-yah-ho,*" he said and glanced anxiously toward

the lodge, where he could hear Laughing Girl's cries of pain. "How is it with my *ni-sisah*?"

"Gray Wolf, the medicine man, is with her," Buffalo Runner replied, "and my mother and sisters."

"Then all goes well?" Jamie asked, for the young man's face was twisted with worry.

"No!" Buffalo Runner cried out the word. "She is small and the child is large."

A chill ran down Jamie's spine, because Meadowlark had died trying to bear a child who came wrong. Sometimes the baby could be turned, but not that time. Sometimes there were medicines to widen the birth canal. He knew all this from his own loss, and from the wisdom of Cutting Woman.

But Cutting Woman was also the year's Medicine Woman. Just now she would be taking her nightly ritual sweat. She would be in isolation until after the ceremonies, fasting and praying. She could not leave, or she would destroy the ceremony and bring disaster on the people.

"Cutting Woman feared this, I think," Buffalo Runner said morosely and reached to feed the fire burning in front of the lodge. "She told my mother what must be done, but no one has Cutting Woman's skill."

From inside the lodge came the sounds of the medicine man chanting his prayers of healing and the jerky rhythm of his bone rattle. He would be dressed in the costume revealed to him in the vision that had made him a medicine man. Suddenly the chanting was drowned by the screams of Laughing Girl. Jamie jerked open the lodge flap and went in.

Dressed in his grotesque costume of a wolf skin, a sacred rattle in his hand, the medicine man paused and glared at the interruption. Laughing Girl lay on her pallet, knees bent, legs spread apart, the rawhide support belt all pregnant women wore laid aside. Her naked body gleamed with sweat and the flesh seemed to have drained from her face, so that there was only skin over the bones. Jamie drew in a horrified breath.

Water Bird, Buffalo Runner's mother, and one of his sisters held Laughing Girl's slack arms. Jamie squatted beside Water Bird. The woman's face was wet with tears.

"Have you done all Cutting Woman told you?" he demanded, ignoring the outraged medicine man. After a moment, the man began shaking his rattle and chanting again.

"I have tried all she said," Water Bird protested tearfully. With a racking sob, she covered her face, so that Jamie could scarcely hear the words "She will die."

"Follows the Eagle." The contraction had eased and Laughing Girl gazed up at him, weary eyes pleading. "Help me, my brother," she whispered through cracked and swollen lips.

"I'll bring help to you," he told her, reaching to smooth the disordered hair back from her face. "Be strong, ni-sisah, my little sister, until I come back."

Again the medicine man glared at him for interrupting, while Buffalo Runner's mother looked at him in disbelief verging on anger.

There was help, Jamie told himself as he hurried to saddle his horse. Laughing Girl must not follow Meadowlark to the Sand Hills. At Fort McLeod there was a white woman doctor with medicine the Blackfoot could not know. If Laughing Girl could be saved, Kate Maginnis would do it. He prayed she was still there.

The wind had died and the air inside the surgery was hot and still. Carefully sorting her father's medical instruments from those belonging to the Mounted Police,

Kate was again filled with sorrow for his death, her everlasting loss. She had decisions to make before McLeod's return. She couldn't live here when the new doctor arrived, and there was no place at the fort for her.

Yesterday she'd spoken candidly of her situation to Mr. Conrad at I. G. Baker's store. He was a kindly man who had taken an Indian wife, perhaps only for a season, as so often happened. To her surprise, he'd urged her to stay.

"McLeod is growing and when settlers move in, they'll need a doctor." Smoothing his whiskers, he gazed at her thoughtfully. "I could rent you the lean-to next door that I use as a storeroom if you want to hang out a shingle in McLeod." With a wave of his hand, he indicated the adjacent slant-roofed room attached to the side of the store.

"My father's shingle," she corrected him.

Conrad shrugged. "I understand you're a good doctor. Here on the frontier, that's what counts—not a piece of paper from some school back east."

Kate hesitated, thinking that there were only a few settlers as yet. She doubted any of the rough men and women inhabiting the town would seek the services of a woman doctor.

"I'm still thinking of installing a pharmacy," Conrad told her. "You could run it for me in addition to the medical practice."

A crowd of Blackfoot come to trade interrupted them. Kate left the store with Conrad's words called after her. "Think it over, Dr. Kate."

Since that conversation, she had vacillated, hating that she had to decide and hating the alternatives. Now she sat so lost in her internal debate that a knock at the door startled her. She turned, expecting to see a Mountie patient.

Jamie Campbell's tall figure was framed in her doorway and his grave expression made her draw a frightened breath. At the same time her heartbeat accelerated, as it always did in his presence.

"Dr. Kate," he began without preliminaries, "you've delivered babies?"

"Of course," she replied, puzzled by the question.

His tone was urgent. "My sister cannot bring the baby out. She's dying. Will you . . . can you . . . help her?"

Amazed that he would seek her aid, Kate said, "Tell me what's happening with her." The doctor in her took command. Even as she spoke, she reached beneath the table for the bag containing her father's maternity tools, unused these many months.

Jamie's description of Laughing Girl's condition made Kate's nerves tighten with apprehension. She had always heard how easily Indian women gave birth, barely pausing in their work, but from Jamie's anguished description, this young woman was in deep trouble.

"Bring me a horse," Kate commanded. "We'll have to hurry."

They rode through a cloudy darkness, a lopsided moon drifting in and out of the thin clouds. Jamie led her horse part of the way so they wouldn't be lost from each other. It was said among the Mounties that Jamie Campbell had a kind of second sight. It was as though he had truly flown with the eagle above this land, so that he knew every mile of it by heart, in daylight, in the darkness of night or in the midst of a blizzard.

The size of the encampment stunned Kate when she saw the many campfires from a distance. They rode straight through, ignoring barking dogs and curious stares from the few people still awake. She lost count of the number of lodges. Jamie had briefly explained that this was the Blackfoot summer encampment, a gathering of all the bands in the brief respite between the summer hunt and the beginning of the great fall hunt. Still, she hadn't guessed at a village of tepees that seemed to go on forever.

"Buffalo Runner!" Suddenly Jamie leaped from his horse to shake a man sleeping beside one of the lodges. The man groaned and sat up.

"We wait." Buffalo Runner groaned the bitter words. "My mother sent the medicine man away . . ." He bowed his head.

"Good!" Jamie declared. "I've brought the white doctor to help my sister." Ignoring Buffalo Runner's amazed expression, Jamie helped Kate dismount, quickly untying her bag from the saddle and urging her into the lodge.

Even the sweet grass smoldering on the low fire could not erase the stink of blood and sweat. Kate gazed in horror and pity at the naked girl who lay on a pallet, unmoving except for an occasional moan of pain. A gray haired woman sat beside her, bathing her drawn face with cool water. She stared in surprise at Kate. "*Kyi!*" The woman turned her questioning gaze to Jamie and spoke rapidly in Blackfoot.

"They can do no more." He choked on the words. "Now they wait for her to die."

"No!" Kate cried, and dropped to her knees at the foot of the pallet. Death was her enemy whether in a mansion or in a buffalo-skin lodge. She would fight death for this girl and for her child.

A quick examination left her fearful of the possibilities. The girl had not dilated sufficiently, probably would not because she was so small. And the child was turned so that its shoulder appeared in the birth canal. First turn the baby, Kate told herself, all her being concentrated now on what must be done. She glanced at the young woman's worn face and knew she dared not give her anything to kill the pain.

Laughing Girl screamed and writhed in agony as Kate slid her hand into the birth canal, searching for the top of the baby's head. Jamie and the gray-haired woman, Water Bird, seized Laughing Girl's arms and held her steady. At last Kate's searching fingers found the fuzzy head. She worked carefully, gently, to bring the head around and push the shoulder back inside. Finally it was done. With a sigh of relief, she looked up to see that Laughing Girl had fainted, and she met Jamie's fearful eyes. "Now we must bring the baby out," she told him with pretended confidence.

"*Kyi!*" Water Bird cried out in alarm when she saw Kate pick up the surgical scissors.

"Tell her it's all right," she said to Jamie. "I will just make room for the baby to come out."

Only partially convinced, the woman settled back to bathing the girl's face, watching Kate apprehensively.

Quickly, Kate completed the cuts for the episiotomy, remembering with a pang how her father had taught her this procedure. She blotted blood from the incisions and regretfully drew the forceps from her bag. Her father had never liked to use them, nor did she. Too often they brought a damaged child into the world. Tonight there was no alternative.

Laughing Girl was conscious now, tears seeping down her pale, drawn face. "Can she help me?" Kate asked the frightened older woman, forgetting the language barrier. "I need her to push."

"She will help," Jamie assured her, tenderly wiping away his sister's tears. "Tell us what to do."

It was agonizing . . . the girl's screams, punctuated by the woman's wailing and Jamie's urging his sister to try to push. Slowly, carefully, Kate fit the forceps to the baby's head and tugged. Exhausted as Laughing Girl was, Kate admired her bravery as she forced her worn-out body to push on Kate's command.

At last the head was free; then, in a great gush of blood and mucous, the baby came. Hurrying for fear the child had been in distress for too long, Kate cleared the mucous from its throat and blew her own breath into the tiny lungs until she was rewarded by a protesting cry.

After she had tied the cord, Kate handed the baby to Water Bird, who was weeping, muttering over and over, *"Ston-i-tap . . . ston-i-tap . . ."*

Laughing Girl had fainted again. "Bathe her face with cold water," Kate told Jamie and hurried to sew up the incisions while the girl was still unconscious.

The lodge of Buffalo Runner was crowded this morning, all his relatives there to celebrate the birth of a son. Laughing Girl slept and the infant slept on her breast, both worn out by the ordeal of birth. Everyone had to see, and to repeat the story of how the white woman doctor had cheated death this night.

Buffalo Runner greeted them with undisguised pride and offered the feast his sisters quickly made.

Exhausted herself, Kate sat outside the lodge, leaning against the willow backrest Jamie had brought for her. The sun rose in a cloudless sky of intense blue. Her skirt was dark with blood, her back ached and her hands still trembled from the effort of the forceps. But her heart sang with the joy only a successful healer knows.

Gratefully, she took the mug of coffee Jamie offered, knowing that the drink in itself was a tribute, so rare and valued was coffee on these plains.

Jamie stood above her, silent, studying her with a grave expression.

''What was it the old woman, Water Bird, said when I gave her the baby?'' she asked, smiling up at him. ''I don't think she really trusted me at first.''

The intensity of his gaze made the breath catch in her throat and her pulse race. ''*Ston-i-tap*,'' he said softly. ''Something wonderful . . . a miracle. You have made a miracle, Kate.''

❦ 15 ❧

Skin drums kept an eerie, hollow rhythm, accompanied by bone rattles and whistles. Voices chanted and shouted. The commotion startled Kate awake. At once she knew where she was and, to her amazement, she felt no apprehension. The religious ceremony Jamie had spoken of must have begun.

From the hot light pouring through the opening made by the raising of the lodge cover to let in cool air, she guessed she had nearly slept around the clock. She vaguely remembered Jamie coming last evening to bring her food.

Turning onto her back, Kate gazed up at a patch of blue sky seen through the smoke hole at the top of the lodge where the lodge poles came together. Yesterday she had been too tired to take much note of Crowfoot's lodge, where Jamie had brought her. The bed was Jamie's, she was certain. It had the scent of him, an odor like wind across sagebrush that she remembered vividly from the night of the blizzard.

A circle of stones in the center of the floor contained the fire pit, banked now. Around the walls hung an inner wall of tanned skins, brightly painted with figures that seemed to tell a story, and next to the wall lay the couches, or beds of the occupants. The larger couch opposite the door opening was obviously that of the chief. On either side two more beds lay against the wall, all divided by a device made of willow in the shape of an inverted V that seemed to be a storage place for the occupants' clothing. Cooking pots and provisions were neatly stacked in rawhide parfleches near the doorway. The floor was covered by rugs of buffalo skin, hair side up.

As her eyes surveyed the room, Kate was suddenly aware of the young man seated in the doorway as though guarding the entrance. Stone Calf, son of Cutting Woman and Crowfoot, born after the measles epidemic.

"This is Crowfoot's lodge," Jamie had told her when they had at last broken away from the grateful family of Laughing Girl and he had led her across the camp. "You can rest here," he continued, and grinned at the young man who suddenly appeared before them.

"This is Stone Calf," Jamie said, and Kate shook the eager boy's hand. "He will keep watch outside so you aren't disturbed. The *I-kun-uh-kah-tsi* are patrolling the camp. There will be no trouble.

"He doesn't talk except for a few words," Jamie went on as the boy stared silently at Kate, "and he understands only if you speak very loud. I've asked him to look after you. I think you can figure out the sign language he uses."

She had seen such children in her father's practice— the round moon face, the bright darting eyes—all with some damage to their wholeness. The boy might have been thirty or thirteen. Obviously he was fond of Jamie. After they spoke to each other in sign language, Stone Calf nodded and turned smiling, to Kate. With a sweep of his hand he showed her he would be guarding her at the door of his father's lodge.

A small, gray-haired woman with a weathered face appeared, waiting timidly until Jamie reached out to take her hand. "And this is Crowfoot's number two wife, Little Fox. She will look out for you, too."

Shocked by his words, Kate stared at the smiling woman as they shook hands. Sometime she must have been told that the Blackfoot practiced polygamy, but the reality of it staggered her.

When Little Fox went to build up her cooking fire in front of the lodge, Kate asked Jamie in dismay, "Crowfoot has two wives?"

"Four," was the offhanded answer. Then, seeing her expression, Jamie smiled and explained. "Little Fox was the wife of his brother who was killed in battle. The others are also widows of relatives." He gave her a searching look. "Warriors are often killed in battle or in the hunt. A woman cannot live without a hunter to bring food. Crowfoot is a wealthy chief. He can afford to take these women into his lodge."

He turned away then to speak to Little Fox, dismissing the fact of his uncle's polygamy as if it were nothing.

Kate stared at him in disbelief. What would be a moral outrage among her own people was accepted here as natural. How could she feel so drawn to this man who was part of a savage people, easily accepting their savage customs?

But when he led her into the lodge to show her where she would sleep and turned to go, she was filled with sudden panic. "Where are you going?" Kate asked, failing to keep the tremor from her voice. She was weak with fatigue, and the thought of being alone in this strange village where no one spoke her language was frightening.

"I'm part of the Sun Dance," Jamie answered somberly. "Tomorrow the Medicine Lodge will be built. I must fast and pray tonight and tomorrow. I've made a vow that can't be broken. Until the *Okan*, the Sun Dance, is ended, I can't leave here to take you back to Fort McLeod."

Their eyes met and held there in the dim light of the lodge. She understood he had made a commitment and that his honor bound him to it. Honor . . . the memory of his tenderness toward his suffering sister made her eyes sting. Wearily, she nodded. "I need to sleep now."

Fully awake in the hot afternoon, Kate sat up, holding the blanket to cover the drawers and chemise she had slept in. "Hello," she called to the silent boy who sat in the lodge opening, watching her. She wondered why Jamie had been so sure they could communicate.

Stone Calf stared at her in silence. With apprehension, Kate saw that her bloody gown had been taken away. "My clothes," she said to him, trying to indicate her meaning with gestures. He replied with signs seeming to ask if she wished to bathe. At the inviting thought of washing away the sweat and blood of the birthing struggle, Kate nodded vigorously. Perhaps one of the women had taken her gown to wash it and would bring it back soon.

Stone Calf led her to a secluded spot among the willows bordering the creek, then left her alone. Shedding the blanket she'd wrapped around her, Kate plunged in, drawers and all. It felt wonderful. The cool water swept away her fatigue. After she let her hair down and washed it, she clambered back up on the grassy bank. Quickly, she wrapped herself in the blanket once more.

Back at the lodge, Little Fox was busy hanging strips of meat to dry on a willow rack over a low fire. Inside the tepee, Kate saw that clothes had been laid out for her. Not her own cotton gown, but a Blackfoot dress of pale doeskin as soft as velvet. An intricate geometric pattern of beading outlined the neck; an ermine tail dangled from each shoulder. Short sleeves were trimmed with fringing, as was the hem of the skirt. Beneath the dress she found a pair of moccasins beaded on the toe in the three-pronged pattern she had been told represented the three tribes of the Blackfoot confederacy. There was no underwear.

Kate looked down at her soaking drawers and chemise, knowing they must be hung out to dry. It occurred to her that they would likely look strange beneath this native costume and that Blackfoot women probably did not wear underclothing. What had her father said? "When in Rome, do as the Romans do." She smiled, remembering, then wondered if he'd think his homily appropriate here, and if he'd extend the thought to polygamy.

She dressed quickly. The velvety leather clung luxuriously against her bare skin and the moccasins were as soft as bedroom slippers.

Her black leather medical bag was sitting next to the storage at the head of Jamie's bed. A bright blue calico shirt she had once seen him wear when the day was hot lay stuffed into the space, something rolled inside it. With a glance to make sure she was alone, Kate drew it out. Wrapped in the shirt were two well-thumbed books, the staples of the frontier: *The Collected Works of William Shakespeare* and the *Holy Bible, King James Version*. Since he had no permanent home and few possessions, these books must be valuable to him. With gentle fingers she stroked the worn leather covers, picturing Jamie's dark head bent over the pages, by firelight or alone on some sunlit hillside. Hands trembling, she replaced the books. Each new discovery about this man deepened the sense of kinship she felt toward him. Sighing, Kate took up her medical bag and went outside to find Stone Calf.

By imitating a mother holding a baby, she was able to tell him she wanted to see Laughing Girl. They set off beneath a glorious summer sky dotted with white cotton clouds drifting from the west. He led her through the jungle of skin lodges where Kate knew she'd have been lost in a minute. In front of most of the lodges there were women busy cooking or working skins. Many of them called greetings to her, and she could only wave back.

At the lodge of Buffalo Runner, she was greeted by enthusiastic cries of welcome and urged into the tepee. The new mother was nursing her child and smiled tiredly at Kate. Water Bird, the mother-in-law, hurried to bring Kate a wooden bowl of stewed meat. Suddenly aware that she was famished, Kate took the offered backrest and sat down to eat. When Water Bird realized Kate had no knife to eat with, she drew her own from her belt and held it out. Not sure where the knife might have been last, Kate took it gingerly. She dared not wipe it off for fear of insulting the giver. The buffalo meat had been cooked with wild onions, which gave it some flavor, for the Blackfoot rarely used salt. But Kate was hungry enough to eat it all and forget her fears about the knife.

On examining Laughing Girl, Kate was filled with pride at the work she'd done by firelight in the most primitive of conditions. Before she returned to Fort McLeod, she would remove the stitches, and Laughing Girl would be well and whole again.

More visitors came and went, each of the women speaking to Kate respectfully, admiration in their dark eyes. They seemed to share Water Bird's opinion. The white woman doctor had made a miracle.

Kate could only smile in response to their unknown words and shake the offered hands. All the time her eyes stung with unshed tears. Here in this primitive place, among a savage people, she was what she'd always sought to be—a doctor.

A sudden uproar of shouts and singing came from the distance. Remembering the word Jamie had used, Kate asked, "*Okan?*"

"*Okan!*" Water Bird stood, nodding vigorously. "*Okan!*" She seized Stone Calf's shoulder where the boy still sat eating, her gestures indicating that he should take Kate to the *Okan* at once.

The great circle of the encampment stretched across the grassy prairie as far as Kate could see. Stone Calf trudged ahead of her, past running children, barking dogs, groups of women gossiping at cooking fires. Near the edge of the camp, they came to the place chosen for the Medicine Lodge Jamie had told her about. Stone Calf placed a restraining hand on her arm and indicated they must go no closer.

A tall tree trunk of peeled cottonwood, forked at the top, lay in the center. All around it, men in brilliant costumes were busy erecting the lodge itself, what would be a roof resting on pole stringers connected to smaller cottonwood trunks set in a rough circle around the center.

Ignoring the workers, a group of drummers took their place beside the Sun Medicine Lodge. Their rawhide drums gave forth a deep, mellow tone in perfect rhythm. Dancers appeared, each man costumed more elaborately than the last. Their deerskin tunics and leggings were brilliant with beading, hung with ermine tails and feathers, painted with war signs. As they began their jerky, strangely graceful dance, singing what seemed to Kate a mournful chant, she wished desperately for an interpreter to tell her the meaning of the ceremony.

A crowd of spectators had gathered around the lodge when the drumming slowly ceased and the dancers moved aside. An air of expectancy emanated from the crowd, which suddenly fell into respectful silence.

"The Medicine Lodge Woman comes," said a voice at Kate's elbow.

Kate was so relieved to find Jamie standing beside her, she seized his arm and held on fiercely. He wore only a breechclout and moccasins, his bare brown chest gleaming with sweat in the late-afternoon sun. Around his neck hung a necklace of blue beads, and on each wrist there was a bracelet of beading and fur. The sight of that muscular, half-nude body sent a flush of heat through Kate, so intense it nearly unnerved her. Deliberately, she looked away.

He bent to speak softly near her ear. "It's time for the Bringing Forward of the Tongues. Cutting Woman has organized the Medicine Lodge. All summer she collected the buffalo bull tongues and dried them for this ceremony. For four days she has fasted and prayed. Now she completes the cycle."

Kate stared as Cutting Woman moved slowly toward the Medicine Lodge, her head bowed. She wore an elaborate elk-skin dress and robe, with a fantastic headdress of eagle feathers arranged like a crown, weasel tails dangling from the headband. "She brings the sacred root digger," Jamie was saying, "brought to the Siksika by the bride of Morning Star. Her husband assists with her duties." And following the Medicine Woman was Crowfoot, his face and body painted black except for the half-moon device on his chest. Chanting prayers as they went, the party finally came to a halt at the western opening of the Sun Lodge.

The women who assisted the Medicine Woman placed

the parfleches they carried on the ground beside Cutting Woman. Slowly, and in perfect order, women, children and men came to her bearing gifts. Each petitioner was prayed for and painted with black on face and wrist.

"They ask the blessings of the holy ones." Jamie spoke softly beside Kate. She found herself choked with emotion, caught up in the reverence with which this pagan ritual was being enacted.

Still chanting prayers, Cutting Woman reached into the parfleche at her side and took out a dried buffalo tongue. She faced the sun, now low in the western sky, and chanted a prayer with such power, it made Kate tremble to listen. Taking her knife from her belt, Cutting Woman cut off a piece of the tongue and held it toward the sun. Then she ate a bit of the meat and buried the rest in the dirt at her feet.

"An offering to the Sun god, and an offering to Ground Man," Jamie said.

With the help of her women, Cutting Woman sliced all the dried tongues. A piece was given to each of the spectators, who came reverently forward. Kate's throat tightened as she watched this solemn and sacred act so like Holy Communion.

"Now they raise the center pole," Jamie told her as four groups of men came forward, singing to the rhythm of the drums as they advanced. With the stout poles they carried, they pried the heavy center pole upward until it dropped into the hole dug for it and stood upright. A great sigh swept through the crowd.

Jamie smiled down at Kate. "It is well. If the pole fell, Cutting Woman would be disgraced."

The men began pounding dirt around the center pole as Cutting Woman was led away by her assistants.

"Now she will break her fast," Jamie said, "but she must stay in the Medicine Woman's lodge for four more days. Crowfoot goes to take a sweat . . .'' He pointed to the four small rounded huts of woven willows. There were two on either side of the half-finished Medicine Lodge, each one adorned with a painted buffalo skull. ''Then his part of the ceremony is finished.''

People were drifting away now as the long summer dusk fell over the prairie. There would be feasting and smoking in the lodges. Stone Calf signed to Jamie, who shook his head. Answering in sign, Jamie then turned to Kate. ''I won't return to the lodge with you, but Stone Calf will watch over you again.''

Kate longed to know more about this ceremony that had touched her deeply in some part of her that surely remained as primitive as the Blackfoot. There were so many questions she wanted to ask. Stone Calf was not a very satisfactory companion. ''Why won't you come?'' she demanded.

''I must go to the sweat lodge,'' he replied. ''I must fast and pray again until I fulfill my vow to the Sun god.''

Seeing her distress, Jamie took her hand. ''You will be safe in Crowfoot's lodge.''

They stood a little apart, surrounded by people, yet somehow only the two of them existed. His dark eyes held hers. The gleam of his naked chest, the musky male scent of him, aroused in her a fever unlike anything she'd ever known. Kate was drawn to him as if by an irresistible force. A kind of singing ran along her veins . . . and yet she was afraid. Waiting . . . waiting . . . for what she didn't know.

With an effort, Jamie tore his eyes away from hers. Silent, he stared fixedly at the Medicine Lodge, now receiving the final touches—a leafy roof of cottonwood branches.

Kate studied his face. He was preoccupied, already

gone from her to the sacred ceremonies to come. A frisson of fear went down her spine. What did it mean to take part in the *Okan*? Before she could ask, Jamie touched her shoulder reassuringly and was gone. She stared after him, trembling, suddenly lost without her only connection to this world that was so different from her own, and yet a world in which she felt oddly at home.

❧ 16 ❧

"Night Singers come tonight," Laughing Girl had said in her stumbling English. "Do not be afraid." She had been unable to explain further, merely piquing Kate's curiosity.

Now a full moon rode high in the night sky, flooding the encampment with silvery light. Kate stood before Crowfoot's lodge to watch the mysterious Night Singers pass by, for she had awakened to the distant singing.

A young warrior in beaded leggings and a feathered necklace was riding past in what Kate guessed was another part of the seemingly endless ceremonies of the Medicine Lodge. The young man's wife rode in front of him on the horse, wearing her husband's full-feathered war bonnet. Bells on their wrists and ankles jingled a soft accompaniment to the melancholy air they sang. At once joyful and sad, the music touched something inside Kate so that her eyes stung with tears even as she smiled and waved to the passing couple.

They seemed not to see her and rode on, the melody fading in the distance. Kate turned to find Stone Calf watching beside her and wished with all her being that Jamie were there to share the moment. Even more she wished he had time to explain to her all the mysterious ceremonies taking place. Tomorrow he was to be part of his own ritual. Then, surely, he would answer all her questions.

Several times in the night she was awakened by the passing of singers and the jingling of their bells. The sound was somehow reassuring, so that she slept again at once.

Morning dawned clear and hot. In the distance the sound of drums and chanting continued, sometimes punctuated by shouts and war whoops. Little Fox, Crowfoot's number two wife, had risen early to cook but Kate ate scantily, knowing that when she went to check on Laughing Girl, Water Bird would expect her to eat there, too.

Water Bird was waiting, sitting in front of the lodge, holding the baby. She sang a soft, tuneless lullaby, gazing lovingly into the tiny face.

"Eat," she said, standing up as soon as she saw Kate and Stone Calf. Always hungry, Stone Calf nodded enthusiastically. While Water Bird dished up their buffalo meat from the cooking pot, Kate examined the baby. She saw with relief that his misshapen head was returning to normal and the bruises left by the forceps were fading. His eyes were bright and alert as he stared at her for a long moment before he began to wail.

"He'll be all right," she said aloud, reassuring herself as much as his worried grandmother. She handed him to Water Bird and took the offered food. Again the meat was saltless, almost tasteless, and Kate ate sparingly.

Buffalo Runner came out of the lodge dressed in all his finery, carrying his decorated weapons. Laughing Girl followed with his eagle-feather headdress. She was pale and moved gingerly. Obviously performing an important wifely duty, she fit the headdress on her husband's head, drawing the band tight and carefully arranging the weasel tails that hung from the beaded headband. He turned to her as though for approval, and she gazed at him with fond pride just as another warrior rode up, leading Buffalo Runner's horse.

"He dances," Laughing Girl informed Kate when the men rode away. Pride in her young husband filled her eyes as she added, "Warrior . . . count coups."

Kate smiled and nodded, though she had no idea what "count coups" meant. When she was with Jamie again, she would ask for an explanation. In the meantime, she would try to learn some Blackfoot. In school she had been very good at languages—Latin in grade school, German at Normal School and French simply because of her father's many French-speaking patients.

While she examined her own patient, Kate wondered if perhaps the pad of moss Laughing Girl wore had a healing quality, for the incisions were knitting quickly. "Good, very good," she told her when she had finished. Unexpectedly, Laughing Girl grabbed Kate's hand and held it affectionately to her cheek. Misty-eyed at that gesture, Kate emerged from the lodge to find Stone Calf jumping up and down with excitement.

He held out a hand to her, at the same time signing urgently to Laughing Girl. "*Okan*," she said to Kate. "He take you to the *Okan*."

Stone Calf set such a pace, Kate was breathless when they arrived at the Medicine Lodge. Buffalo Runner was there with a group of warriors on painted and decorated horses, waiting at one side, watching the performance. A warrior in ceremonial dress stood before the fire, acting out a story with war whoops and chanting. It seemed to be a story of horses as he imitated riding; then he cast a stick on the fire. Again he told of a battle, acting out his part in the fight and casting another stick on the flames. Counting coups, Kate thought; that's what it means. He's telling of his exploits and counting them for his audience. At last he seemed to have finished, and there were shouts of approval all around.

An expectant hush fell over the crowd, which had grown since Kate's arrival. Stone Calf took her arm and led her through the crush of spectators until they were inside the Medicine Lodge itself. In the dim light filtering through the roof of leafy cottonwood branches, she could see a line of people standing before the medicine man's willow booth at the far side of the lodge, waiting for his prayers and the sacred paint. Like Catholics at the confessional, she thought, amazed at the diversity and similarity of humankind.

A shocked gasp broke from her lips and her heart seemed to stop when her gaze found Jamie. Three aging men led him to the north side of the lodge and spread a blanket for him. He wore only a breechclout, his body painted white with black dots on legs and arms and cheeks. A crescent-moon symbol decorated his forehead beneath a wreath of sagebrush. Garlands of sage were tied around his ankles and wrists. He looked so completely the savage, she wanted to cry out in protest.

When Jamie lay on his back on the blanket, the three old men knelt beside him, chanting to the steady beating of the skin drums. Two held his shoulders pressed to the blankets. The other drew his knife, offered it to the sun, then made two small incisions on either side of Jamie's chest just above the breast. Jamie gave one grunt of pain and was silent even as blood poured from his wounds.

A strangled sound came from Kate's throat. It took all her strength to stand still and watch this primitive torture Jamie had chosen for himself. Nothing he had told her had prepared her for the sheer savagery of the ritual. She wanted to cry out, to stop them from hurting him. Involuntarily, she leaned toward him and felt Stone Calf's hand restraining her.

The old men now inserted a short willow skewer through the incisions on each breast. Kate could see Jamie's mouth tighten and his eyes squeeze shut as the blood flowed down his chest, brilliant red against the white paint.

Rawhide ropes attached to the center post of the lodge were brought out and tied to the skewers in Jamie's chest, first on the right side, then on the left. One of the old men grabbed the ropes, jerked them hard and tight, then called out an order to Jamie. Slowly and deliberately, he rose, and Kate felt tension gather in her, fearing what was to come.

Jamie walked to the center pole, face lifted to the sky, chanting as he went. Then he walked slowly backward until the ropes were taut. Leaning back against the ropes until he seemed suspended only by the skewers in his chest, Jamie began a swaying dance, chanting in a hoarse voice. Tears of pain smeared his painted face as he moved to the inexorable rhythm of the drummers. Blood flowed from his wounds, down his chest onto his white-painted legs. Yet he never faltered in the swaying, surging dance, his body supported by the rawhide ropes.

The awful scene, the agonizing dance that seemed unending, filled Kate with such horror that she turned sick and dizzy, reaching out to Stone Calf for support. A scream rose in her throat and Stone Calf's hand clamped across her mouth, strangling her cry. The world turned dark and she was falling . . . falling.

With slowly returning consciousness, Kate became aware of the increasing intensity of the drumming, of voices calling approval and encouragement to the tortured dancer.

He will die of it, was her first thought as she struggled to sit up with Stone Calf's help. As her vision cleared, she realized that no one was paying her the slightest heed. All attention was centered on this test of a warrior's vows.

"Stop!" She croaked the word in a desperate voice. Again Stone Calf's hand covered her mouth, his expression disapproving. She had no idea how long she'd been unconscious; it seemed like hours. "How long?" she tried to ask and remembered there was no one to tell her. The answer was there in the lowering sun beyond the Medicine Lodge entrance.

"Jamie," she murmured as Stone Calf reluctantly removed his hand from her mouth and helped her to her feet.

Sick with fear for him, she saw that Jamie still danced, his movements slower now in spite of the increased tempo of the drums. From the west toward the lodge doorway and back again he moved, his body painted with blood.

"It is a religious ceremony," he had told her. "I made a vow and I must fulfill it." A religious ceremony . . .

Closing her eyes, Kate recounted to herself the Catholic saints of her childhood who had suffered so, even practiced self-flagellation. Her mother had been devout, but after her death the Church was no longer part of Kate's young life. Thomas Maginnis's agnosticism was unremitting and Kate had been his apt pupil. Now she saw a kind of repetition of the martyr stories of her childhood, and thought it was true . . . there was nothing new under the sun.

She could watch that agonized face no longer and closed her eyes against it. But when Jamie cried out, she opened her eyes to see that at last the skewer on the left side of his chest had torn from his flesh. The rawhide rope fell slack; fresh blood flowed down his body. He faltered for only a moment. Kate heard murmurs of approval all around as he danced toward the doorway, swaying and surging, then back again. The drums went on endlessly.

Just when it seemed to Kate that the torture would never end, that surely Jamie could bear no more, the right skewer broke loose. With an anguished cry, Jamie fell to the ground and was still.

All her instincts bade her go to him, and in that instant Kate knew she loved Jamie Campbell with a love that transcended worlds. As though sensing her need to be at Jamie's side, Stone Calf held her arm in a bruising grip.

The three old men, chanting songs of praise, rushed to Jamie. One of them trimmed the loose flesh from his wounds and handed the pieces to him. Another cut the wreaths of sagebrush from his head and ankles and placed them in his hand. Carefully, as though each movement was excruciating, Jamie walked to the center post of the lodge, which was already hung thick with offerings from other warriors. There he offered the flesh and the sage to the sun in a now familiar gesture. Turning, he picked up his blanket and went out of the Medicine Lodge at the same slow pace.

Stone Calf's grip relaxed, for now Buffalo Runner came before the audience to recite his war stories and count coups. Without a thought, Kate shoved Stone Calf away and ran from the lodge.

Jamie made a lonely figure against the lowering sun. Anguish filled Kate's heart at the sight of him stumbling through the sagebrush toward the horse herd. When he staggered and fell, she cried out and ran to him. Before she reached his side, Jamie had struggled upright and continued his dogged way toward his horse.

"Jamie!" Kate seized his arm. "Oh, God—Jamie!" The agonized words burst from her as his glazed eyes met hers. Sweat and tears stained the grotesquely painted face. Great streaks of blood had turned his white body paint pink. He was exhausted and in pain. All Kate wanted was to take him in her arms and soothe his wounds.

"Come to Crowfoot's lodge with me," she begged. "I'll take care of you." For an endless moment he stared blankly at her. With a stab of pain, she sensed that he had gone away from her, just as he had the other night. At that moment he was all Blackfoot; no white blood flowed in his veins.

Through a sick haze of pain and exhaustion, Jamie stared down at Kate's pleading face. It passed through his weary mind how pleasant it would be to lie in her comforting arms, where she would ease his agonies and bring him rest. "*Kyi!*" he croaked from a dry, aching throat, bringing his inner self to attention. Because of this white woman, he had failed in his Blackfoot duty to revenge Pretty Bird's murder; because of her, he had lost his medicine. Now he had regained his power in the most difficult ritual of a Blackfoot warrior. He could not let her lead him from the Blackfoot way again.

"I will fast and pray alone tonight." Jamie's voice was firm even as the world spun around him. With a supreme effort, he turned away from her. "Tomorrow I will return to Crowfoot's lodge."

Golden light stained the eastern sky. Little Fox and Stone Calf still slept. Crowfoot had come in the evening and gone again to the Medicine Woman's lodge, where Cutting Woman would remain until the ceremonies were ended. As the sun rose above the distant horizon, Kate sat before the door of the lodge, a blanket from Jamie's bed around her shoulders against the chill of early morning. She had slept little, and the Night Singers' songs had seemed so mournful she could scarcely bear their passing. Now she could only wait. Jamie had said he would return and she had watched him go with fear in her heart, even though she understood that he must do what the ritual demanded.

At the soft sound of a slow-moving horse approaching, Kate jumped anxiously to her feet. The sight of Jamie slumped on the horse's back, chin on his chest, brought a cry from her throat. Taking the reins from his inert hand, she cried out again as he slid from the horse's back and lay unconscious on the ground.

Awakened by Kate's cries, Stone Calf and Little Fox hurried from the lodge and bent over Jamie, Little Fox chattering excitedly. Stone Calf calmly helped Kate carry Jamie into the lodge and place him on his bed.

Kneeling beside him, Kate gazed with horrified pity on the drawn face of the man she loved. His lips were cracked and swollen from the long fast. The incisions on his chest looked swollen, too, as though infected. A hand on his forehead confirmed her fear that he had a fever.

"Water," she shouted to Stone Calf, wondering if the boy would understand. In a moment he set a buffalo-skin pail of water beside her. Working quickly, Kate tore a strip from her discarded petticoat, dipped it in the cool water and carefully washed Jamie's haggard face. Slowly, he revived, his eyelids fluttering open. Kate lifted his head and held a cup of water to his lips. "You must drink, Jamie," she said. He nodded vaguely, sucking at the water that dribbled down his chin. "Not too much at a time," Kate cautioned and set the cup aside.

She saw that Little Fox had kindled the fire inside the lodge. From the pot she'd set on the flames came the pungent odor of sage. A twist of sweet grass smoldered on the coals. Kate sensed the woman meant to help in her own way.

With gentle hands, Kate continued to wash away the smeared blood and paint, carefully cleaning the scabs that had formed on his wounds. His breechclout of soft tanned deerskin was filthy with blood and dirt, stained with black-and-white paint. After a moment's hesitation, Kate stripped it from him, quickly covering his groin with a blanket. You are a doctor, she scolded herself, her whole body aflame from that brief glimpse of his maleness.

After her washing, Jamie's incisions were open and seeping blood. Frowning, Kate thought for a moment, then reached for her father's black bag. In the bottom was a pint bottle of whiskey he always carried for medicinal purposes. She had to clean those wounds. Setting her lips determinedly, Kate poured whiskey into each of Jamie's incisions. His shout of pain shook her. She took his face in her hands, terrified that she might have hurt him beyond repair. Jamie's eyes were shut tight, his mouth a thin, agonized line, his chest heaving as he gasped for air. After a moment he stilled, opened his eyes and waved away Little Fox, who was at Kate's shoulder, scolding vehemently.

Again and again Kate bathed his burning body, fed him water a little at a time and tried not to let it hurt that he seemed scarcely aware of her. Little Fox insisted the sage water be used to bathe Jamie. When it had cooled, Kate obeyed. Perhaps it had some healing property she was unaware of.

"*Hai-yah-ho.*" Kate saw, with relief, that the speaker was Crowfoot, still in full regalia. He crossed the lodge to look down intently at Jamie's inert figure. "*Mut-siks*," he muttered approvingly. Again Kate wished for knowledge of the language, but from his tone she guessed that Crowfoot had expressed pride in his adopted son.

Once more Crowfoot spoke in his own language, holding out to Kate a small doeskin bag she instantly recognized as one of those carried by Cutting Woman back at Fort McLeod. Opening the drawstring, Kate saw that the bag contained a strong-smelling herb. With eloquent gestures, Crowfoot showed her she must make a poultice of the herb for Jamie's wounds.

Nodding her understanding, Kate turned to Little Fox, who was already offering her a mixing pot. Busy blending the herb with warmed water, Kate scarcely noticed Crowfoot's departure. She applied the herb to Jamie's wounds, binding the poultice in place with another strip of her diminishing petticoat. Then she bathed his heated body with the cool, clean-scented sage water.

People came and went throughout the day, but Kate was scarcely aware of them. With the approach of evening, Jamie's fever diminished and he fell into a profound slumber. A healing sleep, Kate told herself wearily as she rose to go out of the lodge and take the food Little Fox urged on her.

Crowfoot was fortunate in his wives, Kate thought, smiling her thanks to the hovering woman. Cutting Woman was an honored medicine woman. Little Fox had been at Kate's side all during the day, seeming to know what was needed for Jamie—water or thin broth from the day's stew. And surely the women were lucky to be cared for by a chief and a great hunter, not struggling on their own as they would have been in the white world. That last thought brought a twinge of dismay as

Kate wondered at her growing acceptance of savage customs that should have been unacceptable.

Stone Calf had brought a clean breechclout, giving Kate a sly grin as he slipped it over Jamie's hips. Covering her patient again, Kate stroked his forehead, flooded with relief that the fever had abated. Now she feared an infection in the wounds. If the whiskey had cleaned those wounds, which the old men had neatly trimmed, and if Cutting Woman's herb was effective . . . if . . . She knew she could do nothing now but wait. Sitting beside Jamie's bed, Kate offered a prayer to her own God for the life of this man she had come to love.

First light slanted through the open flap of the lodge and Kate stirred awake, her legs cramped from sitting beside Jamie's low bed. Dimly she realized she'd fallen asleep there, her head pillowed near Jamie's shoulder.

A hand rested softly on her head, and Kate looked up into the warm, dark eyes of Jamie Campbell. There was no need for words in what passed between them. Kate leaned toward him, his big hand cradling her head, and touched her lips gently to his. Jamie sighed beneath her kiss and with his other hand drew her closer until their mouths melded and her tongue caught the taste of sage and blood.

Slowly, reluctantly, her heart pounding so she could scarcely breathe, Kate let him release her from that all-consuming kiss.

"*Nat-o-ye,*" Jamie whispered, lifting her loose, disordered hair in his fingers, so that it gleamed red-gold in the shaft of morning sun. "You have brought down the sun."

17

"Hear, O Sun!" Crowfoot stood at the entrance to the Medicine Lodge, his eagle-feather headdress ruffling in the breezes. Like golden fire, the sun stood just above the western horizon in a cloudless sky.

It was the fourth and final day of the *Okan*, the Sun Dance. Everyone had been prayed for, everyone had made his or her present to the Sun god, warriors had swung from the center post to prove their vows, the sacred tongues had all been consumed. Now the ceremony ended with the farewell speech of the *Ni-Nah*, Crowfoot, chief of the Siksika.

"Hear, O Sun!" he cried again, lifting his arms in supplication. "May this people go safely while traveling afar. May they find plenty buffalo. May we all live long and be friends. May we meet and be happy together again."

Jamie interpreted the words for Kate in a low, reverent voice. On the day after he was tortured in the *Okan*, Jamie had stayed in the lodge, submitting without question to Kate's ministering. He slept a great deal, awakening to follow her movements with eyes that told more than words could ever convey. In the evening she sponged his body with the fragrant sage water and straightened his bed. When she eased his sore body back onto the blankets, Jamie gently trailed his fingers down her bare upper arm. His touch was as soft as thistledown, as hot as fire. Such a rush of joy poured through Kate that she thought she would melt away. Their eyes met and she drew an aching breath, for that rugged face was totally transformed by tenderness, the black eyes glowing with warmth. ''Katie,'' he had said, and her name became a love word. Time hung suspended as that meeting of eyes seemed to join their souls. Then Little Fox bustled in with the fresh sage she had gathered. With a sigh, Kate turned to give Jamie the valerian tea she had made, and he was soon sleeping.

This morning he'd risen with the others and gone to the creek to bathe. When she changed the poultice on his wounds she knew he was in pain, but he refused to wince. The rest of the day had been taken up with those who came to consult the white doctor, including a small boy with a broken arm, the result of racing a pony in imitation of his elders.

Despite Kate's misgivings, Jamie had insisted on joining these final ceremonies of the Medicine Lodge. Now it was ending . . . that terrible, savage, heart-touching, incredible ceremony. Crowfoot was ending it with his great booming voice. ''Joy in your hearts, my people, no troubles, many buffalo. What I speak with my mouth, I feel in my heart. Farewell!''

After a long moment of profound silence, everyone began talking at once. People drifted out from beneath the wilted roof of the Medicine Lodge, pausing here and there to visit.

Without speaking, Kate and Jamie walked slowly back toward Crowfoot's lodge. Along the way, finely dressed warriors stood before their lodges, shouting out invitations to feast and smoke with them, naming the guests.

The lodge was deserted. "They've all been invited to a feast," Jamie informed her. He sat down on his bed with an effort. The sides of the lodge had been lifted and a cool evening breeze poured through. For the first time that day, Jamie looked directly at Kate.

"I was told how you fainted when I danced," he said, adding sternly, "Stone Calf should not have taken you there."

"I was afraid you would die." Kate couldn't keep the tremor from her voice.

"No one dies," Jamie told her. He paused and frowned as though searching for the right words. "What I did was a religious offering to Natos, the Sun god, the fulfillment of a vow I made . . . a sacred promise. The man who danced before me gave thanks to the Sun god for sparing his sick son. He had made a vow, too."

The intensity of his voice, the solemn expression on his face, told Kate how deep the emotional meaning of the ceremony was for Jamie. She could never tell him how it had both fascinated and horrified her. Even though she was aware she might be intruding on his privacy, she had to ask, "Why did you do it?"

He was silent for so long, she thought he had refused to answer, his thoughtful face turned away from her. At last he gave her a wry look and shook his head. "How can I explain to one who isn't Blackfoot?"

"I will listen," she replied quietly. The sudden warmth that leaped in Jamie's eyes quickened her heartbeat. Kate sat perfectly still against her willow backrest, afraid to break the moment.

"The Blackfoot religion is very complicated and makes no sense to white men. But it's important to us to observe the ceremonies at the proper times. And it gives the people a code of honor that rules the tribe.'' He fell silent, groping for words, and Kate wondered if he could bring himself to speak of his own honor.

''I had been among the white men too long,'' Jamie said and felt his heart squeeze in pain. How could he tell this beautiful, unattainable woman that it was his desire for her, his need to be near her, that had led him from the Blackfoot way? It hadn't been her fault, only his. ''I had forgotten my Blackfoot duty.''

Slowly, painfully, he related to her the story of his mother's murder. Kate gazed at him wide-eyed with horror as he spoke, and her face grew pale. ''It's a matter of honor,'' he finished. ''The murder of one's relatives must be revenged.''

''Revenged how?'' she asked in a choked voice.

The truth could not be told, Jamie thought. He hadn't prepared her for the Sun Dance. If she had been so deeply affected then, she could never accept the idea of Blackfoot justice—a life for a life.

''I vowed to the Sun god I would swing in the Medicine Lodge if my medicine was renewed.'' He had evaded her question and spoke quickly. ''After the Sun Dance, in the night when I fasted and prayed, the old vision came to me . . . the eagle . . . and I knew my prayers were answered.''

Her gray eyes were enormous, swimming with unshed tears. A man could drown in those eyes, and Jamie's heart contracted painfully, for the yearning that tormented him was reflected there in her lovely face.

It cannot be, he told himself angrily, and forced himself to look away.

Cutting Woman moved slowly along the creek bank, the morning wind stirring her long black hair and catching at the fringes of her gown. Watching in fascination, Kate followed. So dignified and regal was the medicine woman, yet now she was like a young girl on an outing, avid in her collecting of the herbs she'd promised to show Kate. She was a teacher, as Jamie had said before they left this morning. It was the first thing Cutting Woman had asked when she returned to the lodge last night: "Does the white woman doctor still wish to learn Blackfoot medicine?"

Kate did, and she was glad to be out in open country, her mind occupied with new things. The nightmare had returned last night as she lay alone in the small sleeping lodge Little Fox had erected for her. Screams of terror, caught in her throat, awakened her in the quiet darkness. Bathed in sweat, Kate hugged herself, relieved that it was only a dream, and tried to force the ugly images back into forgetfulness: her mother's limp figure, trampled and bleeding; the gleaming flash of a knife, and a man's throat became a gaping wound where the red flood of his life poured forth. She closed her eyes tightly, rejecting the awful memories.

It was Jamie's story of his mother's murder that had brought it all back, Kate knew. With trembling hands she stroked the cougar skin, wanting it to be Jamie lying there, his arms ready to comfort her. He had seen horror just as she had. He would understand when she told him her own story.

As she burrowed into her blankets, seeking sleep once more, Kate remembered his use of the word "revenge." What did that mean? She knew only that every word, every look, drew them closer in heart and mind.

Here in the bright prairie morning, the nightmare faded, and there was only the happiness of now.

Soon, Jamie had said, Crowfoot's clan would be moving on, searching for buffalo to begin the fall hunt. Some of the bands had gone already amid a cacophony of shouting men, crying children, barking dogs, travois grating along behind the horses. The medicine woman's family would be the last to leave the summer encampment. Jamie would take Kate back to Fort McLeod. Something wonderful would be ended.

Ahead of her now, Cutting Woman bent to pick a small green plant from the creek bank. Holding the twig up like a trophy, she turned to Kate.

"Mint," Kate said, and reached to pick some for her own collecting bag. Cutting Woman waited expectantly.

Kate sniffed the pleasant odor of the mint she'd picked and dropped it into the bag Cutting Woman had provided. "For the stomach," she told her waiting teacher, and rubbed her own stomach to demonstrate.

Cutting Woman laughed and repeated the word "stomach." Her enthusiasm was infectious. Unaccountably, Kate thought, She's as good a teacher as my father. For a moment her eyes stung; then Cutting Woman pounced on another plant and held it out to Kate.

"Wild ginger," Kate said, identifying it and wondering how to explain that her people used it for menstrual pain. When she rubbed a hand across her lower abdomen, Cutting Woman's laughter was unrestrained.

"Woman pain," Jamie's aunt said, nodding.

Laughing, Kate nodded, too. It was ironic that she had yearned to learn medicine in faraway Philadelphia; now she was learning a very different kind of medicine at the side of a wise Blackfoot woman in the wilds of Canada.

They strolled companionably along the creek bank beneath a gloriously blue sky. A horned lark sang somewhere so high in the air it was entirely out of sight, floating down at last only to flee upward in a burst of melody.

I am happy, Kate thought in sudden wonder, and I

am free. I have made a delightful friend in this woman. I love a man—and her happiness was stilled at the thought of Jamie. All the emotion that blazed between them remained unresolved, and perhaps there was no way to resolve it.

They came back to the lodge in the afternoon, skin bags full of herbs. Many of the plants awaited Jamie's interpretation between the two women, but the friendship that had blossomed needed no words.

"*I-so-kin-uh-kin*," the woman said, proudly displaying her baby, who no longer wailed with colic. Ducking her head shyly, she added, "*Natosin-nepe*." Yesterday, Kate had given the last bit of chamomile from her small store of medicines to ease the boy. Now she would have to consult Cutting Woman on what to give a colicky baby.

They had no sooner returned from the herb gathering than Crowfoot's lodge was crowded with people bringing in their illnesses to the white doctor who had so miraculously delivered Buffalo Runner's son and saved the life of Laughing Girl.

"She says you are a fine doctor, better than the old men." Jamie interpreted the woman's words. He leaned against a willow backrest beside Kate. "She also says the people have given you a Blackfoot name—Natosin-nepe, which means Bring Down the Sun." His face softened as he added in a low voice, "A name I would have chosen myself."

Busy sorting the fresh herbs and tying them in bundles to dry, Cutting Woman glanced up and smiled indulgently.

When the woman spoke again, Jamie said, "She wishes to pay you now that her son is well."

She held out a pouch of soft, tanned deerskin, heavily

beaded in an intricate design and fringed at the bottom with strings of tiny beads.

"Ahhh," Kate breathed in appreciation of the beauty of the work, and the woman's face lit up. "It is too much," Kate murmured to Jamie, but he shook his head.

"It pleases her that you like it. Now you must take it, or she will be disgraced and her feelings hurt."

"Thank you," Kate said and Jamie translated. Smiling, the woman rose to go. Kate stood and walked out of the lodge with her. Impulsively, she bent to gently kiss the sleeping baby's forehead. Her face glowing, the woman turned away to her own lodge.

"You are an honored medicine woman among my people." It was Jamie's voice beside her, for he had followed.

The emotion flowing between them was so intense, Kate dared not look up at him. She stared straight ahead at the scabbed-over wounds from the Sun Dance, then tentatively placed her hand against his chest, just below the wounds. When her eyes met his, she saw such pride and love she was shaken to her depths.

They hadn't touched each other in that way since the early-morning kiss when he'd first awakened after the Sun Dance. Now it seemed they were drawn together by some force beyond their control. Jamie clasped her shoulders with gentle hands and bent his head to find her lips with his. A surge of longing poured through Kate; her whole body yearned toward his. Jamie held her apart from him, touching only her mouth in the long, sweet kiss that spread fire through her veins.

When he drew away abruptly, Kate opened her eyes to see Crowfoot watching, smiling knowingly.

What was to become of her? Kate asked herself in amazed disbelief. She, who had always been so proper, so self-contained and in control, found herself wanting a totally unsuitable man with a passion she would never have dreamed she could feel. Erotic dreams troubled the night, dreams she blushed to recall on awakening.

Looking down at her nude body, she saw that her nipples were hard and erect. Her groin throbbed, hot and moist. All the time she bathed in her small lodge, she had been thinking of Jamie, remembering the touch of his hands on her shoulders, his mouth on hers. Deliberately, she tried to thrust the memory from her mind, to still the yearning ache that filled her body. Quickly, she toweled herself dry.

Kate was grateful for the privacy of her own lodge, where she could bathe from a pail of water. Bathing in the creek had been an ordeal, with the other women staring in fascination at her white skin. Now she pulled the beaded deerskin dress over her head, smoothing its softness against her body. She had come to love the feel of it, the freedom of nothing beneath it. The blood-stained cotton gown she'd worn while attending Laughing Girl had been washed by one of the women, but it remained rolled up and tucked away. Her underclothing, petticoat, drawers and camisole had served to make bandages for Jamie and her other Blackfoot patients. Still amazed at the transformation she had undergone in the past few days, Kate lifted the lodge flap and stepped outside, meaning to join the evening meal at Crowfoot's lodge.

In the glowing dusk that lay over the prairie, Kate stared in surprise at the four fine horses tethered beside her sleeping lodge. Each horse had something thrown over its bare back. They were well trained, for they stood quietly as she stepped forward to examine their burdens. One carried an eight-point Hudson's Bay blanket, the heaviest made and worth many beaver skins; another bore a head-and-tail buffalo robe that required great skill on the part of the skinner to take the hide in one piece; the third horse carried a blanket of soft, lustrous beaver skins so cleverly sewn together as to seem one skin; and the fourth bore the thick pelt of a cougar.

Kate drew in a tremulous breath, knowing from her time among the Blackfoot that the horses were a gift and a proposal of marriage. Startled, she became aware that she had an audience watching her reaction. Cutting Woman and Crowfoot's three other wives. Stone Calf, Laughing Girl and Buffalo Runner stood there, along with several of her patients—the small boy with a broken arm and his mother, the young wife who had been beaten by her husband for being too free in the Kissing Dance, the old woman whose arthritis reminded Kate painfully of her father.

A smiling Crowfoot stepped forward to face her. He still wore his beautiful ceremonial costume, except for the feathered headdress. With one hand he indicated the horses. "A bride price for my nephew," he said, obviously having memorized the English words.

Jamie appeared at his uncle's side. His dark eyes locked with Kate's as he slowly shook his head, his face unreadable. "You have only to refuse. Although it was Crowfoot's idea, he won't be angry . . . and I will understand."

In those dark eyes Kate saw a longing as deep and compelling as her own. In this far place, among a savage people, she had found the love and freedom she had dreamed of but thought would never be hers. Here, she was an honored medicine woman, and she was beloved by the bravest and gentlest of warriors. There was only one choice, and from her observations of the customs of the camp, she knew what to do.

Taking the Hudson's Bay blanket from the horse's

back, she imitated the Blackfoot maidens she had seen being courted by young warriors. While Jamie stood tense and unmoving, Kate wrapped the blanket about her shoulders, then faced him so close she could hear the thump of his heart. With both arms she embraced him, taking him inside the blanket with her . . . a symbol of her acceptance.

The crowd that had gathered to watch the negotiations broke into laughter and cheers, then slowly began to drift away.

Beneath the heavy blanket, Jamie's arms were around Kate, holding her close, his cheek pressed against her hair. Eyes closed, Kate leaned against that strong-muscled body, feeling the heat of him with a joy that was beyond dreams. The ache in her groin spread through her body until her breath came in hot gasps. They stood for what seemed an eternity, absorbing each other. At last Jamie cupped her head in his hands and found her lips with his. His devouring kiss left her faint and trembling with desire.

"Beloved," he said, caressing her cheek and looking into her eyes. "Be sure this is what you want."

"With all my heart," Kate answered and lifted her face for his kiss.

His breathing hot and fast, Jamie reluctantly ended the kiss and moved a little away from her. He stroked her hair, smiling tenderly into her upturned face. "Tomorrow the camp will move to where the scouts have found buffalo. Tomorrow we will be wed and go our own way. But tonight I go to the sweat lodge. I will fast and pray. Cutting Woman will instruct you."

"I love you, Jamie," Kate said, and he seized her close in a kiss that left her weak with longing.

Jamie groaned as he pulled away from her, and Kate knew they were both at the edge of self-control. He wrapped the blanket gently around her, touched her face with his fingers, murmured, "Until tomorrow," and hurried away.

All the women were making ready for tomorrow's move, packing the rawhide parfleches with cooking utensils, food packets, clothing and other household goods. After dark, when Kate had packed her own few belongings as well as she could, they came to her lodge. Cutting Woman, Little Fox and Crowfoot's other wives, along with Laughing Girl and Water Bird. From their own belongings they had brought her the things a Blackfoot woman needed to set up housekeeping: cooking pots, skin buckets, horn dishes, cups and spoons, as well as neatly made parfleches to carry goods on the packhorses that were part of her marriage price.

Cutting Woman brought skin packets of healing herbs. She put them in Kate's hands, then took off her beautiful necklace of elk's teeth, a prized possession, and placed it around Kate's neck. Tears filled Kate's eyes at the loving gesture and she embraced Cutting Woman without thinking. The enthusiastic hug she received in return told her she had done the right thing.

When all the gifts were arranged, Laughing Girl unrolled hers—a gown of white antelope skin, soft as velvet and elaborately beaded at the shoulders and breast, the sleeves and skirt edged with long beaded fringes. Leggings and moccasins were decorated with beading and fringe. From the mixture of Blackfoot and English the women contributed, Kate understood that this was her wedding gown. She must wear it tomorrow morning when Jamie came to claim her.

After she was dressed to suit them, Cutting Woman brushed Kate's hair with a brush made from porcupine tail and braided it in two long braids similar to her own hair style. The kindness of the women, their obvious pleasure in helping her, touched Kate's heart. There were tears in her eyes as she said good night to them and they left her alone in her sleeping lodge, dressed in all her wedding finery.

It was impossible to know what lay ahead. She should have some plan, Kate thought in the sleepless darkness. But she could think only of tomorrow, of being in Jamie's arms.

A Blackfoot wedding was astonishingly brief. Just after dawn, with the camp already on the move, Jamie rode up with their four horses. Little Fox at once began loading the packhorses.

When Jamie met her in front of Crowfoot's lodge and took her hands in his, Kate's heart leaped into her throat. He was so incredibly handsome, dressed as she had seen him at the great council at Fort McLeod, in his full warrior's regalia: beaded and fringed tunic of tanned deerskins, beaded leggings and moccasins, an eagle feather in his braided hair.

Her trembling hands rested in his strong grip as he looked down at her, his eyes dark and serious. "Are you sure, Kate?" he asked in a low voice. "If you wish it, I'll take you back to Fort McLeod today."

"I love you, Jamie," she answered simply. "I want to be your wife." A flame of joy shone in his eyes. Desire pulsated between them and Kate's whole body longed for him.

Crowfoot came out of his lodge, wearing for the occasion his great feathered headdress. Jamie took Kate's elbow in his hand and together they turned to face the chief. Lifting his arms to the rising sun, Crowfoot sang a prayer. Then he turned to Kate and Jamie.

"*Nit-o-ke-man*," he said earnestly in a deep voice as

he took Kate's hand and placed it in Jamie's.

"Wife," Jamie interpreted in a low whisper.

"*No-ma.*" And Crowfoot joined their free hands together.

"Husband," Kate said, guessing the meaning of the word.

Crowfoot lifted their joined hands in tribute to the sun and spoke in a falling tone that meant he had finished.

"Follows the Eagle and Brings Down the Sun, now you go in peace together." Jamie interpreted the words, turning to look into her eyes, holding both her hands. They stood there, lost in the wonder of belonging to each other until the bustle of the camp aroused them. The women were already taking down the great lodge of the chief and preparing to load it on the waiting travois.

Stone Calf brought up the horses and stood shyly nearby until Kate leaned over to kiss his cheek. Blushing furiously, the boy ran to hide behind the lodge.

Smiling, Jamie touched Kate's face, his dark eyes soft with love. Her hand clasped lovingly in his, he led her to the waiting horses. "We will go now," he said. "*Nit-o-ke-man*, my wife."

~ 18 ~

The great caravan moved northward. Chief of chiefs Crowfoot and his family led the way. Warriors, armed with their weapons, rode on the flank and protected the rear. Other families fell in behind the chief's entourage, all with their travois, pack animals and riding horses. Loose horses were herded by the older boys; babies slept in cradleboards on their mothers' backs.

Scouts had ridden far ahead, searching out the buffalo. The dust of their passing was a distant blur on the horizon.

Kate and Jamie headed west, leading two packhorses. It scarcely passed through her mind that Fort McLeod was to the south. For the first time in her life, she went with no thought of the consequences of her actions. The future didn't exist. There was only the moment. All her being was focused on the man who rode beside her, all her senses yearning for the moment when she would truly be his wife.

Crowfoot's band at last moved beyond sight and sound, disappearing beyond the curve of the earth. Kate and Jamie were alone beneath a deep blue sky dotted with goose-down puffs of cloud. Wind stirred the dried buffalo grass and brought the scent of sagebrush. In the distance a meadowlark called, sharp and clear in the warm air. Suddenly a raven broke from the wild-rose bushes ahead of them and soared into the sky.

"A good omen," Jamie said, smiling at her. "The raven is powerful medicine." He squinted at the sky. "The weather will hold."

Reining her horse closer, Kate reached out to lay her hand on his. "Where are we going?" Even as she asked, she thought that it didn't matter as long as they were together.

Jamie took her hand and pressed it to his cheek. The gesture made Kate's heart leap against her ribs. "Nit-o-ke-man," he said, smiling. Wife . . . he made it a love word. The rugged face, the deep eyes, all filled with love and desire and caring, so intense that tears stung Kate's eyes.

"Jamie," she murmured breathlessly, longing to stop the horses here in the middle of the dusty prairie, to take him in her arms . . .

Still holding her hand, Jamie let the horses move apart. "There are two places," he said thoughtfully, staring into the distance, "that are important to me. I want to share them with you."

Kate tightened her fingers on his hand as her heart twisted with pleasure at the words. This was another of those unexpected revelations that had brought her to love him beyond reason and logic. To share what was important to him was surely a gesture of love beyond price.

Twilight gathered over the prairies before they stopped. The sun was gone, but lavender light lingered in the western sky. Jamie had chosen to camp beside a small creek edged with a tangle of willows, alder and red birch. Quickly, he unloaded the horses and tethered them near the musically flowing stream. Then he kindled a fire, arranging the parfleches nearby. Kate watched, realizing that if she were a Blackfoot woman, she would know exactly what to do to make a camp—the things Jamie was doing now.

When they'd stopped briefly for nooning, Kate had thought he'd take her then. She'd wanted it. But Jamie had only kissed her with gentle restraint, then helped her mount, obviously anxious to move on. Now . . . she thought, and trembled.

Jamie picked up the bedroll and turned to her with the smile that made her bones melt. "Let's make our marriage bed, *nit-o-ke-man.*" Half dizzy with happiness, Kate followed him up a slight rise from the creek bank where an outcropping of rocks loomed against the darkening sky.

Together they made the bed. A heavy buffalo robe, skin side down, came first, then another with hair side up, then the precious beaver-skin blanket and two Hudson's Bay blankets. A tanned buffalo skin covered all. She wanted to fall onto the bed, hold him, surrender her whole being.

"Are you hungry?" Jamie asked, and Kate sighed. With an arm around her shoulders, he led her back to the fire. Kate suddenly realized she was famished. They'd eaten only dried buffalo jerky all day. Jamie opened the parfleche stuffed with bundles of food and arranged for her a horn bowl of pemmican. Sitting beside him at the low fire, she ate hungrily of the mixture of dried buffalo meat, marrow and buffalo back fat, pounded with berries. Back at the encampment, she had tasted this Blackfoot staple gingerly. Now she ate it as if it were the nectar of the gods. The meal was finished with a tin mug of water Jamie brought from the stream.

Why had he distanced himself from her? Kate wondered as she watched him bank the fire. They were man and wife, yet all day he'd scarcely touched her except to hold her hand as they rode. As though he heard her thoughts, Jamie reached out and drew her close to him. Desire flamed through her at his touch. "Jamie." Her voice was ragged with longing.

"This is the place of my *nits-o-kan*, my vision," he said softly, almost reverently.

Shaken that he would bring her to a place she had learned all warriors held sacred, she closed her eyes and clasped her arms around him. "Can you tell me about the vision?" she asked, looking up into his serious face. Darkness lay on the land, so that only the last flickering of the fire lit the black eyes that seemed to be seeing inward.

Still holding her in his embrace, Jamie lifted his head to the sky as though offering his words to Natos. "It is the custom," he began, "to fast for four days and nights, and to pray to the Sun god for a vision. On the fourth day I despaired, certain my half blood made me unworthy. Weak from fasting, I fell into a kind of trance. A great and powerful eagle came to me then, lighting on the rock there." And he pointed to where they had made their bed on the grassy rise.

"The eagle signed that I must come with him. I started to protest that I couldn't fly when suddenly I was flying, soaring over the plains. As we flew, the eagle pointed out the landmarks, the mountains and streams. 'Remember it all,' the eagle told me, 'for where I go, you will follow and show others the way.'" Jamie's voice fell. "When I awakened, the sun was rising."

"*Sto-ni-tap*," Kate whispered, awed by his story, using the word from her growing knowledge of Blackfoot that meant things strange and wonderful.

Jamie nodded. "It has been as the eagle said."

In that half-light before full dark, their eyes held as though they would see into each other's hearts.

"*Nit-o-ke-man*, wife . . ." Jamie whispered. Cupping her face in one hand, he covered her mouth with his.

The kiss deepened as Jamie's other hand slid down her back to press her hips against his hot hardness. Kate's whole body went soft, pulsing with the desire that was at once pain and joy.

A long sigh shook the length of him as Jamie took her hand and led her up the rise to their bed.

The moon had not yet risen, and the night sky was black velvet, studded by a multitude of stars. The Milky Way, which the Blackfoot called the Wolf Trail, was flung like a gauzy scarf across the darkness. Somewhere a night bird called, and the wind brought the sweet scent of damp grass.

Gently, caressingly, his face intent in the starlight, Jamie removed her beaded headband and the elk-tooth necklace, placing them in a parfleche. Bending, he caught the hem of her antelope-skin wedding gown and drew it over her head. Trembling with anticipation, she stood naked before him, clad only in her moccasins. With a groan from deep in his throat, Jamie brushed his lips across her breasts as he bent and with one arm caught the backs of her knees and laid her on the soft beaver skins.

Earlier in the day, Jamie had removed his tunic because it chafed the healing wounds on his chest. Now he stripped off leggings and breechclout. An involuntary cry broke from Kate's throat at the sight of his tall, nude body, totally aroused in the dim starlight. In caring for him, she had stroked the length of that hard-muscled body again and again. She knew the feel of him. But this was another Jamie . . . her husband . . . lover . . . wanting her. The evidence of his desire for her kindled her need into a raging inferno. Feverishly, she reached out to him. Jamie dropped to his knees, tugged off her moccasins, then lay beside her, enfolding her in strong, demanding arms.

"*No-ma*, husband," she said to the dark face looking down into her own. With a hand on his cheek, she brought his lips to hers. Their mouths devoured each other, their bodies straining to be closer. Kate's hips arched against him, her blood pounding, the aching emptiness demanding to be filled.

Wanting him closer still, Kate stroked his muscular back and pressed her lips against the wildly beating pulse of his throat. Jamie loosened her braided hair, gathered the strands in his hand and, with a long sigh, buried his face in its softness.

With a gentleness that belied the wild pounding of his heart against her breast, Jamie's hard, callused hands moved over her body, caressing her breasts, the flat of her stomach, the curve of her hips and soft inner thigh. There his searching fingers found the center of her, hot and wet, so completely aroused she cried out in pleasure when he touched her.

His tongue traced the hollow of her throat, teased her aching nipples, his whole body trembling with a need as deep and urgent as her own. Instinctively, she reached to stroke his heated maleness. At her touch, he groaned as though in pain. The heat of him burned her fingers, igniting a flame that surged through her body with such intensity Kate knew she could wait no longer. Wrapping her legs around his hips, she took him into her, unaware of the pain, aware only of her frenzied need.

"Kate!" he cried, then grew perfectly still. Sensing his struggle for control, she waited breathlessly. After a moment, his tortured breathing eased. His mouth found hers. His hands cupped her hips, lifting her to meet his thrusts. With each thrust the sweet madness grew until Kate wept and laughed and called his name with growing urgency.

"Jamie!" She cried his name to the stars and was lost among them in a vortex of ecstasy, her whole being shattered by a joy of unbearable intensity.

A shudder shook his body as Jamie thrust deep, gasping her name. Kate felt his hot seed spill within her, sending a new wave of ecstasy along her limbs.

"*Sto-ni-tap,*" Jamie whispered as his body went slack against hers. "It is magic."

"Magic," Kate murmured. Stunned by the power of what had passed between them, she lay with eyes closed, clinging to the glory of the moment.

Tenderly, Jamie smoothed back her damp, disordered hair and kissed her eyelids. "My woman . . . my wife," he murmured and pillowed her head on his shoulder. Their legs intertwined, Kate settled, sated and content, against his heated body. "I didn't want to hurt you," he began and she quickly placed her fingers on his lips.

"No," she said. "No, it was only that I wanted you so much I couldn't wait." With a deep, shaken breath, Kate continued, her voice trembling. "I never guessed . . . never knew . . . the power of it . . ." Words failed her, but she looked into his eyes and knew he understood.

"Beloved wife." Jamie's voice trembled with emotion as he raised himself on one elbow to look down into her face. "The power of it is in a true mating . . . in what has brought us together since I first looked on your beautiful face."

"I love you," Kate told him and was answered by a gentle kiss.

Pulling a blanket over them, Jamie settled her in his

arms. Smiling, he kissed her lips and eyes. "Sleep now," he said.

The drawn-out, eerie notes of a coyote's howl echoed beneath the night sky. Startled awake, Kate felt a tingle of dread run down her spine. Instinctively, she moved closer to Jamie to find him already awake. He gathered her protectively in his arms and kissed her long and tenderly, that kiss slowly growing in intensity.

"There's no danger," he told her, ending the kiss breathlessly. "Wolves and coyotes are the people's friends. Sometimes they travel along with the moving camp. If a person is hungry and sings the wolf song, he will soon find something to eat. But if a man goes out of camp at night and a coyote barks at him, then the people look out and are careful, because it's a sure sign something bad is going to happen."

"This one didn't bark," she said, the tension of her sudden awakening draining away. The pressure of Jamie's warm, nude body next to her own brought a rush of heated wetness to her groin. Longing ran along her veins. After all her initial boldness, Kate felt suddenly shy and pressed her face against his shoulder, waiting for him to make the next move.

"Then I think something good will happen," Jamie murmured as his mouth caressed her breasts, "and it will happen now."

"Soon . . ." Kate whispered. Running her fingers through his thick hair, she opened her lips to him. Their mouths joined in a deep, devouring kiss.

Driving passion swept through her heated body, and Kate lifted her hips to take him into the center of her being. A rising tide of rapture caught her, blind and deaf and lost to everything except the exquisite pleasure of loving. The sky itself seemed to explode in her eyes as

Jamie's seed burst inside her. Holding him fiercely to her, Kate wept for the joy they had found together.

Kate's slumber was so profound she scarcely stirred, her breath deep and soft against his cheek. Burying his face in the glorious hair spread in wild disarray on the cougar skin, Jamie breathed in the sweet, musky scent of her. Gently, he caressed the curve of her hip, still warm and damp from loving. In that time-suspended moment between the searing climax of their lovemaking and satisfied sleep, Kate had murmured, "I didn't know it was possible to be so happy."

Nor had he, Jamie thought as he stared sleepless at the waning moon rising in the eastern sky. No other woman he had ever known lost herself so completely in passion, and none had ever brought him such total fulfillment. In this girl who was so alien to his world, Jamie knew he had found his true mate. In sorrow and adversity, among the Blackfoot or the Mounties, and now in the joy of their joining, he had seen that she was strong and true. He had been right to wait to take her here in this sacred place. A long night lay ahead and there was love to be shared through the dark hours. When she sighed in her sleep and moved closer, Jamie knew he loved her beyond any fantasy of love he'd ever had, yet his heart recognized how fragile this happiness was.

A stolen piece of time . . . that was what they shared now. Tomorrow he would take her to the blue lake in the Shining Mountains. And his heart fell in the knowledge that that time, too, would be stolen. Soon they must return to the real world. Sometime they would have to speak of the future if they were to have one together.

A night-hunting bird swooped by, its wings beating the air. The eagle . . . Jamie's throat tightened. An omen. A reminder that his heart was Blackfoot and that he had a Blackfoot warrior's duty to perform. He had rededicated himself to that duty in the *Okan*. Then he had let desire rule him, and nothing had meaning but his need to possess this woman. For that he could have no regrets, even though Blackfoot justice had not been done.

At the encampment, he'd learned that Big Rib and Good Young Man were living among the southern people on the Blackfoot reservation in Montana. When the encampment broke up, he should have gone south to find them and take vengeance. Instead, he had given himself, body and soul, to this white woman he loved and wanted more than anything in the world.

Sighing, Jamie tightened his arms about his beloved wife. The struggle between his two selves, white and Blackfoot, was not ended, despite his sacrifice at the Sun Dance.

19

The horses picked their way through the shade-dappled forest of pine and fir. Following close behind Jamie, for there was no trail in the soft forest floor, Kate couldn't keep her awed eyes from the cloud-piercing mountains towering above the trees.

Last night they had camped on the banks of the wide, peaceful Bow River. The wind off the mountains, still snowcapped in early autumn, had a bite to it. Lingering beneath the heavy blankets until the sun was high, they made love, slept and made love again. An elk with a massive rack of horns had been grazing beside the river when Kate went to bathe. He continued placidly chewing grass and staring at her until, as Kate laughingly told Jamie, he had made her blush.

Ahead of her now, Jamie slowed the horses. Through the trees Kate caught a glimpse of sun glinting off water. This must be where Jamie meant to camp, although it was early in the afternoon. Perhaps it was the surprise gift he'd promised when she asked again where they were going. Dismounting, he tied the horses and came to lift her down from the saddle. A little gasp of pain escaped her for the tenderness in unexpected places, places unused to the demands of a man's body as well as the bruises she had caused herself in her frenzied passion. On that first morning when the sun rose on their lovemaking, Jamie had laughingly told her they looked as though they had battled. His Sun Dance wounds had broken open during their wild loving. Blood was smeared across his chest, matching the smears on her breasts. And there was dried blood on her thighs from the piercing of her maidenhead.

"This is my blue lake in the sky." Jamie's dark eyes glowed with anticipation. "Come." Taking her hand, he led her through the thick stand of trees. They came out onto a rocky shore beneath low-hanging fir branches.

With a cry of amazement, Kate clasped her hands together. Tears filled her eyes and blurred the beauty lying before her. The lake lay like a milky-blue jewel in a setting of tree-dark mountains. On the farther shore a river of ice poured down a great snowy mountain. The water was perfectly still, reflecting sunlight in a luminous glow.

She saw that Jamie was watching her intently. He wanted to share this beautiful hidden place with her as he had shared his vision. Impulsively, she threw her arms about him and kissed him. "Thank you," she whispered. "A wonderful gift."

He smiled. "Shall we stay, then?"

"Could we stay forever?" she asked, perfectly serious. Laughing, Jamie tweaked her ear and went to bring the horses.

While Jamie made camp, Kate sat on a rock beside the shore and feasted her eyes on the incredible beauty of his blue lake in the sky.

Darkness fell and hunting birds swooped above the lake surface, where all the stars gleamed back at the sky. The evening star rose above the pines to find its reflection in the still water. They had feasted on the rabbits

Jamie shot this morning beside the Bow River. Replete and content, they sat before their small fire, Jamie with his back against a tree trunk. Kate lay against his bare chest, embraced by his arms and legs, his cheek pressed to hers. From across the lake, the plaintive cry of a loon broke the silence.

The words came from Kate's deepest heart. "If only we could stay like this forever . . . never go back."

"If only . . ." Jamie echoed, kissing her ear. Sighing, he tightened his embrace, his hands pressed to her small, neat breasts. Through the soft deerskin he felt her nipples harden.

Guilt grew in his heart. After she delivered Laughing Girl's son, he should have taken her back to Fort McLeod at once, should have ridden away from her forever. And he should have at least argued against Crowfoot's naive desire to see them wed . . . Should have set her free of him. Kate was a passionate woman. There would have been another man for her . . . a white man . . . perhaps Cavendish, who had been so attentive . . . anyone but a savage half-breed. A sick pain ached in his chest when it came to him that she would return to censure and disapproval. Among her own people, Kate would pay heavily for these few days of passion and perfect happiness. He feared she had not even considered that.

His mind cast wildly about for some way he could protect her from what lay ahead. Kate's voice interrupted his painful thoughts with a mundane question.

"Why is the water that strange, beautiful shade of blue?"

"The glacier . . ." Jamie let his anxieties go and pointed to the ice-clad mountain across the lake gleaming in the faint moonlight. "It's a river of ice, very thick and very heavy. It grinds the rocks to powder as it moves. The powder dissolves in the water and changes the color."

"Umn," she said and turned to smile up at him. "How did you know that?"

Jamie stroked her loose hair lovingly, his mind suddenly transported back to Rocky Mountain House. "Alec Campbell was an educated man. Whichever missionary was at the fort was expected to teach me all he could. In the long winters when I was a boy, we read lots of books. Alec taught me many things, most of them useful, some merely interesting—like the glaciers."

"Were you happy, growing up there?" Kate asked, snuggling the top of her head against his neck.

"Happy?" Jamie reflected on the question. "Not unhappy," he finally answered. "Lonely, I suppose. Alec and his wife were kind to me. When he died, she went back to her people. But I always knew I was a half blood, that I didn't truly belong anywhere. From the beginning I was determined I wouldn't be like the other half bloods—worthless, lying drunks."

"So you went to Crowfoot?" she prompted softly.

Jamie nodded, his eyes distant with remembering. "They welcomed me, taught me . . . but I didn't really belong there either."

"Even when you married?" A catch in her voice made him bend to kiss her cheek reassuringly. How could he explain the difference between that love and this one?

"I was eighteen when I wed Meadowlark . . . young to marry, but she was carrying my child. Within the year she was dead in childbirth."

Covering his hands with hers, Kate pressed them tightly to her breasts. "I'm sorry."

"It wasn't like this, Kate." Jamie's voice deepened, urgent in his need to make her understand the depth of his love for her. ''Nothing was ever like this. You're my heart, my soul . . .'' Cupping her face with one hand, Jamie turned her to meet his kiss. Desire poured through him and he knew that, whatever the consequences, he could never have denied this love.

Kate leaned into his kiss, opening to the sweet, smoky taste of him. The lonely little half-blood boy and the solitary, studious doctor's daughter would be lonely no more, she told herself. In this great, lone land, under circumstances she could never have dreamed, she had found her soul mate. This was forever.

One big, gentle hand stroked her loose hair, a sensation so endearing Kate closed her eyes and gave herself over to the pleasure of his touch.

''I know you didn't want to go back to Toronto without your father.'' Jamie broke the contented silence. ''Were you unhappy there?''

As she was held in his loving embrace, his lips caressing her hair, all Kate's natural reticence fled. With tears welling in her eyes, she told him of her mother's tragic death; of the lonely, responsible, ambitious child, always different, always an outsider; of her unwomanly ambition to be a doctor, a true healer, and how she'd been thwarted at every turn. She even told him about Curtis, how her one venture into conformity had brought only hurt.

Jamie's arms enveloped her as though to protect her from unhappy memories. After a silence, he spoke softly. ''So you were lonely, too?''

''Until now,'' she answered fervently. Filled with joy at the truth of her words, Kate turned her face, seeking his kiss. The need to share herself in love with him was suddenly more urgent than ever before. It was as though sharing their inner selves had brought them to a new plateau of oneness.

Against her back, she felt his hard erection and she turned in his arms, pulling him down on top of her. In the hot wetness between her thighs, the demanding ache grew in intensity, the ache only one man could ease. He filled her then, completed her. Kate gave herself into wild, blind passion and a soaring climax made more complete because they had shared their hearts.

Eden itself could not have been more perfect. Kate laid aside the wild rhubarb she had gathered to roast for supper and once more let her eyes drink in the beauty of Jamie's blue lake in the sky. Eden . . . yes, and she was a wanton Eve who could not get enough of loving.

This morning the two of them had bathed in the lake, the icy water making them shout as they hurriedly finished. Shivering, they clung to each other and fell laughing to the grassy shore, where they made love as the sun climbed the morning sky. Spent and sated, they lay together naked in the warm mountain sunlight. A soft breeze sighed through the pines, cooling their heated bodies until desire rose again. Together they drowned once more in the sweet madness.

Afterward, reluctantly bestirring himself, Jamie said they needed meat and he went by himself to hunt. At his suggestion, Kate gathered the rhubarb, then set a stewpot of wild onions and dried buffalo jerky to cook. Filled with pride, she looked at the camp she had made neat and the stew steaming on her small fire. She would make a good Blackfoot wife. If Jamie chose that life, she'd go with him gladly. His people honored and respected her as a healer. Her husband was a renowned warrior. It could be a happy life . . . the best of worlds.

"The eagle followed us," Jamie called to her as he came tramping through the trees, the hindquarters of a small deer slung over his saddle. Kate had heard only one shot, far across the lake. Swimming birds had flown up from the water in a flurry at the sound.

Before he unloaded the meat from his horse, Jamie crossed to meet her beside the fire. Kate went into his arms, her face lifted to his, wanting his kiss with all her being . . . wanting more.

Reluctantly, he drew away from her eager mouth. "The eagle left a gift for you," he told her. "I found it where I found the deer." He held up a prized eagle feather, as long as his hand, gray and white with black tipping. Then he carefully inserted it into one of her braids. With a loving smile, he held her face in his hands and looked into her eyes. "The hand of Natos is over you. That is the meaning of the eagle feather."

Kate's arms tightened around his neck as his mouth claimed hers again in a long, devouring kiss that left them both throbbing with need. She turned her face to kiss the palm of his hand. "*No-ma*," she murmured. "It's not the hand of Natos that pleases me, but your hands."

His eyes glowed at her words and Jamie kissed her again, then held her away with a soft chuckle. "We have meat to care for, *nit-o-ke-man*. After that, my hands are all for you."

A loon's cry awakened Kate to a pearl-gray morning sky. Gleaming like silver in the pale light, the lake was a still mirror reflecting the glow of the morning star above the great mountain of ice.

"The Morning Star." Jamie spoke softly. He was awake and watching her with tender eyes. The air was chill and he tucked the blankets around their nude bodies. As he gathered her into his arms, his mouth found hers. "Son of the Sun and the Moon," he murmured between teasing kisses.

Intrigued by the concept, Kate sighed with pleasure as Jamie's lips moved to the base of her throat. She stared up at the gleaming light of the only star in the pale gray sky. "Tell me about Morning Star," she whispered.

"Morning Star." Jamie lifted his head and looked down with an indulgent smile. He began in the cadence of a storyteller. "Morning Star lived with his mother and father in their land beyond the sky. It was a beautiful land of happiness and plenty. But Morning Star was sad and lonely. His parents, the Sun and the Moon, had each other. From his place in the sky, Morning Star could see the lovers on earth lying in each other's arms . . ." As though to demonstrate his tale, Jamie's hand moved gently down Kate's body, coming to rest tantalizingly between her thighs.

"At last, Morning Star went to his parents and asked if they could find a wife for him because he was so lonely. Well . . ." Jamie groaned with pleasure as Kate reached to stroke his growing erection. A long, satisfied sigh came from Kate's throat as she felt him harden beneath her fingers.

"Morning Star's parents loved him and wanted him to be happy," Jamie continued, his voice a little uneven. "They searched the earth below until they found a young woman who was beautiful, virtuous and wise. Morning Star fell in love with her at once and wanted her above all things. Many fine gifts persuaded her father to grant permission, and so they were wed. The beautiful girl came to the land beyond the sky. She was wife to Morning Star and for a long time they were happy . . ."

"As we are." Kate pressed him back against the blankets and kissed him hungrily on the mouth, then on the strong pulse at the base of his throat. With a ragged groan, Jamie pulled her on top of him. Impulsively, she straddled his hips, then bent to nibble at his ear.

"Do you want to hear the story?" he asked with laughter in his voice.

Kate raised her head and smiled down into his face. "Isn't that the end?"

Shaking his head, Jamie went on determinedly. "All the women in the land beyond the sky were harvesting wild turnips for the winter. In the center of the turnip field there grew a huge turnip, larger than all the others, growing bigger each day. Again and again the Sun and the Moon warned the wife of Morning Star that she mustn't touch the sacred turnip. Finally, her curiosity was too much. Taking a long digging tool, she uprooted the turnip and made a hole in the sky."

Kate grew still, certain now that Jamie's story had a meaning beyond mere words.

"Kneeling down, the girl looked through the hole and there she saw her family down on earth, going about their daily tasks. Homesickness overcame her and she wept bitterly, for she missed her family and the camp life she had left behind when she wed Morning Star."

"But she loved Morning Star," Kate interrupted, suddenly fearful of where the tale was leading.

After a moment's hesitation while he looked intently into her eyes, Jamie continued. "The homesick girl went to the Sun and to the Moon, begging them to let her return to earth. Remembering how lonely their son had been before the girl's coming, they refused. So she went to her husband, weeping, and asked to go back to her family. Because he loved her so, Morning Star granted her wish. She climbed down through the hole in the sky the turnip had made and went back to her people."

When Jamie fell silent, Kate raised her head from his shoulder and frowned at him. "That's the end?" she demanded, and when he nodded, she protested, "The ending is wrong."

Amused by her vehemence, Jamie chuckled. "It's an old myth. The ending is always the same."

"It's wrong," Kate declared emphatically. Looking into his questioning eyes, she lifted her hips to ease his hot erection inside her. He groaned with pleasure, his hands clasping her waist as he thrust deep into her melting sheath. Jamie reached to grasp her bare shoulders, drawing her down to meet his demanding kiss.

Deliberately, Kate drew away. "First, *no-ma*, I'll tell you the true ending." She began in a low voice choked with emotion, as though she told her own story. "Because she loved Morning Star, yet longed to be with her people, the girl went to the Sun and asked a boon, which he granted. He made her into the Evening Star. Each night she is there to say good night to her family. When Morning Star fades from the sky, they are together, loving each other all through the day."

Kate's hair was a bright curtain in the growing light as she looked down into Jamie's intent face. "Neither of them," she said, her voice trembling with the intensity of the feelings pouring through her, "neither of them will ever be lonely again."

꩜ 20 ꩜

An ominous moving cloud of dust hung above the prairie, muddying the deep blue autumn sky. Kate stared at it in dismay, remembering the stories of terrible prairie dust storms that blew everything before them. She shivered with apprehension, wishing once more that they could have stayed forever in the mountains. She had asked that question of Jamie only this morning when she disconsolately watched him packing the horses. In answer, he had pointed toward the thin rime of frost on the grass beside the lake. It was melting already as the sun rose. They had scarcely noticed the cold of the night in their heated need for each other as they came together again and again.

"Only hibernating bears can survive the winters here," he'd answered with an amused smile for her foolishness.

Bridling a bit at his condescension, Kate protested. "I have nothing to go back for—no one who cares whether I come back. Jamie . . ." When he turned to her with soft eyes, she slid her arms around his waist and pressed her face against his chest. "I know we have to go," she said tremulously, "but I will leave a part of my heart here."

Jamie stroked her hair lovingly and kissed her eyes. "And so will I, my Katie," he murmured, holding her close. "But there are responsibilities . . . decisons to be made." He drew a deep, aching breath and tilted her chin to claim her kiss. They moved apart then, damping down the fires that kiss had ignited. "What we shared here has made us one, beloved. You are my *nit-o-ke-man*, in my heart and soul and body. Always, forever, I will care for you and keep you safe from harm."

That vow was made with such intensity, Kate was shaken to her depths. Love for this man filled her with an overpowering joy. Again she took him into her arms, holding him fiercely as she whispered her own vow, "And I will always care for you, beloved *no-ma*."

The enchanted blue lake in the sky was far behind them now, that place Kate found herself thinking of as their home . . . the home of Morning Star and Evening Star. Despite their leisurely pace, stopping to watch a fishing bear on the Bow River, they had left the mountains long ago.

Apprehensive, Kate reined in her horse and stared at the dust cloud. A sound like distant thunder came from that direction—not thunder, for it was a steady roar, gradually increasing in volume. "Jamie?" she asked and pointed.

"Buffalo!" he answered and urgently beckoned her to follow him. They rode quickly toward a copse of willow and alder surrounding a spring trickling from the lee of a low hill. With the horses safely tethered among the trees, Jamie took Kate's arm, his black eyes dancing with excitement. "We can watch from here," he said and led her up to the brow of the hill, where he spread the cougar skin for her to sit on.

As far as the eye could see were the endless, rolling prairies, dun-colored now as autumn came on. Only the dust cloud marred the clear blue sky, thickening as it neared and the thunder of running buffalo increased.

"Here they come!" Jamie cried. He stood beside her, staring with eager eyes across the prairie. Kate's throat tightened and her heartbeat accelerated as an enormous brown tide of running buffalo poured over a rise to the north. The rumble of their hooves echoed across the plain, making the earth beneath her feet tremble. The cloud of dust they had seen from far away rose from beneath those pounding hooves, blurring the sunlight.

Behind the fleeing beasts came the Blackfoot buffalo hunters. Like the centaurs of fable, the hunters rode in wild pursuit, copper skin gleaming in the sunlight, black hair streaming. Repeating rifles gleamed metallically as they were lifted for the kill.

The stout, fleet horses kept pace with the stampeding buffalo herd. "They ride their best horses," Jamie told her, "the ones trained as buffalo runners."

The sharp sound of gunshots echoed above the incessant roar of running buffalo. Slain animals dropped from the fleeing horde to lie in death throes, then unmoving on the torn earth.

Jamie's excitement at the spectacle of the chase was infectious. Kate couldn't sit still, and both of them stood, straining to see. Jamie had brought the rifle from his saddle. He held it now in the crook of his arm, his body swaying as though he rode in the chase himself, totally absorbed in the scene playing out before them. If he had his own buffalo horse, he would surely have ridden to join in the hunt.

Taking a deep breath to relieve the sudden tightness in her chest, Kate reminded herself that she well knew of the savage part of this man she loved. It might even have been much of what drew her to him. For this moment, Jamie seemed to have forgotten her, even to have gone in his mind to some place where she could not follow. A foreboding fell over her and she shivered in the hot autumn sunlight.

Finally the massive, trampling herd of buffalo and their pursuers faded into the distance across the plains. The sound of gunshots diminished and the dust cloud blended with the southern horizon. Kate saw that the hunters had been followed by women and older children bringing up packhorses and travois. They all set to work immediately, skinning dead buffalo, cutting up the meat and loading it onto their pack animals. The women's arms grew red with blood as they worked, and it flowed thick into the dust and dry grass.

Transfixed by the bloody business taking place down on the plain, Kate was startled by Jamie's touch on her arm. The medicine bag he always wore tied to his belt was in his hand. "My buffalo stone," he said. "I should have been with the hunt."

In the hard brown palm of his hand lay an odd shaped grayish stone. Peering close, Kate touched it with a tentative finger. In shape and markings, it looked like some strange kind of beetle. Perhaps it was one of the ancient fossils she had read about.

"A buffalo stone is powerful medicine and brings its owner good luck." Jamie's fingers closed over the stone possessively. "It gives the owner great power to find and kill the buffalo." He smiled. "Shall I tell you the story?"

Sensing his need to explain and to share, Kate took his arm and pressed her cheek against his shoulder. "Tell me."

"Long ago," he began as they walked slowly back

toward the waiting horses, "the buffalo disappeared. The snow was deep and the people were starving. One day a young woman was walking along the path to the river to get water when she heard a beautiful song. She could see no one, but the song seemed to come from a cottonwood tree. There she found, jammed in a fork of the tree, a strange-looking rock, such as this one. The singing stopped and the *i-nis-kim*, the buffalo rock, said, 'Take me to your lodge, call all the people together and teach them my song.' That night the people sang:

> *"The buffalo comes down from the mountains to the plains.*
> *The mountains are his medicine.*
> *The buffalo is my medicine.*
> *He is very strong medicine."*

The forceful song ended and Jamie continued in a quiet voice. "Soon the people heard the tramp of a great herd of buffalo coming. They rode to the hunt, killed many and ate well."

He paused beside the restive horses flicking their tails against the swarms of stinging deer flies, and smiled down at Kate. "Are you weary of my stories?"

"Never," she answered, looking into his eyes, her body warming as always from his loving glance.

"It's very lucky to find a buffalo stone. Whoever finds one guards it with care, for that man has the power to find buffalo to feed the people." He threw the cougar skin back over her saddle and adjusted it carefully.

Watching, Kate wondered that he took so long at such a small task. When he turned to her, the smiling story-teller was gone. His face was stern, the dark eyes guarded. "Now we must decide," he told her in a care-fully controlled voice, and Kate felt a chill of apprehension run down her spine. "If we're to be together . . . where will it be? Tonight we can sleep in Crowfoot's camp and feast on the buffalo, or . . ." His voice trailed away and he looked down at his hand clutching the buffalo stone as though it were an amulet.

Straightening his shoulders, Jamie lifted his chin and looked into the distance over Kate's head. "Or we can go south to Fort McLeod."

The dreaded moment had come. Suddenly their worlds were divided again. During all the days with Jamie, Kate had refused to let herself think of the decision to be made. The passion she'd found with this beloved man had possessed her completely. Nothing else in all the world mattered except the perfect joy of their mating.

"Katie?" He took her face in his hands, forcing her to look at him. Tears pricked behind her eyes as her heart swelled with love for him. There was no choice. Kate flung herself into his arms, kissing him with wild abandon, holding him against her as though she would fuse them together.

"I'll never leave you," she cried hoarsely between frantic kisses. "Never . . . Jamie . . . *no-ma*, my husband, my love."

His silence as he held her close was more disturbing than any words. At last she quieted, scrubbing her tear-wet face against the soft deerskin of his tunic.

With a gentle hand, Jamie smoothed the windblown locks that had escaped from her braids and tilted her chin to kiss her softly. "*Nit-o-ke-man*, beloved wife," he murmured against her hair. "I didn't mean for you to leave me," he soothed her. "We go together, my Katie."

Jamie drew in a deep sigh and when he spoke, she knew he had made the decision. "McLeod needs me and I have given him my promise. There are things you must

see to at Fort McLeod. When we've settled our business
there . . . '' His voice trailed off and Kate knew their
future was still in limbo.

But they had now, this moment. At the thought, desire
poured through her, so potent she could feel the pulsing
of her veins and every nerve sang with longing. "Tonight we stay here," she told him.

Beneath a brassy sky, the horizon seemed to melt and
run into the earth. Around them as they rode, small prairie creatures scurried to their burrows—prairie dogs and
field mice and stately, burrowing owls. Across the immense sky, an endless wind blew towering white clouds.
That wind was filled with autumnal scents—dried curly
grass, ripening chokecherries. It ruffled the feathers of a
calling meadowlark perched on a wild-rose bush heavy
with red pips. Along the little creek a flock of yellow-
headed blackbirds lifted into the air, riding the gusts with
practiced ease.

Peering from beneath the light summer buffalo robe
Jamie had given her for protection from sun and wind,
Kate met his dark, tender gaze. A rush of heat flooded
her body. Surely they'd stop for nooning soon, maybe
make love beneath that vast, overpowering sky. The
thought made her heart race and she sighed, remembering the tea Jamie had made for her each morning. Today
she'd finally asked him why he insisted she drink it
every day.

"Cutting Woman gave it to me," he replied, turning
away. Without looking at her, he added, "While you
drink it, we won't make a baby."

Kate stared at his averted face, not sure whether to be
angry or sad. Incredibly, she hadn't even considered the
possibility of pregnancy. Swallowing the rest of her tea,
she went to him and took his face in both her hands,

looking deep into his eyes. "I would welcome our child, Jamie."

With a rueful smile, he caressed her cheek. "Not yet, *nit-o-ke-man,* my wife . . . not yet."

In answer, she embraced him, pressing her body hard against his so that he knew she wanted him. They had made love again while the sun climbed the sky and the horses waited.

Now Jamie seemed anxious to keep moving. He took some jerky from his pack and they ate as they rode. By midafternoon they were riding in the lee of rocky hills rising abruptly from the floor of the plain. At the bottom of a tall cliff there were bleached bones and buffalo skulls scattered about.

"It's a buffalo jump," Jamie replied to her puzzled question. "In the days before horses, the people would drive a small herd of buffalo, trying to stampede them at exactly the right time so the animals would run off the cliff and be killed in the fall. Or they would be crippled, so that it was easy for the hunters to finish them off." He smiled grimly. "Hunting buffalo on foot with bow and arrow must have required great skill."

As they rode on, Kate turned in her saddle to look back at the piles of bones. Somewhere she had read that the Spaniards first brought the horse to the new world. In those days the Blackfoot would have been a primitive people, forever on the verge of starvation. Now they were rich by the standards of the frontier—and growing richer as they gained back what they had lost to the whiskey traders.

"There's a stream," Jamie called now, interrupting her thoughts. "We'll water the horses here."

After she had dismounted and led her horse to the water, Kate hurried to Jamie's side. The need to be near him, to touch him, was always there, but it had grown

sharper as they traveled south toward her other life. In
the heat of the day he had taken off his tunic. Kate slid
her arm around his bare waist, the palm of her hand
moving sensuously over his warm, damp skin. Jamie
sucked in a breath and she expected to be seized in his
arms and kissed.

But his head was raised . . . like an animal sniffing the
wind, alert and wary. His tension communicated a sense
of danger. A frisson of fear went down her spine and
Kate froze beside him. "What is it?" she whispered,
then heard the faint sound of hoofbeats in the distance.

They both turned toward that sound and saw the riders
coming fast around the foot of the hills. Red coats
gleamed brilliantly in the hot afternoon sun. "Mounties," Kate breathed, and her knees went weak with relief.

Frowning, Jamie watched as the men approached at a
gallop. There were a half-dozen horsemen, and David
Cavendish reached them first.

"Thank God!" he cried, leaping from his horse and
seizing Kate by the shoulders. "Thank God we found
you. Are you all right?"

Stunned speechless by his abrupt greeting, Kate stared
up into the thin, aristocratic face that she saw was filled
with concern for her. "Of course I'm all right,
David . . . " She finally found her voice, then cried out
in protest when she saw that two of the men held Jamie's
arms while a third was tying his hands behind him.
Shoving David away, she flew toward them. "What are
you doing?" she demanded.

Jamie's face was impassive, but his black eyes burned
with rage. He didn't struggle, simply shrugged the men
away contemptuously.

"David!" Kate screamed, turning to Cavendish.
"What is this?"

Pointedly ignoring her question, David faced Jamie. "You're under arrest, Campbell . . . for abducting a white woman."

"No!" She grabbed David by the front of his jacket, trying futilely to shake his tall, immovable frame. "You don't understand. We're married. Jamie didn't abduct me—he's my husband. You have no right—"

The disbelief on David's face might have been comic if the situation weren't so terrible. "It's true, David," Kate cried.

His face flushed with anger, David glared at her. "You're lying to protect him, Kate. God knows why." Abruptly, he turned toward the men holding Jamie. "Take him straight to the fort and throw him in the stockade. The arrogant bastard needs to be taught a lesson."

"You're a fool, Cavendish." Jamie's voice was low and threatening. "McLeod will deal with your stupidity, and then . . ." The menace in his cold, angry face sent a chill along Kate's nerves and she drew in a sharp breath. "Then, Cavendish, *I* will deal with you."

Seizing Kate's arm in a bruising grip, David jerked her away. "You," he said in the harsh voice of command, "you foolish woman, will come with me."

⤜ 21 ⤛

"**F**or God's sake, change your clothes." David's voice was low and furious. "You look like a bloody heathen."

He had led her horse across the fort to the surgery, where she hurriedly dismounted, disdaining his assistance. Ignoring his demeaning comment, Kate glared at him. "Why are you doing this, David? I've told you a hundred times that Jamie and I are married. It was no abduction. I was with him willingly." She added bitterly, "McLeod will have your head for this."

On the other side of the fort, the stockade gate clanged shut behind Jamie and his escorts. Involuntarily, Kate took a step toward it. David grabbed her arm in a painful grip. A low moan escaped her. With all her being, she needed to go to her love, to somehow free him from this awful humiliation. It was crazy—as she'd explained to David over and over. He refused to listen.

"We found your quarters like this," he said, pushing open the surgery door. Her half-packed trunks still stood in the middle of the floor. With a pang, she saw the neat pile she'd made of her father's clothes to be given away. "Two weeks ago you were seen riding out of the fort with Campbell. *Two weeks*," he emphasized, tight-lipped. "When you didn't return, it was obvious you'd been abducted. We traced Campbell to the summer encampment, but it was deserted when we arrived."

"Listen to me!" Kate's voice took on a hysterical edge. "Let me tell you again. Jamie came for me to help deliver his sister's baby. I stayed because he couldn't leave until the Sun Dance ended. Crowfoot married us. Jamie's my husband and I love him." The last words ended on a sob.

The dubious expression on David's face added to Kate's frustration. "Find Crowfoot and ask him," she demanded.

"God knows where Crowfoot is now. The fall hunt has started and Indians are moving everywhere." David's words had a ring of finality. For some insane reason, he had no intention of listening to the truth.

"David . . ." she began again, her voice pleading.

Anger flared in his blue eyes and his mouth tightened. "You can stay here for the present, Kate," he told her in a hard voice. "Finish packing. McLeod is expected back soon and he will deal with you." Without looking at her again, David mounted and, leading her horse, rode toward the stables.

"You bloody idiot," Kate muttered to herself. But anger gave way to tears of frustration and fear as she closed the door of the surgery behind her.

After being refused contact with Jamie, Kate spent an unhappy and sleepless night. In the morning she defiantly crossed the compound carrying the breakfast she'd made for him. She was uneasily aware of David watching her from in front of his quarters, aware of the barely concealed anger on his drawn face. They did not speak and he didn't try to stop her.

The stockade was built of palisaded logs all around.

A small dwelling against the inside wall held only rough bunks and an iron stove. Jamie ate standing in the narrow yard of his prison beneath the cold gray autumn sky.

"Why is he doing this?" Kate demanded of Jamie, watching as he mopped up the last of the fried venison with a crust of bread. "Surely he knows McLeod won't allow it."

Jamie gave her a long, considering look. "Don't you know, Kate?" He touched her cheek with one finger. They hadn't kissed or held each other here. Too many eyes were watching. "He wants you for himself. The man is sick with jealousy."

"No!" Kate shook her head vehemently. "You're wrong. David's a gentleman. He'd never . . ." Her protests trailed off as she met Jamie's ruefully tolerant eyes. To her inner horror, she remembered her father's amused assessment of David's attraction to her, the constant attention David had given her from the time they moved into the fort—and only recently, his promise that they would meet in Toronto next year. How could she have been so blind? If she had been more experienced with men, perhaps she would have been aware of the depth of his feelings for her. The painful truth of Jamie's words stilled her denials. She had to believe it, if only to understand David's motives.

Jamie shrugged and set his empty bowl back on the tray she had brought. He seemed to have accepted this incarceration philosophically, certain McLeod would end it as soon as he returned. Perhaps only Kate was aware of the banked fury behind his eyes. The pride of a Blackfoot warrior had been wounded, she knew, and the thought of consequences was a cold fist of fear in her chest.

Tight-lipped, Jamie muttered, "McLeod will have his hide . . . or I will."

Kate remembered that threat with a thrill of fear two days later as she hurried toward McLeod's office through the early morning bustle of the fort. The commissioner had returned yesterday afternoon. Word had been sent ahead of the party and a scarlet-clad line of Mounted Police had been drawn up on the parade ground to greet him, the inspectors and the three wives come to Fort McLeod. The small band played "God Save the Queen"; the women were escorted to the newly completed married officers' quarters. Kate had watched from the doorway of the surgery. No doctor appeared to take over; none seemed to be with the arriving party.

She had meant to face McLeod as soon as possible, but there was no chance. The door to his quarters had closed firmly behind him and his wife, and remained closed as darkness settled over the fort. Kate could hear the Mounties on guard duty making ribald remarks. Sighing, she sought her own bed, vowing that early tomorrow she would have it out with McLeod and that jealous fool, David Cavendish.

But when she took breakfast to Jamie, the stockade was empty. There was not even a guard she could ask for Jamie's whereabouts. Dropping the tray of food, she ran straight for McLeod's office.

Flinging the door open, Kate demanded, "Where is he?"

McLeod looked up from the papers lying on his desk and regarded her with mild reproof. "Sit down, Kate. I was about to send for you."

Instead of sitting in the offered chair, Kate placed her hands flat on the desk and leaned toward him. "What have you done with Jamie?" She was aware of the hysterical edge in her voice and struggled to calm herself.

McLeod leaned back in his chair, stroking his heavy dark beard and studying her coolly. "Campbell has taken the extra horses to Sun River just as he did last fall."

"Why didn't he tell me?" she cried, tears pricking behind her eyes. "Is he all right? What have you done about the outrage David Cavendish committed?"

"Inspector Cavendish has been reprimanded," McLeod replied. Again he waved a hand toward the chair. "Calm down, Kate. In spite of the fact that he overstepped his authority in my absence, Cavendish had ample reason to be concerned about you."

"But to arrest Jamie," she protested. "A reprimand isn't nearly enough punishment for what he did."

McLeod's piercing eyes slid away from her angry gaze. "Campbell explained everything to me." He drew in a deep breath. "Now calm yourself and sit down so we can discuss this."

The commissioner's reasonable attitude was somewhat reassuring. Trembling with frustration, Kate finally sat down. She leaned anxiously toward him and asked, "Did Jamie tell you we were married?"

Something on the ceiling seemed to occupy McLeod's attention. When he didn't answer for so long, Kate felt her nerves go taut with apprehension. Thoughtfully, he stroked his beard, delaying his reply. At last he spoke in stern, fatherly tones. "I feel responsible, Kate. After your father's death, it was certainly my place to see to your comfort and safety. If only you'd agreed to return to Toronto and gone to Fort Benton with me, none of this unfortunate incident would have happened."

Unfortunate incident? Kate stared at him in disbelief that the most important event in all her life could be labeled an "unfortunate incident." "I'm Jamie's wife,

Commissioner." Her voice trembled with emotion.

The commissioner shook his head, denying her. "Perhaps you were led to think you were married."

"Crowfoot himself performed the ceremony," Kate countered. The trend of McLeod's thoughts was beginning to dawn on her, and indignation flamed through her. How dared he disbelieve her, call Jamie a liar and a seducer? Before she could voice her wrath, McLeod shook his head sadly.

"Why, Kate? Why did you do it? Campbell's a half-breed, savage, uneducated . . . so far beneath you . . ." His words trailed off as he gazed sorrowfully at her.

Tight-lipped, shaking with anger, she stood to face him. "I am not a fallen woman, sir. I am the wife of Jamie Campbell and I expect to be treated with respect."

Drawing another deep breath, McLeod faced her across the desk. "All right, Kate," he conceded reluctantly. "You are Mrs. Campbell for now. You are also the only doctor we have, because Dr. Samuelson went on to Fort Calgary, where there's an outbreak of typhoid. You may stay in the surgery until he returns and take care of whatever medical needs the men may have."

He paused, his bearded face stern. "Agreed?"

"Agreed," Kate answered grimly, meeting his eyes without flinching. When Jamie returned, she promised herself, they would go away from here. McLeod would find how helpless he was in the vast Northwest without Jamie Campbell's guidance.

"In the meantime," McLeod was saying as he took her arm and led her toward the door, "it might be wise for you to consider your choices. I'm still willing to arrange your passage back to Toronto."

You can go to hell. Kate swallowed the words she longed to throw in the commissioner's face. Her only satisfaction came in slamming the door hard behind her.

*   *   *

Kate kept to herself, seldom leaving the surgery during the seemingly endless days following McLeod's arrival. The three women were apparently busy settling in and she saw little of them from across the fort. Her patients were few and she thought most came out of curiosity rather than illness. Young Bagley arrived with a cut finger he could easily have cared for himself. While Kate bandaged the cut, he stared at her in an unnerving way. Finally he gained the courage to ask, "Is it true, Miss Kate? You married the half-breed?"

Kate's fingers turned cold at the words, so that the bandage fell and rolled on the floor. Picking it up, she answered in an icy voice, "His name is Jamie Campbell."

Bagley gulped audibly and said no more. He went away looking disconsolate. Kate sighed as she watched him go. If the troopers could make ribald jokes about their commander, she was certain they wouldn't spare her.

After a lonely and unhappy week of waiting, Kate received an invitation from McLeod to have tea with his wife and the other two ladies. She could scarcely refuse. But from the moment she sat down and accepted a cup of tea and a sweet biscuit, Kate was certain all the women had heard the various versions of her story.

Mrs. McLeod was a plump, pleasant woman with kindly eyes. The other two were obviously aware they were being entertained by the wife of their husbands' superior officer and were at great pains to make a good impression.

The bustling Mrs. McLeod had already transformed her rough log dwelling into a pleasant home. There were white curtains at the two windows siding the front porch. Bright rag rugs covered the plank floor. A large, cushioned rocking chair stood beside the fireplace, obviously meant for the master of the house. Mrs. McLeod and her guests took four straight chairs with needlepoint cushions around the low tea table by the fire.

Kate asked about their trip and listened politely. With a surreptitious glance at the ornate ormolu clock on the mantel, she wondered how soon she could excuse herself from this uncomfortable gathering. At last Mrs. Shurtliff found the courage to ask what they all must have been dying to know.

"Did you find life in the Blackfoot camp interesting?"

The underlying meaning of the words wasn't lost on Kate. Swallowing her irritation, she smiled politely. "The Blackfoot are a remarkable people." She hoped they would drop it there.

Instead, Mrs. Winder leaned forward, her eyes avid. "I understand your husband"—there was the slightest meaningful hesitation before the word "husband"— "was raised by the Blackfoot."

"Mr. Campbell"—Kate emphasized the "mister" and hated herself for trying to impress these women— "was raised by the Hudson's Bay factor at Rocky Mountain House . . , Alec Campbell. After he was grown, he lived among the Blackfoot for a time."

Arched eyebrows and smiling nods greeted that statement. She could stand it no longer. Smoothing the skirt of her blue bengaline, a gown she had once loved and now found hideously uncomfortable, Kate rose. "I'm sorry, Mrs. McLeod, but I have a patient coming in for minor surgery. I must go make ready."

There was a flurry of pleasantries. "Thank you . . . so nice . . . good-bye . . ." Outside, hurrying across the compound in the unseasonably cold wind, Kate berated herself. Jamie was her lover, her husband, the only happiness in her life. Why had she tried to make him fit those women's image of what a husband should be? When he returned from Sun River, they would go away from here, she vowed. In the camp of Crowfoot, she was an honored healer and her husband a renowned warrior. Although that life was hard and primitive, it held far more rewards than this place.

Flames licked at the wood in the small iron stove, casting dancing lights in the dark room. Certain there would be no patients seeking help, Kate hadn't bothered to light a lamp when darkness fell. The low flames brought memories of a fire beside a blue lake in the sky. Her longing for Jamie was so deep and so painful, Kate rose and pulled off her clothing. Quickly, she drew her deerskin wedding gown over her head and smoothed it against her body. Jamie's hands had smoothed the dress in the same way. No, not the same—and a sob escaped her. Soon he would return, she reminded herself, and for now, the caress of the soft deerskin comforted her. Weary with her unhappy thoughts, she sat beside the fire, her fingers smoothing the velvety dress against her knees.

A knock at the door startled her. Disoriented, Kate looked around her . . . at the embers of her fire, at the one window of the surgery, filled only with windy darkness. She must have dozed.

David Cavendish stood at the door, the wind tugging at his fair hair. "May I come in, Kate?"

"Do you need something?" she asked coldly, for they had not spoken since the return to Fort McLeod.

David pushed past her, closing the door behind him. He bent to stir up the fire and add more wood. The flames caught, illuminating his tense face.

"Why are you wearing that?" he demanded in a

strangled voice. "You look like—like an Indian whore!"

Shocked, Kate tried to draw away from him, but he gripped her arm fiercely. A feverish light burned behind his blue eyes, and she caught the scent of liquor as he leaned toward her. Sudden fear ran cold along her nerves.

"You are, aren't you?" His voice was hoarse and slurred.

"David!" she protested, trying to pry his hand off her arm.

"Campbell's whore—that's what you are." With unexpected strength, he jerked her up close to him, peering into her face. "You might as well be mine, too." Roughly, he shoved her backward until her knees buckled at the edge of her cot, and he pressed her down onto the blankets.

Terror engulfed Kate. She shoved fruitlessly against his weight, which seemed about to crush her. "David!" she cried, frantically trying to escape the hands groping her body. "For God's sake, David—stop it!"

He seemed not to hear her frantic pleas, grunting in his effort to subdue her. Desperately, Kate turned her face away from his searching mouth. Sick and scared, she knew what she must do when he half rose to loosen his trousers. She brought her knee up with such force that he fell backward on the floor, doubled over and crying out with pain.

From one of the bags she had left packed, Kate took her father's Northwest Mounted Police pistol. Very deliberately, she loaded it as he'd taught her, contemptuously watching the man writhing on the floor.

"You won't die of it, David," she told him coldly when his moans finally eased. Straightening her clothing, she seated herself, the pistol in her hand, and waited for him to recover.

The dark room was silent except for David's labored breathing as he finally pulled himself to a sitting position and rested his head on his knees.

"Why, David?" she asked, looking down at him with loathing. "How could you do such a thing?"

His glance was hostile and unforgiving. "You should have been mine, Kate. I meant it to happen when the time was right."

Kate could only stare at him, amazed that behind his proper English facade there lurked this kind of unbridled passion. She'd grown fond of him, and she'd enjoyed his attentions, even occasionally letting herself consider the possibility that he might court her, marry her. But that was before Jamie, and those fancies had been born of desperation. She hadn't really taken them seriously. If only she'd been wise enough to see the depth of his desire, she might somehow have avoided this kind of unforgivable behavior.

"I loved you." David groaned and laid his head down on his knees again.

Past tense, Kate thought wearily. He loved her no more. She had violated all the proprieties. She was a fallen woman in his eyes.

David staggered to his feet and opened the door. An icy wind swept through. Kate scarcely felt it for the coldness within her.

"We could have had a life together," David said, pausing beside the open door, his eyes accusing. "You have ruined everything."

~ 22 ~

*I*n the ten days since McLeod had so summarily
sent Jamie to Sun River, autumn had blown across
the land in a rush. Along the river, cottonwood
leaves glowed golden in the cold sunlight. Each morning, frost lay on the north side of the surgery. From the
autumn sky the melancholy honking of southbound
geese foretold the winter that would soon follow them
down from the northlands. Now the buffalo hair would
grow long and Blackfoot hunters would gather the valuable winter robes in their urgent effort to recoup the
prosperity lost to the whiskey traders.

None of the Mounted Policemen said anything to Kate
about her time among the Blackfoot, but there were sly
glances and meaningful grins as she passed on her er-
rands. While she waited impatiently for Jamie's return,
she kept to the surgery, except when it was necessary to
bring supplies from the commissary. Her patients were
few, obviously reluctant and embarrassed. As David had
so cruelly said in that ugly confrontation, they thought
her a whore. He had gone on patrol the day after his
attempt to rape her, a circumstance for which Kate was
thankful. She doubted she could bear to face him again.

When Jamie came back, Kate decided, they would go

to Crowfoot's winter camp. The discomforts of Blackfoot life seemed to her nothing compared with her growing unhappiness here. She was determined to prove to the world that she and Jamie were truly husband and wife. If Father Scollen came through again this winter, she would have him perform a marriage ceremony, even though it would mean less than those brief words of Crowfoot. In the meantime, she could only wait for her love's return from Sun River.

Late-afternoon light slanted through the window onto the medical book Kate was trying to read to crowd out her melancholy thoughts. Outside, the sky was a dull, threatening gray. No rain had fallen, but a cold wind blew from the north.

The mournful sound of the wind was broken by a sudden commotion on the parade ground. Horses arriving, cheers, shouts and curses. Kate's heart leaped with the certainty that Jamie had finally returned from Sun River, and she hurried to peer out the door.

Hope drained away when she saw that the Mounted Police patrol had just returned, the one led by Inspector Cavendish. They were being greeted boisterously by a crowd of troopers milling about in front of McLeod's office, shouting questions at one another. At the hitching rack, two men sagged on their horses, hands tied behind them: prisoners.

Mrs. McLeod, who had asked Kate again to tea and tried to be kind, had told her there were rumors the whiskey traders were moving north again. "The commissioner says the Americans are testing the resolve of the Mounted Police," she advised Kate, her loyal little face resentful of those who would contest her adored husband.

Trooper Bagley rode toward Kate from the crowd of policemen, his young face flushed with excitement. "We caught 'em,'' he told her. "Whiskey traders with a cart-load of alcohol and a cart full of skins.'' He waved to-ward the gates, where two creaking Red River carts were being pulled inside. "It's Cal Dodd.'' He indicated the burly man being dragged from his horse by two of the troopers. "He's a bad one, they say. Been selling whis-key for a long time.''

The other prisoner sagged awkwardly on the ropes tying him to his saddle. "That's an Injun,'' Bagley in-formed her. "Got shot up pretty bad. None of the Mounties were hurt,'' he added proudly. "Inspector Cavendish was upset that one man got away. We think he was an Injun, too.''

"What about the injured man?'' Kate broke into his excited story. Even as she spoke, the prisoner slid from his saddle to the ground, obviously unconscious.

"Oh . . .'' Bagley looked embarrassed. "Inspector wants to know if you'll treat him, even though he doesn't think the b—the man will make it.''

"I'm the doctor,'' Kate said briskly. "Have them bring him to the surgery.'' She hurried inside to set wa-ter to boil and lay out her instruments. Working swiftly, she spread the cot kept for patients with a much-washed blanket and donned her heavy apron.

Two policemen staggered through the door she'd left open, one holding the prisoner's feet, the other his shoul-ders. They slung the injured man onto the cot as they might have handled the carcass of a slaughtered deer. He lay inert, totally unconscious.

"The other man—Dodd—was he hurt?'' Kate asked as she picked up her scissors to cut away the Indian's bloodstained buckskin shirt.

"A scratch.'' The trooper shrugged. "Inspector Cav-endish bandaged it. He'll be all right.'' He stared down at the injured man without compassion. "Too bad we didn't finish this one off. Save everybody's time and trouble.''

Such callousness appalled Kate, even though this man was a criminal. Pausing in her work, she glared at the speaker. "He's a human being," she said curtly.

With a mirthless chuckle, the trooper replied, ''Naw, he's an Injun.'' Without a backward glance, the two men left the surgery, closing the door firmly behind them.

The bullet wound in the man's broad chest was large and ragged. It had bled copiously by the look of his clothing. Now the blood seeped slowly, and faint pink bubbles rose from the wound with each shallow, labored breath. Turning him onto his side, Kate saw that the bullet had gone completely through him. She cleaned and bandaged the exit wound. Then she stood studying him, trying to decide her next move and knowing how little chance she had of saving his life.

He had a coarse, heavy face and wore his thick black hair in traditional braids. Groaning with pain, he muttered a few words she recognized as Blackfoot. Unlike most Blackfoot warriors, this one ran to fat, a roll of belly hanging over the belt that held up his breechclout and leggings. The fat would make his wound more difficult to dress.

For a flash that seemed to last forever, Kate stood looking down with pity at the man, her mind racing back into the past. Long ago a terrified little girl had watched her father and the nurse labor to save her dying mother. She fetched and carried for them, longing to take part in the struggle—anything to save her beloved mother. It had seemed to her then that death was a menacing, hovering presence, the enemy to be fought and conquered. Afterward, when the sorrow had dulled, Kate often thought that was the moment when she had determined she would be a doctor, a fighter against death.

It should be no different with this man, she told herself now. He was her patient, a human being with a right to live, a victim of mindless violence as her mother had been. She was the doctor with the healer's mandate to fight death with all her skill.

Darkness fell, made deeper by the rain that came blown on great gusts of cold wind. Kate lit the lamps and barred the door, as she had done every night since David's unwelcome visit. Fear that some of the other men might feel as he did—that she was a whore for the taking—lay always beneath the surface of her mind. She'd debated whether to go to McLeod with the story, but reluctantly decided he would only tell her again that she should go home to Toronto. And she knew she could never tell Jamie.

By lamplight, Kate cleaned her patient's wound with boiling water, telling herself to put other things from her mind. She placed a moist compress of healing herbs over the pulsing lung wound, then bound it all tightly.

With a warm, wet cloth, she carefully cleaned his scratched and dirty face. At the dampness against his lips, the man reacted, licking thirstily at the moisture. Black eyes flickered open and stared up at her face framed in the lamplight. "*Nat-o-ye,*" he muttered hoarsely through cracked lips. *Of the sun,* Kate mentally translated and, without thinking, touched her hair, which all the Blackfoot had thought like the sun itself.

Lifting his head, she tried to help him drink. After the first swallow, he choked and coughed violently, spitting up bright blood. His body went slack and unconscious. He's dying, Kate thought, and knew she could not accept that verdict. All life deserved life. Death was the enemy. Somehow, she would save this man.

Night deepened and the sounds of the fort faded into silence, with only the occasional snort of a horse or the distant cry of a coyote to break the quiet. Her patient's fever rose. Kate bathed his face and chest with cool sage water again and again. Sometimes he muttered incoherently, but he did not regain consciousness. "You will live," she told him fiercely. If this man lived, it would prove her worth as a doctor even more than her work with Laughing Girl. He had to live.

Sometime in the early hours before dawn, he began to shiver violently. The fever dropped. Kate hurried to build up the fire and warm the stones she and her father had once used to warm their beds on winter nights. Wrapping the hot stones in towels, she placed them next to her patient, then brought more blankets to cover him and restore living heat to his shivering body.

At last he quieted and fell asleep. This night had seemed to go on forever. Her apron was soiled with blood and sweat. The stink of the man filled the small room. Exhausted as she had never been, Kate sat at the table, thinking she would simply lay her head down for a minute. She was instantly asleep.

Dawn stained the window when she awakened to the gasping of the Blackfoot. On her feet at once, she went to his side and saw how he struggled for breath. His heartbeat was wildly erratic—then suddenly it beat no longer. "No!" Kate told him angrily. "No—you won't die!" Placing her palm over his heart, she pushed with all her strength, again and again, willing the heart to beat once more. Slowly, faintly, it began. She had won. Through the window she saw the fort stirring into the awakening day. Tears poured down her weary face as she tucked the blanket around the unconscious man.

Kate raised her head from the table, wondering how long she had slept this time. She saw that her patient hadn't moved, but he still breathed, long-spaced, shallow breaths. The threatened storm had blown past, and brilliant noon light lay on the parade ground. With a weary sigh, she rose. She must report to McLeod. A glance in the mirror at her drawn face and disordered hair told her it would be best to clean herself up first.

She had just changed her dress and was arranging her hair when someone tried the barred door. Someone come to check on the prisoner, she thought, and hurried to lift the bar. Sunlight poured into the dim room, blinding her for a moment. Then she saw that Jamie stood in the doorway.

With a cry of joy, Kate leaped into his arms. His rain-soaked buffalo robe slipped to the floor and he kicked the door shut behind him as his mouth devoured hers. "Jamie," she murmured when she could breathe again. "Jamie . . ." She repeated his name again and again as she held him close and rained kisses on his grinning face.

"*Nit-o-ke-man*, beloved," he said, and kissed her with such passion that her knees went weak and she leaned against him. "I'm back." He looking lovingly into her eyes and smoothed her hair tenderly.

"Jamie . . ." She couldn't stop saying the name, or stop kissing his face. "I was so afraid when you went away without telling me."

"Damn McLeod," Jamie growled. "He insisted I leave immediately. I think he hoped to ship you off to Toronto before I came back."

"Never," she told him vehemently, taking his face in her hands and kissing him with all the pent-up passion of their days apart. That kiss stirred him as deeply as it did her. Jamie took a shaky breath and held her away.

His dark glance took in the room and froze at the sight of the figure on the cot. "He's wounded," Kate explained, following his shocked stare. "A detachment arrested him with whiskey and brought him here.''

Jamie went perfectly still. His arms fell from around her as he stared at the wounded man. ''Big Rib,'' he said in a hollow voice.

''He was shot in the chest—a bad wound,'' Kate said, puzzled by the sudden change in Jamie. ''I've worked all night to save his life. I'm not sure yet.''

''In Montana they told me he was dead.'' Slowly rising anger rasped in his voice, and Kate shuddered at the furious glitter of his eyes. ''I meant to kill him then.''

With those words, Jamie lunged toward the bed and grasped the unconscious man by the throat.

Kate's horrified screams filled the room. Seizing Jamie's broad shoulder, she struggled desperately to pull him away from her patient. Her strength was nothing against his as he lifted Big Rib from the bed. Staring with murderous rage into the blank face, Jamie shook the man as though to awaken him to meet his death.

''No, Jamie! No!'' Even as her screams of protest echoed in the small, dim room, Kate heard the death rattle in Big Rib's throat and knew all her efforts had been in vain.

His face twisted with fury, Jamie threw the body back against the cot. Kate confronted him as he turned away, tears streaming down her face. ''You've killed him!'' she cried in painful accusation. ''I saved his life and you killed him!''

The rage drained out of Jamie as he looked into her beloved face, hostile now with accusation. He reached out for her, but she shoved his arms aside. They stared at each other for an endless moment and Jamie felt a cold sense of loss fill his heart. Wearily, he told her, ''Big Rib and Good Young Man raped and murdered my mother. Blackfoot justice demands a life for a life.

Big Rib knew I searched for him. He ran and kept running.''

"Now he's dead. You have your Blackfoot justice and you are a murderer," she cried. There was no love in the gray eyes that had once softened with passion for him—only loathing, a repugnance that added to the growing emptiness within him. Once more he reached out to touch her, and she cringed away from him.

"Understand, Kate . . . please." She must see; he must reach past the horror in her eyes. "There's a code of honor all Blackfoot warriors live by. I would be less than honorable if I didn't take revenge for what was done to my mother." His pained glance went to Big Rib's body. "This man was filth."

"And you are a savage." Kate spit the words at him. "Get away from me."

Drained and numb, Jamie could only gaze into the beloved face filled now with contempt. All that had been between them—her tenderness in caring for his wounds, the glorious, loving days beside the blue lake—all were nothing if she hated what he really was.

He drew a deep, anguished breath. Anger stirred in him, for if she loved him as she said, she would at least have tried to understand his motives. Shaking his head as though to shrug off the pain, he told himself he had always known it couldn't be. They were of different worlds, with different values. What they had shared was stolen from time. Now it was lost forever. He would go back to his own—to the Blackfoot. In one swift move, Jamie picked up the wet buffalo robe and went out the door.

Stunned, frozen where she stood, Kate stared at the closed door, Jamie's departing figure imprinted on her brain. She had convinced herself they could make a life between their two worlds. Now she knew those worlds could never be reconciled. Jamie was always the warrior and he had taken the life she'd struggled to save. She was a healer; it was the whole meaning of her life. To take a life for any reason was a betrayal of all she stood for. The overwhelming passion she had shared with Jamie Campbell could not survive the fundamental differences in their cultures.

With that agonizing realization, Kate gave way to wild weeping. The aloneness she had felt before those enchanted days with Jamie was nothing compared with the emptiness that filled her heart now.

23

"The rumors in Montana are that the whiskey traders are coming back." Jamie leaned his chair against the wall and looked into the commissioner's glum face. He knew the commander was annoyed that he hadn't reported at once on his arrival. Kate had to come first, and Jamie steeled himself against the pain every memory of her brought. In an exchange so ugly he couldn't bear to think of it, he'd lost her, finally and forever.

Stunned by Kate's violent reaction, he'd fled Fort McLeod as though pursued. At Crowfoot's lodge he had found, as always, unquestioning acceptance even of such a black mood. This morning Constable Turner had arrived there, bringing the commissioner's summons to report. Despite his reluctance to return to the fort, Jamie knew he owed McLeod that much. Perhaps any activity was better than sitting here tearing himself apart.

Fully under control by the time they'd ridden to the fort, he was doing his job now—reporting what he had learned on his journey to Sun River. Behind his desk, McLeod frowned on hearing Jamie's news.

Outside the office window, a blustery autumn wind stripped dry leaves from the cottonwood trees surrounding the fort and rattled the windows. Jamie leaned over to feed another stick of wood into the stove.

"Bloody hell!" McLeod thumped a fist on his desk. "Thought we'd taught them a lesson. There's too much money involved. They can't leave it alone."

"They think the Mounties have shot their wad," Jamie said laconically, "and they're gambling you won't bother them."

"Then the bastards lose." McLeod's voice was thick with anger. "This time we'll wipe them out for good."

Jamie regarded him with cool irony. "I've heard the Americans said that, given free rein to sell whiskey, they could solve Canada's Indian problem in two years." In reply to McLeod's probing look, he added, "Drunken Indians would kill each other, or they'd die of poisoned whiskey. If all the Indians are dead, the problem is solved."

"Americans!" McLeod spit the word in disgust. He stood up decisively. "We'll stay on full alert. You can contact the Indian camps for information on any whiskey sellers moving in. I want them wiped out before they get started trading this fall."

"Then *I* might as well get started." Jamie rose, anxious to put distance between himself and Kate. After that agonizing parting, he had intended to go back south and search for Good Young Man. He would finally complete his duty to his murdered mother. Now it seemed McLeod needed him again.

In the months they'd worked together, Jamie had come to respect the commander's forthrightness, honesty and strict discipline of himself as well as his men. He and McLeod had a common goal—to rid the Northwest of the whiskey traders. This fall the Americans would learn that the Mounties were in control here. They would have to keep their vile business on the other side of the Medicine Line.

"Don't leave yet." McLeod held up a staying hand. "We've other business to take care of." As if his words were a signal, someone knocked at the office door.

Jamie sucked in a steadying breath when David Cavendish entered in response to McLeod's "Come in!" Impotent rage shook him as he watched the red-coated inspector salute his commander and wait at attention.

Before he left so hurriedly for Sun River, Jamie had demanded of McLeod exactly how he meant to deal with Cavendish's treatment of him and Kate. "He'll be reprimanded," the commissioner had replied stiffly. Jamie had wanted to shout at him with all the anger boiling inside him.

"Reprimand," he'd managed to say sarcastically. "Damn weak punishment for arresting an innocent man." When McLeod had answered only with grim silence, Jamie added, "But it was only an innocent half-breed, wasn't it?" And he'd ridden away before he took his wrath out on the commissioner.

So McLeod had decided not to let the matter lie, he thought in surprise as he studied Cavendish through half-closed eyes. He took his chair again, leaning negligently against the wall, his face like stone.

"Inspector Cavendish," McLeod began in his most military tone, "in the interest of harmony among the troops, we have some unfinished business here between you and Campbell."

Cavendish's face flushed, nearly as red as his jacket. His lips tightened and his blue eyes darkened. "As I told you before, sir," he replied stiffly, "I was merely doing my duty as I saw it."

McLeod muttered something into his beard and shuffled the papers on his desk. "Quite so," he finally said and cleared his throat as he stood up again.

"Gentlemen," he began, his glance going from Jamie to Cavendish, "in my experience it's best to stop trouble before it begins. Campbell here"—he indicated Jamie—"feels he has been badly treated. And you, Inspector, were more than a little hasty in your conclusions and your actions."

Tension vibrated in the room as Cavendish stared blindly at his commander, unable to conceal his resentment. Jamie rose from his chair, nerves taut as a bowstring, as he watched this amazing scene.

"Sir . . ." Cavendish began, and McLeod stilled him with an upraised hand.

"An apology is in order, Cavendish." The words were a command. The silence following those words was so filled with hostility it was almost palpable.

Stunned that McLeod would actually expect one of his officers to apologize to their half-breed guide, Jamie stood frozen to the spot. His respect for McLeod rose to new heights.

Obviously unwilling and struggling to hold back his anger, Cavendish turned to Jamie. "My apologies, Mr. Campbell," he said as though the words burned his tongue.

Jamie merely shrugged an acceptance. Under McLeod's fierce glare, the two men shook hands. That would be the end of it as far as the Mounted Police were concerned. But Jamie knew he would not forget his own humiliation, nor would he forgive.

Watching a rigid, resentful Cavendish stalk out the door, Jamie's heart went cold. Would he go to Kate? Had she forgiven the man and made friends with him again? He couldn't believe she would, but then, he'd never have believed she'd denounce him for venting his fury on a dying man. Kate was a doctor. She should know he hadn't killed Big Rib. The man was dying before Jamie had ever touched him.

"Is there anything else you wanted to discuss with me?" McLeod asked, breaking the silence filled only with Jamie's unhappy thoughts. Obviously, the whole incident with Cavendish was ended as far as the commissioner was concerned.

Moving to the window, Jamie looked out across the parade ground to the closed door of the surgery, closed against him just as Kate had closed him out of her heart.

"About Kate . . ." he began, his back to McLeod.

He heard the commissioner clear his throat in an embarrassed manner. "I spoke with her yesterday when I was trying to find you. She said she didn't know where you were and didn't want to know."

Pain lanced through Jamie and he closed his eyes tight as though he could shut out reality. With an effort, he composed his face in stoic lines and turned to McLeod.

"I want to know she's safe and well cared for," he said in a surprisingly steady voice.

"It was unwise, Campbell, unbelievably foolish," McLeod said. Some sense of Jamie's anguish must have reached him, for he paused. When he spoke again, it was in a tone of reassurance. "I'm trying to convince her to return to Toronto. I think that would be best."

The thought of her so far away, forever beyond his reach, tore Jamie's heart. He could only mumble, "Has she agreed to go?"

"She's a damn stubborn woman."

At the disgruntled exclamation, Jamie tried desperately not to smile, not to let himself hope. "Yes," he agreed. It was all he could bear to say.

After a moment of silence, McLeod spoke, this time as commander of the Northwest Mounted Police. "I need you to go to Fort Calgary and bring Dr. Samuelson back. Perhaps when he's here to take over the surgery, Kate will see she has no choice but to accept my offer of passage back to Toronto.''

On the stoop in front of McLeod's office, Jamie paused to secure his wide-brimmed felt hat against the wind. Once more, inevitably, his eyes went to the surgery across the way. Smoke rose from the chimney into the cold blue autumn sky, but there was no other sign of life within.

There was some comfort in knowing McLeod was a man of integrity. He would see that Kate was safe and sheltered. With a deep, aching breath, Jamie tore his hopeful gaze from that door and mounted his horse. He had nearly reached the fort gates when the longing for Kate overcame his pride. Perhaps there would be some way to make her understand his Blackfoot-warrior sense of honor and duty. Turning the horse, he rode quickly to the surgery and dismounted.

"What do you want?" Kate demanded of him, her gray eyes as cold as a winter sky. She held the door barely open, not welcoming him inside.

"You're my wife, Kate," Jamie answered softly, forcing himself to ignore her obvious rejection. "My love . . . we can't end what we've been to each other."

"You ended it when you became a murderer," she replied hoarsely, tears welling in her eyes. "How could you do such a thing to a man already half dead? The nightmares I told you about—my mother and the riot— now I have another nightmare." She caught back a sob and turned her face away.

Jamie stepped into the room, closing the door behind him. His heart aching for her pain, he took her by the shoulders, seeking to draw her into the comfort of his arms.

"Don't!" Kate placed both hands against his chest, holding him away from her. "I can't bear to look at you." With a strangled sob, she bowed her head.

Sick with the certainty that nothing he could say would bridge the enormous gulf between them, Jamie gazed down at her, longing to caress that bright head, to hold her.

"I explained to you," he managed to say in a ragged voice. "Blackfoot justice demands retribution. My honor is at stake."

With a furious gesture, Kate brushed the tears from her face and stared coldly at him. "Then your honor is all you'll have, Jamie."

For what seemed an endless time, their eyes locked in a battle in which there could be no victor. Kate's words of rejection echoed and reechoed in Jamie's brain. It was ended . . . all the joy of her, all his loneliness vanquished by her love . . . all the pleasure they'd shared in each other's bodies . . . Ended.

Taking a deep breath, Jamie spoke at last. "You are free, Kate." His voice was low, strangled in the bitterness of what he must say. "A Blackfoot marriage means no more in the white world than Blackfoot justice."

Covering her face with both hands, Kate turned her back to him. Jamie allowed himself one last, long look at her beloved figure before he walked out the door into the cold and lonely future.

The pity in McLeod's eyes only served to arouse Kate's ire. She wanted no pity, especially from a man who'd just sent for her to tell her again how foolish she'd been in the matter of Jamie Campbell. She'd spent a sleepless night agonizing over her parting with Jamie, certain it was forever, and even more certain she couldn't bear that she had lost her one and only love.

"It's a problem, Kate," McLeod was saying as she sat stiff with anger before his desk. "Yesterday I sent Campbell to Calgary to bring the doctor back here for the winter. He'll be moving into the fort surgery. The riverboats won't run again until next spring, and I'd hesitate to send you south to the American railroad because of the hostiles."

She hated this, hated having her actions enumerated and criticized. If she'd made mistakes this past year, she would have to live with them. She'd already told McLeod that her relationship with Jamie had ended. Now there was no indication what McLeod was leading up to, but he probably intended to impose some decision of his own on her.

"It was Adela's suggestion," he said, and his deep voice softened at the mention of his wife's name. "She's always been one to care for the lamb that has strayed."

Kate's face turned hot with anger and humiliation at those words. She was no one's stray lamb and she was perfectly capable of taking care of herself.

Blandly, the commander continued. "She proposed that we build a room for you onto our quarters. You would be our guest until spring, when you would go back to Toronto."

"Charity, Commissioner?" Kate asked without a trace of gratitude in her voice.

He frowned and protested lamely. "Not really, my dear. Just a solution to the problem that confronts us." A solution, she guessed, that he cared for even less than she did. His adoring wife had scarcely arrived. Any man would resent company when he had a year of loving to make up for.

When Kate didn't reply, merely sat looking down at her hands clasped in her lap, he cleared his throat. "Well?"

"Your wife is very kind," she finally managed to say, her throat tight. She rose from her chair, avoiding his probing glance. "I'll finish packing now."

Her shawl pulled tight against the cool autumn wind, Kate walked quickly across the parade ground. She hadn't promised anything. Kindness was a fine thing, but she couldn't bear to be the object of charity no matter what name McLeod gave it.

It was too late in the year to go east, and she couldn't stay in the fort—couldn't bear to, even if a place was made for her. There was only the town of McLeod. Conrad's name came into her mind then, and the conversation about her father's practice . . . the pharmacy. Suddenly hope buoyed her spirits. Kate lifted her chin determinedly and turned her steps toward the stables. She'd ride into town at once and talk to Mr. Conrad.

"Kate! Kate!" Breathless from her dash across the parade ground, her skirts held high to avoid the litter of horse dung, Adela McLeod confronted Kate. "What on earth are you doing?" she demanded, eyeing the two packhorses Kate had just finished loading.

Kate struggled to hide her dismay at this interruption. In the two days since her interview with McLeod, she'd quietly packed all her belongings. Arrangements had been made with Conrad. He'd promised the place would be ready today. She'd hoped to slip out of the fort unobserved, without explaining or justifying her decision to anyone.

The horses were hers, she'd told the young Mountie in charge of the horse herd. She didn't add that they had been given as her bride price. That memory hurt too much. The parfleche filled with the wedding gifts given to her by the Blackfoot women brought hurtful memories, too. In the end, she couldn't bear to leave them and added the pack to her horse's burdens.

Now Adela had caught her in the act of leaving. Kate sighed resignedly. "I'm moving, Adela," she said matter-of-factly. Kate knew she looked dreadful in the worn old brown stuff dress, her hair tied up in a scarf. Mrs. McLeod, always dressed as though expecting company, had been extraordinarily kind since her arrival. It might have been on her husband's orders, but Kate thought her kindness came from the heart. She was certain the other women simply followed Adela's lead.

"You can't move," Adela protested in dismay. "Where will you go? Not . . ." Her eyes widened, so that Kate was sure she had been about to ask if she meant to go to the Blackfoot winter camp upriver.

While she tied the last of her bedding from the surgery to the saddle, Kate explained. "Mr. Conrad, who runs I. G. Baker's store in town, wants to start a pharmacy. He's asked me to take charge of it. There's a room for me in the back and I can treat patients there—if any come to see me."

"But, Kate . . ." Adela wrung her hands together in real distress. "Please wait until the commissioner comes back from patrol. The town is no place for a woman alone."

"I *am* a woman alone, Adela," Kate replied stiffly. Seeing that Adela's distress was genuine, she relented, reaching out to pat the woman's shoulder reassuringly. "You mustn't worry. I have a job and a place to live. That's all I need for now."

"Kate . . . the commissioner . . ." Adela's voice fell as Kate mounted her horse.

"Give him my regards," Kate said ironically. She was determined not to show any weakness, nor to reveal the pain roiling inside her.

"Will you come see me?" Adela laid a detaining hand on Kate's knee. "I'll worry about you."

"Of course," Kate replied, not really promising. Leading her packhorse, she rode out the gates of Fort McLeod, under a cold gray autumn sky, for what she thought might be the last time.

In the short year since Fort McLeod was built, the town on the opposite bank of the river had burgeoned. A biting autumn wind kicked up dust from the wide street as Kate rode along, considering the uninviting prospects ahead of her. She'd make the best of it, she reminded herself; do what had to be done. When spring came, there might be other possibilities. The thought of Jamie rose with painful clarity and she shoved it away. Foolish, the commissioner had said. Perhaps he was right, but that didn't stop the yearning, the dreams that filled her restless nights, nor could she ever erase memories of those brief, enchanted days with Jamie.

T. C. Power from Fort Benton had erected a store to compete with Baker's—one of the reasons Conrad was anxious to add the pharmacy. There were Mounted Police horses tied in front of the ramshackle billiard hall. Male laughter drifted from inside. A blacksmith was hard at work next to the livery. The chair in the tiny barbershop was occupied. The hitching rack at the rustic one-story hotel was filled with horses. A few shacks had gone up away from the main street to house arriving settlers and those who worked in the town. Conrad had built himself a stout log cabin. From a distance Kate heard a woman call to her children. Somehow the sound gave her hope that the future would work for her.

"I hope this will do, ma'am," Conrad said, his beefy face doubtful as he showed her the quarters he'd arranged for her in the lean-to stockroom at one side of the store. Already he'd nailed up a sign over the street entrance a few feet from the front door of I. G. Baker's: PHARMACY. The interior connecting door had been boarded up.

Shelves had been built against the walls of the narrow room, some already stocked by Conrad. A rough counter ran across the front, where a small, rectangular iron stove struggled to provide warmth. A sagging, frayed curtain separated her living quarters from the store. There, Mr. Conrad placed her trunks at the foot of a folding cot. An upended wooden crate held a kerosene lamp.

"It's the best I could do just now." Conrad's voice was apologetic. "Even though it's late in the year, it might be possible to order some furniture out from Helena on the next bull train. In the meantime, I'll ask my carpenter to build you a table and benches and anything else you think you'll need."

"You're very kind," Kate said, laying her bedroll on the canvas cot. She hadn't been able to locate the bedroll she and Jamie had brought. Perhaps it was just as well . . . too many memories. Conrad waited expectantly. "This will be fine," she told him in positive tones, giving him a reassuring smile. It would have to be fine. There was nothing else.

"Well . . ." Conrad set down the last of her cases and brushed his hands together. "I'll let you settle in, then. My woman will bring something for you to cook. And I'll have my handyman take your horses to the livery if you like."

"Thank you," Kate said. "I'll see the liveryman tomorrow about their board."

"Well . . ." he said again, ill at ease. "I'll be going."

"Thanks for your help," Kate repeated, and added in

a businesslike tone, "We'll discuss the stock you'll need tomorrow after I've made up a list."

Late-afternoon sunlight spilled through the new window set on one side of the room. A pungent odor of new, green lumber rose to her nostrils, along with the lingering scent of the animal skins Conrad had once stored here. Despite all her brave resolve, the sight of the barren, uninviting room brought a flood of tears. Her mind filled with the memory of Crowfoot's lodge . . . the soft fur couches with warm Hudson's Bay blankets, the buffalo-skin rugs covering the floor, brightly beaded medicine bags hanging from the lodge poles and, in the center, the flickering of the warming fire that brought everyone together in quiet comfort.

For the first time, Kate surrendered to despair. Huddled on the cot, she wept until there were no more tears.

Tears were useless, she reminded herself sternly, and she rose to wash her face at the bucket of water Conrad had left on the counter. Her father's black bag sat there. Kate opened it with trembling hands and took out the smooth wooden shingle with gilt letters reading: T. MAGINNIS, M.D. Sorrow washed over her, and longing for what was lost. Then she shrugged her shoulders, tightened her mouth and went outside. Beside the door she found a nail protruding from the rough lumber. With tears blurring her eyes, she hung the shingle. T. MAGINNIS, M.D. He would have been the first doctor in all the Northwest Territory. Now his daughter would try to take that place in her own way.

❧ 24 ❧

Gradually, in a town where there was little to do, curiosity brought customers to the pharmacy. For Kate, that meant company, people and talk. Mounties bought headache powders and laxatives; townswomen bought patent nostrums for female ills. Almost everyone bought the sarsaparilla drinks Kate mixed from the jars of syrup Conrad had enthusiastically added to her stock. Mounties would wander over from the billiard hall for a glass of sarsaparilla and stand around the warm stove exchanging gossip. At first, Kate thought they seemed uneasy, unsure of how to treat this white woman who had once gone away with a half-breed. One or two men made overtures, but Kate quickly put them in their place. The word must have got around. Now they treated her respectfully, if a bit warily.

In an attempt to make the place less Spartan, Kate hung a brightly printed calico curtain at the window and another to close off her sleeping space. A jar filled with bright October leaves stood on the table Conrad's carpenter had built. Above it he'd added shelves for her books and medical instruments. A treasured cougar skin was draped over her one chair. The parfleche of Blackfoot gifts remained stored beneath her cot.

On the counter, Kate had set up her father's chess game, along with a cribbage board. Often there would be a crowd around both ends of the counter, giving advice to the players or bemoaning a bad move. From last winter, Kate knew how boring life could be at Fort McLeod when the men weren't on patrol. They seemed to enjoy themselves in her little store, although the profit to Conrad was small. She was certain sarsaparilla couldn't compete with the beer at the billiard hall for very long, especially after McLeod had brought the payroll from Fort Benton.

"That new doctor ain't a hair to you, Miss Kate," the rough-hewn Turner said, leaning against the counter and savoring his drink.

Kate managed a tight smile. Dr. Samuelson, whom she hadn't met, lived in the fort surgery and cared for the Mounties now. In the two weeks since she had hung out her father's shingle, Kate had had one patient—a croupy baby named Harry, who belonged to the Jacksons, who ran the livery stable.

"Fact is, he ain't got much hair a'tall," another Mountie offered to appreciative laughter all around.

"Complains all the time. Campbell was damn glad to dump him on McLeod when he brought the old boy in from Calgary and took off again."

There was a sudden silence in the room. Someone coughed in embarrassment. Kate busied herself with wiping spilled sarsaparilla from the stained counter.

The barber's wife came in then, wanting some cascara pills. By the time she left, the tension had gone out of the men. Kate was certain her relationship with Jamie was discussed in the barracks, but they were usually careful to avoid mentioning his name in her presence, even as she listened desperately for news of him. Hating what he'd done hadn't dampened the yearning for him that haunted her lonely nights. Over and over again in those dark hours, she tried to somehow reconcile his values with her own.

"Campbell's gone?" she asked. Again there was silence as the Mounties exchanged uneasy glances.

"Told McLeod he had personal business ... down south. Wouldn't say when he'd be back, so I heard." Turner slanted her a questioning glance, then looked away.

In a quick movement, Kate picked up some of the used drinking glasses and turned to rinse them in the pan simmering on her stove. She couldn't trust her face to hide the emotions she had no intention of revealing to these men. Jamie had gone in search of the other murderer. She knew that beyond a doubt. When he found the man, he would kill him. Sickness grew from the pit of her stomach and crowded her throat as she considered that the man she loved was capable of murder.

Cold air swept through the door as young Bagley entered the store. The boy had apparently forgotten or forgiven Kate's brief transgression with the half-breed. He stood for a moment, adoring eyes fixed on her face. "Brought you a note, Miss Kate," he said, shifting shyly from one foot to the other.

For a flashing moment Kate thought it might be from Jamie and she nearly tore it from Bagley's outstretched hand. It was not from Jamie; it never would be. She chastised herself for such futile hopes and opened Mrs. McLeod's invitation to tea on Friday.

Cold autumn rain followed the wind after darkness fell. Kate pulled the calico curtain over the window and bolted the door. Conrad's handyman had filled her woodbox and now the little stove fought valiantly to warm the drafty room.

It was at this time of day when she felt most alone. Everyone else in the world seemed to have a place to go—Conrad home to his Indian wife, the Mounties to their barracks. She ate a little of the buffalo-meat stew that had simmered all day on the stove. The table built for her to serve as an examining table doubled as her dining table. Setting the stew away, Kate laid one of her father's medical books beside the lamp and drew the chair close. She had nearly memorized the book, but read it again for company—and perhaps for patients who would come after the mother of the croupy child told about the wise woman doctor. That was something to hope for.

As she opened the pages, she thought of Jamie's treasured books and wondered if he still carried them in his saddlebags. Eons ago, or so it seemed, by a blue lake in the sky, they had spoken of those books. "They're company when I'm lonely," he had explained, and he'd listened with tender eyes as she read a sonnet from Shakespeare:

"For thy sweet love remembered such wealth brings,
That I scorn to change my state with kings..."

It was too painful now to remember sweet love after it was lost, Kate thought, and tears blurred the familiar pages of *Gray's Anatomy*.

The sound of someone at the door startled her from sad thoughts. Drunks had knocked there before. That was the reason for the strong bolt and for the peephole the carpenter had cut for her. Whoever was there knocked again, more forcefully this time.

With her usual caution, Kate approached the door and eased open the peephole. Jamie stood there in the dim light, rain dripping from the wide brim of his hat, his dark face inscrutable. Kate's heart lurched painfully.

After a charged silence, he spoke. "I thought you'd need these, Kate." He indicated the bundle under his arm. "Cold weather's coming and I'll be gone . . ." His voice trailed off as she hesitated, then closed the peephole and unbolted the door.

While she locked the door again, he silently surveyed her quarters. Watching his face, she knew he was comparing this poor dwelling with a snug buffalo-skin lodge, just as she had done. Frowning, he turned to her. "Are you comfortable here? Will you be all right?"

So formal, she thought, and remembered when they were last together. After the terrible things said that day, it wasn't surprising there was constraint between them. "It does well enough," she answered coolly. Never would she let him know the loneliness and despair she'd felt in this room.

Jamie laid his wet hat on the counter and stepped into the room. Unrolling the bundle he carried, he revealed a buffalo-skin rug. Kate could only think how warm it would feel when she stepped out of bed in the frosty mornings. Wrapped inside it, safe from the rain, was the beaver-skin robe and the heavy Hudson's Bay blanket from her bride price. Threatening tears burned her eyes at his kindness. How could a man bent on revenge and murder also care for the comfort of the woman who had been his wife?

Refusing that painful thought, Kate took the beaver robe and held its soft warmth against her face.

At once she was flooded with memories of lying in

Jamie's arms on this same robe beside a blue lake that shimmered beneath a star-filled sky. Trembling, she forced herself under control. "You're cold and wet. I'll make some tea."

Ignoring his quiet "No," Kate stoked the fire and put the kettle on. She took the tea caddy from a shelf and set the blue-willow teapot that had been her mother's on the table.

"I only came to bring the things to you," he protested.

Kate turned and their eyes met for an instant that might have been eternity. The fire his presence ignited in her was reflected back in the depths of his dark eyes.

"Take off your coat," Kate commanded in a ragged voice, spilling water on the table as she attempted to fill the teapot. "You'll catch your death."

Jamie gave a short laugh. "I've been out in worse, as you well know." But he took off the wet buffalo coat and dropped it in the corner.

Raindrops blown by the wind rattled against the window. From the wooden sidewalk in front came the steady rhythm of falling rain.

Jamie watched in silence as she made tea. Even as she worked, Kate's eyes were filled with him. He wore a plain, undecorated buckskin tunic and trousers, leather boots instead of moccasins. Lamplight flickered across the planes of his lean face and caught in the gleam of his black hair. The aura of him enfolded her so strongly, Kate grew dizzy, with the familiar ache in her groin. It was madness, she told herself. She should tell him to go away, and quickly. But she could not.

When she handed him the mug of tea, he sipped it slowly, watching her over the rim with smoldering eyes.

Trying to look everywhere except into those eyes, Kate spoke distractedly. "They say you're going south."

He nodded, his expression unreadable. "Are you well, Kate?" he asked, obviously changing the subject. "Is there anything you need?"

Her whole body trembling, Kate shook her head. The silence stretched between them, eyes holding as though mesmerized.

"*Nit-o-ke-man.*" Wife . . . that word, spoken in a soft, caressing tone, shattered all Kate's defenses. She was pierced by a need so fierce and so urgent it could not be denied.

"Jamie!" With a sob, she flung herself against him, frantic with the longing that poured through her.

His arms went around her with such violence she feared she would break in two, and his mouth claimed hers in a savage, devouring kiss. Through the folds of her skirt, through his buckskin trousers, she could feel his hot, hard, answering passion. With a sweep of his arm, Jamie caught her behind the knees just as he had that first glorious time, and laid her on the beaver-skin robe.

Jamie fumbled futilely with her white-woman clothes until she pushed his hands away. While he pressed hot, hungry kisses on her eyes, her mouth, her throat, Kate untied, unbuttoned and pushed off skirt, petticoat, drawers, kicking off her shoes. She was blind to everything but her need to hold him within her, to know again the blazing joy they found together.

Somehow, Jamie's boots and trousers were gone and he lay between her thighs, the hot, pulsing pressure of his erection adding to her madness. No time now for gentle, teasing seduction. They sought only surcease from a need too long unsatisfied.

Kate cried out with pleasure as he entered her and lifted her hips to meet his thrusts. Together they rode the spiraling storm within, until Kate heard herself call Jamie's name and the lamplight burst in a white-hot blaze of joy so intense she thought she would die of it.

Jamie's breath came out in a rushing sound as his body shuddered and went slack against hers. Replete, boneless, Kate stroked his back as her breathing gradually eased. He moved as though to withdraw and Kate embraced him fiercely with her legs. "Don't go," she begged, her mouth searching for his and claiming it in a compelling kiss.

"Don't go," she had said. Jamie yielded to her urgent embrace, certain that her words carried more meaning than her longing for him to stay inside her. Did she mean, don't go south to hunt for your revenge . . . don't go to the Blackfoot duty that separates us?

Still bathed in the moisture of the seed he had spent within her, Jamie felt himself harden again with desire. Gently, he probed her hot, welcoming depths. They lay quiet in each other's arms, letting the sweetness of that joining radiate through every nerve and muscle.

"*No-ma,*" Kate whispered. "My husband, my love. When you take me, we are one being."

"A being not of this world," Jamie murmured, his lips against her pulsing throat. He gasped as she lifted her hips to take him deeper into that heated void.

"Morning Star." The name came naturally to her lips, her breath accelerating as they moved together in measured perfection. "*No-ma . . .* Morning Star." She cried out the words and then could speak no more. With a primitive cry of passion, she stiffened and arched against Jamie. He could hold back no longer. A deep, shuddering groan tore from his throat as his seed burst within her and he was undone.

In the long, singing silence that followed, they lay as though melded together, limbs intertwined, slick with loving. Kate's bright hair had escaped the pins and spread like a glowing sun across the dark fur of the beaver pelts. Jamie moved to lie beside her warm, passive body, bending to kiss her mouth and her throat.

"Don't leave me," she whispered without opening her eyes. Clasping his head, she brought his lips to hers, murmuring softly against his gentle kiss. "You're my husband, Jamie." Her voice was drowsy, on the edge of fulfilled slumber. "Never go away from me again."

His only answer was a kiss. Jamie pulled the blanket over them and held her close as she sighed into sleep. The lamp guttered out, so there was only the light from the flickering flames in the stove. For a long time Jamie lay there in that half dark, holding her, smoothing her hair and pondering her words.

It was as she had said. At the moment of climax they were one being, complete as neither of them was alone. And yet—he sighed and his breath stirred her hair—it was impossible. In the throes of passion, she had half said what she would say on awakening: "Don't go, Jamie . . . give up your Blackfoot honor, your revenge. A life for a life is wrong."

With a soft moan of renunciation, he eased out of her embrace, drawing the beaver fur close around her inert body, covering her with the bride's-price blanket. As he silently dressed, he watched her smiling in her sleep and his heart shattered with the certainty that he would see that smile, hold her in love, no more.

Even during the years at Rocky Mountain House he had felt himself to be more Blackfoot than white. In

Crowfoot's lodge he had become a Blackfoot warrior with a warrior's privileges and a warrior's duties. He had given his vow to the Sun god and now his duty lay to the south, in the death of Good Young Man.

❦ 25 ❧

*P*ale morning sunlight seeped through the thin calico curtain. Surfacing slowly through layers of sleep, Kate murmured, "Jamie . . ." and reached out for him. An icy shaft of fear pierced her consciousness. He was gone. She sat up, staring wildly around, searching for some sign of his presence. There was none—only the blankets he'd wrapped about her.

Closing her eyes, she called up last night . . . the passion they'd shared, the ultimate joy. How could he have gone away after that? Suddenly bereft, she felt the coldness of the room seep into her heart. Gone without a word, or a sign that he would ever return. Had he regretted that wild joining last night? He couldn't have . . . any more than she could regret what they had shared. She only wanted him back in her arms, loving her always, again and again, forever.

"Jamie!" She cried out his name in aching frustration and pounded her fist on the spot where the imprint of his dark head still lingered. A small, hard object lay there. Kate picked it up and tears came to her eyes when she saw it was Jamie's *i-nis-kim*, the tiny beetlelike buffalo stone; his lucky stone that helped him find buffalo and kept him safe. He had placed it there for her while she slept, leaving behind his luck to become hers. Even though the stone told her how deeply he cared for her, she knew then that she had lost him. His way could never be her way. Each of them would be alone, just as Morning Star and his mortal wife would be alone despite their love for each other.

You can't weep for him forever, she admonished herself futilely as she hurried to build up the fire and set the room to rights. Numb with sorrow, she washed all traces of him from her body, certain that body would never again hold him in a loving embrace.

Yesterday's note from Mrs. McLeod still lay on the table. Kate sighed resignedly when her eyes fell on it, knowing she was obligated, if only because Adela had been so kind to her. Moving mechanically, she dressed in her best black skirt and white shirtwaist. From the small leather case in which she kept her few valuables, she took the gold locket that had been her mother's. For a long time she stared at the two small photographs it contained . . . her beloved parents. Then she carefully fit the *i-nis-kim* between the photos, snapped the locket shut and hung it around her neck, pausing for a moment to press it hard against her aching heart.

No customers came to the door. When the hands of her father's gold watch edged toward three, she locked the door and told Conrad she was going to the fort. As she made her way to the livery, Kate told herself that though her heart was in shreds, life still moved on. The commissioner's wife had invited her to tea. She could not stay in her poor little room weeping for a dream that would never be.

"You look pale, Kate, dear," Mrs. McLeod greeted her. "I'm afraid you're not eating right, living there by yourself."

"I'm fine," Kate replied absently, watching through the window as an orderly led her horse across the muddy parade ground. She saw that David was making his rounds as Officer of the Day, side arm and rifle at the ready. They had scarcely spoken since the awful night he'd tried to rape her. Unthinking, she sighed for a friendship lost.

"See, there!" Adela McLeod exclaimed. "You're short of breath. Probably need a blood tonic."

Kate smiled, removing her gloves and folding her shawl. "I'm a doctor, Adela," she reminded the plump, concerned woman peering at her. "I'll take care of myself, I promise."

"There'll be just the two of us today," Adela informed her as they moved into the parlor, where tea was waiting in front of the fireplace.

Kate sagged with relief. Today she couldn't have faced the inquisitive and prying Mesdames Shurtliff and Winder, not with the memory of last night still hot in her mind.

On the tray there were plum cake and lemon tarts and little smoked-fish sandwiches. In this far outpost, Adela was re-creating home. Kate found she was famished, and only courtesy prevented her from eating everything in sight. She sipped the strong, hot tea and listened absently to Adela's prattle, which was punctuated liberally with "The commissioner says . . . The commissioner thinks . . ." Gradually it dawned on her that, as a military wife, Adela had been delegated to convey the commissioner's wishes and persuade Kate to accede to them.

". . . the unfortunate incident with the Indians . . ." Adela was saying. With a start, Kate restrained her hand from fondling the locket and stared at her hostess. Adela flushed.

"We know y-you were abducted against your

w-will," she stammered without meeting Kate's eyes.

"That's not true," Kate protested, but Adela rushed on.

"The commissioner thinks it isn't safe for you to be living alone in town. That man . . . that Indian . . ." Adela's face was scarlet and there was sweat on her upper lip. "He might bother you again."

All Kate's self-control barely kept her from breaking into hysterical laughter. Bother her again? What would Adela and the commissioner say if they knew that last night she had lain on the floor of her ugly little room, lost in passion with "that man"?

Determinedly, Adela continued. "Since you don't want to stay here at the fort, if you agree, the commissioner will make arrangements for you to stay with Mrs. Thompson this winter. You can go to Fort Benton with the next bull train, and take the first downriver boat back to Toronto." She leaned over to pat Kate's hand. "It's the best thing for you, my dear. You see, my husband feels a certain responsibility for your welfare."

Kate gave her a vague smile. She was no longer a resident of the fort, no longer under military control. McLeod couldn't make her do anything she didn't wish to do. But she knew it was futile to argue with Adela, who had no power. So she simply smiled and said, "We'll see."

If she didn't leave now, Kate feared Adela would begin making plans for her, so she stood. "It's been lovely, Mrs. McLeod, but I must get back to the store."

"I'm glad we've settled things," Adela said as Kate donned shawl and gloves and they moved toward the front door. Settled things? Kate thought with irony. She wished anything were settled in her life, especially her feelings for Jamie Campbell.

"Is the prisoner, Dodd, still here?" Kate asked to change the subject.

"John Weatherby refuses to pay his fine," was the tart reply, "so the commissioner refuses to release him. Those Americans will have to come to terms with Canadian law."

So John Weatherby was a whiskey trader. It seemed a hundred years had passed since Kate had met him at the landing in Fort Benton and been repelled by a sense of evil.

She and Adela waited on the front stoop for the orderly to bring Kate's horse. After last night's rain, the October sky was deep blue with a few stray clouds scudding across it. The air felt clean and crisp. Smoke from the fort's chimneys rose above the denuded cottonwoods.

With the shortage of uniforms, the Mounted Police now wore their scarlet jackets only when on guard duty or on special occasions. Otherwise, they had come to dress like any other frontiersmen. Just now, a red-coated guard unbolted the gate to the stockade and led the prisoner out. Dodd was a dark-skinned, burly man, towered over by the tall Mountie. He was dressed in buckskin pants, a soiled white Hudson's Bay blanket capote over his flannel shirt.

A surly, almost desperate expression on his face, Dodd marched with his guard across the muddy parade ground toward McLeod's office. The gates of the fort stood open, as they always did during the day.

Kate's eyes went to Inspector David Cavendish, who stood in front of the guardhouse watching the prisoner, then to the orderly bringing her horse from the stables. She wished she'd left earlier and hoped there would be no opportunity for her and David to meet.

A shout startled her and a chill went down her spine.

The prisoner had broken from his guard and was running frantically toward Kate's saddled horse. For an awful moment the scene seemed frozen in place, a tableau from one of the penny-dreadfuls with tales of the Wild West. Everything before her eyes moved in slow motion.

David raised his rifle to his shoulder and took aim. "No!" Kate screamed, sensing his intention. "No, David—don't!" If he heard, Cavendish ignored her cries. Very deliberately, he squeezed the trigger. The sound of his shot reverberated in the still autumn air. Dodd fell forward into the mud, the back of his white capote suddenly scarlet with blood.

A cry of horror broke from Kate's throat. Her knees went weak and she reached out to support herself against the doorjamb. Adela gasped and put a hand to her throat. At once the compound was filled with Mounties. The wide-eyed orderly tied Kate's horse to a hitching post and ran to join the group looking down at Dodd's unmoving body. With one booted foot, David turned the body over. Dodd didn't move.

"Inspector?" Adela called.

David looked up, frowning. "Go inside!" he commanded harshly. "The man's dead."

"How could you, David?" Kate was shouting hysterically, but couldn't stop herself. "He wouldn't have hurt anyone. Why did you kill him?"

"It was my duty!" David glared at her, furious that she would question his actions. "He was trying to escape."

"You didn't need to kill him!" Kate wailed.

With a peremptory wave of his hand, David ordered, "Mrs. McLeod, take her inside. She's raving."

Adela grabbed Kate's arm, pulled her back into the house and closed the door. "They'll take him away now," she said, trying to appear calm, although her breath came in little gasps. "He was a fool to try to escape, but I guess he saw your horse and thought he had a chance."

She went on talking endlessly as though to ease her own nervousness, urged Kate to a chair and poured luke-warm tea for both of them. Stunned, her whole body as cold as ice, Kate was scarcely aware of her companion. Her inner eye was filled with the horrifying image of David Cavendish, a man of background and education, carefully aiming his rifle to kill a man.

"Inspector Cavendish acted very decisively," Adela was saying approvingly. "The commissioner will be pleased with him." She tasted the cool tea she'd poured and grimaced.

Kate stared at her in amazement. "But he killed the man," she protested.

"An escaping prisoner," Adela admonished as she set the kettle to heat again.

"He was only a whiskey seller," Kate protested once more. "David had no right to kill him."

Adela took Kate's hand, patting it soothingly. "Now, now, my dear . . . you've had a shock. A cup of hot tea will set you right." She stood up straight, her plump face stern. "Inspector Cavendish was doing his duty, the honorable thing. It's what's expected of him. He's your friend. You should be proud of him."

Proud? Kate thought, and shook her head in disbelief. But Adela's words "duty" and "honorable thing" echoed inside her head, calling up those same words on Jamie's lips. Closing her eyes tight, Kate tried to hold back the painful memories. Even now the man she loved, her husband, searched for a man he meant to kill. The Englishman who had been her friend and wished to be her lover had killed a man before her eyes. I am a healer, she reminded herself. I cannot love a man who takes a life.

Adela was pouring fresh tea as Kate rose and drew on her shawl. "I must go," she said and started for the door.

Adela followed, reaching out a detaining hand. "You're too upset to be alone, dear. Sit for a while."

"I must get back." Kate cut her short, knowing only that she had to be alone or she would never make sense of the turmoil in her mind.

The door bolted, curtains pulled, fire blazing, Kate sat at the table and stared at the medical instruments neatly arranged in the makeshift cupboard. Tools for saving lives. In this violent land whose vast prairies and enormous skies she had come to love, could she ever be a healer, a bringer of life? Was it possible to reconcile her reverence for living things, her hatred of death, with the realities of life?

"If you wish to be a doctor, you must accept death as a part of life." Her father's wise words, words she'd never come to terms with. Perhaps it all went back to the tragic death of her mother. The bereft girl-child Kate had been could never really understand or accept a loss so devastating. Nor could she deal with the violence that had brought about her mother's fatal injuries. Now her father was gone, too, and Kate knew that this time she must accept the reality. Jamie had spoken once, in those magical days beside the lake, of the Blackfoot circle of life . . . birth and death, unending through ages of time.

"Jamie." She spoke the beloved name into the dim silence of the room and knew she had wronged him. He was no savage murderer, for Big Rib had been dying of his wound. Jamie's duty and honor were as deeply inbred as those of David Cavendish. Both men could take a life in the name of those two words. But Jamie sought revenge for the ugly murder of his mother; David had killed a man for trying to run away. If she condemned Jamie, she must certainly condemn David.

The reality was that her battle against death could not always be won. Surely the loss was to a power greater than her own. It was a truth she had tried to avoid, but now it grew in her heart, bringing a strength she'd never imagined she could feel. A sensation of comforting warmth enfolded her as though she was in loving arms. There in her cold and lonely room, Kate at last knew she was not alone.

Somehow, some way, she would be with Jamie again. They would mend the breach between them and once more be lovers . . . man and wife as they were meant to be.

An urgent knock at the door brought Kate out of her reverie. She hurried to answer.

"It's my little Harry, Dr. Kate," Mrs. Jackson told her through the peephole. "He's havin' trouble breathing."

A rush of unreasonable joy poured through Kate as she flung open the door and took Harry Jackson's small body into her arms. She was a healer. There was a place for her.

∽ 26 ∾

*T*he smoke of many fires rose from the lodges of the Blood camp, bringing the sweet odor of burning cottonwood. In a blue sky burnished gold by the setting of the sun a long V of geese winged southward, fleeing oncoming winter.

Jamie dismounted in front of the lodge of Red Crow, chief of the Bloods, and waited for acknowledgment of his presence. The ride had been long and his muscles ached for respite from horseback. One of Red Crow's wives, a fine-looking young woman, lifted the lodge flap and bade him enter.

He found Red Crow reclining against his willow back-rest opposite the doorway of the lodge. The fragrant scent of sweet grass rose from a small fire burning in the center.

"Welcome to my lodge, Follows the Eagle," Red Crow said, a smile on his heavy, aging face. He indicated that Jamie take the honored seat on his left and to his wife to bring his pipe. "It is long since we fought together to kill the Cree." Three other men drifted into the lodge and took seats while Red Crow reminisced about the great battle at Belly River when the Bloods and the Blackfoot wiped out the attacking Cree. As he talked, Red Crow meticulously cut up the tobacco to be stuffed into his long-stemmed pipe.

One of the women brought Jamie a bowl of roast buffalo hump and he ate it quickly, knowing the pipe ceremony could not begin until he had finished. What he had to ask Red Crow and the other Bloods would have to wait until the appropriate ceremonies were complete.

Red Crow lit the pipe with a coal from the fire, drew in the smoke and blew it out again to the four winds and to the sun overhead. Then he passed the pipe to Jamie, who repeated the ritual. At the doorway, the pipe was passed back to begin its circulation on the right side of Red Crow. When the pipe again rested in the chief's hands, conversation began.

There was talk of the successful buffalo hunt, with much bragging about how many robes each had taken, some good-natured chaffing of a young man who was courting an unwilling maiden, some touting of individual buffalo runners. At last, Red Crow ostentatiously knocked the ashes from the pipe and uttered the useful Blackfoot exclamation that meant all things: "*Kyi!*"

It was a dismissal and the men rose to leave.

"You will sleep the night in my lodge," Red Crow told Jamie.

When he had unsaddled and taken his buffalo robe and blanket, one of Red Crow's young sons led Jamie's horse away to join the horse herd.

Back in the warm lodge, seated beside his host, Jamie could hear the women talking and laughing around the outside fire. In the distance a baby cried and a dog barked. Those were the comforting, familiar sounds of his life. Some of the tension drained out of him.

"I have come seeking the murderer of my mother," Jamie said in answer to the questioning gaze from Red Crow's deep-set black eyes. "He is called Good Young

Man, and I was told he'd come to live among the Bloods."

Red Crow frowned into the fire, his dark, heavy face filled with anger. "He is gone from here. I banished him. No warrior brings whiskey to my camp, for that brings trouble and death."

So Good Young Man still followed the whiskey trail, Jamie thought, and asked, "Does anyone know where he is now?"

"I will ask among my warriors tomorrow," Red Crow replied. "If he killed your mother, Good Young Man must die."

Both men stared thoughtfully into the fire, Jamie thinking of tomorrow, what he would learn of Good Young Man, and the trail he must follow wherever it led.

"Your people have killed many buffalo this hunt?" he asked Red Crow, who nodded with pride.

Jamie had known that from all the rotting carcasses he'd passed on his way here, and everywhere he'd ridden across the prairies. "Too many, perhaps," he told Red Crow. "There will be other hunts, other winters when the people need food and hides. The hunters should spare some buffalo for the future."

With a careless shrug, Red Crow replied, "Once the people of the Blackfoot confederacy were rich, far richer than the Cree or the Assiniboin or the Crow—the richest people on the prairies. Then the whiskey traders came and made them poor, stealing their robes and horses for their poisonous whiskey. Now the Redcoats have sent the Americans away and my people wish to be rich again. The more buffalo robes they have to trade, the sooner they will have many horses and fine lodges again."

Greed, Jamie thought, a thing unknown or condemned

by this people when he was a boy. Now greed for the good life ruled a people impoverished by their greed for whiskey. He could not rid himself of the sense of foreboding. Greed could destroy the all-important buffalo, and destroy the future.

"You will see," Red Crow assured him. "The Blackfoot confederacy will again be the most powerful nation on the plains." With that final comment, the chief called to his wife to come to his bed. "We sleep now," he told Jamie as the woman banked the fire.

Even when Red Crow's other women had settled into their beds on the opposite side of the lodge and the fire had fallen into embers, Jamie could not find sleep. The gentle flapping of the lodge ears rimming the smoke hole nudged at the edge of his mind. Closing his eyes, Jamie turned restlessly. Tomorrow he would follow the trail of the murderer, and tomorrow go farther in every way from the woman he loved. In the week since he had reluctantly left her sleeping, he'd failed to banish her from his mind. At night, at odd moments in the day, he was suddenly overwhelmed by the memory of her body against his, enclosing him, loving him with wild abandon.

"We are one," she had murmured in the darkness. But in the light of another day and time, she had told him she could not love a man who killed another man. It is done with, Jamie told himself, and cursed softly as he felt himself harden in response to the remembered image: her warm, sweet face; her pale body against the dark beaver fur; her bright hair spread about her as though she had brought down the sun.

It was David's first visit to the pharmacy, and a week since Kate had watched in horror as he deliberately shot the whiskey seller, Dodds. When she asked with restrained politeness if he wanted something, he merely shook his head, then stood in a corner, watching. His brooding presence made Kate so uneasy, she even found the banter of her three young Mountie customers unnerving. They finally departed, and the store was empty before David finally spoke.

"Commissioner McLeod wants you to go to Fort Benton with Baker's next bull train. You need to be aware of the hazards of travel on the plains in winter." It was Inspector David Cavendish delivering an order. He had worn his scarlet jacket and his white helmet, Kate was certain, to emphasize that he was there on official business.

"McLeod is not my commander," she answered sharply and glared at him accusingly. The words burst from her. "Did he approve your killing the whiskey seller, Dodd?"

"Of course." David stared at her in surprise. She saw that he didn't comprehend her meaning, nor would he ever understand how she hated that he'd killed a man. With an inward sigh, Kate surrendered to that reality and let it go.

After a moment's hesitation, David came toward her with his hands outstretched. Remembering too well the last time they had been alone together, Kate quickly put the counter between them.

Unexpectedly, David groaned when he saw that obvious move. "God forgive me for the way I behaved that night, Kate. Can you ever forgive me?"

Kate studied his unhappy face, saw the heartsickness in his blue eyes and felt her anger drain away. "Whatever made you behave like that, David?"

As though he found the words difficult to shape, he delayed his answer for a long moment. He still could not seem to meet Kate's eyes squarely, for he stared out the window into the blue autumn day.

"I couldn't bear it," he began in a voice so low she could scarcely hear. "To know he'd held you in the way I longed to hold you drove me to a kind of madness." He drew a deep, shaky breath. "I was crazy with jealousy, Kate." He turned to her imploringly. "It won't happen again, I promise you. Only forgive me."

"I forgive you, David," she replied and, with trembling hands, took a glass to mix a sarsaparilla for him—anything to occupy her attention while she regained control. How could she have guessed that behind his proper facade there raged the kind of passion that could lead him to try to take her against her will? His attentiveness to her had been flattering. Even though she'd sometimes mused on the possibility of a relationship, there had never been the kind of inner fire she felt with Jamie. With a sense of guilt, Kate wondered if she'd innocently done something to inflame his feelings, but she could think of nothing she'd offered except friendship.

When she handed him the glass of sarsaparilla, he looked surprised but took it, drank sparingly and set it aside.

"You never spoke of your feelings, David," she said quietly, hands steady now as she folded them on the counter. "I never guessed. You were my father's friend, and, I thought, mine, too."

"I loved you. I thought you knew that," David replied. He leaned across the counter, looking with longing into her face. "I'd even dared dream that someday you'd be my wife—go back to England with me."

With a rueful smile, Kate shook her head. "Your world in England is as different from mine as that of the Blackfoot. It couldn't be." She didn't add that it couldn't be because there was only one man in all the world she could ever love, one man who possessed her body and soul for all time.

"It could have been," David answered sadly, studying his hands placed flat on the counter between them. "I loved you, Kate. It still could be . . ."

She met his eyes for the first time. "Perhaps we can be friends again. But that's all."

Beneath the neat mustache, his mouth twisted wryly. "That's all?" When she didn't reply, he spoke brusquely and with authority. "Will you go to Fort Benton as Commissioner McLeod has requested?"

"No," she answered, giving him a smile she saw annoyed him more than her words. "Never."

"This is no life," David protested, indicating the bare, primitively furnished room. "Not for a lady."

He spoke as a friend now, Kate knew, not as McLeod's emissary, but it was no use. She smiled at him forgivingly. "It's my home now, David. I'll stay here."

"Waiting for him?" he asked bitterly.

When Kate couldn't answer, he turned and stalked from the room.

The first snow of the season fell as October ended. This morning it lay white along the narrow ledge of the window. The banked fire in the stove brought little warmth to the icy room. Kate pulled the beaver robe up to her ears and closed her eyes against the queasiness. She wouldn't get up yet, not until the weakness and the nausea passed. In spite of her determination, tears trickled down her cold cheeks.

For the past few days she'd awakened light-headed and sick. When she counted off the weeks, more than a month, since Jamie had been with her and the time since her last flow, she knew it wasn't something she'd eaten.

Cutting Woman's tea, she'd thought, remembering Jamie brewing it for her each morning. But not that last morning when she woke to find him gone and knew it was forever. He'd left something behind in that last night of passion they'd shared. He had left her with his child growing in her womb.

After she had vomited in the chamber pot, Kate built up the fire and crawled back into her bed. The future seemed a blank stone wall confronting her. She couldn't think about it with her head whirling this way, couldn't deal with the obvious consequences of birthing an illegitimate child and caring for its future.

Much later, the slow drip of melting snow from the eaves awakened her. She lay gathering her strength to get up and go about her work when a knock sounded on the door. Donning her wrapper, she opened the peephole. Looking back at her was the calm, handsome face of Cutting Woman.

"Natosin-nepe," Cutting Woman called her by the name the Blackfoot had given her, Brings Down the Sun, and smiled. Sudden tears pricked at Kate's eyes. The warmth in that strong face, the concern reflected in those intelligent black eyes, were exactly what she needed this morning—a mother to comfort her.

Forgetting her attire, Kate flung open the door and drew Cutting Woman inside. Two strong arms embraced her. The dam broke and Kate wept unrestrainedly against the smooth-beaded shoulder of Cutting Woman's doeskin gown.

"*Ni-tun*," the medicine woman murmured, stroking Kate's disordered hair. "Daughter."

At last the paroxysm of weeping passed. Kate wiped her eyes and managed a smile as she gently caressed Cutting Woman's dark cheek. "Welcome," she said, wondering if they could communicate in words, and certain the affection they felt for each other would ease the way.

"Coffee?" she asked, turning to build up the fire and set yesterday's coffee on to warm. Conrad had decided sarsaparilla was a summer drink and that it would be more profitable to sell coffee during the winter. He brought the ground beans and Kate made coffee. She'd even sold a few mugs of her brew.

Cutting Woman's eyes brightened and she nodded vigorously. Coffee was a rare treat among the Blackfoot.

"I must get dressed." Kate signed so that Cutting Woman understood her meaning. Behind the calico curtain, she quickly donned her brown serge skirt, a blue shirtwaist and the old brown sweater that had been her father's. After brushing her hair, she simply pinned it in a knot, quicker than braiding it.

Cutting Woman had moved the chair close to the warm stove and sat, hands in her lap, waiting. When Kate offered her the mug of coffee, heavily laced with sugar, the older woman sighed with pleasure. She relished the salted crackers, too, while Kate nibbled cautiously and sipped cold water.

"I bring gift," Cutting Woman said after they had laughingly attempted conversations with her poor English and Kate's little knowledge of Blackfoot. With great dignity, the medicine woman walked to the counter, where she had left her buffalo robe. She returned to lay on Kate's table a buckskin roll, a twin of the one she had first brought to help Kate treat the typhoid victims.

"Yours," Cutting Woman told her and unrolled the bundle. Inside were the same kind of individual deerskin bags, each painted with a symbol and containing healing herbs collected through the summer, along with the dried herbs they'd collected together that memorable day at the summer encampment.

Unable to restrain her cry of pleasure, Kate touched each bag reverently, knowing this was a gift of great meaning. She turned to Cutting Woman, wondering how she could possibly express her gratitude that she had been chosen for such a favor.

"Thank you." Impulsively, she took the older woman's strong hand and held it to her cheek.

Cutting Woman's dark eyes gleamed with moisture as she took both of Kate's hands in hers and looked into her eyes. "You are medicine woman, too . . . healer. I teach you."

On this cold and muddy day there were few customers to interrupt them. Kate and Cutting Woman sat at the table. One by one, the medicine woman took up each herb bag, explaining in eloquent signs the use of the herb within. Some Kate recognized by smell—sage, wild ginger, red cedar. She listened intently, memorizing signs and meanings as they went. The lore Cutting Woman brought was suddenly as important to her as anything she had learned at her father's side, or any knowledge she might have gained in a medical school.

Conrad's handyman interrupted, bringing wood. The buffalo stew was reheated and as they ate, Kate asked the Blackfoot words for everything in the room. Her eagerness amused Cutting Woman, who ate heartily even as she continued her single-minded teaching.

Darkness fell before they were aware the day had gone. "You will stay the night?" Kate asked with signs, and saw that Cutting Woman understood.

Exhausted, her brain reeling from all she'd absorbed that day, Kate's last conscious thought was of the bitter lady-slipper tea Cutting Woman had made to soothe her. She slept quickly and dreamlessly.

Morning brought her again to her knees beside the chamber pot. Finally, the nausea passed. Kate wiped her mouth and looked up into Cutting Woman's sympathetic eyes. She spoke in Blackfoot, but every word was as clear to Kate as though it were her native tongue.

"Follows the Eagle has given you a child."

Kate nodded as another wave of nausea swept over her, and was amazed by Cutting Woman's joyous smile. Had Jamie told his family nothing of the rift between them, and didn't Cutting Woman think it strange that Kate lived here alone? Under such circumstances, pregnancy wasn't an occasion for joy.

And yet, as she lay back on her cot while Cutting Woman bathed her face with cold water, on some level her heart rejoiced to have Jamie's child in her womb, to have a part of him that would be forever hers.

∽ 27 ∽

"Where the hell is Campbell?" McLeod glared at the Mounted Policemen surrounding his desk, saving his fiercest look for the cowed interpreter who had failed to ascertain the reason an incoherent Three Bulls had come to Fort McLeod. The angry and excited Blackfoot finally waved the interpreter away in frustration. He demanded to speak to Jamie Campbell, a demand he repeated with vehemence.

Inspector Denny spoke up. "Campbell was here yesterday to get his horses. Said he was taking them to Crowfoot's camp for the winter."

"Then go get him," McLeod ordered. "This crazy Indian keeps talking about whiskey. He might have important information."

Dusk fell early in the autumn of the year and the wind was chill. Soon winter would lie on the land, and Jamie thought sadly of Kate's inadequate shelter. Midwinter blizzards would find a thousand holes in that lean-to. A cold gray twilight dimmed the little town of McLeod as he rode through. He could have gone to the fort without passing down Main Street. The two Mounties who had come to Crowfoot's camp for him didn't question the route he chose, nor the fact that he slowed his horse's pace as they neared Baker's store.

Lamps had been lighted in the store and in the little pharmacy, windows glowing golden in the dusk. He had a brief glimpse of Kate's bright head and was transported back to their last night together: her red-gold hair gleaming against the beaver fur; her warm body welcoming his; soaring with her beyond time and space. "We are one," she had said, and his throat ached at the memory.

The scene he saw now, framed by her window, made his heart lurch painfully. Cavendish stood frowning down at a chessboard, contemplating his move, apparently feeling perfectly at home. Kate stood beside him, watching with a half smile. Her hand touched his and she said something. Cavendish looked up as though in surprise, then grinned and moved a chessman. They laughed together, sharing the moment. The rapport he sensed in that exchange tore Jamie's heart. All this time, even while he'd told himself he'd lost her, there had been hope somewhere deep inside. Now she smiled into another man's eyes, a man he hated for humiliating him. The thought of her in Cavendish's arms turned Jamie's mind into a chaos of anger and despair.

The old loneliness that had been eased for such a short time by her love seized his heart like icy hands. She was lost to him forever. It had been a fool's dream. Kate belonged with her own kind. Kicking his horse into a gallop, he startled the two Mounties, who quickly followed as he headed for Fort McLeod.

"Where in the name of God have you been?" McLeod demanded when Jamie entered his office.

Without a glance at the commissioner, Jamie walked over to the glowing iron stove, stripped off his gloves and held out cold hands to the warm flames. "I told you

I had personal business," he growled at McLeod.

Personal business . . . that long and fruitless search for Good Young Man. Everywhere he went, the murderer had already been and gone. That he was in league with the whiskey sellers was a common rumor. Eventually, the Mounted Police would catch him, Jamie knew, but that didn't ease his own frustration or fulfill his vow.

McLeod might have reprimanded one of his troops for such abrupt behavior, but his relationship with Jamie was on a very different level. Pacing, he told Jamie, "We have an informant who can't seem to make himself understood. He wants to talk to you. Maybe you can figure out what's on his bloody mind."

Jamie shrugged. "Where is he?"

McLeod barked a command at his orderly, who had been waiting stiffly by the door. "Bring the Indian." After the young Mountie had hurried to obey, McLeod gazed thoughtfully into the distance. With a sigh, he turned again to Jamie. "Before they get here, I need to ask you about that girl . . . Kate Maginnis."

Jamie stiffened at the words, deliberately wiping all expression from his face.

"Both of you once insisted you were married. Then she said you're not. Now she's left the fort and is living in that terrible lean-to by Baker's store, pretending to run a pharmacy. I've tried to send her home, at least to Fort Benton for the winter. She refuses to leave. I wish I didn't feel responsible for her, but I do." He slapped a frustrated hand on his desk and leveled an accusing look at Jamie. "You're the one who caused all the problems by running off with her. Now I want you to either take her as a wife or persuade her to go back east."

Such a violent turmoil of emotion seized Jamie at those words that he had to turn away from McLeod. For a long time he gazed out the dark window in silence, struggling to control the conflict that tore at him. He wanted her for his wife with every part of his body and soul, yet what he'd seen tonight convinced him he'd lost her. There was no going back to the golden days beside the lake in the sky.

"Well?" the commissioner demanded.

Jamie cleared his throat and managed to speak in a steady tone. "I have no more influence with her than you do. She'll do as she pleases no matter what either of us says."

McLeod's sharp blue eyes flashed with anger at those words. He opened his mouth to reply, when they were interrupted by the guard's appearance with Three Bulls.

The heavyset Blackfoot rubbed his stomach and burped, obviously well satisfied with his supper in the enlisted men's mess.

"See what you can find out," McLeod said to Jamie. "He apparently has information, but he gets so excited in the telling none of the interpreters can make it out."

Jamie motioned Three Bulls to a chair near the stove and sat beside him. They spoke in Blackfoot, and as Three Bulls began his story, the problem became obvious. He had a bad scar on his lip that caused him to lisp, and the more excited he became with his story, the more unintelligible he grew. With many reassurances about the fairness of the Redcoats, Jamie eventually calmed him down enough to make sense of his story.

"Pine Coulee," Three Bulls said, and Jamie nodded, remembering the place two days' ride to the southwest. "Whiskey traders . . . American," Three Bulls continued. "Set up there in the cabin. Lots of Indians come to trade. I trade two"—and he raised two fingers— "horses for whiskey."

Jamie frowned. A good horse was worth two hundred dollars. It didn't seem possible Three Bulls could drink that much whiskey. "How much did you get for the horses?" he asked.

The question set Three Bulls off on another unintelligible tirade. When he calmed down, he admitted he'd received two gallons of whiskey for the two horses.

"And when you sobered up, you figured you'd been cheated?" Jamie asked, groaning inwardly, hating it that some of his people still had such a thirst for whiskey they continued to allow the Americans to bilk them.

"Damn right!" Three Bulls scowled, using up his entire English vocabulary.

"The whiskey sellers are still there?"

Three Bulls nodded vigorously. "They keep a lookout for the Redcoats. Some wild young warriors who get paid in whiskey are patrolling the camp."

Good Young Man! Jamie thought, certain from all he'd heard in his futile search that this was the kind of place his mother's murderer would seek out. "Is Good Young Man there?" he asked. When Three Bulls nodded, Jamie knew the die was cast.

He turned to McLeod, who had watched their exchange with unconcealed curiosity and growing excitement. Jamie stood up and dismissed the guard who had brought Three Bulls. Only the three of them remained in the office. Fort McLeod attracted all the wandering whites and Indians from the plains. They drifted anonymously through the place, satisfying their curiosity and moving on. Any of them could be connected to the whiskey sellers. If an attack on Pine Coulee was to be successful, it would also have to be kept a secret.

When the situation was explained to him, McLeod agreed. "Whoever's behind this is deliberately defying the authority of the Mounted Police," he said grimly. "This time we'll teach them a lesson they won't forget."

Plans were quickly made. Early tomorrow, Inspectors Denny and Cavendish, with ten men, would leave the fort with no announced destination. Jamie would meet them on the trail to guide them and lead the attack on the whiskey traders. Tonight, Jamie and Three Bulls would sleep in the camp of Crowfoot.

Inside the sweat lodge, Jamie sat against the buffalo-hide wall and bowed his head on arms crossed on bent knees. Red-hot stones glowed in the fire ring, the only light in the low, willow-supported structure. The scents of sage and sweet grass emanated from the small container of water beside him. His nude body was slick with sweat, slack and drained.

Once more he sprinkled the heated stones with scented water. Steam rose in a thick vapor, obscuring vision. Lifting his face toward the sky beyond the low roof, he chanted the song of a warrior preparing for battle, a warrior bent on righting wrongs and bringing Blackfoot justice to those who had done evil. Again the hoped-for connection with the spirit of his medicine, the eagle, and with Natos escaped him. Instead, the face of Brings Down the Sun came to him, woven in the threads of rising steam. Kate, beloved wife. The image changed, the lovely, laughing face looking into the admiring eyes of David Cavendish, just as he had seen through the window. Was this the message of the gods, Jamie asked himself in despair, that she was fated for one of her own people, for Cavendish?

Then I must truly let her go, Jamie told himself, and he sang the warrior's song again, concentrating deeply on the words and thinking of the enemy he must slay tomorrow.

When Blackfoot justice had been done, he would go

away from the prairies that had been his home. Perhaps he'd go to Rocky Mountain House again, then west and north to the outposts of Hudson's Bay Company. Far enough to forget what couldn't be.

Frost had painted an intricate design on her window, like a forest of white, icy ferns. Kate admired it for a moment before she scraped off enough to look out into the wintry morning.

Nothing moved in the length of frozen mud that was McLeod's main street. Sighing, she turned away and set water on the stove to heat for tea. Last night for a few minutes she'd forgotten all her troubles. David and several other officers had come to buy her coffee and sweet biscuits. David had challenged her to a game of chess. The joking comments of his comrades had made the game anything but serious. She had laughed—and Kate squeezed her eyes painfully shut—for the first time in a very long while.

Suddenly light-headed, she sat on the chair beside the stove and hung her head between her knees. At least she was no longer nauseated in the mornings, and this dizziness soon passed. Soon—very soon—she must make a decision. Although the bull trains ran to Fort Benton whatever the weather, the trip was dangerous in midwinter. She wouldn't be allowed to go then. She'd refused David's last plea on McLeod's behalf. The commissioner would no longer try to persuade her. Even his emissary, Inspector Cavendish, seemed to have given up in frustration.

Kate knew the alternative to going was to stay here and bear her child, facing whatever condemnation the settlers, the Mounties and the officers' wives might heap on her.

Profits from the pharmacy were small. Likely, Conrad wouldn't continue with it for long. And her hope for patients hadn't been fulfilled. In the past month there had been only a small boy with a broken arm and a young settler's wife who feared she was pregnant but merely had an infection. In every way, Kate thought, her life was at a dead end. Decisions had to be made because next year she would have a child to care for.

Would Jamie welcome the child they'd made in that wild night of passion? Remembering his loving ways with the children at the Blackfoot encampment, she knew he would. Tears burned her eyes with the knowledge that it was she who had torn them apart. Only now did she understand that Jamie's honor was no less than the honor of a Mounted Policeman. She'd admired McLeod for his nonviolent approach to solving the problems of the Northwest, yet she was certain even he would be capable of killing in the name of honor. And she at last recalled the rage she'd felt toward the men who had injured her mother, how she'd once longed to hurt them in some terrible way.

Tears hot on her cheeks, her throat tight with pain, Kate hated how she'd wronged her beloved Jamie. When he came again to Fort McLeod, she would forget her pride and beg his forgiveness. But what if he didn't return? she thought in sudden panic. She would find him, and she swore it to herself. Wherever he might be in the great Northwest, she would find her love.

A knocking on the door aroused Kate. She had wept, then fallen into a restless sleep. Now she pulled her wrapper close and opened the peephole. Cutting Woman looked grimly back at her.

They had parted such good friends after Cutting

Woman had brought the gift of her medicine that Kate was startled by the condemnation in the medicine woman's eyes.

"You didn't tell him!" she accused as soon as she entered the room.

During their shared time at the summer encampment and the two days they had spent together last month, Kate and Cutting Woman had arrived at a kind of language of their own, a mixture of English and Blackfoot interspersed with signs and often understood because of the rapport between them. Kate didn't have to ask whom Cutting Woman meant.

"No." The water was boiling and Kate took the kettle to the table to make tea. Cutting Woman followed, glaring at her with angry black eyes, waiting for an explanation.

"I haven't seen Jamie since . . ." Her voice fell as anguish filled her heart. She hadn't seen Jamie since that night of passion when their child was conceived. But she couldn't tell Cutting Woman that. Lamely, she added, "Since I knew."

Anger drained from the medicine woman's face. "So," she said and took the mug of tea Kate offered. For a long moment she stared into the rising steam as though marshaling her thoughts. When she spoke in her mixture of languages, Kate understood.

"Follows the Eagle went to the sweat lodge last night. He sang the warrior's songs, the songs of those who must kill the enemy or die. He dedicated himself to his mission."

So he meant to kill or be killed in his quest to bring justice to the murderer of his mother. Her soul awash with dread and self-blame, Kate wondered if she could finally accept the reality of frontier life. Had she truly learned that Blackfoot honor and duty were no less than the honor and duty of a red-coated Mounted Policeman? Closing her eyes against the pain filling her fearful heart, she wished she could call back the ugly words, the accusations, that had sent Jamie away from her.

"This morning," Cutting Woman continued inexorably, "he guides the Redcoats to Pine Coulee to arrest whiskey traders. It is said Good Young Man is there." Tight-lipped, she stared at Kate in silence for a long time, then sighed and went on with her story. "After the sweat, Follows the Eagle came to my lodge. He asked that I pack all his belongings for a long trek, and told Stone Calf to bring his best horses to camp to wait for him. Then he gave all the other horses to Stone Calf so that he might find a bride." She paused significantly. "If he knew there was a child, he would never go away."

"Where will he go?" Kate asked, hoarse with shock at this unexpected news. Guilt burgeoned in her heart at Cutting Woman's words. Her hand trembled so she had to set the mug of tea down.

Cutting Woman shrugged. "He would not say." She stared sadly out the window, where the frost had melted into a beading of moisture. "I sang a prayer for him . . . *Haiyah! Haiyah! Natosin! Nach-ki-tach-sa-po-auach-kach-pinna . . . Ita-ma-tau-tat-si-sinna.*" Stumbling over the words, she translated the song for Kate: "Hear, O Sun! May he go safely while traveling afar! May we meet and be happy again!"

May we meet and be happy again . . . Despair filled Kate's heart. Was such a thing possible? Could they ever meet and be happy again? Could he forgive the cruel things she had said and remember only how she had loved him? Through a blur of tears, she looked imploringly into Cutting Woman's expectant eyes. "We must stop him. Can you take me to him?"

Jamie's aunt smiled. "We go to Pine Coulee now. I brought horse for you."

28

*L*ate-afternoon sun slanted through pine trees growing sparsely on the rocky sides of the coulee. It gilded raw stumps where trees had been cut to build the rough cabin, and glittered off water in a small stream flowing among tangled willows.

Smoke drifted from the chimney of the cabin, blending into patchy clouds scudding across the ice-blue sky. A sun dog gleamed among the clouds and Jamie felt the hairs rise on his neck. An ill omen.

He shrugged it off. One could not be guided by omens in the business of attacking a foe, and he had never ceased to think of the whiskey traders as the enemy.

From his hidden place among the pines, Jamie sat on his horse, and surveyed the coulee below. His experienced mind assessed the possibilities of how best to take the place when the time came. The Mounties and Three Bulls were miles behind him on the trail. By the time they arrived, he would be ready.

It was a poor, mean-looking place and seemed deserted except for a few horses in the makeshift stable. Unlike most whiskey forts, no drunken Indians were fighting or lying stuporous on the cold ground still wet from last week's snow. Some of the whiskey traders had learned to protect themselves by giving the Indians their jug of whiskey only if they returned to their own camp to drink it. Perhaps that was the case here. It was protection only for the traders, and the result was often tragedy when drunken fights ensued in camp. Cutting Woman's brother had killed his wife and his own son in such a drunken rage. Red Crow himself had done murder before he quit the whiskey.

The cabin was unprotected, standing bare among the tree stumps. It would be simple enough to surround the place and have done with it—as long as the patrol Three Bulls had mentioned didn't come at their backs. Jamie reined his horse around and rode back to meet the Mounties.

"Three Bulls says there's a patrol out from the whiskey fort, watching for the Redcoats," he told Inspectors Denny and Cavendish when he had once more joined the detachment. "I tried to scout them out, but never saw a sign."

"They wouldn't recognize us as Redcoats," Denny said.

It was true that the scarlet jackets were kept for special occasions, mainly to impress the Indians. All the men now wore warm buffalo coats made from confiscated robes by a tailor in the town of McLeod. Except for dress, they had also discarded the heavy white helmets and the silly pillbox hats for the more practical woolfelt Stetsons.

"Let's get on with it," Jamie growled and led out in front of the detachment.

Once more looking down into the coulee, Jamie glanced behind him at the Mounties awaiting orders. Almost all the whiskey forts had been taken bloodlessly, but it would be foolish to count on a quick and easy surrender.

Inspector Denny rode up beside him. "What do you think, Campbell?" he asked. When Jamie had explained his plan, Denny passed orders on to his men.

As they descended into the coulee, the detachment separated, moving quietly to their assigned places surrounding the whiskey trader's cabin.

Even in the thin sunlight it was bitterly cold, and the men's breath rose like smoke in the icy air. Last night they'd camped on open prairie near a spring with water and grass. With no trees for protection, the wind had seemed to come straight from the North Pole.

As senior officer, Denny rode in front at Jamie's side. They moved cautiously toward the front of the cabin, guns ready. Behind them were four men with loaded rifles. Cavendish and the others edged quietly to the back of the building.

"Wait until they're in place," Jamie cautioned Denny. He had little trust in Cavendish's military ability but no choice. They would have to depend on him and his men to secure the rear of the cabin.

Giving the signal to dismount, Jamie strode to the plank door and kicked it open. Denny was close behind, his pistol ready.

"What the hell?" The exclamation came from a tall, gray-haired man who rose to face them. He had been sitting with two other men at a table in front of a blazing fireplace, a game of cards spread out between them. A whiskey jug rested on the stone hearth and each man had a glass of amber liquid at his elbow.

"Don't move," Jamie growled, leveling his handgun at the startled men. One of them made a gesture toward the holster hanging over the back of his chair, then thought better of it and raised his hands.

With a wave of his arm, Denny beckoned the rifle-bearing Mounties forward. He took a commanding stance and announced loudly, "In the name of the Queen and the Canadian government, I place you under arrest for selling illegal whiskey."

"Be damned if you can arrest us," shouted the tall, imposing man with a drooping gray mustache. "We're in American territory." Jamie stared in surprise as he recognized John Weatherby, one of Fort Benton's prominent citizens.

"A long way from it," Jamie told him, not even trying to conceal the disgust he felt for the greed of this man. Only his profits would matter to Weatherby, with no thought for the tragedy his whiskey spread among what he considered savages.

All the time the three men were being bound hand and foot, Weatherby continued his tirade. "I know you, Jamie Campbell, you half-breed bastard," he raged, "and you know me. Tell these so-called policemen what kind of influence I have."

Jamie's fingers tightened on the pistol he still held, and he fought down the urge to do violence to this man who sold pain and misery to his people. "Where are the Blackfoot you've got riding patrol for you?" he demanded.

Weatherby gave him a furious glance and ignored his question. Already hoarse from shouting his protests, he turned on Denny. "I'll take this outrage to Washington—all the way to the President, if necessary. Do you hear that?"

"You're welcome to go the limit," Denny said mildly, and checked the binding on Weatherby's wrists with unnecessary roughness.

With the prisoners secured, Weatherby still muttering threats, Jamie asked, "Where the hell is Cavendish?"

For all he knew, the inexperienced inspector could have been ambushed behind the cabin.

There was no connecting door to what was obviously some kind of storeroom, probably where the whiskey was dispensed. Jamie picked up his rifle. "Watch the prisoners and stay on alert," he told Denny. "I'll make sure all's well out back."

Moving cautiously around the cabin, Jamie saw that the storeroom door had been flung open. Two Mounties stood guard outside.

"Look at this!" Cavendish exclaimed when Jamie peered into the dim room, which stank of alcohol and animal skins. "A wagonload of whiskey . . . more buffalo robes and furs than I can count." Elation filled his face. "McLeod will be pleased," he added with undue pride.

Jamie had to grin at the understatement, but he only said, "Better report to Denny."

"Follows the Eagle!" a voice shouted as Jamie came out of the storeroom into the cold dusk. It was Three Bulls, and he was leading two fine-looking horses. "I found my horses," he told Jamie in Blackfoot. "Now I go home."

One of the horses had an American brand mark on its hip. So Three Bulls had bettered his bargain, Jamie thought, and grinned at the Blackfoot's expectant face. "Better get going," he said with a shrug. "It's a long way home."

Mounted up, Three Bulls warned Jamie, "Good Young Man and his patrol will be back. You watch for them."

In the fading light, Denny inspected the storeroom. He was as pleased with the plunder as Cavendish had been. One of the men had found a wagon behind the stables. Denny ordered, "We'll load their wagon in the morning and head for Fort McLeod."

With Three Bulls' warning fresh in his mind, Jamie could still feel the uneasiness he had felt since they arrived. According to Denny, his questioning of Weatherby's accomplices had brought no more information on the whereabouts of the Indian patrol.

"We don't know where Weatherby's hired guards are," Jamie protested. "If they catch us in the cabin, we'd be in for a bloody fight. We'd better camp down the draw."

"That bloody Indian, Three Bulls, was half crazy," Cavendish growled, glaring at Jamie. "The men have had a hard two-day march. Here at the cabin there's a fire and food. We'll stay here the night." He walked away in the absolute certainty he had made the final decision.

Fool, Jamie wanted to shout after him, you're not in charge of the detachment. Instead, he turned a questioning glance on Denny, who said wearily, "Fire and food sound good to me. We'll post a guard."

McLeod would have listened, Jamie thought, his anger rising at Cavendish's uninformed and illogical orders, and at Denny for backing him. Then he shrugged, knowing his authority ended with guiding the troops to this place. But he would be on the guard tonight himself. Good Young Man and his wild warriors would be back. The whiskey was here.

Night came on them with frightening suddenness. Cutting Woman had led the way, following the trail Jamie and the Mounties had left across the wet prairies, where snow still lay in shaded nooks. In the fading light after sundown, Kate watched her companion turning her horse in a slow circle. Was Cutting Woman lost? Kate wondered apprehensively. She'd trusted completely in the medicine woman's guidance, telling herself Jamie's aunt had grown up on these prairies. Likely they were as familiar to her as they were to Jamie.

"Camp here," Cutting Woman announced and dismounted.

With a sigh of relief, Kate followed her example, then dared to ask, "Do you know where we are?"

The astonished look she received in reply made her wish she could take back the question.

"Buffalo jump there." Cutting Woman pointed. In the last of the light, the familiarity of that cliff struck a chord in Kate's memory. On another, happier day, Jamie had pointed out that cliff and explained its purpose. That day had brought his humiliating arrest by David Cavendish. Anger stirred in Kate. She'd forgiven David much, even tried to be friends again, but she found she could not forgive his behavior on that day. He had taken advantage of his position to try to remove a rival. Perhaps he'd never understand that there was really no rivalry. Her heart was Jamie's forever and always. She was going to him to tell him so.

While Cutting Woman gathered buffalo chips for a fire, Kate unsaddled the horses and staked them nearby. The bedding rolls she placed close to Cutting Woman's low fire, where already a pot of water was heating. She had once more worn her father's wool pants beneath her skirt, the wool capote over a sweater, and a wool scarf tied about her head. Still, she shivered in the icy wind.

The mint tea was warm and comforting, as was the pemmican soup Cutting Woman made in the same pot. If it tasted faintly of mint, it was filling. They worked with scarcely a word, as though they had traveled together often and knew their parts in making camp.

Wind came from the north, bitter cold and chilling to

the bone. They sat close to the small fire while they ate, although buffalo-chip fires yielded little warmth. Cutting Woman had made one bed. Without asking, Kate knew they would sleep together to warm each other. And she remembered that winter night in Jamie's arms with such a pang, she had to bow her head to hide the tears.

Scarcely heard above the wind came the sound of a rustling in the sagebrush. Kate raised her head and stared across the low fire into the feral, gleaming eyes of a watching coyote. Rigid with fear, she gasped. Cutting Woman turned, saw the animal and placed a stilling hand on Kate's arm.

Mesmerized, Kate looked into the eyes of the wild creature. Then the coyote barked once, turned tail and was gone. The only sound was the moaning of the wind.

"Coyote barked," Cutting Woman said, breaking the silence. She sat like a statue, staring into the black void where the coyote had disappeared. "Death . . ." Her voice was low and haunted. "An omen of death . . ."

Kate's heart froze at the words. Despite McLeod's fears, she had seen the attack on Fort Whoop-up turn into an invitation to supper, but not all the forts had fallen so easily. There had been gunfire when Big Rib was wounded, and at some of the other forts. Foreboding lay like an enormous weight on her shoulders. Someone would die at Pine Coulee. It could not be Jamie Campbell, or part of her would die, too. She clutched her locket. His lucky buffalo stone, his *i-nis-kim*, lay inside it, next to her breasts. Then she sent a silent prayer to Natos, to all the gods she knew, that he would be safe.

❧ 29 ❧

An ominous dream, gone quickly from consciousness, awakened Kate. She was trembling and her muscles were taut with a fear she couldn't place. In the east the sky was just beginning to lighten while darkness still lay on the prairie. At once her eyes were filled with the glory of the Morning Star hanging low above the horizon, its gleaming light somehow reassuring in this world filled with unknown terrors.

Cutting Woman had already risen in the gloom and was stirring the buffalo-chip fire to life. Wrapping a buffalo robe around her against the icy morning air, frost crunching beneath her boots, Kate hurried to join her friend.

"We go." Cutting Woman spoke abruptly. "We must go fast." She handed Kate a mug of steaming mint tea. With her cold hands clasped around the warm mug, Kate stared at the medicine woman's tense face. The sense of foreboding that had awakened her felt like ice growing in her heart.

"What's happened?" she asked, her voice shaky with apprehension. "Why do you say go quickly?"

"Coyote bark," Cutting Woman answered abruptly

and turned away to begin saddling the horses.

In a very short time, Cutting Woman had packed the horses and put out the fire. "Come," she said, handing Kate the reins to her mount. "We must hurry."

At the sight of the dread her words brought to Kate's face, the woman smiled sadly and touched her fingers to Kate's cheek. "Follows the Eagle is there." She pointed to the west. Before Kate could speak, Cutting Woman had mounted and kicked her horse into a gallop. Kate rushed to follow her.

The Morning Star gleamed above her shoulder as she rode, a comforting presence until at last it was obscured by clouds scudding in on the wind. Jamie . . . my Morning Star, she thought, desperate fear raging inside her. Cutting Woman hadn't told her, or perhaps couldn't say, what danger she had divined awaited at the whiskey fort—but Kate knew beyond a doubt that Jamie's life was at stake.

He had to live . . . he had to know she loved him still, that they would have a child. And he must know that she finally understood the sense of justice that had been bred into him. Whatever compromises they must make to have a life together, nothing would ever part them again.

In the gray hours before dawn, beneath a cloudy sky, Jamie paced the perimeter of the whiskey trader's cabin. He had been wrong. No attack had come in the night. But the possibility of the patrol's sudden return kept his nerves on edge.

He'd questioned Weatherby again. "Damned if I know where the red bastards went," the trader growled. "Can't depend on 'em for anything except swilling whiskey."

The two men with Weatherby professed equal ignorance, and Jamie finally gave up in disgust.

He came out into the icy morning air to watch the Mounties loading the confiscated wagon with buffalo robes and furs. The uneasiness that had gnawed at him all through the night increased. The police would be safe once they were out of Pine Coulee and on the way back to Fort McLeod with the prisoners. His duty to them would be finished then and he'd be free to search for Good Young Man—free to end his quest for Blackfoot justice.

"Everything loaded?" Inspector Denny asked as he rode up to the wagon.

"Ready," Cavendish told him with a wave toward the waiting wagon.

The sense of urgency grew in Jamie. "Better get started," he advised gruffly. "You know the trail."

"Right," Denny agreed and turned to signal the troopers to bring up the whiskey trader's horses. The prisoners were helped to mount, hands tied behind them.

"Where the hell's my horse?" Weatherby shouted. "A white-stockinged bay—best damn horse I own. You Redcoats are nothing but horse thieves . . ." His threatening tirade went on and on, ignored by the busy Mounties. Weatherby's accomplices merely looked cowed.

Remembering the bay Three Bulls had ridden away, Jamie hid a smile, wondering how far the Blackfoot had fled by now with his fine new horses.

Constable Brant was driving and the loaded wagon creaked into motion, moving slowly up toward the prairie. Mounties and prisoners rode behind, along with the extra horses from the trader's corral.

After a quick, appraising glance around the cabin area, Denny confronted Jamie's nervous pacing. "I'm leaving Cavendish and two men to help you dump the whiskey, Campbell. Fire the cabin as always. Then you join us."

Jamie nodded agreement and lifted a hand in farewell, thinking that he wouldn't join them, nor would he argue with Denny about it. Barring trouble, they'd be back at the fort before this new storm blew in. But he would be gone from here, searching for his enemy.

Methodically wielding their axes, Jamie and the two Mounties hacked open the barrels of alcohol in the store-room. The reek of it made his nostrils burn. One of the men staggered outside, gagging. Jamie rolled the last barrel into the main cabin, pulled the stopper and let it drain onto the plank floor.

He cast an annoyed glance at Cavendish, who stood watching, giving unneeded orders. Doubt mingled with regrets in Jamie's mind as he wondered whether this was the man for his beloved Kate. Would Cavendish keep her safe from the dangers of the frontier, or would he simply take her away to another alien land? There was nothing he could do now to change what would be. He mustn't think of her, mustn't let himself care any longer. She had made the choice and he would be far away.

An end to it, he told himself, and knelt to shave pitch pine into a small pile on the spilled alcohol. With un-necessary ceremony, Cavendish brandished his flint and lit the shavings. "Here she goes," he said as the pine caught. Suddenly the alcohol took fire with a great whoosh of sound and flame. Hurriedly the four men moved away from the fiercely burning cabin.

Another whiskey trader finished, Jamie thought with satisfaction as he stared into the spreading fire. This winter would see the end of them. The Mounted Police had done the job they'd been sent west to do. The Blackfoot and the Bloods had hunted hard this summer, killing many buffalo. The robes would be a beginning of their return to former prosperity. The goods they'd wasted on whiskey were gone forever, lining the whiskey trader's pockets, but now the people would live as in the old days. At least as long as there were buffalo . . . That was a sobering thought, for on his journey to Red Crow's camp Jamie had seen what was happening in Montana, where the white man's cattle crowded the buffalo grazing grounds. He feared he'd seen the future there, and it filled him with nostalgia for a world that was passing away.

The sound of running horses came from down the coulee to the west. Frowning, Jamie turned to look, wondering if the Mounties had lost control of the herd they'd taken. Through the pine trees he saw them coming at a gallop, heard the war whoops and at last saw the feathered headdresses of the riders. Weatherby's Blackfoot patrol had been on a horse-stealing expedition. With a shout of warning to his companions, Jamie seized his loaded rifle.

Kate and Cutting Woman came upon the Mounties, wagon and prisoners where they had paused for rest. Inspector Denny was obviously dismayed by Kate's sudden appearance out here on the prairie.

Before he could speak, she demanded, "Where's Jamie Campbell?"

Denny's face turned scarlet. Silence fell among the watching men. They all knew her history with Jamie Campbell, maybe even believed McLeod's explanation that she'd been abducted against her will. Yet here she was in the middle of the empty prairie, searching desperately for the half-breed—and with a Blackfoot woman riding at her side. Kate knew how incredible the whole thing must seem. Too bad Denny was embarrassed, but she had to find Jamie.

Denny cleared his throat and held out a tentative hand to help her dismount. "Campbell stayed behind with Inspector Cavendish to burn the fort. He'll be catching up with us shortly. You'd better join us until he arrives."

"We go Pine Coulee." Cutting Woman's face was grim. Whether or not she'd understood Denny, Kate couldn't guess. She only knew her friend had a premonition they both must heed.

"He's my husband," Kate announced firmly. Denny's face turned even redder. "I'll ride to meet him." She kicked her horse into motion, ignoring Denny's pleading cries.

"Miss Maginnis—no—it's dangerous—"

The sun slipped down the sky as they rode, half hidden by gathering clouds. Aching with fatigue and fear, Kate had begun to wonder if Pine Coulee had fallen off the edge of the world.

"Fire!" Cutting Woman pointed to the column of smoke in the distance, blending into the gray sky.

A thrill of apprehension went through Kate. Without thinking, she clasped the locket with Jamie's *i-nis-kim* inside . . . his luck, given to her. Even though she knew they always burned the whiskey traders' cabins, she whipped her horse into a faster pace. With growing dread, the two women barreled across the frosty prairie toward the tower of smoke.

Through the sight of his rifle Jamie saw the face of the enemy he had sought for so long, Good Young Man. In their wild charge, the Indians had lost control of the horse herd. Terrified horses fled in every direction, hooves pounding, squealing and snorting, ruining Jamie's shot. When he pulled the trigger, one of the attacking Indians fell from his mount, his limp figure lost in the mad rush of horses. Jamie cursed. It was not Good Young Man.

Gunshots resounded among the trees. From the corner

of the stables where he had taken shelter, Jamie saw Cavendish go down with a cry, clutching at his bloody shoulder. Sergeant Steele dragged him to safety behind a tree stump.

War whoops faded as another of the Blackfoot sagged in his saddle and fell, a victim to Sergeant Steele's aim. Constable Turner was down but moving, still alive.

Good Young Man whipped his terrified horse forward, his eyes glittering with drunken fury. The unearthly light of the burning cabin lit a face dark with murderous anger. Jamie took aim once more at his enemy, only to see that Good Young Man's rifle was turned on him.

The bullet struck just above his head into the pole support of the stable. Again Jamie cursed, his aim spoiled by his reaction. His own shot had grazed the hip of Good Young Man's mount. The horse reared, squealing in pain. For the first time, Good Young Man seemed aware that his two companions were down. He was alone. With one last, screeching war whoop, he jerked his horse around and rode wildly back up the coulee.

Without thought, Jamie raced for his own horse, saddled and tied among the trees, awaiting his departure from this place. Good Young Man was at last within retribution.

"Don't wait for me," he ordered, stopping the horse where Sergeant Steele was trying to bind Cavendish's wound. "Catch up with Denny and get back to the fort."

"For God's sake, Campbell," Cavendish muttered, weakly trying to take command. "You can't catch that madman."

"Good Young Man is dead," Jamie answered harshly. He whipped his horse into a gallop and fled up the coulee in final pursuit of his enemy.

❧ 30 ❧

Overcast skies deepened the gloom in the narrow gully that was Pine Coulee. From a distance they'd heard the terrifying sound of gunshots and forced their horses to an even faster pace. Kate drew rein and paused for a moment, staring down at the sinking flames of what had once been a cabin. The fitful light of the fire cast eerie shadows over a scene that made her breath stop in fear.

Two bodies lay beside a tumbled rail fence. She could see only their buckskin-clad legs. Moccasined feet, she reassured herself. Jamie would wear boots in this weather.

A shout hailed them and she turned to see David Cavendish staring up at her in utter disbelief. As she and Cutting Woman rode down the slope to where he stood with Constable Turner and Sergeant Steele, Kate saw that he wore a bloody bandage on one arm. Constable Turner looked pale, bloody and bruised. Only the sergeant seemed to be in control, his pistol still in his hand.

"Bloody hell, Kate!" Cavendish said, still staring as if she were an apparition. "What—?"

She interrupted him anxiously. "Where's Jamie Campbell?"

For a moment David's shoulders slumped as though he just now truly realized she had made her choice. "Damn fool," he muttered, winced and placed a hand on his wounded arm.

"The Injuns attacked after we set the cabin on fire," Steele told her, glancing at Turner, who groaned and sat down abruptly. Cutting Woman dismounted and went to his side, helping him to lie back on the ground.

Steele continued. "Their horses went wild and hurt Turner here. We managed to pick off those two." He indicated the bodies she'd seen. "The other one took a shot at Campbell and missed, then saw he was alone and headed out of here."

"Campbell jumped on his horse and followed," David put in, adding sarcastically, "He knew that Indian. Called him by name—Good Young Man."

Kate's heart froze at the sound of that hated name. Jamie had pursued the murderer for months, and he would not give up now. "Which way did they go?" she demanded.

When Steele pointed up the coulee, Kate knew what she must do. Whatever the cost to her, Jamie wouldn't be alone in his final revenge. She slid down from her horse and walked purposefully across to the Mounties' tethered horses. "I'm taking a horse," she announced. "Mine's nearly done in. Cutting Woman will stay and care for your wounds."

The men stood as though frozen in place, staring at her in amazement. Then David laid a tentative hand on her arm.

"Don't!" Kate jerked away. "Jamie's my husband. I'll follow where he goes." Quickly, she mounted the horse.

"Kate . . ." David said, then spread his hands in resignation.

Cutting Woman looked up from working on the half-conscious Turner. "*A-wah-heh*!" She held up a hand as though in blessing. "Take courage!" Kate returned the gesture, then kicked the horse into a gallop in the direction Steele had indicated.

Jamie . . . *no-ma*, she thought, my Morning Star . . . you won't die. I won't let it happen . . . whatever I have to do, I will do it . . . for you.

Good Young Man's horse was tiring. Jamie thought grimly that the animal had been run hard even before the attack at Pine Coulee. When he saw Good Young Man head up the low hills toward the buffalo jump, he knew the chase would end here.

By the time Good Young Man reached the top of the cliff, his tortured mount could take no more. The horse simply stopped moving and stood with muscles trembling, unable to go farther. With a war whoop, Good Young Man leaped down and ran to the cover of the rocks long ago piled to guide buffalo over the cliff to their death.

A rifle shot sang in the cold air. Abandoning his own horse, Jamie sought protection behind a small cairn of boulders. His rifle steadied on the rocks, he sighted and waited for Good Young Man to show himself in order to shoot again. His first shot missed. Good Young Man's return shot sent stone chips flying above Jamie's head as he ducked. Two more shots from each man spent themselves among the rocks.

Silence fell. Only the cold wind stirring the sagebrush moved in this bleak place. Turning to reload, Jamie cursed. In his haste to follow Good Young Man, he'd left his ammunition belt behind. Moving carefully, he drew his pistol. The long silence told him it was likely Good Young Man had used all his ammunition, too. He eased forward around the rocks, knowing he'd have to be closer to make a pistol shot count.

"*I-nit-si-wah!*" The battle cry of a Blackfoot warrior burst the silence. "Kill—kill the enemy!" Good Young Man raced toward him with such suddenness, Jamie could not get off a shot before the man was on him. His face contorted with hatred, Good Young Man leaped on Jamie, his knife raised to strike. Jamie sidestepped, with one foot spilling Good Young Man so that he hit the ground with a grunt, still clutching his knife.

Jamie turned, aiming his pistol at the prone man. The gun misfired. Cursing, Jamie threw it aside. In an instant his long knife was in his hand. Good Young Man had sprung up into a crouch. Like two animals in combat, the enemies circled each other warily, eyes locked as each waited for the other to waver.

"Jamie!" The voice of Bring Down the Sun, high and sharp with terror, cried his name. Instinctively, he looked for her. Seeing his advantage, Good Young Man attacked Jamie. Searing pain tore through him as the knife slashed into his shoulder. Blood poured down his arm, his knife fallen from the numbed hand. Gathering all his strength, Jamie seized the warrior's upper arms and struggled to fling him aside. In a quick movement, Good Young Man tripped Jamie and fell on top of him. With a long, savage cry of triumph, he lifted his knife.

The scream that tore from Kate's throat took her heart's blood with it. Leaping from her horse, she ran toward the struggling men. For one flashing instant she was twelve years old again, trying to protect her mother from men with bloody knives. Jamie's pistol lay in the dust and she stooped to grab it up as she ran.

Even in the cloudy day, Good Young Man's knife gleamed with an evil light. Kate's scream of protest echoed beneath the dark sky. For a moment that seemed to last forever, Good Young Man hesitated, his furious eyes glaring at Kate. Jamie struggled to grasp his opponent's arm. A war cry issued from Good Young Man's throat as the knife descended.

Kate raised the pistol and squeezed the trigger, without thought of consequences, only the need to save Jamie from certain death. The shot exploded, sending her reeling.

A grunt burst from Good Young Man's lungs as he slumped across Jamie, blood pouring from the gaping wound in his chest.

"Jamie! Jamie!" Desperate with fear that she was too late, Kate ran to him. With the strength of panic, she flung Good Young Man's body aside and gathered Jamie into her arms.

After what seemed an eternity, Kate realized Jamie had struggled to a sitting position and was holding her trembling body close to him. She looked at his bloody face, his dark, intent eyes, and the full impact of what had taken place hit her. She turned to stare at Good Young Man's inert body. "Oh, God! Is he dead?" She gasped the question, terrified that the words were true.

Jamie's arms tightened around her. "Yes, Katie," he answered.

Shattered, Kate cried out, "I killed him!"

"Don't look!" Jamie cupped her bare, disheveled head in one hand and pressed her face to his chest, shutting out her view of the bloody corpse. "He would have killed me, Katie," he murmured, stroking her hair.

She seemed not to hear, repeating over and over, "I killed him . . . I killed him," as she sat up to stare in wide-eyed horror at Good Young Man's body.

An icy finger of fear touched Jamie's heart. This beloved woman had killed to save his life. Yet he well knew how deep her feelings went against killing, her reverence for the sacredness of life. Again he turned her face from the sight of the dead man. "Don't," he murmured. "It's done. It was him or me. Let it go, *nit-o-ke-man*." But she still wept.

Jamie rose unsteadily to his feet, his wounded shoulder throbbing now that shock was wearing off. Ignoring the pain, he lifted Kate up into his arms. He must take her away from here, away from this place of death, to a place of life renewal. And it must be done quickly.

Cold darkness fell as they rode. There was no moon and no stars. The wind rose and fell in bitter gusts blowing a storm down from the northlands.

They rode one horse, leading the other; Good Young Man's broken horse had been set free. Jamie had retrieved his hat and guns. He'd pushed Good Young Man's body over the cliff to lie among bleaching buffalo bones. Now he sat behind Kate, holding her close against him, his heart aching for a pain he understood only too well. Strangely, he felt no triumph that his long-sought revenge against his mother's murderer had at last been achieved. Nothing in his life was important now except his concern for this woman, his beloved wife.

Enfolded in his arms, she wept, tears torn from her very depths. Remorse racked her as, between sobs, she tried to reason with her guilt.

"I'm a healer, Jamie." Her voice was low and tremulous. "How could I kill a man? There should have been another way."

"There wasn't a choice," he answered. "It was his death—or mine."

The words eased her, but still the tears came. Her face against his chest, she wept until at last she fell into dazed exhaustion, awakening only when they stopped and Jamie dismounted.

* * *

"Where are we?" Kate asked as he lifted her down from the horse.

"You know this place," he told her, quickly unsaddling the weary animals. "The place of my *nit-so-kan*, my vision."

"Yes," Kate murmured, peering through the darkness. She felt it now, the aura of this sacred spot where she had truly become wife to the warrior known as Follows the Eagle. A place of beginnings. Could there be another beginning for a healer who had killed? The thought shook her so, she gave a low cry.

"Katie . . ." Jamie was at her side, taking her hand. With the bedrolls that had been tied to saddles back in Pine Coulee under one arm, he led her up the well-remembered rise. There he spread their bed in a sheltered place among the rocks, out of the wind.

A light snow began to fall, illuminating the darkness, making it somehow warmer. Still clad in their dirty, bloody clothes, Kate and Jamie slid beneath the buffalo robes and blankets, turning at once into each other's arms.

Jamie's cold fingers stroked her face gently, the pain of his wounded shoulder ignored in his concern for her. "*Nit-o-ke-man*, beloved wife," he whispered. "We are where we began together." His warm mouth covered hers, soothing, comforting.

A sob racked Kate and she buried her face against his throat. "Let it go, my Katie," he begged sadly. "You had to make a choice. And I'm alive because of what you did."

She couldn't answer, couldn't truly grasp the words. She only knew she was a healer who had caused a death. Jamie pulled a buffalo robe above their heads to protect them from the storm. Then he gathered her close against him and held her until at last she fell into exhausted sleep.

In the dream, it seemed she was awakened by the sound of beating wings. There before her, with sunlight gleaming on its feathers, was the great eagle of her *noma*'s vision. Its eyes looked on her with loving kindness and from somewhere a voice echoed in her mind: *Forgive yourself. Remember that you saved the life of Follows the Eagle.*

The dream faded . . . the eagle was gone. Yet Kate felt strangely comforted. The awful pain in her mind eased and a deep, healing sleep claimed her consciousness.

Kate awakened to Jamie brushing the light fall of snow from their buffalo robes. He eased back beneath the covers. At once he drew her into his arms, his eyes searching hers. What he saw there made him sigh with relief and he kissed her gently on the lips.

"The eagle came to me in a dream," she told him. Jamie stared at her, a question on his face, and she smiled. "He comforted me." The blanket fell away, revealing Jamie's slashed buffalo coat caked with dried blood from his shoulder wound. Kate gasped, filled with remorse that she had been so absorbed in herself she hadn't cared for his injury. "You're hurt," she said, touching his shoulder carefully. "The wound must be cleaned."

"Yes." He nodded. "I'll build a fire soon."

Silence fell between them as his dark eyes probed hers. "You killed for me, *nit-o-ke-man*," he said at last in a low voice. "I know what that means to you. Will that be forever between us?"

Kate's heart swelled with regret for the pain she had caused both of them. At long last, she had come to accept the existence of violence and evil in a world she would have wished otherwise. With loving fingers, she stroked the face staring down at her so intently.

"My *no-ma* . . . my love. From you I have learned tolerance and understanding. There has been such happiness between us . . . and such pain. From now on there will be only happiness . . . for all our lives."

Still he hesitated. "Can you live in my world, Kate?" he asked, his voice unsteady, and she knew the import of her answer.

"The Northwest is changing, Jamie, as you have told me. We'll change with it, but together . . . always." His breath went out in a rush, as though he'd been holding it. Smiling, Kate took his face in her hands and brought his mouth to hers. In the tender joy of that long, sweet kiss, there was passion remembered and the promise of passion yet to be shared.

"The eagle dream," Kate said after Jamie had risen to kindle a fire. He slid back into their bed, into her welcoming arms to warm himself against her. "Was that my own *nit-so-kan*, my vision?"

"A good vision for Brings Down the Sun, the wife of Follows the Eagle," he said, his cold face pressed against her throat. Kissing his temple, Kate caressed his hair with loving hands and looked up into the clear morning sky. False dawn had turned the east into a pearl-gray curtain. And there above the horizon glowed the Morning Star.

"Look, Jamie," she said. "An omen for us—the Morning Star." He turned onto his back to look where she pointed. "And there . . ." Kate went on, her face close to his. "See beyond Morning Star, another star follows." Its gleam was faint, barely visible. "The Evening Star, who follows her beloved *no-ma* forever."

With an indulgent smile, Jamie kissed her cheek. Intent on her story, Kate pointed again to the east. "And see there . . . the little star? That is their child.''

Jamie paused in kissing her throat and stared into her smiling eyes. "A child?" She saw that he knew it was their own story she told, and was flooded with joy at the deep connection of understanding between them.

"Our child," she answered, and took his hand to press it against her abdomen. "Growing there even now."

"*Nit-o-ke-man*, beloved wife." Jamie's voice was choked with emotion.

The pale light of the Morning Star reflected in the dark eyes that held hers as though he could see into her heart. A sense of perfect peace flowed through Kate's whole being with the knowledge that, at last, she had found her true home here on the vast prairie in the shelter of a love that was forever.

❧ Epilogue ❧

Bow River, Canada
1878

Thin spring sunlight brought a breath of warmth to the morning as Constable Maybree tramped up the path from the stables. He had left his partner saddling the horses for the next leg of their long patrol. This was number eight on the Mounted Police list of ranches checked periodically by a detachment from Fort McLeod. In the endless distances of the Northwest, with no near neighbors and no telegraph, those men were the settlers' connection and their only hope of help in case of disaster.

Smiling, the young constable looked around as he walked, for this was his favorite stop on the long trail. The snug log house was roomy and comfortable, the food always plentiful and delicious, the hospitality warm and friendly. Last night the lady of the house had read to them beside the fire from Walter Scott's *Ivanhoe*, and then bested him in a game of cribbage.

In the distance beyond the ranch house he could see the cattle that were replacing the buffalo on the plains. They grazed on the grass the ranchers called prairie wool. Beside the nearby creek, five skin lodges were pitched. This ranch was adjacent to the Blackfoot Reserve, the land the Canadian government had set aside for the Blackfoot nation in 1877. He thought wryly that the Blackfoot still hadn't learned to recognize boundaries.

A sweated horse stood at the hitching post before the long front porch, a new arrival since he'd gone to the stables. From inside he could hear a man's high, excited voice.

"The missus says it's her time, Dr. Kate. Can you come with me now?"

The bright-haired lady of the house stood up from the breakfast table, smiled briefly at Maybree and indicated an empty chair to the nervous man. "Have some coffee, Charlie," she said, pouring it herself. "I'll be ready to go in just a minute."

Almost at once, a gray-haired Indian woman took her empty chair. She frowned at the mess the small boy in a high chair had made of his oatmeal.

By the time Dr. Kate returned with saddlebags of medical supplies, her husband was at the door with her saddled horse. She had changed into a buckskin riding skirt, which showed her early pregnancy. Glancing at her, Constable Maybree felt his ears burn. Every Mountie who rode this way fell in love with her, he knew, and he was no exception. When Dr. Kate kissed her husband good-bye, Maybree had to look away in embarrassment, for there was more in that kiss than the dutiful touch of a wife's lips. The look they exchanged made him ache with his own half-formed dreams of love.

The anxious Charlie was already mounted, and the two galloped away toward the west. As he watched the figures fade far across the plain, the constable mused to the man watching beside him, "Your wife is a legend in the Northwest, sir."

There was a world of pride in the man's smile. "Dr.

Kate does what she was born to do," he answered.

The child had escaped his Indian nurse and came to fling his small arms around his father's leg. A strong hand reached down to lovingly stroke the boy's dark head.

"And so are you a legend, Jamie Campbell," the constable said, and started to say more, but the quiet dignity of that strong, copper-skinned face kept him silent. With his reputation for courage and integrity, Campbell was an intimidating figure.

The legend would live, Constable Maybree knew, as long as the Northwest Mounted Police existed. The white woman doctor and the half-breed guide, who had helped make it possible for the Mounties to conquer the Northwest, had made for themselves an enchanted haven of happiness here in the Great Lone Land.

The WONDER of WOODIWISS

continues with the publication of
her newest novel in paperback—

FOREVER IN YOUR EMBRACE

☐ #77246-9
$6.50 U.S. ($7.50 Canada)

THE FLAME AND THE FLOWER
☐ #00525-5
$6.50 U.S. ($8.50 Canada)

THE WOLF AND THE DOVE
☐ #00778-9
$6.50 U.S. ($8.50 Canada)

SHANNA
☐ #38588-0
$5.99 U.S. ($6.99 Canada)

ASHES IN THE WIND
☐ #76984-0
$6.50 U.S. ($8.50 Canada)

A ROSE IN WINTER
☐ #84400-1
$6.50 U.S. ($8.50 Canada)

COME LOVE A STRANGER
☐ #89936-1
$5.99 U.S. ($6.99 Canada)

SO WORTHY MY LOVE
☐ #76148-3
$6.50 U.S. ($8.50 Canada)